THE SECRET LIFE OF *Luke Livingstone*

Also by Charity Norman

Freeing Grace
Second Chances
The Son-in-Law

THE SECRET LIFE OF *Luke Livingstone*

CHARITY NORMAN

ALLEN&UNWIN
SYDNEY • MELBOURNE • AUCKLAND • LONDON

First published in 2015

Allen & Unwin
83 Alexander Street
Crows Nest NSW 2065
Australia
Phone: (61 2) 8425 0100
Email: info@allenandunwin.com
Web: www.allenandunwin.com

Cataloguing-in-Publication details are available
from the National Library of Australia
www.trove.nla.gov.au

ISBN 978 1 74331 838 6

Set in 11.5/15.5 pt Sabon by Post Pre-press Group, Australia
Printed and bound in Australia by Griffin Press

10 9 8 7 6 5 4 3 2

FSC www.fsc.org MIX Paper from responsible sources FSC® C009448

The paper in this book is FSC® certified. FSC® promotes environmentally responsible, socially beneficial and economically viable management of the world's forests.

For Petra King, with my thanks and admiration.

What are little boys made of?
Slugs and snails, and puppy dogs' tails.
That's what little boys are made of.

What are little girls made of?
Sugar and spice, and all things nice.
That's what little girls are made of.

Traditional nursery rhyme

Let me tell you a story. Please hear me out, because it will not be easy for me to tell, nor for you to understand. What happened was the last—the absolute last—thing I expected. I never saw it coming until it smashed into my life. I need you to see why I did as I did. I need you to walk in my shoes.

There was once a girl called Eilish French. She was a noisy child, with a bird's nest of hair and socks around her ankles. Her parents divorced bloodily and expensively when she was very small. Though they loathed one another by the time their private war was over, both of them doted on their only child. I'm afraid she was rather spoiled. In those days she wanted to be an air hostess. Then she thought perhaps she would be a pilot, or a brain surgeon, or a film star, or possibly a nun. Each dream gave way to another, and each was abandoned. In the end, she landed a job in marketing at much the same time as Margaret Thatcher arrived in Downing Street.

Eilish attacked her career with a ruthlessness that shamed her later when she thought back on it. A trade magazine described her as a rising star. Her long-term boyfriend, who was a stockbroker, said rising stars had no time for him and found someone who did. Her mother berated her for her carelessness in losing a very eligible man, but Eilish wasn't sorry to see him go. She could not shake off the feeling that she was in limbo, waiting for something.

And then she met a young solicitor called Luke Livingstone, and knew that the waiting was over. Everyone at the wedding agreed that they were a golden couple, sure to live Happily Ever After; and so it seemed to be. As the decades passed they became parents and even grandparents. Life wasn't all plain sailing, but there was enough love and laughter to carry it along. After all, what marriage is ever without its rough weather? Luke succeeded in his own career, and she forged a new one. It brought her far less income—but far greater satisfaction—than marketing ever had. They lived in a picture-book house. Their pond was a haven for wild ducks; their kitchen a haven for lame ones, who found warmth around its table. At weekends the place rang with the sounds of friendship and conversation.

Girl meets boy. They fall in love, and they marry. That should have been the end of the story.

For thirty years they shared one another's lives.

Thirty years.

Thirty.

I thought I knew that man. I thought I had been shown into every corner of his mind, that he'd shared every fear, every hidden longing. I thought he kept no secrets from me.

Turns out I never knew him at all.

This is his story. And mine.

One

Luke

She answered on the fifth ring, breathy because she'd rushed in from her mowing. I imagined her in gardening clothes: those faded jeans that still fitted as though she were twenty years old, and one of my old shirts, her auburn hair tied up in a silk scarf. My beautiful wife.

'On the train now. I'm finished in Norwich,' I said.

'Wonderful!' She sounded happy. It made my heart ache. 'So you'll be home for supper?'

I had my story planned. 'Look, I've got too many emails marked urgent. I think I'd better stay at the flat tonight, go into Bannermans tomorrow and tackle the backlog.'

'You all right?' she asked.

'Fine.'

'Tired?'

'Not really.' I rallied myself. 'So, school term has ended! How was your—'

A blast of sound rocked the carriage as we shot into a tunnel. The mobile connection was broken. I'd lost her. I would call again later, and find some way to say goodbye.

The train was half empty. Diagonally across from me, sharing my table, an elderly woman frowned at a crossword. And, of course, there was the man in the window. He filled my peripheral vision, floating just beyond the inky glass. I knew he was watching me: middle-aged, middle everything in striped shirtsleeves and a tie; dark hair, now a little grey, sweeping above his ears. Neat features. Good looking, according to Eilish and Kate, though to me he'd always been grotesque. When I turned my head, my eyes met the cavernous ones in the black mirror. We stared at one another in mutual dislike. *Not long now*, I thought with triumph. *I'll be rid of you forever.* Then the tunnel ended, and the grey ghost faded into a grey sky.

There were things to be done. Final things. I dug in my briefcase for writing paper and fountain pen. Neither my mind nor my eyes wanted to focus, but I made myself concentrate. I owed my family that. I had one last letter to finish. It was to my Kate: twenty-two years old, pierced in nose and navel; the most precious young woman in the universe.

I hope you find as much love and happiness in your life as I have with your mother. You have been my joy. Do not change, darling daughter. Do not underestimate your gifts. You have the power to make the world a better place.

I'd crossed out two versions and begun a third when the train checked, slowed, and halted. Silence. The scratching of my pen seemed much too loud, so I put it down. Across the aisle a young fellow in a suit kept rattling his packet of crisps. It's a sound that annoys Kate intensely; if she'd been in my seat she might have leaned over and snatched them out of his hand. The woman across from me seemed to feel the same, because she clicked her tongue at every crackle or crunch.

Minutes passed. The temperature rose. The crisp packet rattled. At last the guard's voice thundered over the intercom: it was a signals failure, apparently. He would like to apologise on behalf of Anglian Trains.

'Doesn't sound very apologetic,' remarked the woman. Her hair was absolutely white. A jacket and beret—in matching crimson velvet—lay on the seat beside her. We shook our heads, and I said, 'Good old British Rail, come back, all is forgiven.' Similar sentiments were murmured all around the carriage as strangers united in their irritation. I loosened my tie and said I was going to get a drink from the buffet, and would she like anything?

She thanked me in the over-loud voice of the chronically deaf, reaching into her handbag. 'What a very civilised idea. Gin and tonic, please.'

By the time I returned, crisp-packet boy had donned a set of headphones and shut his eyes.

'Are you being met?' I asked my table-mate, as we poured our drinks. 'You're welcome to use my phone, if you need to contact anybody.'

'No, no. I shall hail a taxi.' She opened a tiny case, took out two hearing aids and slid one into each ear. They whistled as she adjusted them. 'You don't see those nowadays,' she said, nodding approvingly at my gold pen. 'Proper fountain pens. Proper ink.'

I smiled at the pen. 'This was a present from my children. It's an old friend. They had my name engraved on it, see?'

I pictured Kate and Simon—young then, perhaps twelve and eighteen. They'd wrapped up my birthday present and tied a blue ribbon around the parcel. I still kept the ribbon in a drawer of my desk.

I wished there were another way. I wished I didn't have to leave them.

My companion pulled her knitting from her bag, rolled wool around one finger and began to click at high speed. She talked and knitted, chuckling fondly as she described her great-grandchild Henry, and rather less fondly when it came to Henry's parents, who—she said—cared about nothing but material possessions. She herself was eighty-nine years old, and had been a teacher all her working life.

'My wife's a teacher too,' I said. 'Special needs. In a secondary school.'

'Is she *really*? That's enormously valuable. Aha!' The carriage had jerked, and was inching forwards. 'We may get to London today, after all.'

I may get to die today, after all.

'What's it going to be?' I asked, nodding at her handiwork.

'This? A jersey for Henry. He'd much rather be in a sweatshirt, I expect. With a hood, so that he can go rioting and not be recognisable on the closed-circuit cameras.'

I laughed at this, and she looked pleased. 'You have a family?' she asked.

'Two children.' *Three children*, I always think; but I never say it anymore. People ask what they're doing now, and I have to explain about Charlotte, and can see them thinking, *But she was only a few minutes old! Why count her?*

'Still at school?' asked the woman.

'Good Lord, no! Our second grandchild is on the way.'

She raised her eyebrows. 'You look young to be a grandparent.'

'Eilish and I will have been married thirty years come October.'

'Ah! The pearl anniversary.'

I felt my darkness deepening. 'She's planning a party to celebrate. Marquee, band, fireworks. Half the world's on the guest list. The invitations will be going out any day.'

'Lucky man.' Milky blue eyes were fixed on me as she knitted. Loop, click, another loop.

'Yes. Lucky.'

'You don't sound at all enthusiastic.'

I tried to summon the energy to protest, to insist that I was hugely looking forward to the Big Event; but I hadn't the will. I felt transparent. Perhaps she knew what I was.

A stranger on a train. There was nobody I could possibly have told except a very old woman I'd never seen before and never would again.

'I won't be there,' I said. 'If all goes to plan I'll be gone by tomorrow morning. This signals failure on the line has prolonged my life.'

Her fingers stopped moving. 'May I ask why?'

'Because it's time. Because I have come to the end of a very long road.'

'But you have a choice. There's no need for such drastic measures.'

I drained my drink. It felt rough at the back of my throat. 'You were right when you described me as a lucky man,' I said, and coughed. 'Lucky, lucky. Everyone knows that. People kept telling me so on our wedding day—looking shocked, as though I'd somehow tricked her. Actually, it's true: I *did* trick her. Eilish French could have married anyone at all, but for some reason she chose me. Look—hang on . . .' I felt in the pocket of my jacket and pulled out a black and white photograph.

I'd taken the picture on a winter's evening when I'd just walked in from work and stopped in the doorway of the study. Her head was bent over some child's handwriting, her cheek freckled, her hands strong and sure. A coppery lock of hair had escaped from its velvet tie and brushed her mouth. It was one of many moments in our life together when I'd felt overwhelmed at the very sight of her. She had music playing on the stereo and the room seemed to swell with sound. I could still hear it, rippling across the rattle of the train. I hummed the melody under my breath. Debussy. It poured into me. It made me want to weep.

The woman put on her glasses to look. 'Ah, yes. Beautiful,' she said, before handing the photo back. 'I suppose you're having an affair. How very mediocre.'

'Worse. Much worse. I've been acting a part since the day we met. I'm not who she thinks I am.'

'Who are you, then?'

'I'm . . .' No. I couldn't tell her. My secret shame was too monstrous. 'Take my word for it. If Eilish knew the truth, it would destroy her.'

'Whereas your suicide will shower her with blessings?'

'You think I'm selfish. A selfish coward.'

'Hmm.' She considered the suggestion, her head tilted to one side. After a moment she began counting rows, two by two, and I went back to staring out of the window.

I was the birthday boy, five years old, standing at the top of the very tall tree in our front garden. I felt the trunk sway in the wind but I wasn't frightened. I'd skinned my knee on the way up. A trickle of blood was snaking its way down to my sock. I could see across the garden, across the barns, right to the far end of the farm. They were having a party for me, down there in our house. My mother had invited all the boys in my class at school. I'd run away. I didn't want the party. I didn't want the boys. I didn't want to be me.

Then she found me. I could see the white oval of her upturned face, hear her voice high with panic. *Luke! Oh dear God, dear God. Hold tight!*

Something was whispering in my ear. *You don't have to hold tight*, it said. *You could just let go*. In my imagination it was a mummery figure with a red butterfly mouth. That was my first encounter with The Thought, and it stayed with me from that moment on. Other children had imaginary friends who tempted them to steal biscuits; mine nagged me to run in front of a lorry, or turn one of Dad's guns on myself. *No more*, it whispered each morning when the lonely child—the anxious adolescent—the despairing adult—opened his eyes and contemplated a world in which he didn't fit. *No more being Luke. No more being, at all.*

It was whispering to me right now, as I sat on the train.

'Don't give up,' said the woman across the table. I'd forgotten she was there.

'You're trying to be kind,' I said. 'Thank you. Thank you for your kindness, but you know nothing about me.'

'Perhaps I know something about how your wife will feel.'

'This is the best thing I can do for her.'

'I doubt it.'

I leaned closer, wanting her blessing. 'It's the right time,' I said. 'My father's died. He needed me, so I stayed; but now he's gone.

Our children are grown up. Eilish is a strong woman, and the finances are all arranged—she'll be able to live very comfortably.'

The woman looked severely at me, her brows drawn. 'Think of the poor person who has to scrape you off the railway line, or fish you out of the Thames.'

'No, no,' I said. 'I've thought of that. I've everything I need in our flat in London. It won't be messy. I've planned a way to make sure I'm found by someone who won't care. He's ex-SAS.'

'Even ex-SAS soldiers have feelings, I expect.'

'Not this one. And especially not about this, because he doesn't like me very much.'

She completed several more rows of knitting before she tackled me again. 'You're not quite sure, though, are you? When you spoke before of your family, of your wife . . . there's ambivalence. I can hear it.'

She was right. My family. Eilish. I felt something blocking my throat.

'My husband once made a mistake,' said the woman, laying down her knitting. 'He worked for a charity. He cooked the books; embezzled money to pay our children's school fees, though he never told me we were struggling. They could have gone to the local school, for heaven's sake, it wouldn't have been the end of the world! He meant to pay everything back, his ship would soon come in, but it never did. He thought of the disgrace he was bringing on all of us, of prison; he imagined what the newspapers would print. Those thoughts possessed him. So he drove his car to an isolated spot and piped the exhaust through the window.' She reached into her bag, took out a flowered handkerchief and pressed it to her nose.

'I'm so sorry,' I said.

'So was I. So were our children. So were his poor mother and father. He was thirty-eight years old. Do you think we were grateful? Do you think we cared two hoots about the money when we buried him? Would I have cared now, aged nearly ninety?'

'No.'

'We didn't. We *didn't.*' I could hear her anger, still raw after all these years. 'I dare say it would have been grim—possibly I would have divorced him, though I doubt it—but he would have been alive to give his daughter away on her wedding day. Don't you want to accompany your daughter up the aisle on her wedding day?'

I smiled, despite everything, at the unlikely image of Kate in a white veil. 'She's not that kind of girl.'

'Mine was, but her father wasn't alive to see her married. He couldn't see any way out. That's what he said in his letter. *No way out. No choice.*' She shook her forefinger, admonishing the long-dead husband. 'If he'd asked me, I would have told him! There are always other choices.'

'Not for me.'

'Yes, for you!' Her voice was almost a shout. 'It's been fifty years since Jonathan left me. My children, my grandchildren . . . all of us haunted by that one terrible act. His parents never recovered. They died in grief. When I see him at the pearly gates, I'm going to give him a damned good kick up the backside.'

'I'm sorry. I really am.'

Her eyelids came down for a second, heavily, as though I'd bored her. 'Have you murdered somebody?'

'No.'

'Have you raped or maimed or tortured anyone?'

'No.'

'Well, then. Whatever your "crime", your wife has the right to know about it.'

The unshed tears of decades began to scald my eyes. Eilish was my closest friend. She knew me better than anyone in the world. I longed to confide in her.

'She'd think me a monster,' I said.

'*Are* you a monster?'

The door at the end of the carriage slid open, and a guard came noisily click-clicking. 'Tickets, please; all tickets, please.' He woke crisp-packet boy. The woman tucked her anger away, attacking the knitting with pursed lips. I finished my letter to Kate, slid it into an envelope and wrote her name on the outside.

When the train pulled into Liverpool Street, I stood up and lifted our bags from the rack. Hers was small and very light. She thanked me coolly as she put on her jacket.

'Let me carry your case to the taxi,' I said.

'Don't leave that beautiful woman alone. Don't leave her with unanswered questions. And anger. And guilt. She deserves better. Take it from someone who knows.'

•

It took quite a while to get up the platform and past the barrier. The station was packed with Friday travellers, and my companion was alarmingly shaky on her feet. She used a stick, but even so I was afraid she was going to tip right over. I saw her to the covered rank and waited with her until we were at the front of the queue.

I was helping her into a taxi when she gripped my forearm. 'You will continue living? Promise me.'

I had no answer. No promise.

'There's a drain,' she said, lowering herself into the seat. 'There, by your foot. Drop the keys to your flat down there. Buy yourself a little more time.'

I thanked her, and we said goodbye. I stood irresolute as her cab drew away. Three women waited in the queue behind me. They were dressed to the nines, perhaps for the theatre: sparkling earrings, high heels, swirling skirts. I caught a puff of scent mingling with exhaust fumes, hot tarmac and midsummer dustiness. Their heads were bent together in easy intimacy—if you watch a group of women together, you'll see that they manage this as men cannot—talking very fast, never quite finishing a sentence; never needing to, it seemed. Suddenly all three burst into helpless laughter, and I felt the familiar agony of envy.

The rope was waiting for me. I'd already made it into a noose, already tied the knots in exactly the right way. It's amazing what you can find on the internet: step-by-step guides to suicide by every possible method. I had an email ready to send to Bruce, the retired SAS man turned property manager who might or might not have feelings. I'd be long, long gone before he found me.

The next taxi was mine. The journey would take no time at all. Within an hour, I'd be free.

Now was my time. Now. Tonight.

I reached into my pocket to turn off the phone. I couldn't bear to hear her voice now. Two black cabs pulled in from the road, and the first stopped in front of me. I took hold of the door handle. I could feel the vibration of the engine under my fingers.

All around me, life roared and rolled. The three women waved at the second taxi. I glimpsed a flurry of heels and skirts as they threw open the door and piled inside. My driver looked out and spoke to me.

'Sorry?' I said.

He spoke again, but I heard no words. The sky was billowing. I saw Eilish in the garden, among the roses. She had a silk scarf in her hair, and she was alone. She was alone.

Out on the road, it had begun to rain.

Two

Eilish

I felt the first drops of rain speckle my arms. It was a gentle, happy sensation; a caress.

When the mower ran out of fuel I made a cup of tea, carried it out to the terrace and settled myself on the wooden bench. Honeysuckle grew in fragrant clusters up the old wall of the barn. A tendril dipped into my mug, but I didn't mind. The air was rich with the scents of summer, intensified by wet. Life was good. School term had finished at last. I'd spent the afternoon in the garden, demob-happy amid peace and grass clippings.

Luke made the bench about twenty years ago, when the children were small. Sitting there, leaning against the wall, we could keep an eye on them without spoiling their fun. They and their gang built dens in the bushes beside the pond; we could hear giggling over naughty songs, and the war cries of pitched battles. Beyond the terrace, birds darted around the claret leaves of a maple. Charlotte's tree. One day, we'd told each other as we tucked it into its bed of soil, it would be magnificent. Charlotte's great-nephews and -nieces would hang their swings from its branches.

Luke had phoned from the train, to say that his conference was finished. He was cut off in mid-sentence—a tunnel, probably. He hadn't called back, but I hadn't really expected him to. He hates public phone conversations, doesn't like to draw attention to himself. All the same, something in his tone—a heaviness—unsettled me. I'd call ours a very happy marriage, but Luke hasn't always been a very happy man.

Rubbish. I shook myself, spilling tea. *Why should he be in trouble now?* Life couldn't be better! The mortgage was paid off, the children safely launched into adulthood. We were planning a fabulous party, to celebrate thirty years of marriage. Best of all, he and I had organised three months' leave next spring, to be spent in a villa in Tuscany. I told myself these things, and stubbornly ignored the grasping chill in my stomach.

All at once, the heavens opened in earnest. Drops were splashing into my mug. I gave up on the lawn and took refuge inside, slipping off grass-clogged shoes as I stepped through the folding doors into the kitchen. I tried Luke's phone, hoping he might be at the flat by now, but got his voicemail. He was probably on the tube.

The air was warm despite the rain. If Luke had been home, we'd have shared a bottle of wine and sat out on the bench with an umbrella each. He always said we were like two old peasants in front of their log cabin. Never mind: I'd never been afraid of solitude, and tomorrow would come soon enough.

The sky darkened. The rain was relentless.

Kate

She couldn't believe her eyes.

'Bastard!' she yelled, glaring at the screen. 'You thieving, backstabbing prick.'

The cash-dispensing machine wasn't offended. It asked her if she'd like another transaction. No, she told it, she didn't want another frigging transaction, she wanted her money. Then it spat out her card.

There was some guy waiting in the queue behind her. She could hear him chuckling, and his face was reflected in the screen. He had a ridiculous moustache. What was it with losers and moustaches?

'Overdrawn, eh?' he remarked, as though he and she were good mates.

Jerk alert.

'Looks like you overdid the spending on your holiday,' he said. 'Too many piña coladas in nightclubs.'

'Go stuff yourself.'

There was a wounded silence before he muttered, 'No need to bite my head off.'

'No need for you to be a patronising tosspot,' she retorted, and stomped off to the luggage carousel, where she could see her backpack gliding through the rubber strips.

Moustachio had obviously used both his brain cells to think up an insult, because he sidled up to her as she was heading for customs. 'Watch you don't set off the metal detectors,' he said narkily, 'with all that hardware on your face.'

She didn't have hardware on her face. She had one garnet stud in her nose. Just one. It was a lot less offensive than wearing half a hedgehog on your upper lip. She held up the middle finger of one hand. With the other, she was writing a text:

WTF happened to the bank account???

She sent this message while walking past the mirrored walls of customs. She imagined uniformed officers, rubber gloves at the ready, watching beadily. Or perhaps they weren't; perhaps they were drinking coffee and playing cards while thousands of people streamed past, pulling suitcases stuffed full of heroin and exotic birds.

Owen's response made her jaw drop. *Took your share of the rent.*

She stopped dead, firing off her reply. *Bollocks!! I haven't been there for weeks.*

U never gave notice so am entitled. I have ur stuff in bin bags. Pls collect asap as its in my way. Also extensive damage to my shirt. Vet bills. Welcome home BTW.

So. After two years, their grand love affair had come to this. It wasn't so long ago that she and Owen couldn't spend more than a night apart without phoning one another and babbling. They were like an old married couple—like Mum and Dad, come to think of it—until it all went wrong. She'd hoped to patch things up when she got home from Israel but, God almighty, she wanted to kill Owen now. She was thinking about exactly how much she'd like to kill him as her thumb hit the keys.

VET BILLS???

He was really enjoying himself.

Baffy got chicken bone from bin pierced gut infection almost died emergency surgery cost a fortune. Ur dog too remember?

Well, that was true. Sort of.

She was out, and into the arrivals hall. Not being met at Heathrow, she reflected bitterly, makes you feel like a spare prick at a wedding. Everyone else seemed to have fans yelling at them from the barriers. She was almost knocked over by a family who'd begun crying and throwing their arms around one another; then she had to step around a snogging couple. *Get a room.* It was like being an extra in the opening sequence of *Love Actually.*

She'd taken that flight, a day earlier than those of the others on the dig, because it got her home in time for Mathis and John's party. She was regretting this decision as she headed for the train. She loved Mathis and John, and she loved a party, but she'd been sleeping in a tent for six weeks and had no clean clothes. It had been a long flight followed by an emptied bank account. The last thing she felt like doing was staying up all night, getting ratted, and passing out on a sofa among the empties.

She found a seat on the platform and perched like a turtle, her pack still on. Then she scrolled down to her father's mobile number. It would do her good to moan about Owen, and Dad was the man for that. He and Kate had an ancient alliance. Dad could be counted on to toe the party line and agree that Owen was a sociopath. Her mother had a bad habit of demanding details, maybe even—heaven forbid!—suggesting that Kate could be in the wrong.

'This is Luke Livingstone's phone. Press four if you would like to be put through to my direct line at Bannermans. Otherwise, do leave a message.'

Kate smiled to herself. Lovely Dad, so courteous and gentle. Some of Kate's friends found her father too reserved, but he wasn't at all. Quite the opposite, when you were his daughter.

She rang home, hoping he would answer the phone.

'Eilish here.'

Bugger. 'Hi, Mum. Bit of a rush, I'm just—'

'Darling! Where are you?'

'Still at Heathrow.'

'How was the dig?'

'Fascinating. Hot. I've got hundreds of photos, I'll bore you with them when I see you. Um . . . is Dad there?'

Kate could tell her mother was multi-tasking, filling the kettle, probably with the phone jammed under her chin. 'He's staying at the flat tonight,' she said. 'But I expect you're rushing back to Owen, are you? Or did he meet you at the airport?'

Kate thought about Owen's place, and the bin bags with her things stuffed into them. He'd be hanging around like a moray eel under a rock, waiting for her to turn up so that he could play mind games. Suddenly she wanted to be at home again, wearing fluffy socks, drinking tea in the kitchen with her mum and chortling at *Blackadder* with her dad.

'Um . . .' she said. 'I might come home tomorrow. I have to be there Sunday anyway, don't I, when we plant Grandad's tree? I'll just arrive a day early.'

'Terrific! Wonderful! And Owen too?'

'No.'

'He's very welcome.'

'He can't get away from work.'

Kate could hear her mother's antennae whirling around. That woman had some weird telepathic gift. When Kate had first lit up a cigarette, at the age of thirteen, she knew immediately. Kate had no idea how, because she'd gargled for about ten minutes with minty mouthwash, but Mum went ballistic and stopped her pocket money for a month. Her own father had died of lung cancer, so perhaps it was fair enough. When Kate was being bullied at school, she guessed that too, and went storming off to see the class teacher. It made things worse, but Kate appreciated her going into battle.

'All well between you and Owen?' Eilish asked now.

'Sorry? The train's coming in. Can't hear a thing.'

Eilish started bellowing like a foghorn. 'CAN . . . YOU . . . HEAR . . . ME . . . NOW?'

'It's no good, I've lost you. I'll phone tomorrow. Bye, Mum.'

Bloody typical, Kate thought sourly as she lurched down the carriage, smacking people in the face with her backpack. *Owen's a saint in her eyes. He can do no wrong, even though he's a total dildo.*

It was her last coherent thought before she fell asleep with her head on the shoulder of the Japanese tourist in the next seat.

Three

Luke

Rumbling. A train, passing beneath my feet. The keys were cutting into my fist. They were my certainty, in the darkness and rain. I needed them because everything was ready in the flat. I wasn't afraid of dying, you see. I was afraid of living.

I hadn't got into that black cab. I'd let go of the door, stumbled out of the station and into the rain. Now I had no idea how long I'd been walking, and I didn't care. What did time matter? I was non-existent in the bustle of humanity. I felt so much like a ghost that I accidentally collided with a group of city suits as they stood smoking, huddled under a dripping canopy outside one of the bars near the Barbican. Bless them, they were in a jovial weekend mood. They assumed I'd had one too many; they even offered me a cigarette.

Indecision was tearing at me. I would shatter Eilish by my death or by telling her the truth. Either way, I would lose her. There were no other options. You might find that impossible to understand, but, believe me, there were none. I had twisted and turned and come to this final, inescapable conclusion.

The pubs emptied; the traffic thinned. Blocked gutters became muddy streams through which I waded. People eyed me as I walked past, puzzled by my saturated clothes and aimlessness.

My overnight bag was slung over one shoulder, my briefcase in the other hand. They felt more and more heavy. I thought of dumping the overnight bag into a skip, but there were things in it that I didn't want to be found. If I was going to end my life tonight, I must dispose of them more carefully.

It was long after midnight. There was a blister on my right heel, but I limped on. The night buses were carrying Friday-night revellers home, windscreen wipers flicking, when I turned into Thurso Lane.

Well done! purred The Thought. Its voice was affectionate and understanding, as though coaxing a tired toddler on a long journey. *Nearly there. Soon you can put down those things you've been carrying. You can let go of the tree, at long last.*

The rain was a torrent as I walked down the basement steps. I dropped my bags beside the dustbin. The security light flickered into life, glinting on falling drops. Water coursed down my face.

I fitted my keys into the locks. The bottom deadlock first, and then the Yale.

'This is it,' I said out loud.

I'd made my choice. I wouldn't see how Kate's life turned out, or Simon's. I wouldn't see my grandchildren grow up. I wouldn't grow old with Eilish. Perhaps she'd be angry for the rest of her life, like the woman on the train. It was better than the alternative. Probably.

The Yale turned with a quiet click. The door gave way under the pressure of my hand. The security light went out.

Four

Eilish

After Kate rang off, I danced a little jig. Well! This sounded like very hopeful news. Luke and I disliked Owen more every time we saw him, though we made herculean efforts to hide the fact. There was something infuriating about the boy's mousy nondescriptness. Kate was a free spirit and yet he tried to stifle her with his manipulative poor-me-I've-had-a-rough-childhood clinginess. He'd even brought a crazy little dog home from the RSPCA, in a blatant attempt to play mums and dads. Kate took the bait ('He's never had any happiness, Mum') but Luke and I saw right through the ploy. Our abiding terror was that a real baby would be coming along next.

The whole thing was baffling. Ever since adolescence, Kate's been a feminist of the old school. If Owen had been a rugby-playing banker with a square chin and a Range Rover, she wouldn't have touched him with a barge pole. It seemed ironic that she'd let a needy, controlling boy rule her life just as surely as any bullying mobster.

I hummed a few bars of 'Goodbye Yellow Brick Road' as I tipped salad out of a bag and warmed up yesterday's lasagne. Mm-*hm!* Owen was on his way out, all right. I couldn't wait to tell Luke the glad tidings when he phoned.

But he didn't phone. Every half-hour or so I tried his number, only to get voicemail. Maybe his battery was flat. His charger was here, in the kitchen.

After supper I opened my roll-top desk and designed the invitations for our party. By midnight I still hadn't heard from Luke, so I turned in. I read for a while in bed, wearing the honey-coloured silk slip he gave me on our last anniversary. He actually bought it himself, in the lingerie department of House of Fraser. Now, that shows real courage! A lone man, an alien among all that underwiring and cleavage-boosting, tackling false-eyelashed assistants. He'd been so pleased with himself.

After turning out the lamp, I reached across to his side of the bed and pulled his pillow under my head. I always stole it when he was away. It smelled of him: deodorant, soap and . . . Lukeness. It was the next best thing to cuddling the man himself.

A thousand tiny streams were rippling across the skylight. Putting the window directly above our bed was one of the few things Luke had insisted upon for Smith's Barn. 'I'll lie and look up at the stars,' he said. 'Insomnia will be a privilege.'

I was sinking into the depths of sleep when my bedroom door creaked.

'Don't you dare, Casino,' I whispered. 'Master isn't home.'

A weight landed on my legs, followed by kneading and enthusiastic purrs. *Bloody cat.* Ah, well. It was nice to have the company. I reached onto the bedside cabinet for my reading glasses and checked my phone yet again. No text. No missed call. Not to worry. Luke would be asleep at the flat by now. My stomach grew a little colder.

For a long time, I lay gazing through the watery glass at the blurred glow of the moon. Our bedroom was small and misshapen, crammed under the sloping roof of the barn. Charlotte was born in this room. On this bed. Died here too, a few minutes later. Luke and I also seemed to die for a while. I can understand why tragedy breaks couples apart: agony obliterates love for a long, long time. We stayed together, though. In the end we had a deeper understanding, because we'd shared despair.

A burst of raindrops spattered onto the skylight. I could just make out his cable knit sweater and a pair of jeans, shadows in the milky light, hanging over the footboard of the bed. These were the clothes he'd been wearing the day before he left, when we took the path across Gareth's farm. We wandered side by side in the familiar landscape, close together, our hands sometimes touching. The fields were dotted with cotton-reel bales. We were leaning on the handrail of the footbridge, watching the slow passage of the stream, when Luke did something most unexpected.

'I love you,' he said, nudging his forehead against mine. 'Thank you.'

Love wasn't something we mentioned often. There didn't seem to be any need. Luke and I were a pair—we fitted. I don't think either of us felt quite complete without the other. Why go on about it? Only teenagers and film stars talk about *lerve*.

'You're very welcome,' I said, smoothing his hair. I liked the way it lay over his ears, blue-black and tinged with silver, like a bird's wing. 'I've no idea what I'm being thanked for, but I definitely deserve it.'

Something had changed. The world had grown dark. The rain intensified in a sudden roar, louder than machine-gun fire, and the stream was a mud-brown torrent. Luke was in the water. It was sweeping him away. I grabbed an old tyre from the mud and tried to throw it to him, but he didn't reach for it. I screamed at him to swim, swim, but he didn't. His dark eyes looked straight past me as water poured down his face. He seemed to see something beyond. The next moment I'd been sucked in too. I was drowning. I was shouting for Luke, but he was gone.

Panic woke me, thank God. The blanket was bundled around my face. I threw it off, yelling because I'd lost Luke in the river. Casino was on his feet, bottlebrush-tailed.

'Horrible, horrible,' I gasped, reaching out to touch his warm fur. 'Horrible dream.'

For some minutes I felt breathless, winded by the gallop of my heartbeat. Then the old cat began to lick himself, and eventually he lay down again. His calm was comforting. Above my head, the square patch of sky had lightened to a pale grey. Luke would be up by now. Perhaps he was already heading into the office, to face five hundred emails.

'Pop downstairs and make me a nice pot of tea, will you, Casino?' I asked, but the little tabby just curled a paw across his face. I stroked his head. 'Too early for you? Yes, well. It *is* bloody early. It's—hang on, is that a car?'

Casino and I both pricked up our ears at the crunch of wheels on gravel. I rolled out of bed, pulling on my dressing-gown as I peered out into the rain-streaked morning. Who on earth would turn up at this ungodly hour? I imagined the police, with bad news and solemn faces. I expected to see a panda car parked in our drive.

A moment later I'd charged downstairs and thrown open the front door with a shout of welcome. Luke was walking towards me through the rain, his trench coat over one arm.

'You're soaked,' I scolded.

He looked down at himself. He was wearing suit trousers and his black corduroy jacket. His hair was plastered to his head, and droplets trickled under his collar. He seemed lost, but that wasn't unusual for him. It was one of the things that had struck me about him on the night we met; that, and the strong feeling that I'd known him all my life.

I put my arms around his neck and kissed him on the mouth. 'Wet or dry, I am very, very glad to see you! So you changed your mind about going into work? Well, what a lovely surprise! You'd better have a hot shower.' I led him inside and shut the door on the rain. 'Coffee or tea?'

Casino had heard all the commotion. He lolloped down the spiral staircase, made a beeline for Luke and arched against his legs. He was meant to be the children's cat, but Luke was his idol.

'He's a one-man cat,' I said, taking two coffee cups down from the dresser. They were handmade, painted in red and yellow and with matching saucers. Relief was making me chatty. The cold clutching in my stomach—the drowning nightmare—had meant nothing, after all. I rambled on about the weather and the garden, and Kate and Owen. Luke stood watching me, dripping rainwater onto the tiles.

'Chop-chop,' I nagged, pushing him towards the stairs. 'You'll catch your death. How come you set out so early?'

'I lost the keys to the flat.'

I gaped. '*Sorry?* Don't you have a spare set?'

'They're here. So I went to Paddington and waited for the first train.'

It didn't make sense. 'But . . . you've surely not been sitting in Paddington station all night?'

'No, not sitting. I walked around.'

'All night, in the storm? Why didn't you just go to Simon and Carmela's place? They'd have put you up. For heaven's sake—you could have phoned me. I'd have driven in. You know I would.'

'Yes, I know that.' He seemed to retreat into the hollows of his eyes. I watched him, and that aching chill returned. I'd seen him like this before. It was as though he were being tortured: silently, privately.

'What were you thinking, as you walked all night?' I asked.

He didn't answer.

'Darling man.' Sliding around the edge of the island, I touched his face with the palms of my hands, turning it to face mine. 'Is it back? You know these low times always pass. Why on earth didn't you phone me?'

'I was making a choice,' he said. 'I have made it. And now I have to tell you something.'

The room faded away. There was only Luke, ghost-faced and soaking wet. I remembered the day my father turned up here—standing pretty much where Luke was now—and told me they'd found a shadow on his lung. I'd wanted to weep at the determined optimism in his voice: *It's not a one-way ticket nowadays, the Big C. They can do amazing things with chemo*. Six months later, we buried him. My mother didn't even come to the funeral. Death's powerful, but it couldn't dent her bitterness—though why she'd been bitter when it was she who ran off with somebody else, I never understood. She outlived Dad by ten years before the Big C got her, too.

'Are you ill?' I asked now.

'No.' Luke gave a sniff of laughter. Well, not really laughter. 'Sick, perhaps. Yes. People will certainly say I'm sick.'

I breathed again. Not cancer, then. Not some other terminal illness. Anything else could be borne. 'Are you having an affair?'

'No. No! I'd never . . . there's never been anyone but you.'

I had no idea what was coming. I really thought it was something quite trivial. Perhaps he'd lost his shirt in some dodgy investment? Well, so be it. Money isn't the most important thing in life.

'Sit down,' I said, as I carried our coffee to the table. 'Tell me what's going on. A problem shared . . .'

It's seen some action, our kitchen table. For over a quarter of a century, our lives have revolved around its blue-painted legs and scrubbed oak top. It's seen children's baptisms and birthday parties; it's hosted flaming family rows and teenage revels and endless games of Monopoly. Its face bears the honourable scars of hot saucepans, Kate's henna, and Simon's early attempts at soldering. It knows us all, very well.

Luke didn't sit down. 'You'll be revolted,' he said.

'Try me! Whatever it is can't be so terrible, if you aren't ill and you're not having an affair. Is it financial? Have you lost our pension? Our house?'

'No.'

'Has Bannermans gone bust?'

'No. No.' He held out his hands, palms downward, as though trying to suppress my guesses. 'It's who I am. I have to tell you who I am.'

'You look like Luke Livingstone to me.'

'Yes, I look like him. But I'm not.'

'I think you'll find you are.' I was forcing a smile.

'I've been running from this all my life. I can't run any further, Eilish.'

And then he began to talk; but it was as though he were speaking in some foreign language because I could get no sense from his words. He kept saying that he was not who I thought he was, he had never been who I thought he was; that he wasn't unique, that there were others. *You must have noticed*, he kept saying. *You must have suspected.* Suspected what? I wondered, my mind racing in terror. Noticed what? Luke was a rational man—sensitive, occasionally depressed, but above all rational. *Perhaps he's had a bang on the head. Or—dear God, maybe he's had a stroke? Brain tumour? Must get him to a doctor, right away.*

'Stop,' I snapped. 'You've been talking for ten minutes and I still have no idea what you're trying to say. You seem disorientated. I think I should drive you straight to the hospital.' As I talked I was hurrying around, looking for my bag, fetching my car keys from their hook beside the fridge.

'I think I was meant to be a woman,' he said.

'They might keep you in for tests. You'll need warm, dry clothes. I'll go up and—'

'Eilish, listen. Please listen.' Something in his tone made me stop and turn around. He'd pressed a hand across his eyes. 'I look like a man called Luke. I'm imprisoned inside the body of a man called Luke. But I *am not him*.'

I didn't want to understand. I was afraid to understand. 'Okay,' I said, 'just stay calm. Are you in any pain?'

'Eilish.'

'An ambulance might be faster.'

'I'm not ill.' He sat down heavily, as though his legs wouldn't take his weight any longer. 'There's a name for it.'

'Don't say any more,' I begged him. 'Let's just—'

He spoke over me, so loudly that I couldn't ignore him. 'It's called gender identity disorder.'

Gender identity disorder. I'd heard the term. A couple of years before, at a teachers' conference, I'd attended a seminar on the subject. We spent an entire day learning about boys who wanted to dress, play and be treated as girls; and about girls who longed to be male. Some had help from a clinic—even took hormones, which shocked me. There was lots of trendy discussion about which toilets they should use; one of the people on the course had been in a legal dispute with some parents because the school wouldn't let their boy dress in a skirt and call himself Tanya. I like to think of myself as open-minded, but I didn't really get it. Poor tormented things, I thought. I even—very secretly—suspected that the parents might be to blame.

And as for adults? Well. We've all seen those strange creatures, men with wigs and handbags, lurching along on high heels: the wrong shape, the wrong voice, and always alone. I pitied them—actually, when I was young and cruel I laughed at them—but they had nothing to do with me. They were from another world altogether.

'Enough,' I said now. 'This isn't funny. You aren't a . . . That's got nothing to do with you.'

'It has everything to do with me.'

'No, darling, it hasn't.' I wanted to talk sense into him, as though he were one of my pupils. I sat down next to him. 'That's for children who are still finding their way, their sexuality, maybe trying to please parents who always wanted a boy or a girl. They're just very, very confused young people. It's got nothing to do with middle-aged solicitors with wives and families.'

'I'm female. My body looks male, but I am not. It isn't new, Eilish, I've felt this all my life. I was born with the wrong body.'

He might as well have announced that he was an alien from some far-off galaxy, inhabiting the body of a human. I knew it wasn't true. I didn't know why he was putting on this charade, but I knew it wasn't true.

'I *know* you,' I insisted, with a panicky little laugh. 'I know exactly who you are! You're a man. You're *my* man. This is crazy.'

I'll wake up in a minute, I thought. I tried to shake myself out of sleep, but it didn't work. 'You expect me to believe that you've felt . . . been hiding . . . this . . . what, since the day we met? You wouldn't do that to me. I know you wouldn't. I *know* you. You're Luke.'

He put his face in his hands. Casino jumped onto his lap and began to knead.

'I've got to explain,' Luke said. 'Please let me try.'

I was too stunned to interrupt as he described how he had always thought of himself as female, even when he was a little boy. He said again and again how sorry he was; he would understand if I divorced him, but he could no longer keep up the pretence that he was a normal man. He said he didn't want to lie anymore. He said that he loved me.

I sat and listened without comprehending, and thought about how he'd walked all night in the storm. A nail had begun to work its way out of my chair. Quite deliberately, I pressed my shoulderblade against its sharp tip. The pain was at least real and tangible in that nightmare fog. The world was tipping, and I was going to fall off. Water began hosing against the windows. Spouting's buggered again, I thought, as though it mattered about the bloody spouting.

'Do you mean you're gay?' I asked suddenly. 'Is that what this is all about—you want to sleep with men? You've never really wanted me at all?'

'No. I'm not gay. That would be so much easier.'

I laughed, because it was absurd. '*Easier?*'

'Less complicated.'

'So . . . what does it mean? I don't understand what this means. Are you leaving me?'

My question was still hanging above our heads when the phone rang. It seemed irrelevant. Through the mist, I heard Simon's voice on the answering machine. Poor Simon. He sounded cheerful. He thought his world was still whole.

'Hi, Dad. Hi, Mum. Um . . . I expect you're still asleep, sorry if I've woken you up. Dad, just wondered if you caught the interview on Radio Four just now, about mediation across cultures? Pretty interesting, thought you might . . . er, anyway. You can always listen to it online. Hilarious, what they say about non-verbal communication with Norwegians. Um, Carmela sends her love. She's fine—tired, obviously, but blooming. We'll see you both tomorrow, if we're still coming for lunch? I thought I'd check that's still on, but I'll assume it is unless I hear from you. Hang on . . . Nico wants to say hello.'

A pause. Whispers. Heavy breathing. Then the careful tones of a four-year-old who's been allowed the adult privilege of talking into the telephone.

'Hello, Grandpa . . . Hello. Hello? . . . He's not there, Dad.' There were more whispers before our darling grandson spoke again. This time he used his formal message-leaving voice. 'Hello, Grandpa and Granny. It's fish for breakfast. I have a new baby bruvver or sister coming. When are we going to make the wooden plane? Bye.'

I pictured Nico crashing down the receiver before racing back to his fish-for-breakfast. Then there was silence in our kitchen. Water gushed against the glass.

'Are you going to leave me?' I asked again.

'I think that's up to you. All I know is that I have to change. I can't go on pretending to be something I'm not.'

Then I remembered something I'd read once, in a magazine at the hairdresser's, about a woman who found her husband's stash of women's clothes. It turned out he wore them often, as soon as her back was turned. *It was the worst day of my life*, she said. I read it with prurient interest while they did my foils. The husband had announced that he wanted to be female. There was a picture of two women, and one of them looked downright odd.

'You're married,' I said now, with an obstinacy born of terror. 'You have children and grandchildren. You are *Luke Livingstone*, for heaven's sake! Luke Livingstone—who is very male indeed, I can assure you, and I damn well ought to know because you've shared my bed for three decades, and we've had three children in that time.'

'I've tried to be.'

'No . . .' I was desperately trying to think, trying to make him see how insane this was. 'You are my friend, my lover, my husband. I would have known.'

'I hoped you did know, in some way.'

Memories were imps, their grinning faces forcing cracks in my denial: Luke dressing for a tarts and vicars party, wearing my shortest skirt and putting on make-up with surprising skill. He was the life and soul of the party that day, flamboyant and loud, as though the costume freed him from his usual reticence. *Nice legs!* people yelled across the room, as he danced with our hostess. *You'd make a hell of a babe, Luke.*

'We're so happy,' I said. 'Aren't we? Why tell me this now?'

'Because I've come to the end of my road, Eilish. The very end. I can't go on. I was facing a choice last night: to end my life, or to accept what I've always really been. I am so sorry.'

The nail pierced my back, holding me upright. If I'd been less stunned I might have asked him what he thought would happen next; I might have asked about practicalities—what exactly had he chosen? But such questions were far, far beyond me.

'Tell me,' I said, 'when I was walking up the aisle, and you turned around and smiled at me . . . I've never forgotten that, Luke . . . when our children were born, when we lost Charlotte, when we talked about retirement, made all those plans for our future—' He began to speak, but I held up a hand. 'No. Let me ask. I have to ask. All those times we've made love and fallen asleep in one another's arms, and woken up together, and talked and worried and argued and kissed and laughed at ridiculous things . . . day after day, year after year . . . all our lives, when I thought we were happy together, when I thought you desired and valued me . . . all these years you've been lying about something so utterly fundamental?'

He shook his head. I thought I heard him say again that he was sorry.

'I don't believe it,' I whispered. 'You've been lying about everything you think, everything you feel, everything that you are?'

He didn't respond. He didn't need to. I could see the answer for myself.

The chair clattered as I stood up. Casino leaped off Luke's lap. 'I don't understand this. You are Luke. *You are Luke.* Luke Livingstone. That's who you are. I've given you my whole life.' My voice was rising. 'You are Luke, you hear me?'

Tripping over Casino, I fled up the staircase. Our bedroom has always been my refuge, but now there was nowhere to hide. The nightmare had come with me. I lay across the bed, pressing my face into the pillow that still smelled of Luke. My Luke. The real Luke, not the madman downstairs. My heart wasn't quite broken yet, because I didn't quite believe. How could I believe something so utterly impossible?

I turned over and felt my slip slide up my thigh. Honey-coloured silk. I'd thought it endearing that Luke had chosen it, and brought it home gift-wrapped in the shop's tissue paper and ribbons. *Dear God, dear God, what if he'd enjoyed being in there?*

Those grinning imps were slipping in through the cracks, bearing more insidious memories from down the years. *Didn't you know?* they giggled. *Or didn't you want to know?* My favourite high-heeled shoes, and that clinging woollen dress, all suddenly stretched and too big for me; the day I thought there were traces of lipstick on Luke's mouth but brushed the thought away because it was terrifying; those times when I felt my man was hiding some secret darkness from me, but I was too afraid to ask.

The world was upside down. There was nothing for me to hold onto. I was going to be flung off, into the lonely reaches of outer space.

Five

Simon

Dammit. He should have kept his eye on the breakfast instead of phoning Dad. Smoke was billowing out of the grill, which called for action before the fire alarm went off and woke Carmela. He opened the back door, pelted outside and scraped the burned edges of crumbed fish into the compost. There. Good as new.

Nico was sitting on a stool, running a toy Jeep up and down the kitchen bench. 'Did you burn my fish?' he asked, as Simon produced it with a flourish.

'I chargrilled it, just to add a little flavour. One for you, sir, and one for me.'

Nico looked at his plate with dark wide-open eyes. There was no doubt about that child's paternity. People often commented on how much he took after both Simon and Luke: compact, with a smile that made strangers coo over him. Shame about the pudding-basin haircut, though; it made him look like a girl. Simon had complained to Carmela, but she just laughed. 'He'll be a bloody macho pain in the arse soon enough,' she said, 'and then he can have a six-pack and an American military flat-top, but can't he be pretty now, since he's only four years old?' Simon had shrugged, and given up.

'And one for Mummy?' Nico asked now.

'She prefers yoghurt.'

'Yum.' Nico picked up a bottle of ketchup and squeezed it with both hands. Nothing came out. He squeezed harder, his tongue sticking out, until a jet of red shot onto his pyjama top. 'Oops.'

Simon laughed. 'Your pyjamas were hungry,' he said.

Nico stuck his finger into the largest blob and licked it. 'Is Granny your mummy?' he asked.

'She is indeed.'

'And she's Aunt Kate's mummy too?'

'Well done.'

'Mummy calls her Eyelash.'

Simon kept his face straight. Nico was very alert to being patronised or laughed at; that was something else they had in common. 'So she does. That's your granny's name. Eilish, actually. A bit like Eyelash.'

'And what's Grandpa's name?'

'Grandpa is called Luke. Shall I cut up your fish for you?' Simon made the mistake of leaning across to help, commandeering the child-sized knife and fork.

'Grr!' roared Nico. 'I can do it!'

'Okay, okay. Keep your hair on.'

It was painful to watch the slow mangling of that fish. How did Carmela cope with this kind of thing, day after day? Nico smashed it to a pulp with his fork before stirring in liberal dollops of ketchup. It didn't even look like food anymore. Simon had heard some of Carmela's friends—including the two house husbands she hung out with—complaining that they had put on weight because they couldn't resist eating their children's leftovers. Simon found this incomprehensible. He would have to be starving—literally, crawling across the desert with vultures circling overhead—before he popped one of those mushed-up, masticated, ketchup-smothered delights into his own mouth.

Coffee was a *much* better idea. He made himself a perfect cup with the new espresso machine, revelling in its rich and bitter scents as crema settled in a white film across the top of the black. Simon took coffee-making extremely seriously. Holding the cup in one hand, he slid onto a stool and pulled the newspaper closer. Ah, this was the life. He didn't ask for much—family, work, a decent cup of coffee, and enough time in the summer for cricket. A bat had been put into his hands as soon as he could walk, and his first memory was of him and his dad playing with it on the lawn of his grandparents' farmhouse.

He leafed through the paper. War, sanctions, a row over import tariffs. The test match at Lords. Nico was chattering, but to Simon it was just background noise. He carried on reading, murmuring *mmm* and *wow* at what he hoped were the right places.

'Bruvver or sister?' Nico was asking. 'Dad! Bruvver or sister?'

'Mm?'

'What will our baby be?'

The Aussies were two hundred and five for nine at close of play. 'Human, I hope.'

Nico kicked his feet against the bench, sounding like a herd of buffalo. 'Daddy, Daddy, Daddy! Boy or girl?'

'I don't know. It's going to be a surprise, like when you open a present on your birthday. We'll be very, very happy when the baby arrives, whether it's a boy, a girl, a rabbit, or even a woolly mammoth like you.' Simon reached to tickle his son in that very ticklish spot between his ear and neck. Nico squirmed and giggled, then climbed onto Simon's knee.

Hope it's a girl, thought Simon, picturing a toddling delight in a white dress. Mind you, Kate had never been a toddling delight of any kind. He was six when she arrived, and his one abiding memory was of the power of her lungs. His sister started the way she meant to go on. Opinionated. Strident. She was a burn-the-bra merchant, half a century too late. If she'd been born in 1900 she would have ended up under the king's horse.

'Whatcha reading?' asked Nico.

'I'm not reading anything, because there's a great big ketch-uppy head in the way.'

'Haven't got a big head.'

Simon gave up on the paper. 'How about a bit of cricket in the garden? Hang on, I'll just wipe that face of yours . . . Where's your bat? Got it? Okay, you can show me how it's done.'

Nico didn't show him how it was done. In fact, he missed every ball, as usual. Simon had a nagging fear that his son was pathologically uncoordinated. He'd been anxious enough about this to mention it to Luke the previous weekend, when he and Eilish came for Sunday lunch.

'Was I this hopeless?' he'd asked, as Nico stood picking his nose and watching the ball roll gently by. 'He'll never be a cricketer.'

Luke had laughed, which was good to hear. He'd seemed subdued that day. 'The little chap is only four, Simon. Four! He can't even write his own name yet. I don't imagine Ian Botham was knocking 'em to the boundaries either at that age.'

'But *look* at him! He's not even interested.'

They both looked. Nico had discarded his bat and was trying to touch his ear with his tongue.

Simon felt his father's hand on his shoulder. 'Do yourself a favour,' Luke said seriously. 'Take this one off your worry list.'

'Grandad Livingstone will be spinning in his grave.'

'It doesn't matter. Truly. Please remember that. These things *do not matter.* You must let Nico be his own person.'

As they walked back to the house, Luke mentioned that he'd brought his collection of Biggles books. He was having a tidy-up, he said, and wanted Nico to have them. Simon was touched. His dad had read Biggles to him when he was a schoolboy—read every night for half an hour, no matter how late he'd come in from work. It had taken years, but they'd got through every single one.

Today's cricket game was proving as disastrous as every other. *Look, Dad, a plane! Look, Dad, I can do roly-polies!* When Nico started decapitating hollyhocks with his bat, Simon gave up.

'Let's take Mummy a cup of tea,' he suggested, glancing hopefully at his watch. 'She must have had enough sleep by now.'

He felt virtuous as he rinsed the pot. His pregnant wife had been getting some rest and he was an exemplary father. He handed Nico the biscuit tin to carry, and together they went up the stairs and burst through the bedroom door. The room had been decorated by Carmela as only she could have done, in deep blue and burned orange. She blinked sleepily, her hair a dark fan on the pillow.

'Tea,' announced Simon.

'And biccies,' added Nico, dumping the tin onto her feet. He ripped off the lid and found a chocolate finger.

Carmela yawned. 'You are New Men,' she said. Simon caught a distinct edge of sarcasm in her voice. 'What time is it? Only eight? Hmm, not the longest lie-in in the history of the world.'

After five years of marriage, Simon still found her accent seductive. Everything about Carmela was voluptuous, especially now when she was almost six months gone.

'How're you feeling?' he asked, lying beside her, on top of the duvet.

'Like I've got an elephant in here.'

'No!' He patted her stomach through the bedding. 'Just a walrus.'

She sat up, sticking out her tongue at him. 'Did you call your parents? Are we still going all the way to Oxfordshire tomorrow, just to plant a tree?'

'I left a message, but I'd guess it will be on. The weather forecast is improving.'

'Hmm.' She sipped her tea. 'Everyone will be solemn and serious, because they have to remember your grandfather. Eilish and Luke will be busy looking after everyone. It will be no fun for my poor Nico. I bet your aunt Wendy will be there . . . oh, dear. And Kate?'

'I don't know if she's back from Israel yet, but—whoa, Nico! Three biscuits is enough. Put those other ones back.'

Carmela wrinkled her nose. 'Your sister disapproves of me.'

'No, no.'

'Yes, yes. I have sold the sisterhood down the river because I wear heels higher than an inch, and lipstick, and stopped working when Nico arrived. Oh, yes—I am also a capitalist pig, because I worked for a multinational company.'

'A capitalist sow.'

Pulling the dark mass of her hair over one shoulder, Carmela began to plait it. Even now, wearing a maternity tent, she looked spectacular.

'Don't you worry about Kate,' said Simon. 'She's just my scrawny little sister.'

'She could be pretty, if she didn't work so hard to look plain.'

Nico was kneeling on the pillow, gaping at Carmela's hands as she plaited. 'Can I have a go?' he asked.

'Watch me first . . . over here, and under there. Careful not to pull. Oh, my goodness!' Smiling at Simon, she took his hand and guided it onto her stomach.

'Kicking?' he said.

'Mighty kicks!'

Simon felt a small earthquake under his fingers. It always seemed like a miracle. 'The kid's a karate expert,' he said.

'Who is this, do you suppose?' asked Carmela. 'Who is this new person that we do not yet know?' They sat with their heads close together, contemplating the already-loved stranger in their midst.

His parents' distraction was driving Nico wild with jealousy. He'd given up plaiting and was driving his Jeep up and down Carmela's hair. 'It's the baby!' he yelled.

'Yes, the baby,' said Carmela. 'But who is it really? Who is he or she, in his or her heart? Does she already have a soul? Who are you, little one?'

Nico clearly had no interest in the soul of someone he couldn't yet see. He yanked at the Jeep, which made Carmela clutch her head.

'Ouch!' she cried. 'What's going on?'

Simon took a closer look at the Jeep, and wanted to laugh. 'It's stuck in your hair.'

'Can't you free it?'

'Um . . . Your hair's completely tangled around the mechanism. Hang on, hold still . . .' Gently, he tried to unravel the knots. It was hopeless. 'No, I'm sorry. Might have to cut it out.'

Nico giggled. 'You'll just have to be a mummy with a car on her head.'

'A car on my head, and soon there will be baby vomit down my back,' lamented Carmela. 'How are the mighty fallen.'

Six

Luke

Broken guttering. I needed to fix that. I slumped sightless at the table, battered by the staccato drumming of water.

Why had I allowed a stranger on a train to change my mind? *Why?* I'd known what was right. I'd seen the honourable course. Eilish would have been a widow by now, respectable and dignified and financially set for life. The last instalments of the mortgages had been paid on both this house and Thurso Lane. There was a pension. She would have mourned, and then she would have coped. She would still love me.

The phone on the kitchen wall was ringing.

Rain and darkness. I was back outside the flat. The key turned, and the door opened. Peace waited for me, just a few steps away; but Eilish was standing among the roses, and I didn't want to leave her.

Then I'd slammed the door shut again, and I was running. I was running from death. I staggered up the steps, along Thurso Lane and onto the main road. Here, floodwater rushed along the gutter, bubbling in a murky wave before surging down a drain. I fell face down on the kerb and began to push my keys through the grating of the drain.

Really? screamed The Thought. *You really want to carry on?*

The suffering's only just begun, buddy.

The keys were through. I felt the current snatch at them. I hesitated for one last moment, and then released my grip.

They were gone. They were gone, and so was my promise of peace. The rain seemed to pause in astonishment, then pelted more violently than ever. I don't know how long I lay on the wet pavement. I do remember how that gushing stream glowed red, orange and green in the reflection of the traffic lights.

Much, much later, a night bus disgorged a group of partygoers. I heard them trooping along the footpath. They were singing in raucous alcohol-fuelled voices. When they came close to me, the singing stopped.

'Taking a nap, mate?' yelled a male voice.

I didn't answer.

'Pissed to bits,' declared another. 'Go home, Grandad, you could drown down there.'

I rolled over, and onto my knees. I felt profoundly tired, as though I'd never stand up again. One of them—a girl—tottered closer to me. She wasn't walking in a very straight line.

'You're crying.' Her voice was slurred.

'Just a bit,' I said.

'Why're you crying?'

'Because I'm very, very frightened.'

She leaned down, swaying on her stiletto heels, peering into my face. The others lost interest and began to drift away.

'What're you so shit-scared of?' she asked.

She was about Kate's age. A kind girl, probably. I didn't want to spoil her night out. I managed to smile at her.

'I'm shit-scared,' I said, 'because I've decided to live.'

•

The phone had stopped ringing. The kitchen was silent for a moment, and then our answering machine clicked into action.

'Eilish? It's me.' I recognised the voice of Stella Marriot, a very old friend of Eilish's. 'Um, I'm just off to Cornwall as planned, got to show some interest in this new granddaughter, but look . . . I forgot to ask if you'd feed the bloody cat. Would you, Eilish? The usual routine. Oh blast, the alarm code's been changed; hang on, let me check, yes . . . it's one-four-one-four. Got that? Fourteen-fourteen. Thank you, darling. Perhaps you young things could both come over when I get back? Ages since I had more than a fleeting glimpse of Luke. Works too hard. Time he slowed down, he must be important enough by now! Come for supper, I'll poison you both with my new Thai cookery skills. Okay? Right, better get going, it's a hellish drive down there . . . bye.'

No, I thought. I don't think we could come for supper. I don't think Eilish and Luke exist as an entity any longer.

A few minutes later, the phone rang again. This time it was Kate's voice. Listening to my daughter was far, far worse.

'Anyone there? Mum . . . Mum? Can you pick up the phone, please? Okay, you're obviously out gallivanting . . . I was wondering if you'd heard from Dad. I thought we could take the same train but he's switched his phone off or something. I can't get hold of him.' A sigh. 'Okay. Well, can you call me if you get this?'

I stood up, intending to look for Eilish. We'd taken care of each other through every crisis in our lives. This was another one. I'd reached the stairs when she appeared on the gallery above me. She was wearing a bright, summery dress. I knew it well. In fact—and I'm not proud of this—I'd tried it on several times, but it didn't do anything for me. It looked much better on her. Not today, though. By contrast with its vivid flowers her face was pallid, the freckles standing out unnaturally. Her mouth seemed weighted down at the corners. Her hair wasn't brushed, and it frizzed around her head.

'No,' she said, stopping me with a raised hand. 'Don't come up.'

'Eilish, I—'

'And don't say any more—not to me, not to anyone. I don't want to hear a word of this . . . this absurdity. There's a lot to do. Kate's arriving sometime today, and tomorrow your mother and

Simon and Carmela and Nico and Wendy, and they're all going to be—' She broke off.

The tree-planting. Of course. 'I'd forgotten,' I said.

'Had you?' She began to walk down the stairs. Her steps seemed steady, but I saw how she gripped the rails on both sides.

'I think you should talk to someone,' I said. 'What about Stella? She's off to Cornwall—just left a message about the cat—but she won't have gone yet. She'll come round. I don't mind if you tell her.'

'No.'

She stepped around me, careful to avoid any accidental contact. She was in survival mode. I'd seen it before, when we lost Charlotte. In those first terrible hours we sat in the bedroom, holding our baby—now dressed in the stripey suit we'd so happily bought for her—weeping until we had no more tears. It felt as though Eilish and I were one person: one grieving, shattered person. Then Charlotte was taken away for an autopsy, and Eilish insisted on getting out of bed and putting on her clothes. She said she had a funeral to arrange and it was bloody well going to be a good one. She faced the world, though the world did not expect her to.

On the day of the funeral I looked like a scarecrow. My eyes were bloodshot, my suit crumpled. I'd cut myself shaving. But Eilish was beautifully turned out in navy linen, her hair in an immaculate French pleat, her face closed and rigid. She never noticed, and nobody mentioned, that her shoes weren't a pair. One was a blue court shoe, the other a sandal. I admired her even more, because those mismatched shoes were a window onto her courage.

She had that same closed look now, as she opened the chest freezer and began hauling things out of it.

'This can't just be ignored,' I said. 'You must have a thousand questions, and we have decisions to make. Tell me what you want. I'll do anything to make this easier for you. I'll leave immediately, if you want.'

'Sleep in the study tonight, will you? Tell the children you have a cold.' She was piling the contents of the freezer onto the bench top; piling things up, higher and higher and higher in a tottering pile, without even looking at them.

'Please stop!' I implored her. 'Let's cancel the family. It's only planting a tree for Dad. We can tell them we've gone down with flu.'

'Please don't mention this thing again.'

I was baffled. 'What, never?'

'Not until after tomorrow.'

'But it's going to be impossible—'

'No, Luke!' She slammed the freezer lid. 'No. I'm asking you to let me keep my dignity for another forty-eight hours. My *dignity*. For pity's sake, is that so much to ask?'

'Of course,' I said. 'Anything.'

I watched as she took a kitchen knife and slit the wrapping off a frozen leg of lamb. Her movements were quick and jerky.

'I think you're deluded,' she said savagely. 'Perhaps by tomorrow you'll have found your sanity again. Now, if you'll excuse me, I'd better go and get Kate's room ready.'

'Can I help?'

She shook her head and disappeared upstairs. I wandered into the study. It was tidy; unnaturally tidy, because I hadn't intended to return to it. There were no sticky notes on the filing cabinet, no chaotic piles on my desk. In the top drawer lay a sheet of paper with notes for my executors. There was also a list of everything Eilish might need to know: my online passwords, the location of the stopcock in the flat, the addresses of everyone I wanted to be informed. I wasn't supposed to be here.

I stood with no purpose, in a future I hadn't expected to see. I was an impostor in my own life. Through the window I could see Gareth trudging, his head bent under the rain, as he moved cattle out of the sloping field. He'd be calling to his animals, and they would follow him through the gate in the thick hedgerow because they trusted him; which was ironic, really, as some of them were going to end up in our freezer. Lucky Gareth. He had a perpetually happy girlfriend, and his own small son ran around the farm with him at weekends and on holidays. Rain ruined his haymaking some years, and his tractor was always breaking down, but Gareth knew who he was. He fitted his boots and overalls. Always had, always would.

The phone on my desk rang. I picked it up without thinking.

'Dad!'

The sound of Kate's voice made my breath catch. I was glad to be here, talking to her, after all. I was glad she hadn't just lost her father.

'Hello there,' I said. 'Welcome back to Blighty.'

'Why didn't you answer your phone? I'm after a Dad-hug.'

I smiled. She used to get Dad-hugs when she was tiny and skinned her knee, when her schoolfriends were bitchy, or when she woke in the night and screamed at the sight of a face at her window. The first few times this had happened, I crept outside with a cricket bat in one hand and the other clutching my pyjama bottoms. Finally we worked out that the culprit was the full moon.

'What's up?' I asked.

'Owen turned out to be a complete knob. He had a one-night shagathon with a slapper called Gwen, just before I went to Israel. And *then*—check this, Dad—he claimed it was all my fault because I made him feel insecure!'

'No! What a . . . um, complete knob.'

'Exactly. So I cut a few pieces out of his favourite shirt. You know, the mushy-pea-coloured one. Fake satin.'

'You did *what*?'

'Dolly shapes, all holding hands. So that when he put it on he'd have dancing ladies across his chest. Very arty, very tasteful. I never liked that shirt.'

I was astonished to feel an explosion of laughter in my chest. My marriage was over, and maybe my life too . . . yet somehow I could still appreciate the image of Owen with dolly shapes across his irritating shiny front. Funny thing, human resilience.

'You vandal,' I said.

'I thought that was pretty mild, in the circumstances.'

'I suppose you could have mutilated things that would have caused him more pain.'

'Exactly!' Her laugh was wicked. 'Then I went on the dig, and I thought we'd make it up—because for God's sake, Dad, we've been together two years—and guess what he's done? Cleared out my bank account! Reckons he's owed for rent and vet's bills and damage to his frigging shirt.'

'The man's a cad. D'you want me to call him out?'

'My champion! Yes, please, call him out and run him through. Or you could just collect me from the station at half-past one.'

The house seemed to echo after she'd rung off. No sounds at all. Suddenly anxious, I climbed the stairs and looked into Kate's room. The bed was made, the pillows plumped, bath towels folded at one end. Books and ornaments on the shelves had been straightened. It took me a moment to spot Eilish, sitting in the rocking chair by the window. Her eyes were shut, and she was hugging Kate's polar bear—Mr Polington—in both arms. As I hesitated, a gasping sob burst out of her, quickly smothered when she pressed her face into the bear's soft flank.

I crept away. I had shattered that brave woman's life. The least I could do was let her grieve unwatched.

•

'Okay!' Kate threw her backpack into the boot and stowed herself noisily in the passenger seat. 'What's happening at the old homestead?'

The end of the world was happening.

I searched for a reply as we drew away from the station. 'What's happening? Well, we're planting Grandad's tree tomorrow.'

'Mm, I know.' She sounded gloomy. 'Simon and the clothes horse will be putting in an appearance, I suppose?'

'What's wrong with Carmela? I rather like her.'

'Well, you would, wouldn't you, because you're a man and she has a massive bust and a sexy Spanish accent that she exploits shamelessly. She hams it up, you know. Men can't see past those things. She doesn't patronise you. She doesn't bombard you with advice on how to live your life.'

She yawned, stretching out her legs and complaining of a hangover. Kate is blessed with Eilish's colouring—auburn hair, pale and given to freckles—and is as skinny as a rake. On this particular day she was wearing black lace-up boots, black tights and a black tunic over—I glanced sideways—a charcoal T-shirt, and had on heavy earrings of impressive ugliness. The garnet in the side of her nose was the only colourful glint. Her hair was cut short but asymmetrically, longer on one side than the other. It was as though my glorious daughter—who has regular features, blue eyes and a knockout smile—was trying to erase all the advantages nature has given her.

'D'you miss Grandad Livingstone?' she asked.

I thought about my father. 'He's been gone for a year,' I said. 'And he didn't have much of a life for a long time before that. But, yes, I miss him. He was a good father. I didn't deserve him.'

'I'm sure you did.'

We'd turned into the network of lanes that crisscross our part of Oxfordshire. Our road curved around the foot of Yalton Hill, muddy and narrow between lush hedgerows. The rain had stopped. As I wound down my window, the countryside rushed in—opulent and humid, heavy with after-rain smells of earth and wet vegetation. I'd taken my father for a drive out that way exactly a year earlier, the day before he died. We'd stopped in the Yalton Hill car park and eaten cheese sandwiches with Branston pickle, and talked. We both seemed to know it was our last talk. I wanted him to know that I loved him. He wanted me to know that he was proud of me.

I lied, right up until the end. I let him be proud of me. It was my last gift to him.

'Dad climbed a tree once,' I said now. 'To rescue me. It was the day of my fifth birthday party. I'd climbed up there, and I wouldn't come down. He was afraid of heights but he got a ladder and he climbed right to the top of the tallest tree in our garden. That must have taken every bit of courage he had. I wish I'd said thanks.'

Kate reached out and took my hand. I squeezed her fingers as I drove. *When you know*, I thought in panic, *I'm going to lose you too*.

'You said thanks in practical ways,' she replied. 'You did all that work on their house when he got ill. You put in the ramp. You took care of them.'

'I was only able to do that because Dad taught me everything I know about joinery. He also taught me how to play cricket, how to shoot, how to plough in a straight line . . . above all, he showed me what it means to be a decent human being, even if I wasn't able to be one myself.'

'You *are* a decent human being! You're the best!'

'No.'

Out of the corner of my eye, I saw her head turn to look at me. Of course she'd be surprised: I rarely revealed myself in any kind of depth. If people pressed me I always made some light remark before turning the conversation back to them. I knew this made me seem guarded, but it was a self-preservation thing. My secret was immense, and I'd been hiding it for half a century. I couldn't take risks.

'I'm sorry about you and Owen,' I said.

She folded her arms. 'God, he's such a jerk.'

'What exactly happened?'

She told me the long, sad tale, peppered with indignation and obscenities. I tried to listen properly, but Eilish's misery kept crowding into my mind and blotting out everything else. I tuned in from time to time. I heard about the savage, unforgivable things Owen and Kate had said to one another, and more about how she'd wreaked vengeance on his shirt.

'He made me promise not to tell anyone, but I'm going to anyway,' she said. 'He's got a tattoo of a sailing ship on his arse.'

'Stop right there! That's *way* too much information!'

She giggled. 'Mum wouldn't be shocked. Granny certainly wouldn't be shocked.'

'Well, I am!' I spluttered. I wasn't at all. In fact, I was amused; but I knew what role I was expected to play. I was the straight man in our family.

'I lived with the guy,' said Kate. 'It can't be news to you that I've seen his butt.'

'There are some things a father would *much* rather not think about.'

She rumpled my hair. I could see in the mirror that she'd left a tuft sticking up.

'I do love you, Dad.'

My briefcase was lying on the back seat, immediately behind where she was sitting. My mind flicked unhappily through its contents: dictaphone, laptop, files, periodicals. The farewell notes I'd written and not yet destroyed, just in case they might still come in handy. Gold fountain pen. Flash drive. A couple of squash balls. The Christmas-tree angel Nico made out of toilet rolls and tinsel at nursery school and gave to me as a very special gift.

It wasn't those things that made me burn with shame.

There was a small zip at one end of the lining. You wouldn't even know it was there unless you looked very carefully. Anyone discovering this secret pocket might be puzzled when they saw what was inside: blusher, mascara and a plum-coloured lipstick.

Seven

Eilish

My mother-in-law arrived on cue the following morning. I hurried to meet her, just as she climbed out of her new car. It looked like a giant ladybird.

'Hybrid,' she announced, in her smoke-roughened voice. 'Top notch for fuel economy.'

'Marvellous! Welcome, Meg. And you've brought this heavenly weather with you!'

I was struggling to keep up appearances. All through that terrible night, my brain had been spinning Luke's secret around and around. It chanted that he'd never loved me; it whispered that I'd known all along, and had been complicit in my own deception. My eyes felt as though they'd been scrubbed with sand. From time to time the tears would rush into them, but I'd managed to control myself so far, and intended to keep it that way. I still hoped this thing would disappear, if I ignored it. Like a pimple. Or a headache.

Meg glanced towards the house. 'Luke not at home?'

Even hearing his name brought on a wave of panic. 'He's gone to collect Wendy from the station. Come on in . . . That must be Robert's tree on your passenger seat? Let's get the poor hot thing into the shade and give it a drink.'

The sapling was about a metre high, its roots wrapped in a sack. I lifted it out and led the way inside, nipping into the cloakroom to stand the tree in a bucket of water.

'We'll leave it there for now,' I said, emerging.

Meg had sat down on the antique settle in the lobby. I joined her, laying my hands on the cool wood of its seat. I like Meg. We don't have a lot in common, but we respect one another. She's never indulged in the one-upmanship her role traditionally involves.

'Funny,' I said. 'Seems like only a week ago pairs of tiny red wellies lived under this settle.'

She was squinting at me. 'Look at you! Pale and pasty, and downright wobbly. What's up?'

'I'm absolutely fine. Just got a bit of a cold.'

Her lips pursed. 'Hmm. Change of life?'

'Possibly.' I tried to smile, and almost cried. 'Quite possibly.'

Bless her, she patted my arm. 'If you'll take my advice, love, you'll accept every hormone they offer you. And eat lots of soya. Japanese women don't suffer like we do.'

Meg had just celebrated her eightieth birthday, but you'd never know it. You'd never guess she'd been widowed a year before, either. She was wearing cream trousers, a fuchsia shirt and lipstick to match. Diamantés shimmered in her ears. Her figure was tidy, her hair a shade of grey that could almost be blonde. She skipped around an eighteen-hole golf course three times a week, rain or shine, pulling her clubs behind her.

'Now,' she said, rubbing her hands as she got up and led the way into the kitchen. Lunch was ready, the table laid. 'What can I do?'

'Nothing. Kate's been helping me. Just have a drink.'

I was opening a bottle of wine when Kate's face appeared over the gallery rail. 'Granny!' she yelled, her footsteps clanging on the metal staircase. 'Thank God!'

'This is a lovely welcome,' said Meg, as a human whirlwind shot off the last step and enveloped her. 'Nearly knocked me down, you hoodlum. Let's have a look at you—ah, Kate, love!

Why all this morbid black? It doesn't suit you. And take that thing out of your nose, it makes me feel queasy.'

'And what's this?' Kate plucked at her grandmother's shirt. 'Shocking pink! On a woman of your age! A dowager should dress more seemly and sober.'

Two days earlier, I would have laughed to see the generations sparring so amiably. But now their pleasure in one another intensified my sense of nightmare. These two women had no idea of the horrible truth; no idea at all. The father of one, the son of the other . . . How would they bear it?

Blinking rapidly, I handed Kate the bottle. 'Could you just—' My voice petered out. 'Sorry, sorry, something stuck in my throat. Um, could you look after Granny? Grab some olives out of the fridge.' Those wretched tears kept coming. I spun around, shot out of the kitchen and headed for the cloakroom. 'I'll only be a minute . . . Sorry, upset stomach, just got to nip—'

I fled into my sanctuary.

Kate

The cloakroom door slammed and was locked. Kate and her grandmother looked at one another, their eyebrows raised.

'What on earth?' whispered Meg.

Kate picked up the bottle and glasses, jerking her chin towards the open doors. 'Come outside. She might be able to hear us in here.'

They made camp under the honeysuckle.

'That girl's in quite a stew,' said Meg.

'The pair of 'em!' Kate was sloshing out two glasses of wine. 'She won't even look at him. He slept in the study last night, made some stupid excuse about both of them having a cold, and he must think I was born yesterday, because (a) I haven't heard so much as a sneeze, and (b) I can never, ever remember them sleeping apart. Never. Not even when she had meningitis that time. They just don't do it.'

'Heck.'

'D'you think one of them is screwing around?'

Meg chewed the inside of her cheek. 'Can't imagine that, can you?'

Kate thought about it. Her father was in good shape. He wasn't especially tall, maybe five-nine or -ten, but he had great posture and there wasn't a hint of a beer gut or jowls. He had lots of hair, and he wore it a bit longer than those other stuffed shirts at his work did. Even the streaks of silver suited him. If he added a beret he'd look like a French artist, with his dark brown eyes. Kate wished she'd inherited the Livingstone eyes.

'Dad's still an attractive man,' she said.

'True. He's got the looks, all right, but he's never been a womaniser. He's a one-woman man, and that woman has always been your mum. Anyway, he's too bloody honest. He couldn't manage all the fibbing.'

'Mum couldn't, either.'

'Nope.' Meg chewed her cheek again. 'She's got everything to lose. She loves this house, she loves her job, and I'm quite certain she loves your dad. She's planning her anniversary knees-up and the big Italy trip next year. Why would she throw all that away?'

They lifted their glasses in unison. We must look like a comedy duo, thought Kate: a skinny, hungover student in Doc Martens and an eighty-year-old widow in a jaunty blouse and salon-set hairdo. The two of them had always been as thick as thieves.

Meg's father had been a miner in County Durham. She left the north at the age of eighteen, when she married Robert Livingstone and made a career out of being a farmer's wife. Kate had always thought this was a crime—her granny was a bright woman, could have done anything with her life.

'I'm so glad you're here,' she said fervently. 'It's been fucking awful since I arrived.'

'Tut-tut. Language.'

'*Jolly* awful. I've felt like screaming. All that frozen civility, and both of them behaving as though they were going to burst into tears. Now I know how kids of broken homes feel.'

Meg was digging around in her handbag. 'Doesn't sound good. Mind you, in years and years stuck together, you're bound to have some tiffs. Maybe she wanted a dog, and he didn't. Maybe she turned down a promotion and he thought she should have taken it. Could be any number of things.' She pulled out a packet of cigarettes. 'Want one?'

'No, thanks. I don't smoke tobacco, I only smoke hooch. I've told you this about a million times.'

'Rude not to offer.'

'I can't believe you're still poisoning yourself, at your age.'

Meg flicked a lighter, inhaled that first lungful of nicotine. 'I can't believe you're still nagging me about it, at my age. Anyway, I've cut down. Four a day.'

'Did you and Grandad have many fights?'

'Our fair share.'

Kate leaned back, resting her head against the wall. 'So . . . what do we do, Granny? I can't take much more. All this tension gives me a sense of doom. Should we have it out with them?'

'No,' said Meg, and blew out a plume of smoke. 'No, I wouldn't confront them. Leave them be. The one time Robert and I were in real trouble, our marriage was saved by good old-fashioned sweeping under the carpet. We were both hopping mad but neither of us was honest enough to come out and say so. After a couple of days, we forgot we weren't talking. The day after that, we had a laugh about something—I've forgotten what—and that was that.'

'What was it all about?'

'I didn't want more children. Robert did. He'd set his heart on having a boy. I said it wasn't him that had to carry it for nine months. Gail hadn't been an easy pregnancy, and Wendy almost killed me.'

'Quite right!' Kate straightened her spine in sisterly solidarity. 'A woman's body is her own.'

'All right, you can hop off your soapbox. "Anyway," I said, "what's the point?" Didn't he love his daughters? Did he think he'd love a son more? What made a boy so special?'

'I'm proud of you, Granny!'

'He said . . .' Meg paused, balancing a tall pile of ash on the end of her smouldering cigarette. 'People never have ashtrays anymore, do they? Smokers are a dying breed . . . Ah, a plant pot. Perfect. He said he loved Wendy and Gail to bits but he wanted a son. Someone who would be just like him, a miniature Robert Livingstone. Someone to take over the farm when he was gone.'

Kate sighed. 'Dear oh dear. And this was the twentieth century, right?'

'He imagined them making model railways. Shooting. Playing with Robert's woodworking toys. Running the farm together.'

'His daughters could have done all those things!'

Meg looked doubtful. 'Well, anyway, nature took over. Soon after that argument I found out I was expecting again. You might call it a mistake, or you might call it a miracle. Either way, it was your dad.'

'So, Grandad was happy?'

'A pig in clover.'

'Yeah, well.' Kate shrugged. 'I can forgive him the medieval values, since he was Grandad . . . and since it was Dad who came along.'

The pair fell silent, looking across the lawn. Kate could see the hole her dad had dug that morning, ready to plant the memorial tree. She felt better for talking to Meg. She and Simon used to go and stay on their grandparents' farm when they were small, and it was the highlight of her year.

She was topping up their wine when a black Jeep came crawling through the gateway, navigating around the deeper potholes on the drive. 'Oh God,' she groaned, downing her newly filled glass. 'Here come Simon and Carmela. This calls for sedation.'

'Why would you need Dutch courage to face your own brother?'

Kate swept back her hair—what there was of it—and imitated Carmela's voice. 'Oh, *Kate*, I can recommend a *marvellous* hairdresser. He's a magician!'

'To be honest, love, you do look as though you've sheared your fringe with a pair of blunt nail scissors.'

'They were quite sharp nail scissors, actually. And Simon's not been interested in anyone or anything since he married her. He's got no idea what makes me tick. He just makes snide little remarks. I bet you, Granny, he'll find something sarcastic to say within the first three minutes.'

Meg looked at the Jeep, which had just pulled up. 'I'll bet he won't.'

'You're on. I'll time it.' Kate checked the second hand on her watch. 'A tenner? Starting from . . . *now*.'

Simon

Mum and Dad needed to do something about that bloody drive. It was getting beyond a joke. Someone was going to break an axle.

'Bumpety bump,' yelled Nico. He was holding a toy Piglet up to the window. 'Look, Piglet, there's Grandpa's shed. We're going to make a plane in there.'

'Kate and your grandmother are sitting on the bench. See? They're just watching us,' hissed Carmela. She was brushing her hair. 'You'd think they could wave, or smile, or something. It doesn't matter how far I extend the olive branch, Kate does not want to take it.'

Simon brought the Jeep to a halt and yanked at the handbrake. 'Let's make a real effort this time. Keep the moral high ground. We're here to remember Grandad, after all.'

'I'll drive home. You can drink.'

'Thanks.' Simon exhaled theatrically. 'Okay, I'm going in. My orders are to carry out a section attack and take the guns. Give me covering fire.'

'Will do.'

He leaped out, grinning idiotically in his effort to exude cheerfulness.

'Hi!' he called, and trotted up the terrace steps to kiss Meg's cheek. He was sure she'd shrunk since last time. 'Lovely to see you, Granny.'

Then he looked at Kate, and did a double take. Oh, for Christ's sake! She had a stud in her nose! She looked like a lowlife. Why would she mutilate herself?

'What's this?' he asked, pointing at the same place on his own nose. 'Hormones playing up?'

Kate glanced at her watch, turned to Meg and held out her palm. 'Eighteen seconds. Has to be a record. You owe me.'

Simon didn't understand her full meaning, but he knew he'd put his foot in it. 'Nah, it looks great,' he lied. 'Stylish. Um, how's . . .' He racked his brains, and then remembered. 'Owen?'

'It's ex-boyfriend.'

'Thank Christ for that! He was a total moron, wasn't he?'

He was relieved when Carmela joined them; she was much better at doing the family thing. She was from a massive clan herself—including four brothers and their wives and families—and at the slightest excuse they all met up in Madrid. Simon's efforts to learn Spanish hadn't been very successful, and he couldn't tell furious argument from enthusiastic agreement. His policy was to nod and smile.

'Meg! Kate!' cried Carmela, kissing both women while Nico shot inside to look for his grandparents. 'You look terrific! And, Kate, that haircut is simply . . . courageous.'

Simon saw Kate stiffen. 'Nice shoes, Carmela,' she said. 'I don't suppose kept women actually have to walk anywhere.'

He felt all his good intentions slipping away. 'Kate, that's just bloody rude.'

'Drink?' said Meg, intervening quickly. 'And who's this turning in? Ah! It's Luke and Wendy.'

Simon watched as Nico ran out of the house and bounced

down the steps to meet the car. Yes, there was Aunt Wendy in the passenger seat. Luke's sister, survivor of a string of disastrous relationships, who'd found God in her fifties. Nothing wrong with finding God, of course. Simon was all for it, in theory. The problem was that Wendy had always been neurotic and self-obsessed, and her new hotline to the Almighty seemed to have made her worse.

She sprang out of the car, wearing a flowered skirt and a necklace that looked like a daisy chain. 'Hello, everyone!' she called. 'Isn't this lovely?'

And there was Dad, stooping to pick up his grandson. Nico had an arm around his neck and his legs around his waist, gabbling on about the plane they were going to make together.

Thank God, thought Simon in relief. Dad's home.

Eight

Simon

It should have been a perfect family day. The kitchen table had been set for lunch, with the folding doors opened right out so that they were practically sitting in the garden. From here they could see the new tree, now planted close to Charlotte's.

The death of his baby sister was Simon's earliest memory: a grey, sad time when excitement turned into tears and silence. He sometimes wondered whether his life would have been different if she'd lived. Perhaps she would have been a friend to him in his teenage years. He could have done with one.

His mother brought out the highchair for Nico. He climbed in and perched in splendour, looking like an umpire at Wimbledon.

'Please, can Eyelash and Grandpa sit next to me?' he asked, pointing at the seats on each side. 'Eyelash *here*, and Grandpa *here*.'

'That chair used to be mine,' said Simon, as his parents took their allotted seats. 'You made it, didn't you, Dad?'

His father smiled, but he seemed distracted. 'I did.'

A breeze lifted the edges of the lace cloth, carrying in the heavy scent of oilseed rape from Gareth's crop. Someone—Eilish, Simon guessed—had arranged a bowl of roses as a centrepiece for the table. They were creamy yellow; fallen petals lay scattered on the lace. The scene could have been an advertisement for air freshener.

'This is so *Home and Garden*,' said Wendy. 'You are clever, Eilish. Everything you do is effortlessly beautiful.'

Eilish barely managed an answer. She'd caught a bad cold, apparently, and was feeling lousy. Simon could see that she was wearing more make-up than usual, but it didn't hide how bloody ill she looked. His father had the bug too. The pair of them were behaving like zombies. Simon hoped Nico wouldn't come down with it.

Wendy's remark was followed by silence. Even Nico temporarily stopped chattering as he drove his Jeep along the back of his chair. Simon hated awkward silences. He found them . . . well, awkward.

'Four generations around the table!' he gushed, rubbing his hands together. 'That makes you an uber matriarch, Granny.'

'Makes you an uber prat,' said Kate. She was smiling, though. He nudged her ribs with his elbow. She nudged him back, a bit harder. They'd done a fair bit of elbow-nudging over the years.

'Children, children,' chided Meg, just before he felt Kate kick him in the shin. Childhood games. Kate might be a pain in the backside, but she was his sister.

They were all about to tuck in when Aunt Wendy cleared her throat. 'Aren't we going to thank our great provider for this bounty?' She closed her eyes and held out her hands to each side. A joyous smile played across her mouth. One of her neighbours was Kate, the other Luke, and both kept their hands resolutely out of her reach.

'Off you go then,' said Meg indulgently. 'But get a move on, Wendy, love, because I'm starving and would quite like to make a start on the bounty.'

'Grandpa, will the plane really fly?' asked Nico, speaking around the sausage he'd managed to sneak into his mouth.

'Shush.' Luke tickled his hand. 'Shush for ten ticks, while we say a prayer.'

Wendy wasn't quick, though Simon had to admit she was thorough. She offered thanks for their loving family, for their safe journeys, for permitting them all to live in a land of abundance. Then she offered thanks for Grandad's life, and blessings on the tree they had just planted. Simon had been brought up solidly C of E—confirmed here, at St Matthew's—but in his book, Wendy took it too far. She embarrassed him. Long before she came to the end, Nico had begun chanting the *Postman Pat* tune under his breath. Simon was tempted to sing along.

'Amen,' he mumbled at the end. Then he happened to look across at his mother. She was sitting hunched over. He'd have sworn she was trying not to cry. This was baffling because she never, ever cried.

'Been like this all weekend,' said Kate under her breath.

'Maybe she's really ill?' he whispered back. 'We're going to have to cover for her before Wendy notices.' He raised his voice, and his glass. 'Here's to Grandad! May his tree grow strong and tall—as he did.'

Meg joined in. 'And gnarled and knotted, but good for shade and rest.'

'Yes, to Papa!' cried Wendy. 'What an occasion. He'd be so happy to see all the family here. What a shame Gail can't be with us.'

Another silence followed the mention of Gail's name. She was Simon's other aunt, though he had rarely met her. She'd emigrated to Australia before he was born and never communicated with his father. He caught Carmela's eye and made an agonised face. She was leaning across the table, handing Nico some juice, but she saw his distress signal and came to the rescue.

'So, Kate,' she said brightly. 'What about Israel? What did you find?'

Kate seemed to understand what Carmela was trying to do. She entered into the spirit of things, talking animatedly about the archaeological dig she'd just left. She gave a potted history of the site, which had been occupied for over six thousand years;

she described the implications of their finds; she talked about the blistering heat. When she finally began to flag, Carmela asked about the subject she was planning for her Master's dissertation, which—Simon discovered—was all to do with dating methods with reference to this particular site. She described various techniques, and explained why she'd chosen this site in order to analyse their effectiveness (it had destruction layers to die for, apparently).

As Simon listened, he almost forgot that this was his scrawny little sister. Get her on to her own subject and she was pretty impressive, he had to admit. He was grateful to her, and to Carmela, who kept prompting her to continue. The younger generation was saving the day, while their parents—generally so polished and hospitable—seemed to have gone to pieces. Neither Luke nor Eilish was speaking, or eating, or engaged in any way.

'Fascinating,' he said, to fill the next silence. 'Gosh. Um, when did you get back?'

'Flew in on Friday, just in time for Mathis and John's party—d'you remember, I used to share a house with them? Well, they had their civil union when I was away, and Friday night was the big celebration bash. It was a wedding reception, really. They're so sweet together.'

Wendy had lost interest during the conversation about archaeology, but now her eyes were round and sorrowful. 'Kate, that's terribly sad.'

'Sad? Why sad, Aunt Wendy?' There was a dangerous sweetness in Kate's voice. Simon knew exactly what *that* meant. Take cover, he thought. Trouble ahead.

'They're acting against their natures,' said Wendy.

'They certainly are *not.* Mathis and John are as committed to one another as any married couple I've ever known. And far happier than most.'

'It's . . . you know, it's what they do . . .' Wendy screwed up her face in delicate disgust. 'You're quite right to love them as people, but what they're doing is a sin.'

'A sin.' Kate put down her knife and fork, while Simon mentally donned a tin hat. 'Tell me something, Wendy. Do you know Mathis or John? No, you don't. So what makes you qualified to have an opinion about them?'

'Some things are natural. Some things simply are not. And what they do is—'

Wendy hadn't finished her sentence before Eilish was on her feet, mumbling something about a headache. She charged upstairs, and a moment later the house shuddered as a door slammed shut. Everyone winced.

Mum doesn't slam doors. Kate slams doors.

Silence.

'Why did Granny run away?' asked Nico.

'Excuse me,' said Luke, as he stood up too. 'Sorry. I'm sure she'll be fine. Please carry on without us . . . Kate, Simon, could you make sure everyone has what they need?' He took the stairs two at a time, and disappeared.

'Now Grandpa's run away as well!' cried Nico, and he began to cry.

'Was it something I said?' asked Wendy.

Luke

I found her leaning her forehead against the window, looking out across the drive towards the woods. This room knew everything about us. It had seen a young and hopeful couple setting up their first home together; it had been the backdrop as they travelled through the passing years. It had witnessed passion and grief and helpless laughter, arguments and makings-up, and raucous Christmas mornings with wrapping paper scattered across the floor.

Other things, too. It had watched me at those times when Eilish was out and I'd given in to my desperate need. It knew everything.

She spoke without looking around. 'Why did you marry me?'

'Because I was in love with you. I still am.'

'Oh. Nothing to do with convenience, then? Nothing to do with providing a respectable cover? I think it was that.'

I crossed the room to join her at the window, ransacking my mind for true answers. I had to be honest now. No more secrets.

'Wasn't I enough?' she asked.

'You were more than enough!'

'Obviously not.'

'The opposite is true,' I protested. 'You were so miraculous . . . I thought you could save me. I really thought I could conquer this thing, if I had you.'

We stood side by side, a universe apart. I could almost hear her heartbeat. Noises filtered up from downstairs: a murmur of conversation, the quiet clattering of crockery, and eventually the thud of a car door. Someone was leaving. I really ought to go down there to see them off. It was my duty to play yet another role—that of the cheerful and apologetic host whose wife has suffered a sudden migraine. 'Don't worry,' I would say. 'She'll be fine after a lie-down—she's so sorry, it just hit her—please don't feel you have to leave, let's have a cup of tea.' I knew all about playing roles. I was an old hand.

As Mum's car headed down the drive, Eilish moved listlessly. 'Go on,' she said. 'We still have guests.'

'I don't want to leave you alone.'

She shrugged. 'It's you who's hurt me, though, isn't it?'

She was broken, and I couldn't put her together again.

When I walked downstairs I was met by a reception committee. Kate and Simon were standing by the cleared table, waiting for me. It was years since I'd seen them look so unified.

'Granny's gone. She's dropping Wendy at the station,' said Kate. 'Carmela and Nico are playing on the hay bales. Dad, please. This is awful. Tell us what's going on.'

Simon nodded. 'If one of you is ill, or if there's some serious problem, I think we have a right to know.'

They eyed me with wary determination. My children. This pair, and their mother, were at the centre of my existence. I would die for them if I had to. In fact, that's what I'd intended to do, that very week.

Out in the garden, a thousand birds seemed to be singing. There were roses in a bowl on our kitchen table. I could retire soon, and travel with my beloved wife, and be a sedate grandfather. My children were clever, good, contented people; my grandson was the apple of everyone's eye. And I was about to lose it all.

For one last breath, I wavered. Perhaps it was not too late. Perhaps I could still turn back.

'We deserve the truth, Dad,' said Kate. 'We're adults.'

Nine

Kate

She laughed. She laughed, loud and long. He was obviously joking. Her oh-so-respectable Dad with a wig and false boobs, tottering along the street! Frigging hilarious.

'You *are* kidding.' It was a statement, not a question.

Everything had been cleared away, except Eilish's yellow roses. More petals had fallen. They lay on the lace cloth, curling up as though they were in pain. Kate sat at the table, opposite her father. Simon leaned his hands on the kitchen counter, staring down at the floor between his feet. It wasn't until later that Kate realised he'd been stunned. Literally, stunned. Their dad might as well have hit him on the back of the head with a spade. One minute Simon was waltzing through his smug life—just a normal, boring, basically quite nice guy—and the next minute he was flat out on the ground with a big hole where his respectability used to be.

'Gender dysphoria,' he kept muttering. 'I don't get it.' Each time he said that, Dad patiently found a new way to explain.

'You're having us on,' said Kate. She was still trying to giggle, as though by laughing she could make it all a joke. What she really wanted to do was run away. 'You're my dad. Ergo, you are a man.'

'Yes, I am your dad. And I am a man.'

'Glad to hear it!'

'At least . . . I have a male body; but that body feels completely wrong. It's as though they got the wrong model off the shelf when I was born.'

Kate knew of people who'd experimented with their gender; she'd once had a lecturer who was a trans woman. She wished them well. But this was different. This was her father.

'D'you mean . . . you want to cross-dress?' she asked now, hoping he'd scoff at the idea.

He didn't scoff. He nodded, and she felt her world shake.

'Shit. Have you ever actually . . . ?'

'Yes,' he said. 'Yes, I have cross-dressed.'

No. You can't have. You really can't.

'Look, this isn't about what I wear,' he said. 'It's about who I am. Who I really am.'

This is a weird dream, she thought, and picked up a yellow petal. It was so soft. When she rolled it between her finger and thumb, it crumbled into almost nothing. Funny how roses look loveliest when they're dying and bits are falling off them.

Abruptly, Simon seemed to come back to life. 'What the hell are you playing at?' His voice was too loud.

'I'm not playing, Simon.'

'Please tell me this is a hoax! I've got news for you, Dad. Listen, and listen carefully. You are *male*. You're a father and a grandfather, and a brother and a husband, and you're fifty-five years old. Jesus Christ! It's a bit late to decide you're a screaming shirt lifter.'

'I'm not gay.'

'You want to put on a dress. You fancy men. I've met perverts like that before.'

'Not perverts,' said Kate. 'They're—'

'Shut up, Kate, for Christ's sake! Spare me the political correctness. This is our father, not one of your trendy gender-bender mates.'

Luke raised his hand. 'I don't fancy men. Not at all. This has absolutely nothing to do with my sexuality.'

'What is it about, then?' asked Kate. 'If not sexuality?'

'Gender.'

'What's the difference?'

'The two are completely separate. You *know* that, Kate! Ask John and Mathis.'

Simon had stormed off to the other end of the kitchen during this exchange. He seemed to be in physical pain, unable to stand still. Now he was back, with his fists pressed to the top of his head. 'You dress in women's clothes! How can you do this to Mum?'

'Not . . . all right. Yes, I sometimes do—but the clothes aren't the point. I'm not cross-dressing for the sake of it. I'm not a transvestite. That's a different thing, you see? I identify as female. I actually—'

'*Jesus*.'

'Go on, Dad,' urged Kate.

'I actually think of myself as female. God knows I've tried to deny it, tried to kill it, tried to hide it under layers and layers of other things—but it's the inner core of me and it won't die until I do.'

There was a nasty tightness around Simon's jaw, as though steel cords were knotted under the skin. Kate had seen it before, on her first boyfriend, when he was about to hit her.

'I don't care what labels you stick on this fucked-up weirdness,' he shouted. 'If you've been wearing skirts and high heels, you're no father of mine. You're a freak! You should've been drowned at birth.'

'Hey, Simon,' said Kate. 'Hang on a minute.'

Simon smashed his fist on the table, right in front of Luke. The bowl of roses jumped. Petals rained down. 'What about Mum? Is she collateral damage?'

Suddenly, this boring brother seemed menacing. Kate jumped to her feet, ready to intervene, but she didn't have to, because Carmela and Nico chose that moment to return. Nico's fingers gripped a bunch of wildflowers.

'I picked all of these for Granny,' he announced happily, standing in the doorway. He couldn't quite manage his '*r*'s'.

'Don't come in. Turn around. We're going,' said Simon, barring their way.

'Now?' Carmela looked mystified. 'But why? He has flowers for Eilish.'

'I'll tell you later.'

Give that Spaniard her due, thought Kate, she's no wilting pansy. Carmela wasn't used to being pushed around and she wasn't scared of Simon. Kate couldn't hear what was said, but she could tell from the furious whispering that Carmela was not impressed. While his parents argued, Nico ducked past them and trotted in through the open doors. His face fell when he saw that Eilish still hadn't come down.

'Granny?' he asked, looking all around.

Kate rather liked her nephew. He took no shit from anyone, and she respected that. Now his whole world was about to be turned upside down. Poor kid.

'She's still not feeling very well, little man,' said Luke.

'Aw! Still not very well?'

'I'm afraid not.'

'Flowers will make her feel better.' Nico held out his gift. 'You can have them, Grandpa, if you promise to share them with Granny.'

'Thank you, my friend.' Luke's voice was gentle. 'This is the first bunch of flowers I have ever been given. Please may I have a kiss goodbye, if I promise to share that with Granny too?'

Grinning, Nico hooked his arms around Luke's neck and planted a noisy kiss on his nose. 'Byeee!' he cooed. 'See you later, alligator.'

'In a while, crocodile. I love you.' Luke kept hugging the little boy, as though he might never see him again.

Simon was back. 'Get your hands off my son,' he snarled, snatching the poor little bugger away. Simon didn't sound like himself; his voice was distorted. Kate had a feeling he might be very close to tears, but it was hard to tell. Rage, grief . . . even fear, she thought. They all sound the same.

Carmela had followed. She faced Luke, her gaze incredulous. 'Simon has just told me . . . I cannot believe what he has just told me. Is it true?'

'I'm the same person I've always been,' said Luke quietly. 'I'm not dangerous.'

'See a shrink.' Simon was on his way out, speaking over his shoulder. 'Behavioural therapy. Aversion therapy. Electro-convulsive therapy. Whatever it takes. Please, Dad. *Please.* Just get yourself cured. Are you coming with us, Kate? No? Well, we're going right now. Come *on*, Carmela.'

Nico wailed all the way to the car (*But why, Daddy? Why are you cross with Grandpa? Why, Daddy?*), and seconds later they were off.

Poor Jeep, thought Kate. It wasn't designed to be thrashed like that. The engine screamed as Simon accelerated away.

Her father's head was bent over the table, a hand covering his eyes. He looked defeated.

It was the worst moment of her life.

'That went well,' she said.

Eilish

Simon's hurt seemed to shake the wooden floor beneath my feet. I heard a bellowed *Please tell me this is a hoax*; and, a little later, *You should've been drowned at birth.*

Simon wished his father dead. His father, who had wept with joy when he was born, and never wanted to put him down; who paced the house with him all night when he was colicky; who didn't want to send him to kindergarten (*but he's so* little); who cancelled meetings to go to school plays; who got out of bed at two in the morning on countless occasions—without ever once complaining—to collect a drunken, truculent teenager from parties. This was a father who'd loved his son without question, and never asked for anything in return. This was the father who'd betrayed us all.

Luke was speaking again, but quietly. I couldn't hear his words. They didn't matter. I turned away from the window and looked around the room. Our room. His chest of drawers dominated one wall, with the antique mirror standing on top. Beside that lay his ivory-backed hairbrush, a lint remover, cufflinks, a handful of loose change and a black deodorant spray. Lovely, familiar stuff. A man's stuff.

That was when I began to wonder.

One by one, I opened his drawers and emptied their contents onto the floor. Sweaters. Weekend shirts. Socks. Boxer shorts. All his clothes were in muted colours: black, grey, burgundy, faun. Luke had excellent taste, and there was nothing ambivalent about the things strewn around my feet. These were masculine garments. I lifted the heavy drawers right out and piled them onto the bed, searching for hidden stashes. Nothing.

Outside, a car was fleeing down the drive with a crash of gears. Simon and family, presumably. Good. I was glad they were leaving. Simon and I would talk later, but at this moment I wasn't up to carrying his fear and anger as well as my own.

When Luke and I had bought Smith's Barn, it was just that, a barn, complete with old farm machinery and nesting pigeons. The renovation had been my project. Off one corner of our bedroom, under the eaves, I'd got the builder to make a walk-in cupboard. It's eccentric, with a sharply sloping roof and plastered walls at crazy angles. I kept my shoes and evening dresses in there, and Luke his work clothes and cricket gear. I turned on the light and stood in the cramped space, looking along Luke's rack: suits, ties and striped shirts in an ordered row. His shoes were lined up underneath, sober and polished. Then my gaze came to rest on his leather overnight bag, not yet unpacked from Norwich. He'd dumped it in a corner when he was grabbing things to wear today. I dragged it closer and peered inside: shirts, a tie, pyjamas. His navy-blue jersey, smelling of lanolin and Luke. Oh, how I loved that smell. I buried my face in it, and allowed myself a moment of pretending this wasn't happening.

A John Grisham.

Socks, neatly paired.

At the very bottom, I spotted a calico bag with a drawstring top. I couldn't remember seeing it before but it looked innocuous; perhaps a hotel laundry bag. Later, I asked myself what the hell I'd expected to see in that bag. Laundry, I suppose; maybe damp swimming things. Luke had mentioned a pool at his hotel in Norwich, and he's always liked a morning dip.

I loosened the string, tipped the bag upside down and watched the contents tumble to the floor. They seemed to fall in slow motion.

Kate

'Whisky, gin, or brandy?' she asked, riffling through the cupboard. 'Oblivion is what's called for after bad news. And this is bad news, Dad. This is very bad news, to be honest.'

His voice was muffled by his hands. 'Tea, please.'

'A nice cup of Earl Grey! How homely. See? You're Mr Conventional, after all.'

He smiled: his hesitant smile, which always looked as though he feared he wasn't quite welcome. 'You can have no idea how much I wish that were true.'

One of Kate's ex-flatmates had taken a course in counselling. She used to bang on about the stages of grief: disbelief, anger, bargaining and . . . well, some other things that Kate couldn't remember. Simon seemed to have moved pretty quickly into anger, but she still held out hope that her father was going through some kind of male menopause and would soon snap out of it. She kept glancing at him as she made the tea.

'Dad, this is too wacky. Even for me. And believe me, I've done wacky.'

'I know. And I'm sorry.'

'Don't take this the wrong way, but . . . have you talked to a doctor? I just wondered if Simon might have a point. Maybe your hormones are all screwed up.'

'Actually, yes,' he said. 'I mentioned it to a doctor about five years ago.'

'Not Dr Ryan?' Kate squirmed at the idea of her father facing the family GP across his desk and announcing that he was really a woman.

'Good Lord, no! Don Ryan's a governor of St Matthew's with me. No, I made myself an appointment with a private GP in London when I was going through a very bad patch. I didn't quite come clean with her, but I dropped hints and she ordered blood tests. My hormone levels were just what you'd expect for a man of my age. She prescribed antidepressants. I took them because I was feeling bloody awful, and they got me through.'

Kate's phone was vibrating. She pulled it out of her bra, where she generally kept it.

When r u going 2 collect ur stuff?

'Tosspot,' she spluttered, and turned off the phone.

'Owen?'

'Owen. Never mind him.' She thought furiously as she poured boiling water onto tea. 'This is the twenty-first century, Dad. All those male/female role things, all those stereotypes, they should be ancient history.'

'I wish they were.'

'They *are*. You're not a chauvinist moron, you've always respected everybody equally.'

'Of course.'

'Well then! Gender shouldn't even be relevant in this day and age. Why are you destroying our family for a non-issue? There's no difference between the sexes. Not anymore. You don't have to be a woman, you can be a feminine man.'

He shook his head. He looked exhausted. 'From where I'm sitting, there are differences so fundamental that I've been torn apart.'

She gave him a mug of tea and sat down. 'We all know how it works. Boys get given macho toys like Action Man—look at Nico with that little Jeep he carries around, a miniature version of his dad's—what's the message there? Girls get given bloody Barbie dolls, which tells them it's cool to be bulimic and dress like a princess. They're all forced into roles that may not suit them at all.'

'That last sentence is certainly true. I'm a testament to that.'

'Okay.' Kate felt that she was getting somewhere. 'Okay! Perhaps that's what this is about? You just need to express yourself in ways you couldn't when Grandad was still alive. Have you thought of that? You've been repressing your feminine side. Maybe you should take up . . . I dunno, painting? Drama? Tapestry?'

He didn't reply for a while, which didn't surprise her. Kate had never heard her father give an answer he couldn't stand behind. He didn't shoot from the hip. She wished she could say the same about herself.

'You see,' he said eventually, 'this began long, long ago.'

'How long ago?'

'Before I knew what it was to be a boy, or a girl. I think I was about two when I first went into Wendy's bedroom and got dressed in her clothes. They were too big for me. They trailed on the floor, tripped me up, but I loved them. She had skirts and dresses and lovely white tights. Bangles.' He was almost smiling—a wonky, embarrassed grimace. 'Ribbons for her hair. My family told me off, but I wouldn't stop, so they locked me out of her room. I screamed the place down.'

Kate had been a tomboy, never out of jeans if she could help it, and couldn't see what the fuss was about. She wouldn't have been seen dead in white tights, at any age.

Her father seemed to read her thoughts. 'Please, Kate, try to understand. I longed for those things because I wanted to be like other girls.'

'Other girls? But you weren't . . . Oh. I see. You were.'

'I *was*. Inside me was a laughing girl, with long hair. I called her Lucia. Every time I went to sleep, I prayed that when I woke up I'd have become Lucia.'

'How? You had . . . um.' Kate rolled her eyes and pointed downwards. 'You had a boy's body. Boy's bits.'

'Which I hoped would drop off. One time, I even—well.' Luke stopped and thought for a moment. 'Never mind. I hated them more and more. I was faulty. I needed fixing.'

Kate wanted to shut her ears; she wanted to deny what was happening, to run away as Simon had done, but she couldn't leave her parents in this mess.

'So where do you go from here?' she asked, fearing the answer.

'I don't know.'

'Come on, Dad. You never do anything without thinking it through.'

He picked up a petal from the table and smoothed it on the palm of his hand. 'I can't go on as I am. I don't think I'll survive. Suicide's pretty common among people like me.'

'Don't you dare. Even if you turned out to be a werewolf, you're still *you*. We'd get used to you going all hairy, and baying at the moon and biting people.'

'Werewolves are cool nowadays. So are vampires. Trannies are not.'

Together, they contemplated the waxy petal in his hand.

'Where does that leave you?' she asked.

Instead of answering, he put a finger to his lips. He was staring up at the gallery. Kate listened, and then she heard it too.

Eilish

The cries escaped me before I could smother them. For a time I was paralysed, staring in utter revulsion. Utter fascination. Utter desolation.

Silk and lace. A slip exactly like mine, but pale blue. A pair of sheer tights. An indigo dress with lace edging. Beautiful clothes, with beautiful textures.

Nausea surged through me. I threw down the calico bag and retched, covering my mouth with both hands. These things must have been hidden somewhere in our bedroom, perhaps for years. Every time we'd undressed one another, this secret stash—how far away? Fifteen feet?—was waiting for him. Did he imagine himself wearing these things when he was in bed with me?

I picked up the indigo dress, holding it away from my body as though it were a snake. He'd worn it. He'd slipped it over his head, and pulled up the zip, and twirled around. A faint perfume clung to its folds. Not his deodorant; something else. He must have a bottle of scent hoarded somewhere. Gritting my teeth, I took a fistful of fabric in each hand and tore it from one end to the other. I ripped and tore until the clothes were no more than a pile of rags. It didn't take long; they were all made of delicate fabric.

I was destroying the slip when I heard a movement behind me, and looked around. Luke stood in the doorway, his eyes like craters in his white face. He looked at the rags on the floor, and then at me. He said nothing.

'What did you see?' I asked. 'When you looked in the mirror. What monster did you see?'

'I saw myself.'

I laughed at him. I laughed as loudly as I could. I don't think I sounded sane. 'You saw a man in a dress. For God's sake, Luke, a man in a dress! Don't you understand how ludicrous you must look?'

'Yes.'

'Then why? Why parade around like a drag queen?'

'Because it made me feel normal.'

I hated him. Right then and there, in that moment, I hated him. He was a stranger, a thief who'd cheated me out of everything that matters in this world. He'd taken my love, my youth, my life. I snatched up the obscene remnants and hurled them at him. He didn't move. They hit him in the face before fluttering forlornly around his feet.

'Take your glad rags,' I said. 'And get out of my house.'

Ten

Luke

'I can't let you go off by yourself,' said Kate.

'I'm fine.' I lifted my overnight bag and another suitcase into the car. 'Please, darling. Stay with Mum for as long as you can.'

She was putting on a brave face, but I wasn't fooled. My daughter isn't quite as tough as she likes to pretend. Which of us is?

'You said you were thinking of topping yourself, Dad.'

The noose was still waiting for me. As I'd packed my bags, throwing possessions haphazardly into suitcases, I'd heard the whispering of The Thought. My old enemy was delighted with the turn things had taken. It was still hoping to push me off that stool and into oblivion.

'I wasn't serious,' I said lightly as I shut the car boot. 'The damage has already been done, don't you think? It's a bit late to be bumping myself off.'

'So you'll be at the flat this evening?'

'Yes.'

'Alone?'

Again, the fear in her voice. I laid my hands on her shoulders. 'My Kate. I've caused all this. I'm not the one who deserves your sympathy. Just drop me at the station, please, and come straight back. Mum is blameless, and she is *not* all right.'

'Yes, but—'

'I'll be fine, I promise you. I feel terribly guilty, terribly sad, but I'm all right. I've told the truth—finally, after all these years. Now I have to live with the consequences.'

I'd seen Eilish again, just before I left the house. She was standing in the middle of the kitchen as I carried my bags downstairs.

'So this is the end of our marriage,' she said. 'Death didn't part us. Life got there first.'

I put down the cases and stepped closer to her.

'Just go,' she said, turning away. 'You're breaking my heart. Just go.'

Now, in these final moments, I looked up at the home we'd shared for thirty years. I thought I glimpsed her—a small movement, a shadow behind the kitchen windows. I hoped she might come outside. We'd never parted without saying goodbye.

Kate was following my gaze. 'She isn't coming, Dad.'

'You're right.' I opened the driver's door. 'Let's go.'

All the way to the station, Kate was tapping a frantic rhythm on her knees. She was doing her best to hide her horror, but I could see it in her fidgeting, in the wideness of her eyes—my militant child, who was once suspended from primary school for calling her bullying headmaster an arsehole. Kate had never been afraid of anybody, but she was frightened now.

'You married Mum,' she burst out suddenly. 'You had Simon and me. You've never said a word about any of this before.'

'I know,' I said. 'And I'm sorry.'

It sounded so inadequate. I swung into the drop-off area outside the ticket office, and turned off the engine. For a long time, both of us stared straight ahead. I felt as though my chest were weighted with stones. In the end, I forced myself to get out of the car and retrieve my luggage from the boot. Kate followed me, chewing fiercely on her lower lip.

'You know where I am,' I said.

'Yes. But I don't know *who* you are.'

'That makes two of us.'

'Sod off, old man.' Brave Kate. She forced a smile, and stepped forward to hug me. 'Or old . . . whatever. I'll see you soon.'

For a last moment, I held her in my arms. I imagine we looked like any other father and daughter, saying goodbye at a commuter station on a Sunday night. Then I picked up my things and walked away, into exile.

Eilish

He was gone. Worse than gone. He'd never existed. The Luke I loved was fictional. I'd built my entire life around a made-up character.

Out of some need for order, I began to straighten things in the kitchen. There was little point, of course. It was just a sham. All of it. Thirty years of sham. Even the red and yellow coffee cups we'd bought at a street market because we thought they were fun (or did he think so? Was that just part of the charade?); even the kitchen table, heart of our home; even that photo on the fridge. There we were, drinking coffee outside a Parisian cafe, posing for the street photographer.

I went to stand in front of the picture, a red and yellow cup in my hand. Luke hadn't shaved that day. I remembered feeling happy holiday lust at the exquisite roughness of his stubbled jaw against mine. I could feel it still. The sunshine was making us both squint, and I was grinning. Luke wasn't. He looked as he always did: slightly uneasy, slightly absent, more or less happy. That was Luke. What was he really thinking, as he rested his cheek against mine and gazed into the lens? Was he hating every second of it? Was he dreaming of his secret world?

I'd hurled the first cup before I knew I was going to do it. It hit the tiled floor with a sharp crack and exploded, shards of china spitting in all directions. I picked up another and did the same. Then another, and another, and another. I mourned for them even as I systematically destroyed them. Soon the only one left was my favourite: more red than yellow, with a random pattern that always made me think of musical notes. It lay upside down on the draining board, cowering, awaiting its turn to be broken. I snatched it up.

That last survivor was saved by the phone, which rang as I hesitated.

Hope made me answer it. Maybe it was Luke, already asking to come home? This was all a mistake: a dream, or a misunderstanding, or temporary insanity.

'It's me, dear.'

Not Luke. I sagged against the kitchen counter. 'Meg. Hi.'

'Thank you for a lovely day.'

The social niceties. 'Not at all. Our pleasure. Thank you for coming.'

'Was it a migraine?'

For a moment my mind was blank. Then I remembered. 'Yes. Sorry, yes. A migraine. Hit me like a train.'

'I didn't know you suffered from migraines.'

'Hardly ever.'

'Nasty things.' A pause. 'Is everything all right, dear?'

Well, no. Everything was not all right. Everything was smashed, in red and yellow fragments around my feet.

Meg's voice had sharpened. 'Eilish? You there, dear? Where is Luke—can I speak to him?'

'He's gone,' I whispered.

Eleven

Luke

This time, there was no white-haired stranger to keep me company.

The train was taking me further and further from my home. I felt as though I were wearing a big sign on my chest and everybody at the station, everybody in the carriage, knew of my shame. Giggles escaped from a group of schoolchildren sitting behind me. My shoulderblades twitched. Children were laughing. I was four years old.

•

She woke up in the racing-car bed her daddy had made for her. A million butterflies were dancing in her stomach. After breakfast, Mum got out the clippers and cut her hair (*You want to look smart, don't you?*), and then she had to put on the green uniform—sandals, shorts and a brand-new Aertex shirt. She hated these clothes, they made her feel horrid, but she didn't say so because that would make people sad. Her daddy took a picture with his big camera. My brand-new schoolboy, he said.

Now here she was, in assembly. Real school! This was nothing like nursery. She'd never seen so many children before. The new entrants sat in a ragged line at the front. Somewhere in the great green crowd behind her were Wendy and Gail. She felt happy to know that Wendy was there, but she was scared of Gail.

A boy she knew from nursery had plonked himself down next to her. He was fidgeting. His name was Alex, and he wore glasses. Her best friend, Janey, sat on her other side. She and Janey were holding hands. Their mothers had met in the baby hospital where they were born. Janey smelled of the honey soap that lived in the bathroom at her house. She was wearing a pinafore dress and had a matching green bow in her hair. Luke was sure her own hair would grow long and curly like Janey's, if only they would stop cutting it.

'Your little girlfriend,' Mum was always saying, when Janey came to play.

'I shouldn't be surprised if those two got married,' Janey's mum once said, holding her coffee in one hand. 'They're like twins.' The two mums seemed to like this idea, and started going on about how they would both be mothers-in-law. Luke was pleased. She and Janey would have a house of their own. And a puppy.

A tall woman was clapping her hands for silence, yelling, 'Welcome to the new school year!' Luke knew who this was: Mrs Parry, the boss. She had fluffy hair and sagging cheeks, and she talked on and on. Alex fidgeted more than ever. Luke tilted her head to see the ceiling. It had cracks in it. One of the cracks looked exactly like the scary witch off *Snow White*, the one with googly eyes. She was surprised that her sisters had never mentioned the interesting fact that there was a googly-eyed scary-witch crack at their school.

She could smell the school dinner cooking. She hoped it wasn't liver, because she'd tried liver once and it was so horrible that she'd been sick. Gail had told her they had liver sometimes at school and they had to eat it all, and if anyone was sick the teachers made them eat the sick. Luke hoped this was a fib. She was imagining what sick might taste like when she noticed two older children standing next to Mrs Parry. One was a red-haired boy, the other a girl with a ponytail right on top of her head. Her face looked like Granny's Pekingese dog's, squashed and grumpy as though she'd just run face-first into a wall.

'Moira and Carl are cloakroom monitors,' said Mrs Parry. 'They're going to help you new entrants find your shoe lockers and coat hooks. They'll also show you where the toilets are, and tell you about our toilet rules.'

Luke wondered what a shoe locker looked like.

'Ladies first!' cried Mrs Parry. 'Girls—that's it, up you get—follow Moira to the girls' cloakroom.'

Janey and Luke scrambled to their feet, still holding hands, and joined the other four-year-olds clustering behind Moira. Luke knew she was a girl and Janey knew it too. People called her a boy sometimes, and Daddy said things like 'C'mon, son, let's us blokes go and fix the tractor.' But they'd made a mistake, and now was her chance to put them right.

Mrs Parry was smiling down at her. Luke didn't like the way she was doing that. Then the whole school began to laugh. She looked around, trying to guess what this funny thing might be.

'Not yet, dear,' said Mrs Parry. 'I'll be calling for boys next. They'll be going through that other door. Over there, see? That's the way to the boys' cloakroom.'

The laughing all around her grew into a big wave. She saw children pointing and felt her forehead creasing up. She hoped she wasn't going to cry. She held very, very tightly to Janey's hand. Janey clung to her, too.

'You can sit with your friend when you get to Mrs Mason's room,' whispered Mrs Parry. 'But first, Carl will show you the boys' cloakroom. You've got a peg waiting just for you, with your name already on it! Isn't that fun?'

'But I'm a girl,' said Luke.

Mrs Parry began to look like the witch with the googly eyes. 'Don't be silly.'

'I'm a girl!'

'Shush. Now, come on, let go of your friend's hand.'

Luke wouldn't let go. 'But *why* am I a boy?'

The googly eyes flickered down to Luke's new sandals and back again, as though she were checking. 'Because God made you one.'

'I think God made a mistake.'

'You will go through *that* door with the other boys. And that is final. Now, let go!' Mrs Parry was cross now. She leaned down to drag Janey's hand away.

Luke couldn't bear it. She had to make them understand. She yelled at the top of her voice, '*God made a mistake!*'

The crying thing was happening. She couldn't stop the howl from coming out of her mouth, nor the tears and snot from running down her face. Janey was being led away through the forbidden door. She was crying, too. She stumbled along with her head turned, looking back. Then Luke was all alone, and the whole school was laughing at her. The whole world was laughing. She stood wailing in front of the crowd, feeling ugly in her green shorts. She wished she was dead.

Someone must have gone and got her sister, because she heard Gail's voice in her ear. 'You stupid, *stupid* little bastard.'

'Tell them I'm a girl.'

'Shut up!' Luke could hear the smack in her voice, and covered her bottom with both hands as Gail dragged her over to join the boys. 'And turn off the waterworks.'

Luke couldn't turn off the waterworks. She cried when Carl showed her a peg with *Luke* written beside it. She cried when they showed her the shoe locker, which was just a place to put shoes. She cried when she saw the boys' toilets, with a pool of wee and soggy toilet paper on the floor where some boy had missed. Eventually she stopped crying out loud, but she carried on crying in her stomach. This gave her a stomach ache. She thought she would cry forever, because she'd learned something on her first day at school.

God had made a mistake.

•

'Tickets from Cottingwith,' said the guard, holding out his hand.

'Sorry.' I fumbled in my wallet to find my season ticket. 'Miles away.'

He nodded, flicking this particular passenger no more than a casual glance. No doubt he saw a greying man, utterly unremarkable, wearing cotton trousers and a polo shirt.

'Thank you, sir,' he said. He was already moving on.

Twelve

Eilish

I dropped down from the stile and began to walk, feeling the crunch of corn stalks under my feet. Each step sent up a small puff of dust. Day was draining from the sky, but I could still see the whole field, all the way to the footbridge.

I was looking for Kate. I'd glimpsed her earlier, arriving home from the station. She'd left the car door open and run straight out here. She used to do that when she was a teenager, usually after a fight with Simon; screaming with sisterly rage as she plunged through Gareth's precious crop. My policy was generally to leave her to simmer down, but if Luke was home he used to go and look for her. He would sit and listen to her troubles. Then they'd walk back to the house together, and I'd feel like the outsider.

It didn't take long to spot the slim figure on a cotton-reel bale. She was lying flat on her back, like Snoopy on top of his little doghouse. She didn't stir as I walked up. I thought perhaps she'd taken Luke's side and wasn't speaking to me. It wouldn't be the first time. I lowered myself onto the stubble, leaning my back against her bale. I felt calmer out here. The evening sky seemed honest and open after the deceitful shadows of the house.

I heard Kate shift in the straw. 'You okay?' she asked.

'Not really. How about you?'

'I've been telling myself to get a bloody grip. Be cool. Nobody's died.'

'True,' I said. 'Nobody's actually died.'

'It feels like somebody has, though.' Her legs appeared over the edge of the bale as she sat up. 'Nothing's what I thought it was. Up's down. Right's wrong. Front's back . . . I mean, he's my dad. I *know* him. I know he chews all around his thumbnail when he's bothered about something. I know he secretly loves babies, goes all smoochy over them. I know what makes him giggle: Baldrick off *Blackadder.* I know what pisses him off.'

'Holocaust deniers,' I said. 'Insurance companies. Traffic wardens. Arctic oil exploration.'

'Bossy check-in chicks.'

'People who kick cats.' Yet he's a fraud, I thought; a fraud with silky secrets. When nobody was watching, he put them on.

'We used to play British Bulldogs in this field,' said Kate.

'How could I forget?' I smiled at the memory. 'Every teenager for miles around seemed to congregate at our place.'

'Sophie Baxter and I used to sneak off and smoke under that lime tree.'

'I knew about you and Sophie smoking.' I looked across at the tree, covered now in pale blooms. Luke and I had stood beneath its canopy on our last walk, listening to the hum of bees.

'I remember him singing bedtime songs,' said Kate. 'Dad. Taking us camping. Giving cuddles when things went wrong. D'you remember the day he brought Casino home, up his jersey, after he found him dumped at the railway station?'

I did remember that—and a thousand other things: Luke holding the newborn Simon as though he were made of porcelain, tears spilling from his eyes. *He's perfect*, he whispered. *Perfect. Perfect.* I closed my eyes. I could hear the chuckling of the stream.

'A fox!' breathed Kate suddenly. 'See?'

I saw it: a lithe shadow trotting through the half-light. He paused near our bale, swivelling dark-tipped ears. Perhaps he'd caught wind of the presence of humans, but he seemed quite relaxed. I held my breath as he loped by. There was something magical about this glimpse of a wild creature. I felt a tug of sadness when he disappeared into the trees.

Kate and I sat on, watching the slow melting of evening into night, and the glittering of the first stars. I thought I heard the phone ringing back at the house, but perhaps it was only a bird calling. It didn't matter. I was sinking into a stunned stupor. The air was laced with the scent of wild garlic, and owls hooted from somewhere in the dreaming mass of woodland. We'd been so lucky, I thought, and we hadn't known it. So very lucky. We had lived a charmed life.

It was fully dark when Kate sighed. 'How can the world be so beautiful and so shitty, both at the same time?'

Luke

I listened to the ringing tone. One, two, three . . . and the answering machine. Perhaps Eilish had guessed it was me and didn't want to talk.

'It's only me,' I said to the machine. 'I'm . . . Well, anyway, I was wondering how you are. Both of you. Let me know you're all right, will you? Speak later. Bye.'

Life without Eilish yawned ahead of me. It looked bleak.

Evening always came early at the flat because it was almost subterranean; the kitchen window looked out onto dustbins, stone steps and the feet of passers-by. I'd bought the place with a massive mortgage just before I met Eilish, and we'd kept it as a London base. It had a small garden backing onto a railway line. I turned on the overhead light, a pitiless strip of neon, and two flies immediately smashed themselves into oblivion. A wail of sirens swelled and receded into the night.

I heated a ready meal but didn't eat it. I poured a glass of whisky but didn't drink it. I still had to phone my mother, and I was dreading it. She answered at the second ring.

'All Eilish would tell me,' she said, 'was to ask you. So, I'm asking you a straight question, and I'd like a straight answer. What's going on?'

I was getting better at the explanation: better at saying the words, better at coming out with it. She listened without comment until I'd told her everything. Even when I came to the end, she said nothing.

'Are you still there?' I asked. 'Mum?'

'Thank God Robert isn't alive to see this.'

'I know. Poor Dad.'

'Poor Eilish! What did she do to deserve such a slap in the face?'

'Nothing. She did nothing. It's all my fault.'

There was another silence. I heard the flick of a lighter, and an inhalation.

'Let's not pretend I had no idea,' she said. 'Let's not pretend that. You and I have memories, don't we? I'm to blame.'

'You? No!'

'Oh, I think so. I think I am. I'm going to ring off now, Luke, because you've given me a lot to think about and I don't want to cry when I'm on the phone. Don't worry, I'm not having a heart attack or anything. I'm not going to be found dead in my bed. I just think it's best if I . . . Let's talk again tomorrow. You're all right, are you? Good.'

She sounded completely winded. I think I would have preferred tears and recriminations.

After that, the silence screamed at me. The silence and the emptiness, stretching on forever. I felt completely alone. My eyes strayed to the cupboard below the sink. The rope still lay in there, coiled up. There was a hook in the ceiling that would take my weight. My letters were all ready and folded in the briefcase.

I couldn't manage this without some kind of help. It was too much, too terrifying. I was setting out on a journey with no map, compass or guide—and without Eilish.

I slid my laptop out of its case, fired it up and typed into the search bar: *help advice transgender.*

Within a second, those three words had brought up over twelve million results. I blinked, astonished. *Twelve million*? If only Google had been in existence forty years ago! I grew up believing myself to be the only person ever, in the history of the world, to feel as I did. Later I discovered that there were others like me, but I had no idea how many.

I could see forums and chatrooms. Lots of them. I searched for a site that didn't only push online dating and eventually chose one called *TransChatterers*. It looked innocuous enough.

I clicked on the icon for *chat*.

Register now.

Damn. Why did I have to register? It was one thing to sign up to the National Trust or Friends of the Royal Ballet; it was quite another matter for a partner at Bannermans to be hobnobbing on a website called *TransChatterers*. Perhaps my identity could be traced? I might be blackmailed or publicly outed. I didn't even know where *TransChatterers* was based, if anywhere. The USA? Russia? Nigeria?

Still, I was desperate, so I clicked. The next page asked for my email address. No, no, this was asking too much! They'd find me. I imagined an army of men with handbags chasing me down the street, banging on my door in the middle of the night; or perhaps beautiful Asian girls with penises, trying to sell me something I didn't want to buy. I got up and walked five times around the table, chewing my thumbnail.

Listen to yourself, Livingstone! You're awfully bigoted for a man who keeps lipstick in his briefcase.

Right. I was going to do this. I sat down again, typed in my email address and agreed to their terms and conditions. A final message sprang up:

Nearly there! Please enter a username.

A new name, for a new world.

Lucia.

Instantly, the site responded with the clanging of electronic gongs. *You are logged in! Welcome Lucia!* ☺

Euphoria swamped my anxiety. I was Lucia, and I was welcome! I had no idea what to do next. Suddenly, more words appeared on the screen. This time, they were from a real person.

BK: Hi, Lucia!

I didn't expect that. I ducked, as though they could see me; as though I could hide. Someone knew I was here.

BK: What brings you to our community? ☺

Good question. I laid my hands over the keys, took a long breath, and typed.

Lucia: I just need advice.

BK: Ur among friends here. Are u trans?

Lucia: I think so.

BK: Have u come out to anyone?

Lucia: Yesterday. To my wife. Terrible.

BK: ☹ *Sorry to hear that. My parents didn't want 2 know me but my sister came round. Hang in there Lucia.*

I'm not alone, I thought. My God, I'm not alone.

BK: What's next for you?

Lucia: I don't know what to do.

BK: I am m2f, transitioned 5 years ago.

It took me a while to make sense of the shorthand. Ah yes, I'd got it. BK was born male, but she'd been living as a woman for five years.

Lucia: Are you happier now?

BK: Let me answer that another way. Can you go on as you are?

I hadn't yet responded when my mobile rang. It was Simon. He didn't bother with pleasantries. 'I've just spoken to Mum.'

I stood up, eager for news of Eilish. 'How is she?'

'How do you think? How do you bloody *think*? I want you to promise that you'll never, ever give in to these urges again. I want you to see a shrink and get yourself cured. Then she might even have you back.'

'This isn't something that can be cured. I wish it were.'

'Sort your shit out, Dad! You can control this thing, if you really want to.'

'Please,' I said. 'Meet me tomorrow and let me explain better. There's so much to say.'

'If I see you, I truly think I might kill you.'

'You don't mean that.'

'Oh, I mean it.' His breathing sounded ragged, as though he were running uphill. 'I want to kill you for what you've done to Mum. Don't you dare start mincing down the street in a dress. If you do that, she'll be finished. And you'll be dead.'

'Simon,' I said. 'Simon?'

He'd hung up. I slumped back down into my seat, terrified by the new void in my life. That was Simon making threats—my rational, adored son.

The gong sounded on my computer.

BK: U there Lucia?

Lucia: Sorry but I have to go. This is too destructive. Thanks.

I closed my laptop and sank my face into my hands. It was too much; it was impossible. I couldn't go on, and I couldn't go back. I had no future.

Hi, Luke! breathed The Thought, popping breezily into my consciousness.

'Go away,' I said out loud.

It had no intention of going away. It draped itself around me, hypnotising with whispered promises of peace. *Remember Plan A? It's still the best option! Look at your funeral in East Yalton church. The pews are packed for such a well-liked, public-spirited, decent man! See Eilish? She's in the front row, wearing that black dress. Doesn't she look elegant? Such a respectable widow. See Simon? He's standing with one hand on your coffin, talking movingly about the father he loved. And there's your mother, bless her. She still has a son, even if he's dead. They can hold their heads up. Nobody's laughing at them.*

'Shut up. I'm not listening.'

There's your ticket to peace. In that cupboard. You know what to do. It'll be so easy.

'It would be tidier all round, wouldn't it?' I said.

So much tidier. You've even got the letters in your briefcase. Shame to waste all that planning.

The next moment I'd grabbed the rope from the cupboard and was charging through the flat, out of the sitting-room door and into the garden. There was a very high wall at the end, and beyond that the railway line. I pulled back my arm as I ran, swung, and let go. It was a pretty awkward bowling action, but the rope sailed out of my hand and far over the wall. I'd never be able to find it over there.

The letters were next. Back in the kitchen, I slid them all out of my briefcase. I needed a flame . . . ah, the gas ring. The paper caught faster than I'd expected. A few charred scraps were soon left, but they disintegrated and were washed down the plughole.

Then I stood leaning against the sink, head down, exhausted but victorious.

The Thought was sulking. I'd won the battle, if not the war.

In the early hours of the morning, I wandered along to the bedroom and lay down still in my clothes. I was afraid to sleep; afraid of the dreams. My mind felt light yet opaque, like cloud. The robin was singing in Thurso Lane. I'd seen him sometimes, flitting among the branches of the sycamore tree outside the flat, his red breast dulled in yellow street lighting. His song was sweet and clear as water. Sad, too. The poor little chap should have been safely tucked up in his nest, but he had no choice. The traffic noise was so loud during the day that his complex melodies couldn't be heard by other birds. So he had to suppress his nature and sing through the night.

I know how you feel, I thought as I closed my eyes. *What a world. What a world.*

A bird was singing in the forest. We were lost, my baby and I. Howls echoed in the darkness. I made a bed of leaves in the hollow of a tree and hid in there with her.

Don't be frightened. I'll protect you. Nothing will hurt us.

I felt the prickle of milk in my breast, and as I fed her she gazed up at me. I was filled with perfect happiness. I'd never felt such love before.

Then horrors came. I heard the snarls of wolves, and teeth sank into my leg, dragging me out of our safe place. Their faces were shaped like triangles, like devil faces, and their tails were waving merrily. It was Charlotte they were after. I shouted and kicked but I couldn't save my little girl. I was useless. They'd found her and pulled her out. They were tearing her apart with their terrible teeth.

I was in the flat, lying fully clothed and alone. I was sobbing. There was no baby.

After a time, a shaft of morning light found its way onto my pillow; but it couldn't brighten the darkness of that forest. The robin had gone. There was no point in singing now. The world had drowned his melody.

Thirteen

Kate

Was she back in her tent in Israel? The sky outside her window glowed, and birds were tuning up for the bird version of the Hallelujah Chorus. Then she focused on the striped yellow wallpaper, remembered what had happened, and covered her face with Mr Polington. It didn't matter about the birds or the blue sky. It didn't matter about Owen.

After a time she rolled out of bed, pulled on jeans and a sweatshirt, and trudged downstairs in search of coffee. The kitchen doors were folded open. Eilish was sitting on the bench outside. She was wearing her cotton wrap, the white one embroidered with coloured flowers. She wasn't crying. She wasn't moving. She seemed to be waiting for a non-existent train.

She looks after herself, thought Kate. You'd never guess she's in her fifties. All that Pilates. All that gardening. She's got a waist, and nice legs; she even has them waxed, which I'd never do in a million years. She can still fit into her wedding dress. What was it all for? Was it for him?

'Another lovely day,' murmured Eilish.

'So it is.'

'Your father rang.'

'Any news?'

'He wanted to know if I'm all right.' Eilish rearranged her wrap, smoothing it across her lap. 'I said I am. I asked how he is. He said he's fine. He asked how you are and I said you were still asleep. He asked if he could come home and talk to me, and I said no. And then we both said goodbye.'

'Well, at least it was polite.'

'The politeness was the worst thing.'

Kate retreated into the kitchen, wondering what on earth her mum had been hoping for. For Christ's sake, what conversation with Dad could possibly be cheerful in this situation? And where were the bloody coffee cups? They normally lived in a row on the dresser, with all the saucers piled up at one end. The shelf was empty, and so was the dishwasher.

'Where've the cups gone, Mum?' she called. 'Can only find one.'

No answer. Kate gave up and fished out some chipped mugs that they hadn't used in donkey's years. The biscuit tin was in its usual place, though, and well stocked. She took it outside, along with their coffee.

Eilish thanked her, and seemed to try to rouse herself. 'Have you and Owen really split up?'

'Yep.'

'What about your flat?'

Kate dunked a biscuit into her coffee. 'He's the tenant. My things are all in bin bags by the front door. Look, it's okay. Really. Owen's the least of our problems now, and I can always . . .' *Oops.* She'd been about to suggest that she sleep on her father's sofa bed in London for a week or two. 'Um, I could stay here for a while, if that's all right with you. Save me a lot of rent. Term doesn't start until September.'

'But you've work to do.'

'I've got to write a report on the dig, and I want to start thinking about my dissertation, but there's no reason I can't do that from here. I've got my field notes. I'd really like to stay until this mess is all sorted out.'

Stupid thing to say. It made the whole disastrous situation sound like a cutlery drawer that needed reorganising.

'Then stay,' said Eilish. 'I'd like that.'

She sank back into a reverie. She was looking out at Charlotte's tree. A breeze had sprung up, and was tugging at her wrap.

'How quickly things can change,' she said. 'And for you too, I know.'

Kate nodded. 'Friday morning, I woke up in a tent. All I'd thought about for six weeks were: one, the implications for Judaeo-Christian traditions of our finds; two, how frigging hot it was; and three, whether a scorpion was hiding in my shoes. I was looking forward to a flight home, a nice long bath, and a sloppy reunion with Owen.' She blew on her coffee. 'You're right. A hell of a lot can change in three days.'

'I'm sorry.'

'Don't be sorry! How can this be your fault?'

'I don't know,' said Eilish. 'Perhaps I just wasn't woman enough.'

'Woman . . . ?' Kate smacked her hand to her brow. 'Mum! Have I taught you nothing? It is not the role of any woman to be *woman enough* for a man!'

'Why not? I expected Luke to be man enough.'

'No, you didn't.'

'I did! Of course I did. I liked him to smell of coal tar soap, not Chanel. I loved the five o'clock shadow on his jaw when he came home in the evenings. I liked to see biceps when he took off his shirt. I wanted him to stride along in brogues, not totter in six-inch heels. I wanted—' Eilish looked towards the front gate. 'Oh, no. Please, not now.'

A red car was meandering up the drive.

'You shoot upstairs and hide in the shower,' offered Kate. 'I'll field Granny.'

'I can't do that,' said Eilish, as she got to her feet. 'He's her son. I can't imagine what that would be like. I hate to think, if Simon turned out to be . . . I have to face her, and she has to face me. It won't be the first time she's seen me in my nightie.'

Meg pulled on the handbrake and almost fell out of the car. She wasn't her usual sprightly self.

'Kate, love,' she cried. Shock was spilling from her in a breathless rush of words. 'Oh, my poor girl. Such a terrible thing, Eilish, such a terrible thing. I could tell things were in a mess, but this is . . . Oh, you poor girls.'

'Come inside,' said Eilish. 'There's a wind getting up.'

The yellow roses were hanging their heads. Meg sank into a chair while Eilish drooped against the kitchen counter. Kate felt rattled. These two women were the unshakable ones of her childhood. They weren't allowed to fall apart! Tea, she thought, and reached for another mug. A nice strong cup of workman's for Granny, with extra sugar; that's what she used to dish out when I was upset.

She was dropping a teabag into the bin when a flash of red and yellow caught her eye. She looked closer, saw what it was, and wanted to cry. She'd solved the mystery of the whereabouts of her parents' special coffee cups. Not cups anymore, though. Just a pile of broken rubbish. She reached in, retrieved the largest piece and slipped it into the pocket of her sweatshirt. A memento; a jaunty souvenir of normality before everything was smashed.

'Luke told me you found some of his secret things,' Meg was saying. 'Must have been terrible.'

'It was so . . .' Eilish shuddered. 'Meg, you have no idea.'

The older woman looked away, out into the garden. She sipped her tea. Then she said quietly, 'That's where you're wrong.'

Kate and Eilish both stared at her.

Eilish spoke first. 'You mean . . . sorry, Meg. I must have misunderstood. You don't mean to imply that you *knew*?'

'I hoped he'd changed.'

'No, Granny!' Kate felt bewildered. 'No, no. You can't have known he was like this. You would have said. You would have warned us, wouldn't you?'

Meg seemed to shrink into herself. 'It isn't as easy as that. These things aren't cut-and-dried. I only had the one boy, remember. Just the one. Just my Luke.'

Kate felt the ground shift under her feet, and abruptly sat down. A gust of wind shook the folding doors. She had a vague idea that she ought to get up and close them.

'He never wanted to be a boy,' Meg was saying. 'Two years old, he wasn't like other boys. He just wasn't. If we went shopping he always headed straight for the girls' department. He used to love the pink princess clothes.'

'I've *never* dressed up as a princess,' protested Kate.

'True, love. True. But you had a choice, you see? You could've if you'd wanted. And it was all my Luke ever wanted. One time I lost sight of him in a department store, and when I found him he'd got a basket. That basket was almost as big as he was, and it was so full he could hardly carry it. He'd put in a ballet dress and a diamond tiara and a wand. He was overjoyed with it all; I remember his face was one great smile. It's just about the happiest I've ever seen him in his life. And you know what I did?' Meg was very close to tears. She had to stop and swallow more tea.

'It's okay,' said Kate, wanting to comfort her. 'Don't worry, Granny.'

'I smacked his bottom! I was so frightened, you see? Can you see that? I snatched his precious basket out of his hands and I dragged him out of that shop by one arm. His little heart broke. He wailed all the way home. He begged me please please *please* could he have the tiara for his birthday. He was turning three. He didn't want anything else, just that.'

'I suppose you didn't get it for him?' asked Kate.

'How could I? We gave him a cricket bat. He cried again when he saw that bloody thing. I sent him to nursery school because I hoped he'd play with the other boys and be, you know, normal—but it backfired, because he was one of the girls, played dress-ups and dolls. They accepted him without question, especially Janey. D'you know her, Eilish? Janey Patton, that was. She's Janey Jamieson now. I think she was at your wedding.'

'I've a vague memory,' said Eilish. 'We get a Christmas card from her every year.'

'In those days, Janey and Luke could have been twins, wouldn't be parted for the world. He was hardly out of nappies, but he was always borrowing her sparkly clips and putting them in his own hair. And if he got the chance at home, he'd go into Wendy's room and dress up in her things.'

'He told me about that,' said Kate.

'Did he? He remembers, then. When I growled at him he looked all confused. He used to say . . . he used to . . . Oh dear, I'm blubbing again. I've been blubbing since he told me, it's all so . . .' Meg pressed her knuckle to her mouth. 'He said to me, "But I want to look *pretty*."'

That last word was too much for her, and it turned into a sob.

'Shh, Granny. Don't cry. It's all right,' Kate begged, anxiously rubbing her grandmother's arm.

'It's not all right, love. It's not. It's not.' Meg pulled a tissue from her pocket and mopped her eyes. 'Gail kept saying he was a little freak. But he wasn't a little freak. He was my son, and I loved him. Anyway, what was I meant to do? I'd never in my whole life heard of such things! I'd have believed in mermaids before I believed in boys who were really girls.'

'Didn't other people notice, though?' asked Eilish. 'What about the nursery school?'

'"It's a passing phase, Mrs Livingstone."' Meg imitated the singsong tones of some long-ago nursery teacher. '"He's a bright wee fellow. He'll start running around with toy guns and yelling 'bang-bang-bang' soon enough."'

'Did you believe them?'

'I had to.'

'And later—when he started real school?'

Meg shook her head. 'He stopped trying to be a girl, but he also seemed to lose all his joy. I don't think it ever really came back. He became sort of colourless—that's the only way I can describe it. He never smiled anymore. He wouldn't talk to me about what was wrong; he wouldn't talk to anyone. I was worried. That's why . . . oh dear. I'd better go. I think I've said enough.'

'Go on,' prompted Eilish. Her face was chalk white. 'We need to know. We need to understand.'

'All right. Well . . .' Meg took several breaths. 'He had this den in the attic. And in the den he had a tuckbox. He kept it locked, but I found the key hidden among his socks. One day when he was about . . . fourteen? Yes, he was fourteen . . . I climbed up the ladder and I unlocked the box.' Her mouth was shaking so much that she could hardly form the words. 'I knew I shouldn't. I knew I had no business prying, but I was so worried, and he used to look ashamed when he came down, like he'd been doing something dirty. I *hoped* for girlie mags. Girlie mags would've been just fine! Maybe cigarettes. Even a bottle of whisky.'

Kate and Eilish were both frozen, waiting. Meg screwed up her eyes as though the next few words were going to explode.

'A petticoat. A frock. A bra.'

In the silence that followed, gusts of wind seemed to harry the house. The folding doors swung once, twice, smashing against the trellis outside. Kate got up to pull them shut. It was wild out there. Her grandad's tree was taking a hammering: bent double one minute, springing up the next. Poor thing. It wasn't having an easy start in its new life.

Dad hid a bra when he was fourteen. Dad had a petticoat.

'I locked up that box,' Meg said. 'I came down the ladder. I hid the key away again. I tried to forget what I'd seen, and I never, ever said a single word about it to anyone. Not until now.'

'Not to Robert?' asked Eilish.

'*Especially* not to Robert! It would've broken his heart.' Tears roamed among the wrinkles on Meg's cheeks. Kate had never seen her grandmother cry before. 'My poor Robert. My poor Luke. So much hurt. Can you wonder that I shut up that box, and tried to forget I'd ever looked in?'

Fourteen

Lucia

It was ten o'clock on a Wednesday morning, near Mile End tube station. The army of commuters had already set off on their daily route march. Only the stragglers and unemployed, the elderly and the young were left.

She leaned against the bedroom windowsill, craning her neck to look up at the railings. It was as quiet out there as it would ever be. A heather-coloured skirt and blouse lay on the bed, along with knickers and a padded bra. They were all rather dowdy but that was fine with her. She didn't want to draw attention to herself.

Her fingers shook as she buttoned the blouse. It was long and hung loosely around her hips, but was caught in under her bust. According to the website she'd been consulting, this would help to disguise her lack of a waist. BK from *TransChatterers* had sent her the link. She was grateful, because the site was a mine of useful information.

She'd shaved her legs again that morning, blunting several disposable razors, and then rubbed handfuls of body moisturiser into them. She took a guilty pleasure in their new smoothness as she sat down on the bed to pull on a pair of tights. Tricky things, tights. She wondered how other women managed to get them on without sitting down or falling over. The secret seemed to be to lasso them with her toes and then wrangle them up her legs. Once they were almost on, she stood up and did several pliés, hoisting them higher up her hips. Not elegant.

Her shoes were clumsy boats, bought in Oxfam. They weren't quite large enough for her feet but the leather was soft and could be stretched. She walked towards the mirror, remembering the advice she'd read online (*Walk from your hips, be relaxed and loose, keep your upper body still, don't jut your chin. Draw your shoulders back*). Then she began to brush her hair, moving the parting to the centre so that dark waves framed each cheek. There was plenty of it, enough to cover her temples and disguise the male hairline. Gold knots clipped easily onto her ears, although—*ouch*—they pinched like billy-o.

Now. Make-up. With awkward care, she brushed on a powder foundation. The website had been right: it softened the coarseness of her skin. Next, mascara on her lashes. Finally, she formed her mouth into an 'O' shape and added the plum-coloured lipstick. She'd acquired her first lipstick as a teenager (Gail's cast-off, recovered from the bin) and was quite a dab hand.

There.

She regarded the dark-eyed woman in the mirror. Her jaw was slightly too heavy, her shoulders slightly too broad, her bust not quite the right shape. She didn't seem to know what to do with her arms.

'You look ludicrous,' she said aloud. The woman smiled fearfully.

Lucia picked up her wallet and dropped it into her sky-blue handbag. She'd spotted the bag three years ago, when wandering through the scents and sensations of Peter Jones. It had a William Morris–patterned lining and was made in New York. She'd bought it because she thought it was beautiful, and hidden it in the flat with shame and delight. A man could buy his wife or mistress a handbag, earrings or a silk scarf and raise no eyebrows. Oversized shoes and clothes were rather more difficult.

With the bag over one arm she made her way out of her bedroom, down the short passage and through the kitchen. There was nobody watching her yet, but she felt crippled by self-consciousness. When she reached the street door she stopped dead, her hands clenching and unclenching—hopelessly big hands, on hopelessly long arms. She hadn't painted her nails.

The world lay on the other side of that door, ready to laugh its head off.

She had been through this same routine yesterday, and the day before. She'd tidied up her eyebrows with a pair of tweezers, which was far more painful than she'd expected. She had tried combinations of clothes, and experimented with her hair and make-up. She'd practised walking in the unfamiliar shoes. She'd got herself completely ready—but every time she reached this door, her courage had deserted her.

Today. It must happen today.

'Get on with it,' she muttered, and was suddenly aware of the deep tones of her voice. What a giveaway! Who did she think she was going to fool? She would never be able to speak. Never. She could never go out there.

She must go out there.

Okay. A deep breath in, and out. Lift your hand. Turn the Yale. Open the door . . . well done.

Lucia had never been outside in her life. Sunshine lit up the area steps and she felt its friendly warmth on her face. She'd count to three, and then she'd take that final step across the threshold. She would do it this time. She would.

One. Two. Th—

Footsteps sounded like jackboots, marching along the pavement above. Several pairs of feet. She retreated instantly, a clam into its shell. The steps passed. The street was silent again, yet still she hid.

Now. It had to be now. *Now.*

And then she'd done it. She was standing outside in broad daylight, and the door had closed behind her. Terror and exhilaration thudded in her chest. Her foot was on the first step. The second. She reached the level of the street and, to her horror, there were people nearby. Two women in burkas, pushing toddlers in pushchairs. She glimpsed strappy sandals under their hems. They knew what it meant to cover up their femininity. Neither of them glanced in her direction as they passed.

She hauled the strap of her bag onto her shoulder and set off along Thurso Lane, feeling the grittiness of the pavement through her soles. She took small steps, remembering not to stride out as though she were in lace-ups and a pinstriped suit. She'd researched everything: how to walk, how to move. How to talk. How to pass. Every tiny nuance mattered. *Hold your head high*, the anonymous chatroom friends had advised. *Be confident. Smile. Hide your fear. Nothing marks you out more than your own fear.* She had been acting a part all her life; now, it seemed, she must act another.

After a couple of hundred yards, Thurso Lane met the main road. She could hear children chanting in the school playground, hidden behind fortress-like gratings. Two men were unloading furniture from a van. One nudged the other as she passed by. She heard exaggerated laughter, followed by a wolf-whistle. She knew exactly what they were seeing. She'd seen it herself, in the mirror. Her spine felt cold and exposed; some primal instinct expected an arrow in her back. She wanted to run, but forced herself to walk.

Her destination was the cash machine outside the newsagent's. She'd planned this as a first challenge. She wouldn't go into the shop and buy a paper. Not today. If she could only get herself as far as the cash machine, use it and come home again, that would be enough. The machine had never seemed so far away. Two hundred metres. One hundred. Fifty. She was there.

She took her card out of her handbag, soothed by the familiarity of routine. The hole-in-the-wall didn't care how she looked, so long as her PIN matched the card. It spat out a pile of notes and a receipt. So far, so good. As she tucked them into her wallet she heard movement, very close behind her. Somebody was standing there. Gripping her bag, she turned around.

It was someone she knew, someone she often spoke to.

'*Big Issue*?' he asked.

She nodded dumbly, took a magazine and paid. She regularly bought a copy from this seller as she emerged from the tube station; sometimes she even read it. He had tightly curled hair and smoked roll-ups. Whatever the weather, he wore a red T-shirt with a picture of Che Guevara.

'Thanks,' he said, taking the money. That was when his eyes flared in recognition. She waited for him to laugh, or spit, or abuse her. She wanted to sink into the ground.

'You're all right, love,' he said quietly.

She was running. A shoe came off, slapping onto the pavement—wretched thing; she was forced to hop along as she pulled it on again. The two delivery men were arguing over a washing machine, too engrossed to notice as she darted past them and into Thurso Lane. *Down the basement steps—watch the slippery one with the mould—where's the key? Get this bloody door open.*

The key was in the lock. It was turning . . . there! She was in. She slammed the door behind her and leaned against it, laughing. She felt as though she hadn't breathed at all in the past fifteen minutes.

She'd done it. She'd *done* it.

Luke

I went bungee jumping once, when I was much younger and still had things to prove. I've got the photos somewhere.

We were on holiday in New Zealand. Simon was about five; Charlotte had died the year before, and that darkness was still with us. This was an attempt, I suppose, to move on. By the end of the holiday, Eilish was pregnant with Kate, so perhaps it achieved its purpose.

Our guidebook said bungee jumping was a must-do. Eilish said it was a mustn't-do.

I was appalled when I saw the platform, cantilevered from a cliff fifty metres above a river, but I had my pride and couldn't back out. A couple of super-cool youths buckled straps around my ankles. They were singing along to very loud, palpitation-inducing music, but I didn't join in. I shuffled to the very edge of the dizzying drop and stood like a condemned man at the scaffold, trying not to look down. My God, that cliff was high.

Eilish and Simon had run off down the hill, hoping to get better photographs. I was glad they weren't there to see my terror.

Behind me, the bungee crew counted down to take-off: *Three . . . two . . . one . . .*

This is madness, I thought. *Madness. I'm a father. I'm a husband. I'm going to die.*

As I hesitated, I felt a sharp shove in my back—the super-cool duo had obviously decided it was time for me to go—and then I was diving through thin air. As I plunged into that terrible abyss, my body told me I was finished. This fall was not survivable. I was too terrified even to scream.

Then the bungee stretched, and held. As I rebounded, I yelled and yodelled for the pure joy of still being alive.

It was the ultimate adrenaline rush. Simon thought I was a bloody hero.

But it was nothing compared with a walk down the street in Mile End, on a sunny morning in July.

Fifteen

Eilish

So. What do you do when your husband announces that he's a woman?

I'll tell you what I did. I raged at him, I blamed him, I blamed myself. Then I asked Google, and found that I wasn't unique. There were women all over the world in my position—wives, girlfriends, daughters, mothers. Some had always known; some guessed; others discovered the secret by chance. Some were bitter, and some forgave.

I was astonished to read about wives who behave like shining saints. They listen, and they compromise, and they love, and they continue with their sex lives, and they try to understand. They go with their cross-dressed man to cross-dressed social weekends in motels on the M25, where—presumably—they watch him prancing around in their clothes while they compare notes with other shining saints. I bet they hate it, I thought. I bet it gnaws at their souls.

Good women do that. Good, loyal wives. I was not a good woman. I threw Luke out of my life. Then the pain began in earnest.

I'd loved the man; that was the trouble. Every inch of Smith's Barn held a memory of Luke. Every song on the playlist. Every

DVD, every painting, every scratch on the kitchen table. The swing—he'd made it, and pushed Simon and Kate in the summer evenings. The rosewood box on his desk, full of photographs of Nico's christening. His wellies (I threw them up into the attic in the end, because they reminded me of our last walk together). I'd changed the sheets, but his clean, male smell was not quite gone from our bed, and it lingered in the clothes I'd put away in his drawers. He was still here, the traitor.

He kept phoning me, wanting—wanting what? My blessing? It hurt to hear his voice, so I let the answering machine take his calls. Simon phoned too, desperate to hear that his father was sane again. Meanwhile, Kate and I supported one another and lied to the world. We had an official story: Luke was up to his ears in a massive deal, very intense, lots of overnighters—he just didn't have time to get home. Everything was fine in the Livingstone family.

My friend Stella returned from her trip to Cornwall to find a note from me, and called straight away. We arranged to meet in the car park at the foot of Yalton Hill. I'd managed to hold myself together for the past fortnight, but as soon as dear Stella hauled herself out of her car, I burst into tears. Bless her, she was so kind: hugging me and squeezing my shoulder and gasping, 'Good Lord, he's lost his mind.'

Stella Marriot has been married three times, and I've been her bridesmaid—maid of honour, whatever you call it—twice. Her first husband, Bob, was the father of her two daughters. He had a massive heart attack when he and she were playing in the final of the mixed doubles tournament in the Yalton club. Their opponents were Luke and myself, but she's never held that against us. The next, Hugh, was still in love with his first wife and turned to Stella on the rebound. The marriage was less than a year old when he and Stella agreed that it wasn't making anybody happy.

The third husband was more newsworthy: Steve Marriot, an affable charmer who managed a chain of pubs. Stella married him at the age of fifty and he gave her a Siamese kitten as a wedding present. She was deliriously happy until the day Steve was arrested for a series of bank robberies. The police found two sawn-off shotguns and a balaclava in the boot of his car, and he was sent to prison for fifteen years. Stella divorced him because he was absent; she seemed less worried about the fact that he'd turned out to be Oxfordshire's Most Wanted. Steve had languished in various prisons over the years, but wherever he was, Stella still visited him once a month.

'I can't believe it,' she said now. 'A cross-dresser? *Luke?* Is it April Fools' Day?'

'I wish it were.'

'What is he *thinking* of?'

'Turns out he's been doing it, or at least wanting to do it, the whole time we've been married. He's not just a cross-dresser, Stella. He says he feels he's a woman, trapped in a male body.'

She snorted. 'We all like the opposite sex. It doesn't mean we have to become one of them.'

We began walking up the hill. Stella's a well-padded woman, and the climb was a challenge for her. For some time she didn't have any breath to spare for talking, but I did. I felt as though I were turning a tap, letting the words stream out. I told her everything.

When the path levelled off, Stella managed to speak. 'D'you think he's serious?'

'I don't know. He says so. But . . . how can he be? It's crazy!'

'What about your anniversary party?'

'I've cancelled it.'

She paused, pretending to look at the view, though I was fairly sure she just wanted an excuse to catch her breath. 'He'll never go through with this.'

'You think he won't?'

'Nah. Look at what he's got to lose! His family and his work. Those are the two things he really cares about—they're the things that define him, aren't they? And I know he's not a proud bugger, but he won't want people to spit on him in the street. He'll have nothing. He'll *be* nothing. Holy moley, this hill has definitely got steeper since I was here last. I need to get myself back to zumba.'

'You okay?'

'Stitch.' She bent over, pressing a hand to her side. 'Whew. Perhaps it's male menopause. They do go a bit funny.'

'I'm in the middle of female menopause,' I retorted, 'but I haven't had a sudden urge to destroy my family.'

Once we were walking again, Stella seemed to get a second wind. 'Look, I'm the undisputed expert on husbands around here, and my money says he'll see sense once he's looked into the void.'

'I hope you're right.'

'The question is, my friend, what are you going to do when he turns up at your door and promises to be one hundred per cent male from now on? Would you take him back?'

I still hadn't come up with an answer when we reached the trig point at the summit. Stella sank onto a rock. I leaned my arms on the marker, feeling the wind whip against my cheek. The Chilterns rolled on and on into a hazy horizon, dappled by the racing shadows of clouds.

'I just want him to come home,' I said. 'I want him to be his old self again. D'you think I'm a fool?'

'No. The man's an absolute gem.' Still puffing, Stella ticked off Luke's good points on her fingers. 'Not dead. Not in love with someone else. Doesn't even point shotguns in people's faces.'

'He wears dresses, though.'

'Mm.' She considered this fact. 'And that has to stop. You can hardly be expected to find a man attractive when he's cavorting around in a petticoat—so no more of that kinky stuff, thank you very much. That's not negotiable. I'll bet he's having second thoughts already and doesn't know what to do about it. Go and see him, Eilish! Tell him his bridges aren't burned. Good Lord, you've been together long enough. You must know how to get through to him.'

You can see for miles from the top of that hill. The miniature houses of East Yalton looked chaotic, straggling around the limestone church with its square tower. Beyond them lay fields and woods, and Gareth's farmyard. I could just make out the roof of Smith's Barn.

'The last time I came up here was with him,' I said. 'New Year's Eve. We opened a bottle of bubbly and stood right here, by this marker. We didn't need a watch to know when it was midnight.'

'Fireworks?'

'Spectacular! All over the countryside, all at once. Mind you, it was bloody freezing.'

It had been all I could do to get Luke to come with me up the hill. He'd been going through a low patch. Even getting out of bed had seemed an effort.

'Another year gone,' he'd said, as we huddled together under his overcoat.

'And another begins!' I reminded him, and began to prattle on about my plans for the year ahead. I was used to these dark moods of his; they were just a part of him. I honestly thought the right strategy was to be Tigger to his Eeyore. Was that where I went wrong?

Now, standing by the trig point, I found myself gazing at the roof of Smith's Barn. Perhaps he'd already come home. I imagined walking into the kitchen to find him waiting for me; and that, by some miracle, he was his rational, handsome, male self again.

Sixteen

Luke

The Bathgate Road surgery was jammed between a pawnbroker and a betting shop. It had eight GPs, and a receptionist so short she could barely be seen above the counter. She said I had to fill in a form since I was a new patient. My hand shook uncontrollably as I wrote. The waiting was over. In a few minutes' time I was going to say the words out loud.

The receptionist smiled warmly when I handed back the form. Of course she did: I must have appeared a well-turned-out, well-spoken chap, more than welcome in her waiting room. I wondered whether she'd be so polite if she knew what I was.

'You'll be seeing Dr Ford,' she said, and gave me a ticket with a number on it, as if I were in the delicatessen at a supermarket. My number was sixty-six. People sat on plastic chairs, staring at breakfast TV on a large screen. I stood, chewing around my thumbnail and trying to distract myself by reading the message boards. There were notices for carers of dementia patients, for diabetics, for people who didn't speak English. There was one for teenagers who thought they were gay, and others offering help with depression and addictions and eating disorders. I could see nothing at all for people whose bodies didn't match their minds.

Once, long ago, I thought my body and my mind might be in harmony after all. I was young, and it was summertime. Eilish and I had booked five days in a little hotel in the Dordogne. We were—I apologise for the cliché, but there is no better way for me to say this—madly in love. Madly, but also sanely. Before her I'd had several girlfriends, all of whom complained that I shut them out. Eilish was unlike anyone I'd ever met. She quelled my inner conflict. With her, I could be a man.

I wasn't yet a partner at Bannermans, and was expected to be at my desk from eight in the morning until all hours of the night; sometimes all night. At the time I was working on a merger with a corporate partner called Benjamin Rose. I liked and trusted Benjamin—I still do—and he was the one person I told about my plan to propose to Eilish. He laid a fatherly hand on my shoulder and suggested a little jeweller's shop he knew off Chancery Lane.

'Off you go,' he said, in his rumbling voice. 'No time like the present.'

The ring was an antique, with three emeralds. It could have been made especially for Eilish, with her green eyes. I bought it on sale or return (the jeweller winked at me, said he was sure it wouldn't be returned) and smuggled it back to my desk. For the rest of the day, I felt the box next to my hip, but my mind kept sneaking away, leading me to Thurso Lane and pointing accusingly at the suitcase I kept under my bed. That's where I kept my precious stash, gathered over the years; those things that brought comfort when masculinity became unbearable.

I didn't need it anymore. It had to go.

That night, I carried my treasures out into the wilderness that I called a back garden. I pushed them into a dustbin, doused them with petrol and set them alight. I even did a little victory dance around the fire. I'd beaten the addiction. I would be a man forever.

I so wanted it to be true. I wanted to be normal. I wanted to be happy. Who doesn't?

The electronic board was flashing: 66. Hoof beats in my chest. *Come in, number sixty-six, your time is up. Come in and confess your shame.*

•

Dr Ford had sparse hair and an air of near-retirement. 'Morning, Mr . . . er, Livingstone. Take a seat. What can I do for you?' he asked, looking me over with professional politeness. He'd be seeing nothing unusual, just a pair of chinos and a stripy shirt. Men who looked and dressed like me were probably two a penny to him. *Prostate?* he'd be thinking. *Heartburn?*

I gripped my knees. Then I did it. I said the words.

'I believe I have gender dysphoria.'

'Sorry?'

'Gender dysphoria. I identify as a woman.'

He coughed. 'Are you joking?'

'No.'

He leaned back in his swivel chair. 'You don't look remotely like a woman.'

'I know that, but nevertheless . . .' I remembered the script. I'd canvassed BK in the chatroom before this visit, and knew what I wanted to achieve. 'I would like you, please, to arrange for me to be referred to a gender identity clinic. I believe I'll need a psychiatric assessment.'

'And what would be the point in my doing that?'

I was taken aback. I hadn't expected open hostility from a GP. 'I've battled with this for decades,' I said. 'I've had depression. I desperately need help. Please help me. *Please* help me.'

'Look,' said Dr Ford, pinching his nose between forefinger and thumb. 'I'm not au fait with the terms you people like to use, but let me tell you that this is an emotional problem, not a physical one. Are you married?'

'Yes, but—'

'Sex okay?'

'Why is my private life relevant?'

He rolled his eyes in exasperation, as though I were a rebellious teenager. 'There's no point in your coming to see me if you disregard my advice. I assume you have a problem with erectile dysfunction?'

'No.'

'It's very common at your age. I can help you with that.'

'No thanks.' I'd stopped feeling nervous. 'This has nothing to do with my sex life.'

'D'you have children?'

'They're adults now.'

'Lucky you,' he said. 'Many of my patients have no family at all. They go through life completely alone—which is what you'll be if you don't snap out of this nonsense! What are your children supposed to think when their father swans in looking like Dame Edna Everage?'

Keep calm, I told myself. *Don't storm out.*

'Now.' Ford was jabbing his biro in my direction as though trying to take out an eye. 'In my professional opinion, you haven't given this enough thought. I can examine you if you like, give you a clean bill of health.'

'Not necessary.'

'I can also take some blood tests, to exclude some kind of hormonal imbalance.'

'That won't help.'

'Then let me give you some advice. What you are experiencing is a midlife crisis. I think you need to take more exercise. What about cycling? Many men of your age find that taking up cycling has all sorts of benefits. Good for your waistline, your fitness levels and your libido. You could join a club. A colleague of mine has found a whole new lease of life. He's just cycled across the Andes.'

'Are you going to refer me or aren't you?'

He was typing now; he wanted to be rid of me. I sensed deep anger in the man. 'I can give you a private prescription for Viagra. That should sort out any little, er, problems with sexual function.'

'No thanks.'

'Don't be a fool, Mr Livingstone. You don't want to lie on a slab and have your genitals chopped off! You don't seriously want them to turn your bits inside out?' He shuddered. 'Of course you don't.'

'I'm not necessarily looking for surgery.'

'What, then? Female hormones? You can buy those over the internet, as I'm sure you know. I expect you already take them, do you? If so, stop. D'you know what effect they'll have? They'll shrink your testicles—it's basically castration. You'll lose your sex drive and you'll grow breasts. You'll become a she-male.'

'A *what*?'

He curled his upper lip. 'A she-male. Neither one thing nor the other. For heaven's sake! Go home to your wife, be grateful for what you have, and let me get on with my job.'

I almost gave up. I got to my feet, wanting to be out of that room. Then I stopped.

'Actually, no. I'm not leaving,' I said, sitting down again. 'Not until you refer me to someone who *will* help. I've waited an entire lifetime to have this conversation. I don't think you have any idea how difficult it's been for me to walk in here and tell you about myself. If you don't know how to refer me, look it up. That's what I do when I'm out of my depth in my professional life.' Then—riding on a sudden wave of inspiration—I added, 'I'm a solicitor. I hope I don't have to make a complaint.'

I sat glaring, expecting an explosion. Perhaps the tiny receptionist would turn out to be a karate expert and I'd be thrown out bodily. Ford tapped his pen on the table. When he finally spoke, he did so without looking at me.

'All right. I have a colleague in this practice who seems to collect people like you. I'll speak to her. She'll be in touch.'

'Thank you.'

'I'd like you to leave now, please. There are a lot of genuinely sick people in my waiting room.'

I stood up. My hand was on the door handle when he fired his final shot. 'Mr Livingstone.'

I looked back at him, wondering what further insults he had in store.

'Be careful what you wish for,' he said.

Seventeen

Eilish

I stood in front of the wardrobe, staring at my clothes. I didn't want to look as though I'd tried terribly hard. Heavens, I certainly didn't want him coveting my outfit! Perhaps that was what he'd been doing, all these years? Maybe I'd been no more than a mannequin in a shop, modelling all the things he longed to wear. Then again, I had to make some kind of effort. I needed to guard my remaining self-respect.

The linen trousers and a loose shirt. They would do. Smart, but not too feminine.

Luke had been gone about three weeks when I took Stella's advice and suggested we talk face to face. He sounded hopeful and offered to come out to Smith's Barn. He needed to be in the village on Wednesday evening anyway, he said, for a school governors' meeting. Perhaps he could drop by?

'I'd rather we talked in no-man's-land,' I said.

'We're not at war, are we?'

We are, I thought. Of course we are.

'Meet me at Paddington,' I said. 'We can find somewhere for lunch.'

I was slipping on the shirt when a splash of primrose yellow peeped out at me from the far end of the wardrobe. My breath caught as I dragged it from its hanger, a sundress with a very full skirt. This old friend! I supposed it was terribly dated—eighties—but, oh, it took me back.

This dress. A hotel terrace in the Dordogne, the smell of strong coffee, and a table with a blue linen cloth. And Luke saying, 'Um.'

I remember being mesmerised by a bird as it glided in the ravine, far below us. I could see the sun on its wings. The river was a glittering thread of silver, half-hidden by skeins of mist.

'What is that bird, Luke?' I'd asked, pointing. 'A kestrel?'

He was trying to pour coffee from a ceramic pot, and the lid clattered. 'Probably. Look. Um. I'm not sure how to . . . Blast!' The lid came off and a small flood of coffee spilled onto the tablecloth.

'Tut-tut,' I said, laughing at him as he dabbed furiously with a napkin. 'Can't take you anywhere.'

'You can't,' he said, reaching into his pocket. 'Look. Bit soon, I know, and you'll probably say no, but I've got to ask at least, because I can't imagine a future without you.'

Three decades later, I stood in our bedroom and surveyed the ruins of my dreams. I could still see the dark liquid spreading across that sky-blue cloth, and the wings of a hunting bird as it wheeled and balanced in the haze. I could still feel the magic, raising the hairs on my arms. I could still see Luke's anxious smile as he held out the box.

I'll never forget this moment, I'd thought, as I took it from his hands. Never.

The ring was too big, but I wore it on my thumb until we got back to London and I could have it altered. He'd chosen it himself: emeralds, he said, to match my eyes—but, of course, if I didn't like it I could choose another.

I was wearing it now, as I stood in my bedroom. This ring was on my hand at the start of our life together, and it would be there at the end. The vicar who married us had said in his sermon that a ring was a symbol of our never-ending commitment. He didn't use the word *love*. He wasn't that kind of vicar. *Commitment.*

That, he'd said, was the key. Hold onto that, and we would make it through until death parted us. He was an optimistic soul.

I remembered an odd thing Luke's best man said to me on my wedding day. Toby was Luke's only first cousin, a broker of some kind who lived in Singapore. He'd weaved up to me, holding his own private bottle of champagne, a little squiffy and maudlin.

'You've got a good man there,' he said. 'I envy you. You're the only person who's ever got close to him.'

I laughed. 'Rubbish, Toby! Half this crowd are his friends or family.'

'Ah, but do they know him? He's built a bloody great wall around himself, ten feet thick.'

I didn't have time to ask what he meant, because the next moment he was buttonholed by my mother, who wanted to introduce him to someone. I'd thought little of it at the time, but as the years went by, I saw what Toby meant. Luke was kind and welcoming to our friends without ever letting them into his mind. He was a terrific listener; I often found people pouring out their hearts to him, but his own remained locked and bolted. As it turned out, even I hadn't broken through that ten foot wall.

I was shutting the wardrobe doors when Kate looked in.

'Mum, you look great,' she said. 'You could have got dolled up in a bin bag, though, and Dad wouldn't care. He thinks you're the loveliest woman in the world.'

'Not lovely enough, evidently.'

She pretended to growl.

'I know, I know,' I said, slapping my own wrist. 'This hasn't happened because I wasn't good enough. This has happened because your father's gone mad.'

'Better. What are you going to say to him?'

'That depends on what he has to say to me. I'd better get going if I want to catch the twelve-eighteen.'

She walked me out to the car.

'Have you heard from him?' I asked.

'Just the odd text.'

'Any news?'

'Nothing interesting.'

She was being evasive. I recognised the blank look on her face. It was the same expression she'd worn at the age of five when accused of eating the chocolate buttons off Simon's birthday cake.

I felt my heart sinking.

'Have I lost him?' I asked.

Kate

She watched her mother drive away. Casino had followed them outside and was winding around her calves, claiming that he hadn't eaten in days—even though he was shaped like a football with legs.

Her mum looked so pretty. She'd tied up her hair, with little ringlets around her face. But that yellow dress! Kate hadn't seen it in aeons. It was a bit retro for lunch in Paddington and, to be honest, it was on the young side. Perhaps it was a favourite of Dad's, or something.

Taking her phone out of her bra, Kate scrolled down to the text he'd sent that morning.

On my way to see another doctor, to talk about my future. Hope you and Mum can forgive me.

Poor Mum. 'I think she's lost him,' she said to Casino.

Luke

After my disastrous appointment with Dr Ford, I decided to treat this whole thing like a work project. My new doctor—Nina Cameron—had phoned me at home and booked a double slot for the consultation. There was just enough time before I had to be at Paddington to meet Eilish. I arrived with a list of questions scribbled in my diary, along with a printout of a protocol for GPs. I wished I'd been so well armed before, because Ford had broken every possible rule.

Dr Cameron's voice on the phone had sounded youthful, and she'd described herself as having an interest in gender identity, so I'd expected someone on the young and trendy end of the spectrum. I was wrong on both counts. The woman who rose to greet me looked a vigorous sixtyish, with no-nonsense hair.

'Ah,' she said, nodding at the protocol in my hand. 'I see you've been doing your homework. That saves us a lot of time.'

What followed could not have been more different from the meeting with Ford. Nina Cameron was another species altogether. She wasn't what Eilish would call touchy-feely—in fact, her manner was decidedly businesslike—but she didn't dislike me for what I was.

'Now,' she began. 'Tell me about what's brought you here.'

'I don't know where to start.'

I detected a faint smile. 'At the risk of sounding like Julie Andrews, why don't you start at the very beginning?'

So I told her about the longing that had pervaded my life, all my life. I told her about my depression. I told her about stealing my sisters' clothes, and wanting a peg in the girls' cloakroom at primary school. I described how, as an adolescent, I stood naked in front of a full-length mirror and shouted obscenities at myself.

'What exactly did you hate so much?' she asked.

'Everything. My masculinity. My hairiness. My voice. Myself. I opened my eyes in my bedroom every morning, with all the posters of Pink Floyd, and wished I'd died in my sleep. I was a battleground. That battle's raged ever since, with occasional ceasefires.'

'And your sexual orientation?' she asked, in the same tone of voice she might have used to ask me what the weather was doing outside.

'I'm, um, straight. Heterosexual.' I hesitated. She had a piercing gaze; it made me feel shifty. 'I really am. Sounds a bit odd, I know, coming from someone who thinks they're female.'

'Not odd at all,' she said. 'Sexuality is entirely separate. And gender is a continuum, not a binary thing. I've worked with people who feel they are without gender altogether.'

'That makes my situation sound simple.'

'Indeed. This is why pronouns are such a minefield. Some people want a gender-specific pronoun—"he" or "she". Others choose to refer to themselves as "they", even though it's plural. I heard of someone who went for "Ze".'

'Ze?'

'It's gender neutral.'

'Good Lord.' I scratched my head. 'How baffling. I must be very conservative. I can't even cross-dress without being a boring twit about it.'

She laughed politely. I hoped she might be warming to me. 'The next question, of course, is where you want to go from here—if anywhere.'

'What do other people do? Others like me?'

'No two people are alike. I'd strongly suggest counselling, whatever else you do. Ultimately, some people transition in the sense that they live in the new gender, but they never make any physiological changes. Some feel that hormone therapy is key. A very few go on to have surgery. There's no one size fits all.'

She picked up a pen and began to write down my options. I could scarcely believe I was having this matter-of-fact conversation. She mentioned hormones, and I confessed that I was tempted to buy them online. Some of my correspondents on *TransChatterers* had done this on and off for years. Nina looked down her hooked nose and said it wasn't safe. We talked about the NHS versus the private system, and what things might cost. She wrote down the name of a private clinic.

As we talked, I had an extraordinary sensation. A vast pair of gates were opening, very slowly. I could see them in my mind's eye: heavy, medieval city gates with metal studs. There was dazzling sunshine beyond. Then something came rushing up to punch me, knocking the breath from my body. I think it was hope.

Nina was watching me. She'd asked me a question and was waiting for the answer. I blinked, shaking my head, unable to speak, feeling the tears begin. Stupid, I thought. Stupid. Why cry now, after all these years? Whoever really cries with hope?

'Sorry,' I whispered, wiping my eyes. 'Completely overwhelmed.'

'Quite all right. Take your time.' She pulled a tissue out of a box on her desk and handed it to me.

'I thought I was the only freak in the whole world,' I said. 'I was so lonely. I couldn't tell my poor parents. I couldn't tell my wife. Endless shame and hiding, and the fear that the whole facade will come tumbling down . . . I go about my daily life, and people respect me, and I think, "If you knew what I am, you wouldn't even speak to me."'

'You've never had a normal conversation about this before?'

'Never. *Never.* This is the first time I've told someone who wasn't shocked. You've no idea what this means to me.'

'Well.' She tore her notes from the pad. 'I've a feeling it won't be the last.'

Eilish

He was waiting for me. As soon as we saw one another through the throng of people, he hurried towards the barrier. He was ready to throw his arms around me. I felt such loss, and such longing.

'Hello,' I said, stopping well out of his reach.

He dropped his hands. 'Darling. You look wonderful.'

'I doubt it, but thank you.'

He smiled sadly, and my heart was squeezed. 'That dress.'

'Ah yes, this dress.' I looked down at the frivolous thing, wishing now that I'd gone for the linen trousers. 'It was all very romantic, wasn't it? In retrospect, I should have chucked your ring into the ravine.'

'Don't say that.'

He was nervous. I knew the signs. He pushed a hand through his hair and a wave of it was left standing upright. I resisted the urge to stroke it flat again.

'I've booked us a table at Parvel's,' he said. 'Shall we go straight there?'

This is obscenely like a date, I thought, as Parvel's waiter threaded through the tables ahead of us. A date with a difference. A goodbye date, perhaps. The man led us to a table in a bay, handing us menus with a flourish. He probably thought this was a romantic tryst—a wedding anniversary, or a birthday, or a clandestine affair.

'Can I get you a drink?' he murmured.

'Um.' Luke picked up the wine list, raising his eyebrows at me. 'Shall we have a bottle?'

'Go ahead.'

'Red or white?'

'For pity's sake, Luke, I don't care.'

Hurriedly, he asked for a bottle of something or other. The waiter took the list and whisked away, clearly trying to look as though he hadn't noticed the tension in the air.

'So,' said Luke. 'Kate tells me that Stella is back from Cornwall?'

Small talk, I thought dully. We're making small talk, while our marriage dies. He asked after Nico and Carmela. We covered such earth-shattering topics as Casino's weight, and the school governors' meeting. We talked about nothing that mattered, and ignored the monster that was ripping us apart. I wasn't listening, even to myself. Someone came over and took our order, but I barely noticed. The background blurred until Luke's face seemed to fill my vision. I imagined tracing the strong planes of his jaw with my finger, smoothing the vertical crease on his forehead. How often had I done this over the years? Thousands of times, probably, in moments of passion or warmth or tender idleness. *Never again. I'll never be able to do that again.*

'Kate hard at work?' he asked.

I couldn't stand it anymore. 'Polite chit-chat,' I burst out. 'Really, Luke? Have we come to this?' I was crying, dammit. I couldn't help it. I felt such appalling bereavement.

He leaped to his feet, and began to hurry around to me.

'No,' I spluttered, waving him away. He hovered unhappily while I fumbled for tissues. Get a grip, woman, I scolded myself. Where's your dignity? Stella's lost three husbands, and you don't see her making scenes in restaurants.

'I don't want to play this game,' I said. 'Let's not do small talk and let's not reminisce. I'm here to ask you to come home. I'm offering to forget what's happened.' I saw his eyes light up, and pressed my advantage. 'Just come home. Be Luke again. It's a good offer.'

For one glorious moment I thought I'd done it. He looked so eager—but then he shook his head. 'I can't be Luke Livingstone again. I can't lie anymore. If I tried to do that, it would finish me.'

The waiter had reappeared, and was displaying the label on a bottle.

'Perfect,' said Luke, without really looking at it. 'Thank you.'

The man didn't take the hint. He opened the bottle and poured a little for Luke to taste, which he dutifully did. Then he complimented Luke on his choice, and the next moment they were in conversation about acidity and oak and the vineyard it had come from. The man was obviously a wine fanatic, and Luke was too kind to tell him to sod off. An ornate mirror hung on the wall to one side, with another opposite. An endless fan of Lukes curved away into infinity: distinguished-looking men with a lot of dark, silver-tinged hair. I wondered which of them was him. Would the real Luke Livingstone please stand up?

None of them was, of course. None of them, not even the one sitting opposite me.

It was while I was looking into those mirrors that it occurred to me there was some physical change in him. Yes . . . yes. I was pretty sure of it. His face was strained, of course. He'd lost weight. There was something else, though; something more tangible. What was it?

Once the waiter had left us alone, Luke reached his hand out to mine, but then drew back again. 'You'll never know how much

I wish I could come home. You're my whole world. D'you really think I'd have done this if I had any choice?'

'You must have a choice.'

'I love you,' he said. 'I cannot imagine life without you. But I can't go on as I am. I won't survive.'

I looked away from him, towards the street door. A large group—an office lunch—was just leaving. There was all sorts of politics about who held the door open for whom, and the net result was that nobody was actually getting out. I might have smiled, on another day. Luke wasn't coming home. I'd failed.

'All right.' My voice sounded faint. 'In that case, I need to know where I stand. I have questions. I want the truth.'

'Of course. I promise.'

'Do you have other clothes—female clothes—stashed in our house?'

'No.'

'But you have some in the flat?'

He obviously didn't want to answer, but he'd promised. 'Yes. I've kept clothes in the flat for many years.'

'I see,' I said, feeling nausea. 'And what else do you keep there?'

'Make-up. Shoes. You know.'

I could have slapped him. 'I *don't* know, Luke. These revelations may all seem perfectly run of the mill to you, but they are, in fact, utterly bizarre. Do you own a wig?'

'Not at the moment.'

'Do you plan to?'

He looked guilty. It was almost comical—a few weeks ago I would have laughed uproariously at the idea of Luke wearing a wig. 'This is early days for me,' he said. 'I don't really know how to do these things. I'm learning.'

'How do you learn?' While he hesitated, a dreadful thought occurred to me. 'Oh no. Have you been going to clubs? I've read about men who lead a double life. They're Larry in one town and Lola in another. Some have . . .' I recoiled from uttering the words. 'Some meet up . . . they have sex with people they meet on the internet. Is that what you've been doing? Have you been fantasising about sex with men, all our married life? Did you think about men when you were with me?'

'No!' He was shaking his head before I'd finished my sentence, looking shocked. 'Come on, Eilish! You know me.'

'I don't, as it turns out.'

'You *do*. I am still me. I haven't changed.'

I could see a couple nearby, gazing into one another's eyes like a pair of cats. They reached across their table to hold paws. Luke and I were like that once, I thought. Those two ought to be careful. They'll burn their joined hands on that candle, and then they won't look so bloody smug.

'This has nothing to do with sex,' insisted Luke. 'Everybody seems to assume I'm planning on behaving like a rabbit on Viagra but—ah. Thank you.'

The waiter had arrived, bearing our meals aloft. He would have had to be stone deaf not to have overheard but, to his credit, he kept a poker-straight face as he refilled our glasses. I was sure my nose was beacon red, and he'd know I had been crying. While the waiter messed about with the pepper grinder, I was watching Luke. What was it about him that had changed? What *was* it? Suddenly, it hit me.

'I don't believe it!' I cried, as soon as the waiter was out of earshot. 'You've been plucking your eyebrows.'

He looked shifty but didn't try to deny it. The effect was quite subtle but now I'd spotted it, the difference was obvious. He crinkled his face in a pantomime of pain, prodding one shaped brow with his fingers. 'Exquisite agony,' he complained. 'And time-consuming. Do women really do this stuff?'

'I go to a threader called Shilpa, at the station. For ten quid she'll give you beautiful curved arches. That'll go down well at Bannermans.'

'Does it hurt?'

'Of course it bloody hurts!'

He stared down at his hands. His poor thumbnail was raw around the edges where he'd chewed it. 'This morning I went to see a GP,' he said.

No. I thought I'd felt awful before, but this was ten times worse.

'I can get help on the NHS,' he continued. 'Counselling, advice, hormones. But they're overstretched. If I go down that route it's going to be extremely slow. It'll be months before I get a first appointment, then more months before a second. I'll probably have to live as a woman before they give me hormones.'

'Live as a . . . What does that mean?'

'Present as a woman in public, every day. They call it the "RLE". Real Life Experience.'

'Real. Life. Experience,' I repeated dazedly. 'Sounds like a computer-simulated game.'

'But it isn't simulated, it's real. It comes with real dangers and real problems and real humiliation. And the thing is . . . the whole process will happen much faster if I pay for my own treatment. I'd like to go to a private clinic. Baytrees. It will cost.'

Ah, I thought. So that's where all this is leading. Money.

'There are financial things we may need to talk about,' said Luke.

I could imagine what Simon would have to say on the subject. He'd already been nagging me to see a solicitor and get the assets tied up. *He's mentally unstable, Mum, he'll drain every penny you have!*

'Are you planning on having surgery?' I asked.

I was pleased to see him wince. 'That's a long, long way down the track. Most transgender people don't go that far.'

'And where does this leave our marriage? You want to kill Luke. You want to make me a widow.'

'No.'

'Yes! What other possible outcome can there be?'

'I've never pretended to be the muscled caveman type, have I? You've always known that. All I'll be doing is taking off the mask. I will still be the same person. And I'll never stop loving you.'

I shoved risotto around my plate, turning his words over and over in my mind, trying to find the flaw in them. The smoochy-cat couple leaned further towards one another and rubbed noses. Her hair was dangling dangerously close to that candle flame.

'What are you suggesting?' I asked. 'That we live together as two women—or one woman and one weird hybrid? Is this really your grand plan?' I shuddered. 'In case you hadn't noticed, Luke, I'm not a lesbian.'

'No, no. I couldn't ask for that. I'm suggesting we stay friends, close friends. All right—not living together, I understand that's not possible for you, but surely we can salvage something? Our marriage wasn't built on sex, was it? It was about love, and understanding, and—'

'And trust, which you have betrayed.'

'Did you love me because I was a man?' He sounded desperate now. 'Or because I was myself?'

'The two are inseparable. Go on with this journey, if you must,' I said, abandoning lunch and picking up my bag. 'But you will be alone. I won't support you in any way.'

The waiter seemed concerned as Luke paid the bill. Had we enjoyed the meal? We hadn't wanted dessert, or coffee? He fetched my jacket and held it out for me to put on; but he didn't hold out Luke's Burberry, because Luke was a man and, apparently, men are capable of putting on their own coats.

Eighteen

Lucia

Evedale College had won the toss, and opted to bat second. Livingstone and Wilson were their openers. Theirs had been a successful partnership all season, the pair of them blasting the opposition bowlers to all four corners of the ground, and today was no exception. They were accumulating runs fast.

Livingstone felt a quiet anticipation as she leaned on her bat, waiting for the fielding team to get their act together. With a bit of luck she'd make a century with this next ball, which would be her third in three successive games. The last person to achieve such a hat trick was her own father, when he was captain of Evedale's First XI. Poor old Dad would be on tenterhooks right now! She imagined him crouched in the scorebox, chewing on his knuckles while muttering maniacally to himself.

A welcome breeze rippled her shirt. She was always happier at the crease, when the human race became a blur of figures in white. It was one of those rare times when she needn't be afraid of giving herself away. Out here she was just another batsman, judged on her ability to hit that ball—and she was good at doing that; she revelled in the tactics and skills of this game. She was fit, too, and that was a great feeling.

Distant shouts floated from a crowd of children playing tag. Half-term began today, and her teammates' little brothers and sisters had come along for the picnic. Parents and teachers were lounging along the perimeter of the ground, pretending to watch while gossiping and knocking back the wine they'd brought in their cool boxes. Getting tipsy, probably. She could see her mother flirting with Mr Van Breda, the music teacher. Lucia thought Mr VB was a pompous twit. Mum thought he was the spitting image of Christopher Plummer, and was always making excuses to talk to him.

At the non-striker's end of the pitch, Dan Wilson peeled off his cricket sweater and handed it to the umpire. Dan was going to join the army after leaving school. Lucia wondered whether she should do the same thing, instead of law. Nobody would ever suspect her while she was in uniform. Her father would be delighted; it might even make up for her not going to agricultural college and taking over the farm. And maybe—just maybe—military life would make her feel like a man.

The Hollyoaks bowler she was about to face was the lankiest boy she'd ever seen; what Dad would call 'a streak of weasel's piss'. He was taking himself very seriously, polishing the ball on his inner thigh while having a confab with his team captain. They kept glancing her way, plotting against her. It was funny, really. These lads were sixth formers; they all had gap years, or apprenticeships, or university life ahead of them. Soon they'd be soldiers and farmers, lawyers and plumbers. Yet right here, right now, winning this game was all that mattered.

At last the field was ready—and so was she. As the bowler began his run, the world seemed to shrink until there was nothing but that ball. She watched as the lanky figure bounded and coiled. When he turned sideways, he almost disappeared. Even before the ball had left his hand, she knew exactly where it was going to pitch. *Yep, here it comes—right on leg stump.*

Always satisfying, that resounding crack, and the knowledge that the ball was sailing to the boundary.

'Century!' yelled Dan Wilson, charging up to slap her on the back. Lucia couldn't keep the jubilation from her face. She wasn't often happy, but she was happy right now. She'd go down in the school record books. Dad would be proud as punch. Mr Van Breda shouted, 'Bravo!', though she knew that was just to ingratiate himself with her mother.

They finally got her out for a hundred and seven. Ah, well. She heard a smattering of applause as she strolled back to the pavilion, but to her ears it sounded weary. The parents were bored, and sunburned, and they'd probably run out of booze. They wanted to go home. Her father wasn't bored, though. He'd taken a break from his duties in the scorebox and was scurrying across to meet her, clapping as loudly as was humanly possible.

'Well played,' he bellowed. 'Good man!'

Her happiness collapsed. It was fragile, after all, and easily crushed by a ton of shame. It was time to become Luke again. It was time to be a Good Man.

So he walked on across the field, a lone figure in white, swinging his bat. When he reached his father, they shook hands.

'Thanks, Dad,' he said.

Luke

I felt his strong farmer's hand clasping mine. He looked as though all his Christmases had come at once. Guilt darkened my victory. The darkness hung over me still, as I woke in my lonely bachelor pad. Today was the day. Sorry, Dad. The shadow was with me while I dressed and set off for the Baytrees Gender Clinic.

It was very discreet; just a short walk from Archway tube station, in a row of identical Victorian houses. There was no sign outside, just the number. You could live next door and not know it was there. I bet the neighbours wondered who these people were who came and went so quietly; perhaps they thought it was the headquarters of some arcane cult.

I rang the bell, and a young woman—discretion written all over her face—showed me into what looked like an upmarket dentist's waiting room, but without that unsettling smell of mouthwash. She offered me coffee, which I declined, and gave me a form to fill in. My medical history, my families' history, my GP's address.

It was like visiting another country. The clinic was a tiny, secret principality in the middle of London where the normal rules didn't apply. After a lifetime of being an alien who might at any moment be unmasked and deported, I'd arrived in a land where I belonged. I was welcome. I had a passport.

There was a carriage clock in the waiting room. It sat above the fireplace, busy with its tick-tick-ticking. We'd had one just like it when I was small. Every Sunday evening, while we were eating our leftover chicken sandwiches, Mum would put up her feet with a cup of tea and the *Radio Times*. Dad and I would reverently lift off the glass dome and wind the clock with a tiny gold key. He had such big hands, but he could do such delicate things.

See, Luke, the key goes into here . . . Now, we have to be careful not to wind it too far. Good boy. Good boy.

The receptionist gave a gentle cough. Mr Brotherton was free now, she said, if I would come this way. I was still thinking about Dad as I followed her.

I'd looked at the website and knew that Ian Brotherton was a clinical psychologist who'd pooled a group of colleagues to set up this clinic as a one-stop shop. The man who met me at the door of the room was perhaps forty, wearing a sleeveless sweater and a tie, and his shape was disarmingly teddy-bearish. I thought I detected a faint Lancashire accent. He motioned me into a leather armchair.

'Now,' he said, sitting down opposite and leaning towards me. 'I have a letter from Dr Cameron, which is very helpful. I know you've already told your story to her, but let's start again.'

I'd never talked about myself so much. Never in my life. It seemed narcissistic, but Brotherton was persistent. He started by asking me about my childhood, my parents and my sisters, and the sort of family we'd been. He wanted minute detail, much of which didn't seem relevant at all. We talked about my work. We talked about my marriage, with the usual embarrassing questions about sex. Perhaps I should get a card printed, I thought, to hand out to professionals: *Yes, I was faithful to my wife. No, sex isn't especially important to me. No, I don't want to have sex with men*. He asked about my general health, and my mental health, especially the episodes diagnosed as depression. Then he changed the subject again.

'You and Eilish have two children?'

'Three.'

His eyebrows went up. He looked again at Dr Cameron's referral letter.

'Two living,' I explained. 'Charlotte died immediately after her birth. It was a very difficult time.'

'I think that's an understatement.'

'Yes. But this isn't something I want to talk about.'

He leaned back in his chair, and it creaked under his bulk. I saw that this was something he *did* want to talk about, and sighed.

'You never quite get over it,' I said. 'Eilish closed up for a long time. I went back to work after a fortnight, which I expected of myself and the world expected of me. But I had difficulty concentrating. I stopped sleeping. When I did sleep, I had dreams.'

'Dreams?'

I looked at my hands. I really didn't want to open this box. 'A baby,' I said shortly. 'And a mother. Anyway . . . it's all in the past. We managed. We had to take care of Simon, who was a preschooler at the time. Later we went on to have another daughter.' I smiled. 'Kate. She is very much alive.'

'And what did you feel when those children arrived?'

I had my stock answer ready. 'Joy, of course,' I said. 'Pure joy.'

It was another lie; just one among the thousands, but it was the one that made me most ashamed. My joy at becoming a father wasn't pure at all. It was poisoned. I'll never forget holding Simon in the moments after he was born. His cheeks were round, and his fingers were perfect, and he was a miracle. The love and wonder seemed too much to fit into my body, and came spilling out of me in tears. I never wanted to let him go. Never. Suddenly a midwife's hands were around him, taking him away from me, giving him to Eilish. 'Come on,' she said, not even looking at me. 'Let's see how Mum does with feeding this little cherub.'

Eilish seemed to know instinctively how to breastfeed a baby. The pair of them were warm in the glowing cocoon of mother and child, Simon gazing up at her face as though she were a goddess. I should have adored Eilish at that moment, but all I felt was envy. I've never felt such envy. It soured and sickened me as I drove home alone to make proud fatherly phone calls. *Mother and baby doing well; yes, nine pounds four! Yes, she's tired but very happy.* I despised myself, I ranted at myself, but I couldn't turn off the bitterness. I felt myself slipping into a trough. It wasn't Eilish who came down with postnatal depression; it was me. I ended up on antidepressants, seeing a counsellor.

I didn't tell anyone about that envy—not Eilish, not our doctor, not the counsellor. I didn't tell Ian Brotherton either. After all, I was lucky to be a parent. Sometimes I wondered whether Charlotte's death was punishment for my ingratitude.

At last, Brotherton came to the subject of gender. I heard my voice droning on and on, digging up the oldest memories. My childhood seemed closer than it had in years. I was young again. I was confused and lonely. It was my first day at school.

'You felt the boys' cloakroom was wrong for you?' he asked. 'Why?'

'Because I knew I was a girl.'

I could hear the laughter. I feared the laughter. I was alone.

'My elder sister was the only one who didn't laugh. Oh no, not our Gail. She was livid. At break time she thumped me in the stomach. Doubled me right over. She said if I ever made fools of our family again, she'd put me down the offal pit on our farm and block up the hole. She said I would die down there and nobody would ever find me. I believed her.'

'How old was this gentle soul?'

'Gail? Ten. I was four. She was very big, and I was very small. She knew the offal pit was my nightmare place. When Dad did a home kill he used to drop the heads and guts and skin down there. She said I would rot away.'

He looked sickened. 'And how did you respond to this threat?'

'With terror. From then on, I had to hide my real self. I think it was my first bereavement. It didn't stop me sneaking into my sisters' rooms to play dress-ups but it had become a frightened, dirty thing. I thought I was the only boy in the world to feel like this. I had no idea there were others. There was no internet.'

I got up out of my chair and wandered to the window. The glass was old; it distorted the sky. There was a tiny courtyard out there where a fountain played. The walls were unusually high. To keep out prying eyes, presumably; or perhaps to keep in the shame.

'I'm not a man who likes to wear women's things,' I said. 'I *am* a woman. I'm a woman who puts on a man's clothes, and speaks in a deep voice, and slaps other men on the back, and pees at a urinal through tackle that shouldn't even be there. All of which, I guess, makes me a freak.'

Behind me, I heard Brotherton put down his pen.

'Where do you see all of this taking you?' he asked.

'I'm not sure.'

'We both know that there's a million websites on this subject. There are books. I'm sure you've researched. I'm sure you have goals.'

'I do.' I turned around to face him. 'But I'm afraid of being thrown down the offal pit.'

He smiled, and waited for more.

'I've used the boys' cloakroom—literally and figuratively—for the past half-century,' I said. 'Now I look at the life I have ahead of me and I see that it's finite. My father died last year. My own generation are starting to go down with heart attacks and cancer. I'm running out of time.'

'What would you like to do about it?'

I knew the answer. I'd known it for fifty years.

'I'd like to walk through that other door,' I said.

Nineteen

Eilish

It was such a beautiful summer. Beauty can be cruel, can't it? Through August, right into September, the countryside around East Yalton was chocolate-box. Day after day I woke, alone, to indigo skies and fields already baking in the heat. The cool waters of the Thames reflected barges with gardens and bright paintwork, and riverside pubs were full of families making the most of the heatwave. Luke and I should have been doing the same.

It's the future you mourn most; the road you always thought lay ahead. People say, *You never know what's around the corner*, and they all nod sagely, but they don't really believe it. I was just as smug. I thought I knew exactly what lay around the corner for me: a long and contented retirement with Luke by my side. I had such plans! Now I'd rounded the corner, and my road had dropped off a cliff.

Life goes on. It has to. We had a new headmaster at Cottingwith High: Walter Wallis. Why would parents with the surname Wallis call their son Walter? He was *innovative* and *energetic* and *dynamic*. At least, that was how he described himself in his CV, and the interview committee were obviously taken in, because we were now saddled with this megalomaniac. I'd have sworn the man had ADD. And one of the innovative, dynamic things he did was to insist that all teaching staff come in at the end of the holidays for a day's professional development. I couldn't think of a good enough excuse to get out of it. So, at eight-thirty on a September morning that was already promising to be a scorcher, I was sitting in the staff car park, summoning the will to get out of my car. Jim Chadwick, who headed the science department, swung in and parked beside me. I was delighted to see him.

'Hello, my friend!' he cried, hopping out of his little green MG. His roof was down. 'Isn't this a waste of a glorious day? Shall we play hooky?'

'That's very tempting.'

He waited as I fished around for my bag. 'We could hire a skiff, and I'll row you down the river. Have lunch at The Lock.' He was warming to his theme. 'Or, if you prefer, we could sit in a classroom all day, get dehydrated, and listen to Wally Wallis's sidekick telling us about learning outcomes.'

Some people question the course their lives have taken. They torture themselves with speculation about what would have happened if they had turned left that day instead of right. What if they'd taken that job they were offered, back in 1995? What if they'd caught that train, been in time for that interview? I know women who've ruined their marriages by imagining the idyllic lives they'd be leading if only they'd married that other man. The other one always seems so much more alluring—so much less likely to have a potbelly, or moan about the cost of petrol, or bite their nails—than their ageing, boring husbands.

I never used to play this game. I couldn't see the point. When I was a young marketing guru, I went with friends to see *Giselle* at the ballet. My ticket was for row K, seat 20. A man called Luke Livingstone happened to be sitting in row K, seat 21. He was embarrassed because the little machine that dispenses opera glasses stole his money. I lent him my set. He bought me a drink during the intermission. If that machine hadn't been faulty, we might never have spoken; but it was, and we did, and that was the end of it. I had this old-fashioned idea that marriage was permanent.

If I had been the type to play the *what if* game, though, it would probably have involved Jim Chadwick. There was an unmistakable spark between us, from the very first time he'd walked into the staffroom at Cottingwith High. He was wearing a blue-and-white-checked shirt, I remember, and it intensified the marvellous colour of his eyes. He had energy. I remember thinking he was . . . well, sexy. We gravitated together immediately. I had no intention of acting on this magnetic attraction, but all the same it made me feel alive. It made me feel young.

Years had passed since then, and the spark had turned into an easygoing—if vaguely flirtatious—friendship. Jim had arrived when Simon was in the sixth form, and he'd had a bit to do with both him and Kate. He also played the odd game of squash with Luke, as they were both in a league that used our school courts. He was a natural teacher, popular and able to control classes that defeated everybody else. He championed children with special needs, because he had a brother with Asperger's. He celebrated with me when Nico was born; I commiserated with him when his marriage came to an end. It doesn't surprise me that people are tempted to have affairs with their work colleagues—of course they are! They're the ones who share in our daily lives. They see us in our element, doing what we do best. Our spouses see us with bed hair, in our dressing-gowns, emptying the cat's litter tray. Domesticity isn't erotic.

'How's your summer going?' Jim asked now.

'Too fast.'

'You and Luke been away? I haven't seen him on the squash courts for a while.'

'Nope.'

I'd begun walking, and he fell in beside me. 'How is the young chap? Still working eighty hours a week?'

Fortunately I didn't have to answer, because we'd reached the classroom where the training was to be held. A gangly man was writing an agenda on the whiteboard. It began with *8.45: Welcome and introductions.* The room was full of teachers holding coffee mugs. We greeted one another gloomily; all except Mick Glover, who taught maths and was always unreasonably bouncy. He travelled to school on a powered skateboard.

'Morning, Eilish,' he called. 'Jim. There are a couple of seats over here.'

Jim and I were just sitting down when the headmaster came bustling in.

'Donald is our facilitator today,' Wally said, grinning fondly at the gangly chap as though he were some kind of pet. 'Let's get started, Don.'

It was a bit like being in an evangelical church. Donald strode up and down, waving his hands around as he talked about 'facing in one direction' and 'tapping energies'. There were around twenty of us in there, and the fan wasn't up to the job. It was a relief when Donald broke us into pairs, giving out chunky pens and paper, and exhorting us to 'workshop this one' before 'coming back to kick our ideas around.' He gave each pair a made-up scenario. Ours was about a teacher who lost his cool and grabbed a third former by the ear.

Jim and I managed to commandeer a shady spot on the edge of the quad. I sat at an octagonal picnic bench. He leaned down to use the drinking fountain.

'*Workshopping*,' I grumbled. 'Who uses that word as a verb?'

'Donald does.' Jim splashed water on his face, then ducked to put his whole head under the stream. It darkened his fair hair. He sat down, dripping, on the other side of the table. 'Has your new grandchild arrived yet?'

'Not due for a couple of months.' I'd picked up one of the big pens and was doodling as we talked. 'Kate's back from Israel. Broken up with the boyfriend.'

'Great news! And how's Luke?'

'Shush. We're meant to be thinking about this wretched child's ear, or we won't get a gold star.'

It took us about two minutes to address the scenario. We scribbled all over the paper in different colours to make it look as though we'd really tapped our energies. Then we got talking about Jim's younger son, who was teaching in Ghana. It was pleasant to sit chatting in the dappled shade. It stopped me from thinking about Luke, and the road that had dropped off a cliff.

Jim had to nip into town during the lunch break. I fled to my room—a small space in a prefabricated block; not salubrious—and made a start on organising my resources for the coming term.

The afternoon's session with Donald was more of the same. It finished at four, and was followed by a mass exodus to the car park. By now, I felt weary and low.

'Well,' said Jim, as we reached my car. 'When I arrived this morning I had no idea what we were expecting to achieve today. And I still have no idea.'

'Team building?'

'It was certainly that. I've never seen such concord. We're all absolutely as one in thinking that was a lot of old cobblers.'

I smiled half-heartedly.

'You in a hurry?' asked Jim. 'Got time for a drink? It'll be heaven on earth right now, at one of those riverside tables at The Lock. There's a white wine spritzer waiting for you in a tall, chilled glass . . . Can't you see the beads of condensation?'

'That sounds wonderful. But not today.'

'Sure you're all right?'

'Sure I'm sure.'

He smiled easily, raised his hand, and walked across to his car. I heard the electronic beep as it unlocked. Before getting in, he paused, looking back at me.

'I'm here,' he said, 'when you're not all right.'

Twenty

Luke

After weeks of heatwave, there was a hosepipe ban. The parks were full of sunbathers. Mirages shimmered above the roads, and the pavements were melting like toffee.

Each morning I put on my Luke mask and took the tube to Bannermans. To the young solicitors there, I was one of the old guard—staid and probably starchy. Each day I battled the urge to phone Eilish just for the selfish comfort of talking to her. And every evening, with the street door locked behind me, I freed Lucia from her hiding place. She was growing in confidence, step by step.

I'd found comfortable shoes and underwear on a specialist website. I'd also given in to temptation and bought a very good wig—just for now, just to know how it felt. It was a rich mid-brown with bronze strands. For the first time in my life I had the sensation of hair curling over my shoulders. I revelled in it. I used to pray for long hair when I was a child. I'd pull a jersey back over my head and leave it half off so that it hung down my back. Prancing about and pouting into the mirror, I'd pretend it was flowing locks. I felt like that child again as I ran a brush through my long hair, and stepped into my feminine shoes. My hair. My shoes.

I'd done nothing permanent yet. No hormones, no hair removal. After all my years of waiting, Brotherton had told me

I must wait a little longer before doing anything irreversible. He wanted to see me again. He also insisted on referring me to the Baytrees in-house counsellor, Usha Sharma.

'I'm getting on,' I protested. 'Lots of your clients are young. They haven't spent half a century thinking about this. They haven't had children yet, so losing their fertility is a big thing. They've got years to dither. I haven't.'

He was unmoved. 'Be that as it may, you won't begin HRT for at least three months. Possibly more. These are my professional rules—international rules—and, believe me, it's a lot quicker than you'd be moving on the Charing Cross route.'

I knew what he was referring to. Charing Cross was the NHS gender identity clinic. It had had mixed reviews.

'You don't need to go full-time before you begin HRT,' he added, 'but you do have to understand how it feels to present yourself as female in public.'

'I've already done that!'

'Been shopping? On public transport? Bought a drink in a pub? There's living as a woman in your head, and there's doing the real thing. Any transgender woman will tell you there's a mighty difference. You may find it isn't what you want, after all. You may want to give your marriage another chance.'

That shut me up, because I thought about Eilish all the time. Often I dreamed I was making love to her—as a man, as a woman, did it matter? The passion and closeness of those dreams would stay with me long after I woke. They were a filter that coloured the day, and they tormented me. If I became Lucia, one thing was certain: I'd never so much as kiss Eilish again.

So I stepped into limbo. I saw an endocrinologist and had blood taken; I met Usha Sharma, who was about my age and on the patronising side. She wanted me to explore my goals, she said, and to do that I'd need to peel away the layers with which I'd covered my true self. I didn't like the sound of this at all, but week after week I jumped through her hoops. She was right about the layers. When you've got a secret as dangerous as mine, you bury it deep. You lie to everyone, including yourself. I was a pass-the-parcel. Each time I thought I'd torn off the last scrap of wrapping paper, I discovered there was more.

We made a list of the positive and negative aspects of transition—no surprises there; I'd been weighing them up for years. We talked about how I felt as a father, a son, a brother, as a human being: a fraud in every role. Of course, Usha broached the subject of my sexuality. What about desires? Fantasies? This was uncomfortable, but not as titillating as you might expect. Like plenty of trans women, I'd only ever felt attracted to women.

'I can't see that ever changing,' I said.

'It might change,' Usha warned. 'If you begin HRT, you may well find you lose libido.'

'I know that. Could be a relief.'

'Your preferences may alter. How would you react if you began to feel an attraction to men?'

'I'd be astonished,' I said. 'Look, Usha, I married Eilish when I was a young man. Since then I've rarely even flirted with anyone else, male or female. Sex for me is about expressing my love for her. That's the vital thing, isn't it?'

'Is it?'

'It's priceless! Thirty years . . . more than half a lifetime. All that shared history, all that understanding, all that life. That's treasure we've built up, Eilish and I. It's rare to get that with another human being. It can never, ever be replaced.'

I felt my hands shaking, and clasped them together. Eilish was my soul mate. Losing our sexual relationship was far less dreadful than the enormity of losing her as a companion through life.

'They think I'm selfish,' I said.

'Who does?'

'Eilish, Simon . . . everyone will think it. I wish there were some other way out of this. I wish I could stay with her, be a normal man.'

'Could you do that?'

I shook my head. Lucia couldn't be amputated. I'd tried that. She wasn't just a part of me; she *was* me. Outside in the street a car horn sounded.

'What does the future look like?' asked Usha. 'I mean, if you transition?'

'Lonely. Terrifying. Wonderful.'

There was another furious blast of honking, followed by shouts. I looked out of the window. A delivery van had stopped in the road while its driver unloaded crates. He was holding up the traffic, which was what all the drama was about. The driver was a cool customer. He just carried on doing his job, whistling. How nice, I thought. How liberating, not to care what people think.

'Turning back would be the most selfish thing I could do,' I said.

'Because . . . ?'

'Because pretending to be Luke is over for me. In a week, or a month, this whole thing would begin again. I know the cycle.'

'You're afraid you'd end up back here?'

'No. I can't put Eilish through a break-up again, that really would be unforgivable. This time it would have to end in my suicide.'

Usha didn't comment. I think she understood that I was stating a simple truth.

'That appointment with the noose was in my diary,' I said. 'I was ready, to the last detail. When you've planned your own end, when you've been so close to it . . . you find you can face other unthinkable things. There was one other choice. Just one. So I made that choice, and here I am.'

Usha murmured something. I heard her chair creak, and knew my hour was up. The delivery man raised his middle finger at one of the yelling drivers before swinging into his van. I watched him hurtle away.

'I can't go back,' I said. 'Can I?'

•

I didn't return to the office after my meeting with Usha. Back at the flat I locked the front door, removed the Luke costume, and—with that guilty, luxurious feeling of relief—let Lucia out of hiding.

I'd decided to tackle the supermarket today. It was the most intimidating sortie yet, which was probably why I found myself procrastinating. I fired up my laptop and sat working at the kitchen table—contentedly, with the soft fabric of my skirt falling around my legs.

I was immersed in work for several hours. One of the trainees had made a mistake and was stressing about it. In the end, I phoned him and disentangled the problem. Then there was a query about a prospective client—a Greek oligarch. According to the risk management unit, he wasn't squeaky clean. Well, I thought, which of us is? I wondered how they'd describe me, if they saw me doing Bannermans work in a dress.

Finally, I got around to reading my private emails. There was one from Wendy:

My dear brother,

I've spoken to my minister. He's a wonderful man, and we prayed together for you. He is absolutely clear: this is not NATURE, it is NURTURE. You can be cured, but first you MUST fight this, as you would any other temptation!!! He suggests counselling, which our church can provide. Please, please come and talk to him.

I sighed. *Facepalm*, as Kate would say.

Talking of Kate, there was a message from her too. This was far more welcome. It was chatty, as all her communications had been since I left. She never mentioned what I was doing; I had a feeling she was hoping the problem would just disappear. She wrote that she was leaving Smith's Barn the following week. Mathis and John had offered her a room in their flat in Swiss Cottage. The place was affordable, but it was the size of your average cat-litter tray, she said, so could she nip over and leave some of her gear with me?

Of course, I replied. *Any time. It would be lovely to see you.*

I scanned the rest of my emails. Nothing urgent. Nothing from Simon. Pity.

Right, I thought as I shut down the laptop. Never mind the Greek oligarch; never mind Wendy's wonderful minister! It's time to go.

I slipped into a linen jacket, found my handbag, and checked my make-up in the mirror.

'Ready?' I asked Lucia.

'As I'll ever be,' she said.

Twenty-one

Simon

It was the hottest day of a sweltering week. Nico seemed to be coming down with something, and had fallen asleep on the sofa. He was due to start school in a few days; hard to imagine their baby as a schoolboy.

Carmela was organising a birthday card for her grandmother. She sat barefoot at the writing desk they'd inherited from Grandad Livingstone. She wore a cotton maternity dress and a pair of reading glasses, and her hair was coiled at the nape of her neck. The combination of the glasses and put-up hair was slightly prim and rather sexy, like a librarian in a porn film—though the effect was rather ruined by the baby bump.

'Which is best for *Abuelita*?' she asked, holding up two cards. 'This one with the lake, or this one with the flowers?'

Simon shrugged and said they both looked fine. He was trying to phone his mother, but was in that extreme state of tiredness when the world seems monochrome. He'd been on call for the past three days, and seemingly every cat, dog and cockatoo in South London had decided to have some kind of medical emergency. His working day had begun at two o'clock that morning: a much-loved family moggy with breathing problems, followed by a red setter with a tricky labour. He'd finished the morning's surgery at lunchtime, and now—thank God—he had forty-eight hours off. His eyes drooped as he listened to the rhythmic lullaby of the ringing tone. His brain began to shut down.

Kate's voice jerked him into consciousness. 'Hello?'

He didn't want to talk to his sister. He was sure she was in contact with their dad. He wouldn't put it past her to be actively encouraging his madness.

'Kate,' he said. 'You're still there, are you? Is Mum in?'

He ought to ask what she'd been up to. He ought to ask how she was feeling about the nerdy ex-boyfriend. But all he wanted to discuss—all he'd thought about for the past six weeks—was their father.

''Fraid you're out of luck,' said Kate. 'She's at some seminar thing at the school.'

'She's back at work, then?'

'Term starts next week. Good thing too, if you ask me. She jumps every time the phone rings. Still hopes he'll change his mind.'

Simon carried the phone across to the window. With the hosepipe ban, the lawn had turned to straw. The neighbour's pug had got in again; it was trotting about, curly tail bouncing like a spring. Bloody animal behaved as though it owned the place.

'I've talked to one of the other vets,' he said. 'He thinks we could have Dad sectioned.'

'You've told people about this?'

'Just Sven. In strict confidence.'

'Yeah, right.'

Simon's hackles rose at the note of sarcasm. 'I bet you've told someone.'

'Mathis and John. They're hardly going to gossip about something like this, are they, since they've been on the receiving end of redneckery in our society? No, Simon. We can't have Dad sectioned. We'd have to get a whole gang of shrinks to say he's suffering from a mental illness.'

'Shouldn't be a problem! He's obviously delusional.'

Kate sighed exaggeratedly. She was such a smart-arse, his sister. 'Bedlam was reformed quite some time ago. We can't lock up our parents just because they embarrass us.'

'*Embarrass* us? We'll get bricks through our windows! How long will it be before everybody knows? Those gossips who run the Bracton Arms—'

'Ingrid and Harry.'

'Ingrid and Harry. That's right. They'll find out any day now, and then Mum might as well pack up and leave the area, because she won't be able to hold up her head.'

Simon heard Carmela's soft steps crossing the room behind him, and then her arms slid around his waist. The warmth of her body carried a breath of scent: Ralph Lauren something-or-other. Her mother gave her a bottle every Christmas. Whenever he smelled that scent, wherever he was, he felt close to Carmela.

'I don't want to take sides,' said Kate, and rang off.

The conversation left Simon jangling. Nobody seemed to get it. Their father was becoming a bloody trans—what was it? Transvestite? Transsexual? Whatever. Soon he'd be gone forever. He had to be stopped before the story got out.

The girl in Moroney's nightclub burst into his consciousness. She'd had stupendous legs, and her eyes were dark blue. She'd made him think of a summer's day. He was nineteen.

'That little mongrel is digging up the pansies,' said Carmela.

'He'll pee on the washing line next.' Simon knocked on the window with his knuckles. 'Oi! Beat it!'

The dog looked towards the window and seemed to grin before waddling off to ferret in the compost heap. He was an enthusiastic fellow—always snuffling, always cheerful. Simon was secretly quite fond of him.

'I want to kill my father,' he said.

'Shh.' Carmela joined her hands in front of his chest, rocking herself and him from side to side. 'No, no. Not that. He is your dad. You love him very much.'

'Ha! He isn't. Turns out I never had a dad. Not sure what that makes poor Mum. Not sure what that makes me, either.'

The rocking continued, and he felt her cheek resting against his shoulderblade. Normally her presence calmed him, but today he wished she'd leave him alone and stop being so bloody reasonable. Then he disliked himself for wishing it. What a mess.

'They're sickening,' he said loudly. 'People like him. *Sickening.*'

'Why does it frighten you so much?'

'I'm not frightened, I'm furious! He's a confidence trickster. Can't believe I share his genes.'

The girl in the club had been a work of art. Simon and his student friends had arrived in a hunting pack, and it didn't take him long to spot her. Denim miniskirt, white sleeveless blouse. The music was so loud, they had to bellow into each other's ears. Simon wasn't confident with girls, but this one seemed to get past his shyness. Her name was Jessica. She was a chambermaid at the White Hart, saving up to go travelling. She was still with him when it came to the last song of the evening. 'Nights in White Satin'. He could feel the smoothness and swell of her body against his.

Stop it! Stop thinking about that. Action. He had to take action.

'I'm going to the flat,' he said.

'I think that's a terrible idea.'

'It's a bloody good idea! He wanted to talk to me. Well, now's his chance. I'm going to have it out with him.'

Simon hadn't felt such energy in weeks, not since his father had lobbed a grenade into the family. It wasn't a pleasant energy—it throbbed, like an electric surge—but at least he had a plan. He strode through to the kitchen, rummaged in a drawer and pulled out the spare keys to the flat.

Carmela followed. One hand was spread across her stomach, shielding the baby from this trouble. 'Don't make a scene,' she said. 'What he's doing may be wrong, but he is a good man.'

'A good man?' Simon snorted. 'That's an unfortunate choice of words.'

'Simon, don't go.'

He stood in the kitchen doorway, bereft, feeling like a small boy. He was going to cry if he didn't control himself.

'I want him not to do this,' he said. 'That's all. I want him to be who I thought he was.'

•

The reedy wail of a saxophone echoed around the tunnel. Simon ran past the busker, arriving on the northbound platform just in time to step onto a train. There were plenty of spare seats but he didn't take one. He needed to keep moving. He stood holding the bar above his head, rocking on his feet as the darkness flicked past.

Lights were flashing. Disco lights. Jessica's dancing seemed to become slow motion, her white shirt iridescent. He could see the black bra underneath it. She swept her hand through the air, and in the strobe it looked like fifty hands. She was mesmeric. *This is lust*, he thought as he slid his hand under her shirt. *Or is it love?*

The escalators had broken down at Mile End, but the electric surge coursed through him and he sprinted up the stairs, past the *Big Issue* seller and out into a blast of heat. The daylight seemed blindingly bright. Soon he was striding along Thurso Lane, down the steps, pounding his fists on the door of the flat. The madness had to end. He hammered again, without success. *Damn*. He cupped his hands and leaned to look in through the window. A laptop was open on the kitchen table. Dad wouldn't go out and leave it there all day, in full view. Either he was in or he'd be back soon. Simon pulled the keys from his pocket and opened the door.

The kitchen smelled of toast. Washing-up lay piled on the draining board. Simon called out, but there was no answer. He had nowhere to put his rage, and it bubbled up. His phone rang. He answered it as he paced around the room, looking for signs of . . . what, exactly? Debauchery? An orgy?

It was Carmela. She sounded agitated; her accent was more pronounced than usual. 'Simon? Did you get to the flat yet?'

He stopped to leaf through a pile of letters and papers. Bills, circulars. Nothing interesting. His fingers were shaking, and so was his voice. 'I'm here. He's not.'

'You haven't really broken in?'

He left the kitchen, checking the other rooms. 'I've got a right to be here. It's Mum's flat too. Hell!' He'd stopped dead in the middle of the bedroom. Suit trousers and a jacket hung over a chair. It was the only tidy corner; the rest of the room was in chaos. Clothes were strewn around as though someone had been trying on different combinations before discarding them. A dress was flung across the bed; colourful things lay in a heap on the floor.

This can't be Dad's mess, he thought. Dad's tidy. He's organised. He has that bloody annoying motto which used to make us groan when we were teenagers: *A place for everything, and everything in its place*.

'What's happening?' asked Carmela.

'Hang on.' Simon nudged the pile with his toe. There were floral garments of some sort. A bra. On top of the chest of drawers he spotted powder, lipstick and other make-up. These things weren't his father's. No. Obviously not. That was impossible. Simon veered away from the unbearable, inevitable conclusion.

'He's got a woman staying here,' he said.

'Leave now, my darling.'

'He's got a mistress.' Laughter leaped into Simon's throat. Hell, what a relief! Some power-shouldered siren from work perhaps, too alluring for Dad to resist. It was despicable, but normal. Thousands of people had affairs. 'I don't believe it—the old dog! He's shagging some woman. D'you think it's another partner?'

'I've no idea.'

'Whoever it is, she's a messy tart,' he said, looking at a collection of silk scarves draped over the mirror. 'Stuff everywhere. This whole sex-change thing's been some kind of smokescreen. Bizarre, isn't it?'

'Good. Terrific. Now leave.'

'Just a sec.' Simon's head jerked around at the sound of a key turning in the front door. 'Someone's coming into the flat. I've got to go.' Ignoring Carmela's protests, he ended the call and moved quietly into the passageway. There were heels on the kitchen tiles—tap-tap-tap—not a man's shoes. He thought he could hear humming too, as he pushed at the kitchen door.

She stood with her back to him, facing the kettle: a tall brunette in an unflattering purple dress. Flowing hair. Quite beefy. His brain was still playing its tricks, stubbornly protecting him from reality. It was hard to tell from this angle, but she didn't look like an illicit lover. Perhaps Dad had a cleaner?

'Excuse me,' he said.

The cleaner stopped humming, and turned around.

Twenty-two

Lucia

She wished she had an invisibility cloak. She used her trolley as a shield, sliding along the aisles with her head down. If she sensed somebody looking at her, she would instantly grab an object from the shelves—a packet of biscuits, a bottle of vinegar—and read every ingredient on the list. In the case of the vinegar, that didn't take very long.

The supermarket's air conditioning felt luxurious. Tights, she'd discovered, were not designed to be worn on such a hot day. The wig was worse. All the same, she caught sight of the tall brunette in the shop's closed-circuit TV monitor and felt a small thrill of joy. She wasn't beautiful. No, indeed, by no stretch of the imagination. She would love to be beautiful, but then didn't many women wish for that? Many men too, for that matter. Still, she dared to hope she might just pass, in the dusk with the light behind her. Passing was what mattered above all else. She hoped she'd get better at it.

It had been a good trip. She was beginning to feel rather proud of herself. She'd managed to find all the things she needed, keeping it small because she wanted to go through the self-service checkout. The supermarket was the place to get things that would raise eyebrows in smaller shops—tights, for example;

moisturiser and hair removal cream. She wouldn't buy any alcohol here though, because the machine would need her age verified and an assistant would have to come over and look at her face to do that. She wasn't ready for people to look at her face.

In the hair-care section, she stopped to choose a bottle of conditioner. She'd read in an article that using leave-in conditioner was a good idea for trans women, because a man's hair tends to be coarser than a woman's. It had to be worth a try. She didn't want to wear a wig forever. She wanted to be real.

Further down the aisle, two lycra-clad mothers gossiped over their trolleys. They looked as though they'd just jogged out of the local gym. One had a baby, and neon-hued trainers. Her friend sipped from a can of Diet Coke while complaining bitterly about the hidden charges on a low-cost airline. Judging by her tone of incandescent rage, you'd think the airline had held her family hostage and tortured them. Her small daughter was dancing up and down the aisle.

Lucia ignored them. She'd never bought leave-in conditioner before—in fact, it was some time since she'd even bought her own shampoo, because Eilish tended to do all that. She had no idea there'd be so much choice. It was fun to browse, reading all the labels. She enjoyed the brushing of her crepe dress against her calves, and the heaviness of her hair at the nape of her neck. Wearing heels made her ankles feel slender, her posture much more feminine. The air conditioning really was heavenly. Soon she'd forgotten to worry about how she looked from the outside. In her mind she was just a woman, taking pleasure in a small but new experience. She was herself. She was content.

A childish voice made her jump. 'What are you getting?'

The little girl had stopped dancing and was gawping up at her face.

'Hi,' whispered Lucia, horribly self-conscious. 'Um, conditioner.'

The gym bunnies burst into gales of laughter at some remark one had made. They were still mid-giggle when the child spoke again.

'Are you a man, or a lady?'

That was when her mother looked around. Her gaze whisked over Lucia. Her eyebrows went up. Her smile switched off.

'Tammy,' she said. 'Come back here.'

Tammy didn't move.

'Tammy!' The woman marched across, grabbed her daughter by the hand and tugged her away. 'Leave the gentleman alone.'

Lucia's illusion of herself was shattered. She was a freak, and the whole school was laughing at her. The whole world. She fled into the next aisle but there were people there too. She felt hundreds of pairs of eyes, thousands, all sneering at her ungainly body, all thinking *Monster, monster.* Every instinct urged her to bolt out of the shop.

Stand your ground, Lucia. Did you think this would be easy?

I need to get away, she thought. Let me run.

If you fail to live as a woman, you will fail to live at all.

She took several breaths and then forced herself to turn back. Her trolley was still where she'd left it, and the lycra women had gone. She steered towards the self-service machines. One of them had broken down. The others were busy. A queue was building up behind her. *Come on, come on, before Tammy and her mother arrive.* An assistant opened another till, unclipping the chain. He was a young man, probably not long out of school. A livid birthmark covered half his face—*Poor lad, I hope people don't bully him*—and he had a ring through his upper lip. Why did young people do that? Lucia fervently hoped Kate would stop at her nose piercing. She tried not to catch his eye, but there was no hope of ignoring him when he beckoned her over.

At first it was all right. He didn't even look up as he put everything into the bags she'd brought with her. When he came to the end he said, 'Forty-two twenty, please.'

She handed him fifty pounds in notes. He cast her a casual glance and instantly knew what she was. His eyes lingered far too long on her face. He was going to smirk, or say something vile. It seemed as though the entire shop had fallen silent. She shrank away.

'D'you have a loyalty card?' he asked.

Confused, she shook her head.

'Would you like one? I can set it up for you in just a few seconds.'

She shook her head again. She couldn't speak. Her voice was a dead giveaway, and others would hear.

'Okay.' He counted out the change. 'Five and two . . . Seven pounds eighty.'

She was ramming the change into her handbag, scrabbling to pick up the carrier bags. 'Thank you,' she whispered.

'You're welcome, ma'am,' said the young man. The words were uttered without irony; without cruelty. It was a simple act of politeness, and it changed everything.

The next moment she was out, hurrying down the high street under a white-hot sun with shopping dangling from each hand. Success! She was officially a member of the consumer society—she'd even been offered a loyalty card. All she had to do now was get herself home. Someone had dropped their leftover sandwiches by the bus stop, and the ground was covered in pecking pigeons. They flew up as she rushed through them. Soon she was passing the tube station, smiling a hello to Mr Che Guevara when he waved. She searched in her handbag to find her door keys, then held them ready. They made her feel less vulnerable. One more row of houses . . . a sharp left into Thurso Lane. Ten metres, nine, eight . . . She was hurrying down the steps, her heels making quick, playful taps on the stone. Her key was in the lock. She was inside, dropping her bags on the kitchen table. *Whew.* Safe.

The flat seemed blessedly cool. She slid her linen jacket off her shoulders and shook it out. It was a truly lovely thing, a classic shape in a crushed-mulberry colour. Even better, it was cut for someone with broad shoulders and fitted easily over the loose crepe dress she was wearing. Here, in her sanctuary, she could be the Lucia she imagined; the real Lucia—not the hybrid clown that Tammy's mother despised. She hung the jacket on the back of a kitchen chair before filling the kettle, revelling in the swing of her skirt as she moved. She'd sit at the table now, with her tea, and get on with some more work.

She refused to be depressed by the reaction of Tammy's mother. The supermarket trip had been a milestone, and the assistant had proved that not everybody hated her on sight. Tomorrow she might even tackle the tube. Lucia wasn't used to feeling such hope. It intoxicated her.

She hummed as she made herself tea. The kettle was hissing loudly. She wasn't on her guard; not at all. Out on the street she was always ready for attack, but not here. She might be lonely in her spartan cave, but at least she was safe.

Until the kitchen door opened.

Simon

The woman looked all wrong. She had his father's face. She had his father's height, his shoulders, the crease on his brow, the aquiline nose. Yet she had a bust, and curving hips. She had waves of brown hair. Earrings. Bold, bright lipstick. She wore shoes with heels, and tights. The components of what he was seeing spun through his mind, but they could not fall into place because the whole was so very, very wrong.

And then she spoke.

'Simon,' she said. 'I didn't expect you.'

Dad's voice, coming from the mouth of that monster, set off a flare in Simon's chest. His rage took control—dancing forward in a blast of energy, smashing his fist into the painted mouth. The face jerked backwards, and Simon felt the jar of impact with a jubilation that frightened him. He heard the creature shouting something, but he didn't stop, he couldn't stop. He wanted to choke it out of existence. He made a grab for the neck—Jesus, there was even a necklace.

'I warned you,' he yelled. 'I fucking warned you!' He squeezed his hands together, feeling their power, feeling the neck begin to give. The curly wig was coming off. It slid sideways, revealing Luke's own dark hair. Simon saw his father's face, with gold earrings and crimson lipstick, smudged now and mingling with blood from the blow to his mouth. He was staring at Simon; not struggling, just staring in horror. *What am I doing?* For a moment, Simon froze, and his foot slipped on the lino floor. At the same time Luke drove his own fist up, hard. It was undeniably a man's fist, and that of a man who was fighting for his life. The blow caught Simon squarely in the solar plexus. He doubled up as the breath was forced out of his lungs. His vision blurred.

For at least a minute, there was no sound in the flat but the two of them coughing and gasping for air. Luke seemed to recover first. He dragged himself over to the sink, poured a glass of water and drank half of it straight down.

'You all right?' he wheezed. His lip was dripping blood, and there was blotchy redness around his neck.

Simon felt bile in his own throat. He'd damn near killed his own father. He'd *wanted* to kill him. 'I'm leaving,' he muttered.

'No! Don't go.'

'You're finished.' Simon waved his hand at the creature in the dress. 'Look at yourself!'

'Don't go. Don't go. I'm sorry you saw . . . I'll get changed.' Luke limped across to the door. 'I'll only be a minute. Look, it's all right. Just . . . please don't go.'

Simon slumped against the wall. He desperately wanted his father back. He wanted him to return in two minutes transformed into his old self, in a sober sweater and polished lace-up shoes. He would be calm, cultured Luke Livingstone. Simon longed to see that man again. He loved and admired that man.

A cupboard door creaked from somewhere in the flat. Simon thought of the colourful clothes scattered joyously, obscenely, across the floor. Christ, Dad must have been trying them on! He'd been outside, walking the streets in a dress. What the hell was he doing right now, in that room full of women's things? Wiping off the lipstick, presumably. Unclipping the earrings before brushing out his wig. There was no calm, cultured Luke Livingstone. There was no father. There never had been. The whole loving-father thing was a lie.

When the door smashed shut behind him, it seemed to shake the sky.

Luke

I pulled on lace-up shoes, fumbling in my hurry. My throat and mouth ached and my heart was still thumping in panic, but that didn't matter now. I had to be quick. There was so much that I wanted to say to Simon. This was my one chance. Perhaps now, in the aftermath of violence, we would listen to one another. If not—if I failed—I was sure he'd never visit me again. I needed to look as male as possible, as fast as possible.

I was reaching for a shirt when I heard the street door slam. I froze, turning my head towards the window. Footsteps ran along the pavement outside. They were blows: fast and heavy and final. I groaned in disappointment, sinking onto the bed. My lip was throbbing. My mind was throbbing.

Cocked that one up, chuckled The Thought. *Can't go back, can't go forward. Might as well throw in the towel. Do your family a favour. Do yourself a favour. You're a zero.*

Simon, six years old, was standing on a chair so as to reach the bench. We'd taken our men's working tea out to the carpentry shed with us, and were making a model biplane. It was almost finished. Simon's task was to glue the struts. He approached this as he did everything, even at that age: with anxious solemnity. The evening sun slanted through the cobwebs in the windows, turning dust motes into a swirling cloud of fireflies. Kate was newborn, colicky and screaming; poor Simon had melted down after the fiftieth visitor asked if he was proud to have such a beautiful baby sister. I'd done the same—privately—because I longed to nurse her. He and I had come out here for some baby-free time together.

When he finished his gluing, I tidied it up a bit for him. He was weary by now. As I worked, I felt his head resting against my arm. I could smell his apple shampoo. Gradually, his whole body sagged against me.

'It's coming along very well,' I said, tousling the apple-clean hair.

'Mm. Yes.' He eyed our creation, yawning. 'It's a terrifical plane.'

'D'you want to go inside now? I'll read to you. Nearly bedtime.'

'Nah.' A little shake of the head. 'Let's stay here. I love woodworking with you, Dad.'

'Just you and me, eh? The desperate duo.'

'One day you and me and Mummy will make a great big plane, and go flying all around the world, and see lions and tigers.'

'Let's do that,' I said.

'But we won't let them eat us, will we?'

Still leaning on me, he picked up the plane and flew it across an imaginary sky. His hand looked small and soft as he gripped the fuselage. Warmth surged from my head to my chest. I must keep my boy safe from the world and its horrors. I vowed to protect him forever.

'No,' I said. 'We definitely won't let them eat us.'

The last brilliance of the day. Dust motes danced in my basement bedroom, as they once had in the shed. *Stupid vow*, I thought as I lay curled on the lonely bed, in the lonely flat. Just another promise I couldn't keep. My lip was torn, my neck bruised by those same enchanting little hands. What a bloody awful mess I'd made.

Something nudged my outstretched arm. It was the crepe dress; Lucia's dress, that felt so weightless and flowing when she wore it. I draped it over myself so that it hung down on either side of me, as though Lucia were embracing me. It gave me comfort. And if I wept, that's my business.

Twenty-three

Simon

Three pints down. Linseed oil and timber resin. Just him and Dad, weaving magic in their dragon's lair. Making that toy plane stood out as one of Simon's earliest, happiest memories. Dad's arm was just the right height for leaning your head on.

Did you have lipstick in your pocket, Dad? Were you wearing lace knickers?

As the years passed they made go-karts, picnic tables, a music box, and, only last spring, a gate for Simon's house in London. As they worked, they talked. Simon used to treasure those times with his father.

After his fourth pint, Carmela phoned, more irritated than worried. 'Are you coming home?'

'Half an hour.'

'You said that two hours ago. Where are you? I know it's a pub.'

'By the tube station. Look.' His tongue wasn't working properly. 'I'm sorry, I got talking to some people. I'll be home soon.'

'What really happened in the flat?'

'As I told you: Dad came home. He was cross-dressed. I left.'

A long, suspicious silence. 'And that's all?'

'That's all.'

Five pints down, and his thought process had begun to splinter. He was far too tired for heavy drinking. Images spun and merged and contorted. It was like living in a kaleidoscope. Aching knuckles. A human face. Blood. He wasn't used to punching anyone, let alone his own father. He winced at the memory of impact. *Crack*. He felt overwhelmed by . . . *no, no*. He bloody well didn't feel guilty. That wasn't Dad back there. That was more like a demonic possession. Tights. *Jesus*. Wig, dress, heels.

I could have killed him. What if his larynx is damaged? Shit, he's by himself.

Once the thought had occurred to him, he had to check. He knew how dangerous strangulation could be. He called Luke's number and while it rang he got to his feet, pulling the keys to the flat from his pocket. *He might have collapsed. I'll have to go back.*

Then Luke answered; his voice was friendly and quiet as always.

'Hello, Simon? . . . Simon?'

Not mortally injured, then. Simon switched off his phone.

Someone was talking to him. The woman from behind the bar, collecting glasses from tables. She was bird-thin.

'All right there?' she asked again.

'Fine.' Simon tried to look fine, wiping his eyes with a thumb and forefinger. He hadn't noticed the tears. 'Thanks.'

'Hayfever?'

'Yep. It's that time of year.'

She cast him a shrewd glance. She must have seen plenty of men like him, weeping into their beer. 'Nice to have the sunshine,' she said.

'Can't grumble.'

Dad getting out of bed at three in the morning to collect Simon from an eighteenth-birthday party; rubbing his shoulder as he threw up in a bush beside the road. *Not to worry, son, don't be embarrassed, it happens to the best of us.*

'People don't like me,' Simon had gasped, between retches.

'I like you.'

'I'm an outsider. They all dance and yell and talk shit. I sat in a corner all night.'

Dad handed him a bottle of water. 'You didn't join in?'

'What's the point? There *is* no point. It's all just . . . shit. Isn't it? Life.'

Instead of going home and back to bed, Dad had driven to a service station on the motorway and bought them breakfast. They sat at a formica table as the short summer night merged into daybreak. It was all a bit of a blur, but Simon remembered rambling on and on about the senselessness of life, of love, of God. Dad didn't talk shit. He listened patiently to his smashed and maudlin son, complete with existential crisis.

Another pint went down, but the alcohol really wasn't helping.

No more pints. The landlady said he'd had enough and it was time he went home. Simon found himself out on the street, though he was struggling to remember which street it was. Heat radiated from the bitumen. The ground didn't seem as flat as usual. He kept tripping.

He was nineteen, in a rain-soaked car park, hiding in the shadows. She'd be here soon. He held a broken bottle in his hand, and hatred in his heart.

Lucia

It was after one o'clock in the morning, but a robin sang from the branches of a sycamore tree in Thurso Lane. A woman let herself out of a basement flat and began to walk towards the post box on the corner. She was neither young nor pretty, but she'd made the most of what she had. Six white envelopes lay in one hand.

A cat called to her from the top of a wall. She stopped to tickle his ears, and he immediately purred. He knew her very well, and arched his back and rubbed his cheek into the palm of her hand. He'd met her every day on her way home from work. She wore different clothes then, but to him she hadn't changed. She was the same person.

She reached the post box but she didn't post her letters. Instead she walked around and around it, whispering to herself, *Go on, go on.*

It wasn't a long letter but it had taken hours to write. She'd typed, deleted, typed—deleted the lot and started again—a glass of whisky at her elbow, the crepe dress folded on her lap. At about eleven, Simon had phoned, only to hang up without a word. All the same, she felt encouraged. Better than nothing.

Midnight had long passed when she printed out six copies of her letter and carefully added a handwritten message at the top of each one. They were ready. They must be posted now, tonight, because already she felt her resolve slipping away. One envelope was going all the way to Melbourne. She allowed herself a vicious smile as she imagined her eldest sister reading the letter. This was going to ruin Gail's day.

A car came cruising down the high street. Its chassis had been lowered to within inches of the road. All the windows were open so that the thumping of its stereo could deafen passers-by. The woman shrank into a shadow, but it was no good. They'd seen her—worse, they'd seen her trying to hide. The driver leaned on his horn while his passengers exploded into catcalls.

'Oi! You got a dick? Tranny! Tra-nee!'

They seemed about to climb out of the windows. Under the shifting city lights, their faces appeared to be daubed with ghostly warpaint. She watched the car roar away. It screeched left at the next corner—handbrake turn—but its music still pulsated in the breathless heat. Then suddenly it slewed back into the high street. They were coming for her.

Throwing her letters into the dark mouth of the post box, she darted down Thurso Lane. She took off her shoes, her breath ragged now, and held them as she sprinted. The pavement bruised her soles. The friendly cat shot away to hide. The night was torn by the howls of those men who hated her so, calling for her as though they were looking for a lost dog. *Tran-nee! Where are you, Tranny?*

She tripped and fell down the area steps. The impact knocked the breath out of her but she forced herself to her feet, fumbling with her keys. *Wrong one, wrong one, bloody hell, where is it?* The security light was a beacon, marking her out to a hostile world. Her tights had ripped; her leg smarted where she'd grazed it.

At last, she had the door open. *Thank God.* As she fell inside, the robin stopped singing and flew away.

Twenty-four

Kate

She wasn't a morning person. Never had been, never would be. The fact that recently she'd been at her old school desk by seven o'clock every morning was testament to just how keen she was to make some progress. She'd spent hours sweating over this write-up, cursing herself for not nailing it when she first got home. She never pulled her finger out until she was staring a deadline in the face. Last-minute-dot-com. Well, she was paying for it now.

Mind you, it was tough to concentrate on the long-buried bichrome pottery of a civilisation that died out three thousand years ago when your own family was smashing pottery right here, right now, in your own kitchen. She had the precious shard of red and yellow on the desk in front of her. It was her talisman.

Simon had got her all stirred up again on Saturday. He'd arrived at Smith's Barn in a state, raving about how he'd seen Dad cross-dressed at the flat the day before. Luckily, Mum was out for lunch with Stella. Kate had never seen her brother in such a mess. He didn't touch the coffee she made him. Instead, he poured himself a couple of very stiff gins and knocked them back. She warned him he'd be over the limit. He said he'd be fine—but he wasn't fine. He was marching around, all over the kitchen, talking and talking.

'The man was wearing tights,' he kept saying. The wig, the earrings and the dress were bad, but it was the tights that had really got to him. 'Tights, Kate. *Tights*. Jesus.'

'What did you do?'

'I walked out.'

'I'm seeing him next week,' said Kate, and explained about her move to the new flat. 'I'll be dropping some stuff off at Thurso Lane.'

Simon looked as though she'd dropped a scorpion down his back. 'Don't do that, for Christ's sake! Don't go near him. Leave your gear with us. We've got space in our cellar.'

'Thanks, but Dad's place is a lot more convenient.'

'Don't be beholden to him. Just don't. It's demeaning, it's . . .' Simon put his face into his hands. His cage had been rattled, all right. 'Tights! Christ. I wouldn't even know how to put on a pair of tights.'

Kate had pretended she didn't mind Dad wearing tights and a wig and anything else he wanted to wear, but it wasn't the truth. Not at all. It was too much to take in. Too much to understand. Just . . . too much.

It was Monday now, and she was coming apart at the seams. No matter how hard she tried to concentrate on work, she kept imagining a pantomime dame—sequinned and feathered and stiletto-heeled, with a clown's painted mouth and false eyelashes. She imagined the dame mincing about, twirling her handbag and talking in a falsetto. It wouldn't be especially funny on a stage at Christmas; it was seriously unfunny when it was your own father. Maybe Simon had a point. Maybe a shrink could retune him, like a mechanic fixing a car. If only life were that simple.

By nine a.m. she wanted more coffee. She *really* wanted coffee. She mustn't stop, though. She had to work until ten before she could reward herself.

Lipstick?

If it had been someone else's father, she'd have been a cheerleader! 'Be true to yourself,' she'd have said. 'You only live once.

Be a man, be a woman, be androgynous—who cares, so long as you're a good person?'

This was different. This was Dad.

The post van turned into the drive. It was all the excuse she needed. Good old Bryan, she thought as she jumped down the last few stairs. Nice, normal, dependable Bryan the postie. They'd gone to school together; he was one of the gang who used to play British Bulldogs in the hay meadow. He had two kids now, though, and a beer gut, and looked shagged out every time she saw him.

He rolled out of his van holding an electricity bill, a bright yellow envelope announcing that 'The Householder was *The Lucky Winner of £1,000,000!!!*', and two identical cream envelopes addressed to her and Eilish. She recognised her father's regular, tidy handwriting. She'd learned at the age of ten that his writing was easier than her mother's to forge, and had put this discovery to good use.

Unfortunately, Kate cannot take part in the cross-country run today. She has a sprained ankle.

Kate was off school yesterday with a vomiting bug and a high fever.

She was finally caught after handing in this piece of literary fiction:

Kate was unable to complete her homework last night, despite her best efforts. We had distant cousin's visiting from Dubai.

It was the apostrophe that led to her downfall. Her primary school teacher smelled a rat and phoned home to ask about the 'distant cousin's', and Kate was rumbled. She spent every lunchtime of the next week in detention, writing lines: *There is no apostrophe in a plural.*

Bryan was in a mood to chat. 'You home for good?' he asked.

''Fraid not. Leaving tomorrow. It's back to the big smoke for me.'

He looked up at the house. 'Mr Livingstone still away?'

'Mm.'

'Haven't seen him for a while.'

'No.'

'Sophie in the pub says he doesn't come in anymore, and my wife Jo—she's parent rep on the school board—she mentioned in passing that he's missed a couple of meetings. He sent his apologies. But, seeing as he's chair, they were a bit surprised.'

'Sorry about that. Flat out at work.' Well, it was probably true. Dad was always flat out at work.

Bryan didn't believe her, of course; it must have been painfully obvious that the Livingstone family were in trouble. It was only a matter of time before the true reason came out. That'll set the lace curtains twitching, thought Kate, as she dropped Eilish's post on the kitchen table.

Then she went back outside, and sat under Charlotte's maple tree to open the letter from her father. Branches shivered above her head, stirred by the breath of a breeze. She wished Charlotte were alive. She'd always imagined a girl with russet hair, like the leaves of her tree. Her older sister would have been wise and calm. If she'd been here, she would have known what to think about all this; and perhaps Dad would have been happier if Charlotte hadn't died. He'd been a lovely father, of course, but for as long as she could remember there had been nights when he didn't sleep and left for work at four in the morning; days when he seemed to be somewhere else, even though he was present. As she grew up, Kate had assumed that this darkness came when Charlotte died.

There was one terrible memory, one she tried never to revisit and pretended was just a dream. This tree must have been much smaller then, but so was Kate. She was little but wiry, tucked in among the leafy summer boughs, watching millions of thistledown heads float up into the blue. She felt happy. No school for weeks, and tomorrow they were off to Wales for their summer holiday at the beach.

Dad was coming across the lawn. He'd been in one of those quiet moods when Mum would kiss him and ask, 'All right, darling?' and he'd say that he was but then go and shut himself in his study. Mum used to explain that it was all to do with the stresses of his job, and nothing to worry about. Ten-year-old Kate wished he'd choose another job. From up in Charlotte's tree, she noticed that his head was down; he was bent over, as though he didn't have quite enough bones in his body to hold him up. He was wearing his nice green jersey that Mum gave him. Kate grinned to herself. She'd wait until he got closer and then give him a fright by leaping down. That would make him laugh for sure, and she wanted him to laugh.

He came up to the tree and stood under it with his forehead leaning against the trunk. Kate was about to jump out when she heard him say something out loud. She caught the words *God* and *hate you*. Who did he hate? God? How could anyone hate God? Then, all of a sudden, he did something awful; something she didn't understand, even years later. He punched himself—not once but lots of times—all over his body, even in the balls, which, according to Simon, was the worst place a boy can get hit. Kate watched with her mouth hanging open, thinking he'd gone mad.

Even when he stopped hitting himself, the terrible thing wasn't over. Kate heard the most frightening sound ever: her dad crying. It was all wrong. Adults didn't cry, children cried. Dad's crying was in a deep man's voice, and it made her feel sick. She knew she was watching something really, really secret, something she should never have seen. Was he crying for Charlotte? Then other, worse, possibilities occurred to her. What if he was dying of cancer? What if he and Mum were getting a divorce?

The next moment, he'd stopped crying and pulled his hankie out of his pocket. He was looking towards the house. Kate looked too, and saw Simon standing on the terrace, holding the telephone.

'Dad!' he shouted. 'Da-a-ad? You out here? It's Grandad!'

Dad pressed the hankie into his eyes and took a deep breath before yelling, *Right you are!* Kate watched as he sprinted across to take the phone. How could he be running, or talking to Grandpa, when he was so sad and probably dying of cancer?

The next day they set off for Wales. The parents shared the driving, while Kate—for once—sat quietly and didn't wind Simon up. Dad seemed all right today, no signs of dying, so Kate pretended nothing had happened. Gradually the memory had lost its sharp edges, and she'd begun to hope she'd dreamed the whole thing.

Full circle. Here she was, twelve years on, visiting Charlotte's tree and shit-scared again. She knew now, of course. She knew what had been torturing her dad that day.

The letter was printed, but there was also a handwritten note in blue ink. Kate was pretty sure he'd used the pen they gave him for his birthday. Simon had had it engraved, and asked if she would like to contribute. Sweet, really. That boy had his good moments.

Darling Kate, this letter explains itself. I have—as you would say—cocked up big-time. Recent events have demonstrated that people must be warned to expect changes in me. If they are not warned, and are caught unawares, they may be very shocked. I must be totally open from now on, every step of the way.

Kate reread this paragraph. The wording bothered her, especially as her dad had a gift for understatement. *Recent events? What frigging recent events?*

I'm sending Mum a copy too, though she and I discussed these things when we met some weeks ago. Thank you for keeping her company. I know it isn't fair to ask you to carry so much. I am only beginning to find out who I am, but I do know who you are. You are my brilliant, tolerant and beautiful daughter. I do not deserve you, but I do love you.

Dad XXXXX

Kate lay flat on her back. She could see nothing but endless blue, dappled by Charlotte's leaves. This lawn had always been mossy. The grass felt like a dry cushion under her head, smelling of herbs. She lifted the letter up in front of her face.

My dear family,

I am writing to all of you so that there are no more secrets. Keeping this secret for so long has been my greatest sin.

The word 'sorry' is hopelessly tame. I'll say it anyway. I am sorry.

It is difficult to write this letter. Difficult, because I am trying to express feelings which I barely understand. Difficult, because I know I am hurting all of you. But I must try. My behaviour will seem like madness, selfishness, or perversion to you. I did not do at all well when I first tried to explain to some of you. I am sorry (there's that inadequate word again) that I was not prepared. The decision to confess took me by surprise—though not, I appreciate, as much as it did you.

In some fundamental way, most people's minds match their bodies. You, Kate, don't like the labels of 'masculine' and 'feminine'. I applaud that in you. But the fact is that you've always been allowed to live, dress, talk, and express yourself freely. I have not been so lucky. I've said that I feel trapped in the wrong kind of body. It's worse than that, really. It's as though the real me is smothered underneath the false one—alive, but unable to speak or move.

Those of you who are female, please try this bit of mental gymnastics: imagine waking up one day and finding that there's been some switch—maybe an alien abduction!—and you now inhabit a male body. You mustn't wear jewellery or make-up anymore. Your hair must be cut. You can't wear feminine clothes or shoes or anything remotely pretty, even underwear. None. You have to pretend you have no interest in those things. Your body is all the wrong shape and size, and you hate it, so you try to avoid mirrors. From now on you're treated as a man by other women. You have to fit in with men. You have to pretend to be one of them. You must talk as they do, be interested only in what interests them. You must never, ever slip up. You live in constant terror of slipping up, and with constant inner turmoil.

Now imagine that this is a life sentence. You will live, love, die and be buried in that wrong body. Nobody will ever know who you really are.

This was me. I became exhausted. I became broken-hearted. I couldn't go on.

That's all very well, you say, but what's unforgivable is the fact that I lied for so long! I have no defence—except to say that I fell head over heels in love with a girl called Eilish French. I was under her spell, and remain so to this day. Everything would be all right, I was sure, if she would share my life with me. I dared to hope. Was I so wrong to grasp at happiness? And, of course, having married her, I had to keep going. And so the years went on, and I kept on burying my real self.

Since I left Smith's Barn I have researched and taken advice. The process is complicated; I don't know exactly how things will unfold. What I can promise is that from now on I will tell the truth.

I'll soon start taking oestrogen and something to block the testosterone. If I can find the courage, I will eventually try to live as a woman. Not just any woman—one woman in particular. I've known her all my life, because she is me. Her name is Lucia.

Each of you will have to decide what this means to you. I fear what lies ahead, and I would welcome your company on the journey. My dream is that you will accept me as I am.

Even if you cannot walk with me, perhaps you could try to forgive me.

With my love always,

Lucia

Kate read the letter three times. Then she shut her eyes and did as he'd asked. She imagined looking into a mirror and seeing a grown man. She imagined being a spy behind enemy lines, in constant terror of discovery. And, just for a moment, she thought she understood.

Eilish was in the kitchen. Her face was set, as pale as the letter on the table in front of her. 'That's that, then,' she said, taking off her reading glasses.

She didn't want to talk. She didn't want a cup of tea. Kate followed her as she marched down to the garden shed. It doubled as Dad's woodwork room, and smelled of timber and linseed oil. Eilish emerged with a pair of clippers and began to slice the heads off roses—all the roses, whether they needed pruning or not. Mostly not.

Eilish

'He's certifiably insane,' yelled Simon, who'd jumped out of his car and was waving the letter at me. 'He's actually signed himself Lucia!'

I completely agreed with him. Kate had gone off to meet a friend in the Bracton Arms, leaving me to wreak havoc in the garden. My hurt throbbed and pulsed and threatened to explode. Perhaps I'd feel better if I screamed and hit things. The foulest words were forming in my mind: things I'd like to say to Luke, things calculated to hurt him back. Seeing it all written down—knowing he had sent the same message to all the family—was too much. He claimed to have fallen head over heels in love with a girl called Eilish French. *Love?* Love didn't mean lying. Love didn't mean hijacking another person's life just to make your own look conventional. Love didn't mean making someone feel diminished and humiliated and used.

'He says he wants hormone therapy,' bellowed Simon now. 'Well, I'll help him with that! I've castrated four dogs today. I'll be happy to oblige.' He made a snip-snipping motion with his fingers. I did the same with my secateurs, decapitating another rose. Soft heads carpeted the ground around my feet. The destruction wasn't as therapeutic as I'd hoped.

I wished Simon hadn't driven straight out here in this towering rage. I had enough rage of my own. He looks ill, I thought. He's too pinched, too shadowy around the eyes. And he smells of alcohol. He must be hard to live with—poor Carmela, poor little Nico. Luke's selfishness is like a pebble thrown into a pond, causing ripples that spread and spread, ruining people's lives. How did I ever love such a self-centred, vain creature?

'You've got to have him sectioned,' said Simon. '*You* have to do it. I can't. You're his wife.'

'What, locked up?'

'Locked up, yes, until they cure him. They'll give him massive doses of testosterone, I expect. Something for psychosis. It has to be curable.'

I knew this idea was ridiculous. I was sure that Simon knew it too, in his heart. Still, the thought of Luke being cured was an attractive fantasy.

'Male hormones,' I said, edging out from between two prickly rosebushes. 'Nice idea. I don't think it's as easy as that, though.'

I headed across the lawn towards the shed. It was another burning day. Simon fell into step. Even his walk was agitated. Sweat darkened his shirt between his shoulderblades. 'Look, Mum, I've asked around and I've got a name for you. A really good solicitor. No connection to Bannermans.'

'To advise me about the Mental Health Act?'

'To advise you about divorce.'

I stopped in my tracks. *Divorce.*

'There's no rush,' I said. 'Plenty of time for that.'

'No, there isn't plenty of time. You need to get on with it, pronto! This woman I've found is meant to be a real terrier. She's in Oxford. I think you should ask for an emergency injunction to protect the house, your savings and the pension. We've got to get the money tied up before he blows it on having himself turned inside out in some weird Asian hospital.'

'He's not a fiend, Simon.'

He began to speak with forced calmness. I found it patronising. 'Mum, we have to face the facts. He's not rational. He's behaving like a kid in a sweetshop. Grab, grab, grab, not caring what damage he causes. How's he paying for these hormones? Can he get them on the NHS?'

Thinking back, I remembered what Luke had said over lunch. 'He mentioned a clinic . . . he wanted to talk about money. I expect he's paying out of the joint account, or maybe with one of the credit cards. We've never divided our finances.'

Simon clutched at his head. 'Oh my God! Call the bank. Tell them to freeze everything. You'll end up on the streets, with your life savings in the pocket of some dodgy backstreet quack.'

Luke's the enemy now, I thought as I logged into our internet banking in the airless study, and ran my eye down the transactions. He was my comrade. Now he's a shadowy foe who'll steal all our money if he gets the chance.

'Found it?' asked Simon.

'Um . . . can't see anything unusual coming out of the bank accounts. Hang on, let's look at Visa. There's a few internet purchases—what are they? And . . . yes. This is it. Two payments, each a hundred and fifty pounds . . . they're to something called *Baytrees Clinic*.'

Simon was looking over my shoulder. 'It's just the beginning. The cost of this will be astronomical. Hormones won't be cheap, and when it comes to surgery, the sky's the limit. You might lose this house.'

'He couldn't take out a mortgage on Smith's Barn without my knowing,' I said, trying to convince myself. 'We own it jointly.'

'Mum, open your eyes! You've got to start fighting back.'

Luke's letter was still lying on the kitchen table. He'd added a handwritten line:

Eilish, I know my lie was unforgivable. But I want you to know that you have saved me, year after year. I wasn't lying when I said I love you. Thank you.

You asked too much, I thought. *You took too much. You have broken me.*

'All right,' I said. 'Let's call that solicitor.'

Twenty-five

Kate

Mathis was driving. He seemed to have no sense of danger at all, and Kate had her hands over her eyes for much of the journey. There was thunder in the air. She was sticking to her seat.

'Turn left here,' she ordered. 'Then at the end of the—Christ's sake, mind that bike!'

Mathis braked sharply, and they all slewed forward. Kate felt lucky to be alive as she staggered onto the pavement outside what used to be her home. Behind her, Mathis reversed the car into a tiny space intended for motorbikes.

John had got out too, and took her arm. 'Wait till he's parked. We need a surgical strike.'

'This isn't an SAS raid,' she protested. 'Owen isn't an evil genius. He's a common or garden wazzock.'

'Kate, we watched you being a nanny to that boy for two years. He's more controlling than any psychopath, and we're not taking risks. We're going to grab your things and get you out of here.'

'I'm the getaway driver,' added Mathis, coming around the car. He did something in radio, and had the kind of wistful beauty that made schoolgirls giggle. John was a cherubic accountant, born with a receding hairline. He finally came out of the closet as a student, when he fell in love with Mathis. They were the only people she'd told about her father. There was nobody else she could trust not to laugh.

'See us as your bodyguards,' said John, 'wearing shades and earpieces.'

They had reached the front door, and were squeezed between dustbins and an overgrown hedge, limp and dusty after weeks without rain. Kate was about to press the bell when the door opened. The last scales fell clattering from her eyes. Owen looked peaky and petulant, and he was wearing an orange T-shirt she'd always loathed.

'Ah,' he said sarcastically. 'What an honour. I was going to dump your stuff at Oxfam.'

'Hilarious.'

'Hello, Mathis, hello, John. Did she tell you she vandalised my best shirt?'

He turned his back and walked down the hall towards a pile of boxes, bin bags and a stereo system. Mathis and John swooped on them and began carrying armfuls out to the car. Kate was following suit when a small, barking object burst out of the bedroom, ricocheted around the confined space and knocked Owen's bicycle right over.

'Baffy's missed you,' said Owen, turning back. He was smiling.

She picked up the little dog, nuzzling his fluffy head while Owen gave her a blow-by-blow account of the night Baffy ate chicken bones and had to be rushed to the vet. She followed him into the kitchen so that she could write down a forwarding address. Before she knew it, they were both sitting at the table. Owen's hair was sticking up and his socks were half off his feet. He looked defenceless. He needed somebody to care for him.

'How are your parents?' he asked.

'Fine.'

'Say goodbye and thanks from me. I'll really miss those weekends at Smith's Barn.'

The words rushed out of her. 'They've split up,' she said. 'He's moved out. She's seeing a solicitor today.'

He looked genuinely shaken. 'You're joking! Those two?'

She shrugged, clamping her lips together in case they quivered.

'Got time for coffee?' asked Owen, putting on the kettle. 'Hell. That was one marriage I didn't expect . . . You must be gutted.'

John came bustling in. 'Grab a box, Kate,' he said. 'No time. We still have to get to Mile End. Your dad's expecting us.'

Five minutes later, the car was packed. Owen came outside in his socks, holding Baffy.

'Thanks for packing up for me,' said Kate.

'It wasn't my pleasure.'

Mathis was a terrible getaway driver; it took an age for him to manoeuvre the car out of its space while Owen and Baffy watched, both of them looking hangdog.

'Lucky we came along,' declared John, as they finally escaped. 'That guy is devious. Did you see his socks? And his hair? It must have taken hours to get the neglected orphan effect.'

Kate felt weighed down. After all, that awkward little scene—these bin bags—were the end of something that had once been lovely. She was dreading the next hour, too. What if Dad was cross-dressed? She wasn't sure she could handle that.

Luke appeared on the pavement as they drove up. He was in his shirtsleeves, with a loosened tie, and Kate felt a great rush of relief. Leaping out of the car, she ran to hug him. Then she stopped. His lower lip was swollen and bruised.

'What the frig's happened to you?'

'Slipped on the steps. Clumsy old sod.' His speech wasn't as clear as usual.

'Which steps? These ones? When?'

'Last week. No harm done. Evening, lads,' he said, turning to John and Mathis. 'It's very good of you to lend your car and your muscle to Operation Rescue Kate from Owen.'

It was an efficient unloading process, accompanied by rolls of thunder and a sullen sky. The flat had only one bedroom but they managed to fit everything behind the sofa. As they worked, Kate kept glancing at Luke. He looked like her dad, he talked like her dad, he behaved towards her friends with his usual self-effacing charm. The odd thing was, though, that thinking of him as female wasn't quite as impossible as it used to be. There was something about him; some kind of ambiguity. Perhaps—she struggled to admit this to herself—there always had been.

'He's happy,' whispered Mathis, when Luke was out of earshot.

'You think so?' Kate made a face. 'He must be lonely.'

'I'm sure he grieves for your mother, I'm sure he has guilt, but . . . no, his spirit is happy. Can't you feel it? There's a lightness about him. He has less weight pressing down on his shoulders.'

The last box had been carried in from the car when Kate noticed a spot of rain darken the pavement. As she looked at it, another arrived. Then another. Within a few seconds they were standing in a downpour. Mathis whooped and held out his hands to catch the drops. Passers-by were running, yelling cheerfully, holding newspapers over their heads. London was weary of drought.

'Hurray!' cried Luke. 'Come in and have a drink to celebrate . . . In fact, can you stay for supper? Yes? Great! We have a choice of takeaway places.'

For a time they stood at the open garden door, watching the deluge. The lawn was so parched that water formed pools, unable to sink in. A flash of lightning lit up the fig tree; they counted the seconds to the next drum roll. Luke went away and came back with a bottle of wine, and invited them to take an armchair each. Soon he and the young men were deep in conversation.

Kate couldn't stop looking at her dad. He'd taken off his tie, and undone the top button of his shirt. The swollen lip frightened her. It made him seem too vulnerable.

'Did someone hit you, Dad?' she asked suddenly.

'I'm just a no-good street brawler, you know me. Always picking fights.'

John leaned closer. 'Actually, Luke, in this light I can see a bit of bruising . . . just here.' He pressed his own Adam's apple.

'Where?' Kate looked too, and saw mottled smudges. A horrible suspicion came to her. 'Oh my God. Did you do that to yourself? Did you try to . . . Dad, did you try to hang yourself?'

'No, no!' Luke was hurriedly buttoning his shirt. 'Don't worry, Kate. I *promise* you this isn't self-inflicted. I just had a misunderstanding with someone, and we got into a bit of a scuffle.'

'You've never been in a scuffle in your life.'

'Well, I have now. Forget it.'

Kate couldn't forget it. Who would attack her lovely dad and do all this damage? She imagined a gang of thugs setting on him in some darkened street. Maybe they'd seen him cross-dressed?

'I don't think you should let this go,' she said. 'Let's report it to the police.'

'It's all right, Kate. What I'm doing upsets people.'

'Who?'

'Lots of people. I'd better get used to it.' Luke raised his hand to show that the subject was closed. Then he turned to John and said something about a cricket tour.

Kate wasn't interested in cricket. She got up and stood in the doorway, holding her hands out to the downpour. Dad was trying to cover something up, that much was obvious. The injuries looked to be a few days old. Simon had been here last week; she wondered whether he'd noticed anything.

Simon was here.

Simon found Dad wearing a dress.

Simon.

She stepped into the rain, pulling out her phone. She was sheltering under the fig tree when Simon answered.

'I'm at Dad's,' she said, without preliminaries.

'Christ almighty—I told you, Kate! He's got a bedroom full of women's clothes.' He'd swung straight into holier-than-thou mode. Jerk.

'He's black and blue,' she said. 'What the hell did you do to him?'

He didn't try to deny it. 'He was out on the streets looking like a frigging pervert. He's going to get himself arrested.'

She could see her father through the open doorway. He was sitting in an armchair, listening intently to John. He didn't look like a frigging pervert. He looked like a kind, anxious man—or maybe a kind, anxious woman, now that she thought about it. Either way, it was her dad: the same person she'd loved all her life.

'Have you read that round robin he sent out?' asked Simon.

'Yes.'

'Mum's going to divorce him. He's going to lose everything, probably end up on the streets. Nobody will give him the time of day. Maybe then he'll realise what a fool he's been.'

'You make me sick!' Kate saw her father glance out at her, and dropped her voice. 'In all the years since you were born, he's never once so much as laid a finger on you in anger—despite the fact that you've been a real little bastard at times. Any other man would have walloped seven bells out of you sooner or later, but not Dad. He's been the most patient, understanding, loving father in the world. Fuck, how many times has he bailed you out of trouble? And now it's his hour of need, and you break into his home and smash him up! Oh, aren't you clever, aren't you brave, aren't you a total fuckwit of a meathead?'

'He hit me too.' Simon sounded like a five-year-old.

'Looks to me like you tried to throttle him! That's attempted murder. I should go to the police.'

'Look, I'm not proud of myself, but if you'd been there and seen—'

'Oh, fuck off.' Kate cut him off, stormed back inside and threw herself into an armchair. Her hair was dripping. 'Frigging Simon! I know it was him, Dad, don't bother denying it. He's just admitted it. Can I phone Mum? She has to hear about this.'

'No,' replied Luke.

'So we let him get away with it?'

'Yes.'

Kate blew out her cheeks. 'Carmela's going to hit the roof.'

'I wouldn't bet on it,' said Luke, who was calmly refilling glasses. 'Anyway, she isn't going to know, because you aren't going to tell her. She's pregnant.'

'She's got a right to know what kind of a tosspot she's married to.'

'No, Kate. No. I'm asking you not to stir things up. Just let it go. Now, how about that takeaway? There's an excellent Thai down the road.'

Kate huffed and puffed, but she had to give in. It was her dad's decision.

They had a great evening in the end. She hadn't expected that, not with so much misery flying around the family. They ate at the kitchen table while Mathis regaled them with celebrity gossip he'd picked up at work. It was getting on for eleven o'clock when Luke's phone rang. Kate saw him look at the number, and immediately smile. There was only one person who could make her father smile like that. There had only ever been one person.

'Eilish,' he said, as he answered.

John and Mathis tactfully got up and started washing dishes, chatting to one another. Kate wanted to listen to her father's conversation, but had no choice but to grab a tea towel and help the lads. Her ears pricked up, though, when she heard her dad mutter, 'Do you want to talk to Kate?'

She moved closer, listening openly now.

'Are you all right?' he asked. 'Shall I come out there to be with you?'

She could hear the murmur of her mother's voice. Luke nodded.

'All right then. I'll tell Kate . . . All right. Stay in touch. I'll be waiting.' He listened for another few moments, then whispered, 'Me too. Me too. Bye . . . bye, darling.'

He spoke so tenderly, so intimately. It was as though the divorce wasn't happening at all. He shut the phone and sat for a moment with his head bowed. Then he looked up.

'Carmela's in labour,' he said. 'It's much too early.'

Twenty-six

Eilish

You know you're getting long in the tooth when your hot-shot no-holds-barred solicitor is no older than your son. She suggested we get the divorce underway immediately, and demand an undertaking from Luke, in order to protect the assets. As thunder rolled outside, she took a history from me.

'I've seen this kind of thing before,' she said.

'What, married men who turn into women?'

She dropped her voice, as though the walls had ears. 'You'd be surprised. One of my colleagues had a client who couldn't understand why her shoes were always too big for her. Even the ones she'd hardly worn. I think you can guess the rest.'

'Yes,' I said faintly. 'Oh, yes. I recognise that.'

I was her last appointment. I left her office and ran through a downpour to my car. Oxford's traffic was a nightmare. I doubt whether it was safe for me to be driving, because I can remember nothing about the journey except the slap-slap as my wipers tried to cope with teeming rain. I was thinking about the night I went to see *Giselle*, and lent a handsome man my opera glasses. Seemed like yesterday.

The church clock was striking eight as I splashed my way through East Yalton. The house looked dark and empty. I walked in, flicking on lights. Casino appeared within two seconds and gave me a fishwife-style telling-off, because it was long past his supper time. I emptied a can of food into his bowl and then sat at the kitchen table, feeling poleaxed.

I was dismayed by what I had begun. I'd been to a solicitor. I had knocked over the first domino, and the trail of fallen hopes would lead to the ending of my marriage. Had I really done that?

Casino jumped up and curled on my lap. I didn't move. I knew Luke. I didn't know Luke. He was a lover, he was a stranger; he was honourable, he was a conman. I feared for him. I pitied him. I raged at him. I loved him. He'd been my travelling companion all through my adult life; how could he walk away from me like this? *It's you who's been to the solicitor*, said a small voice on the other side of my anger. *It's you who's done the walking away.*

I don't know how much time had passed before the phone rang. It jerked me back into wakefulness. *Perhaps it's Luke*, I thought. *Perhaps he's asking to come home. There's still time to stop that divorce petition from being posted.*

'Mum,' said Simon. 'Something's happening.'

Simon

He found Carmela lying on the sofa with her feet on a cushion. Nico was all ready for bed, watching *One Hundred and One Dalmatians*. He jumped up and hugged his father around the waist.

'You're wet!' he declared.

'Just a bit. I walked in the rain.'

'We're watching the dogs. Cruella wants to make them into coats.'

'Not more dogs! I've been looking at dogs all day,' spluttered Simon with mock horror. He squatted down beside Carmela. 'All right?'

'Just those Braxton Hicks contractions,' she said, rubbing her bump. 'They hurt a lot . . . ouch! How was work?'

'Not bad.'

In fact, it had been a hell of a day. The surgery was packed, one of the nurses was off sick, and the new receptionist didn't have a clue. And his dad had taken to wearing tights. He went into the kitchen, poured a gin and tonic and knocked it back. *Tights*. He couldn't get that image out of his mind.

'Eilish phoned this afternoon,' called Carmela. 'She was just going to the solicitor. Ouch.'

He made a hot water bottle for her stomach, and left her resting while he and Nico had supper together. Nico had gone upstairs to look for his favourite story book when Simon's phone rang. It was Kate—she could be such a pain in the arse, his sister—ranting because she'd found out about his fight with Dad. In the end, she hung up on him.

'Christ's sake,' muttered Simon. 'Miss Self-Righteous.'

I won't think about Dad, he decided as he sloshed more gin into a glass. Not now. He was going to fall apart if he didn't stop thinking about his father. Since his visit to Thurso Lane he'd been waking in the early hours, haunted by the horror of the moment when the woman in the kitchen had turned around. What he wanted to do, right now, was forget the whole nightmare and have a happy half-hour with his son. He climbed the stairs to find Nico sitting on his bed, clutching Piglet and looking through his book.

'This one first,' he said, crawling onto Simon's knee. '"The Magic Crayon".'

At the end of the third story, Simon closed the book. Nico made Piglet dance up and down on his father's arm.

'Did you have lots of ill cats today?' he asked.

'Oh, a great army of ill cats. *This* many.' Simon held up the fingers of both hands. 'And dogs. And a snake. And a very fluffy hamster called Vodka. He had bed hair. It stuck up all over the place.'

'Did you make all those animals better?'

'Most of them.'

'I want to be a wet, when I grow up,' said Nico.

Simon nuzzled his nose into the pudding-basin haircut. 'You'll be a very good wet,' he said. 'And now it's time for bed.'

Nico had an armoury of delaying tactics. 'Mummy said "ow" today, when my baby bruvver or sister kicked her.'

'Poor Mummy.'

'Will you read this story now?' Nico opened the book again. 'It's just a teeny one.'

'Tomorrow. How about a flying lesson. Ready for take-off?' Simon stood up and swung the small boy into the air, twirling him around before landing him back on the bed.

'Granny was on the phone,' said Nico, scrambling under the duvet. 'She's got a present for me. I think it's probably another car. I couldn't talk to Grandpa, though, because he doesn't live there anymore.'

'Night-night, don't let the bed bugs bite. Give us a kiss.'

'Is he gone because you told him off when I gave him flowers?'

'I didn't tell him off.'

Nico's brown eyes were wide. He knew a fib when he heard one. 'You *did*. I heard you. You shouted like THIS!' He opened and closed his mouth, silently imitating a lot of shouting. 'Poor Grandpa.'

Simon felt a sickening mix of shame and fury. 'I didn't really shout. There are things you can't understand, and you just have to let the grown-ups worry about those. Time for sleeping now. Goodnight, Nico; goodnight, Piglet.'

As he turned out the light, he looked back. Nico was lying down, holding Piglet at arm's length above his face. He was speaking in a deep, angry growl.

'Getchor hands off my son,' he said. 'Getchor hands off my son.'

•

In the kitchen, Carmela had made a pot of camomile tea.

'Feeling better?' asked Simon.

'Yes, thank you. The hot water bottle worked like magic. I wasn't a happy banana before.'

He carried her tea and his gin back to the sitting room, turned down the lights and put Elgar on the stereo. She lay on the sofa with her feet across his knees, her toenails painted the colour of opals. He wondered how she could even reach them nowadays.

'I should phone Mum,' he said. 'Find out what happened at the solicitor's.'

'Don't do that now.'

It was peaceful in the mellow light and rippling music.

'I heard you reading,' she said. 'I like "The Magic Crayon".'

He stroked her ankles.

'What really happened in Luke's flat that day?' she asked.

'I found him wearing women's clothes.'

'I know that. But what happened next?'

'I left. I went to the pub and had a couple of pints. I came home.'

'Mm?' She wiggled her toes. 'Since that day you have not slept, you have not eaten, you have not smiled. I wish you would tell me why.'

'Because I've lost my father.'

'And he was your wise friend.'

Simon tipped his head back against the sofa, half closing his eyes. The gin was finally taking effect. The pain was dulled. 'No, he was a fraud. Shh. I don't want to talk about him.'

He felt her feet gradually relax, and knew she was dozing off. So was he. They ought to get up, get changed and go to bed. They would. In a minute. The music flooded around him, lifted him up and floated him away.

The lights were flashing. Disco lights. The DJ put on a slow song: 'Nights in White Satin'. Jessica had the sexiest, longest legs he'd ever seen. She leaned close, melting against him. Her mouth was warm.

He kissed her again, and again, as they meandered through the summer-scented night, back to the hotel where she lived and worked. They laughed and talked—nonsense, mostly. They were on the same wavelength. His speech was slurred, he knew, but it didn't matter. He'd fallen in love in the space of an evening, as only a drunk and lustful nineteen-year-old can do. This girl was special. She said he should come travelling with her. He said he would, bugger his career, he didn't want to be a vet anyway. They dreamed of living on a beach in Thailand. He imagined exotic music and flickering lamplight, and the sound of waves on sand, and Jessica lying naked in a bamboo cabin. They'd be so happy.

When they reached the hotel, they fell into the darkness of the doorway. He ran both hands up the smooth curves of her thigh.

'Stop right there,' she laughed, taking hold of his arms.

'Can I come in?'

'D'you want me to lose my job?'

He was going to explode with desire. He didn't want the night to end; he certainly didn't want it to end without him shagging this girl. 'Come home with me,' he begged, as she slid her key into the lock.

'Phone me tomorrow, once you've got over the hangover. Promise you'll phone?'

He promised. The door clicked shut behind her. Her perfume lingered on his clothes.

As he staggered away across the street, he heard somebody groaning. It sounded like a woman, but it couldn't be Jessica. It came again, louder. Somebody was in pain. Somebody was crying. He looked up and down the empty pavement. Who was here? Who was in such distress?

'Simon.' It was Carmela's voice. She was struggling to speak. 'I think something is wrong.'

Eilish

People think of childbirth as routine. Some pride themselves on being blasé. After all, they point out, billions of women have done it. Everybody's mother has done it. Sure, it occasionally goes wrong, but we're so lucky: we live in the developed world, in the twenty-first century. They spout made-up statistics: one in a thousand infant deaths, one in a million. A childless man once blithely told me that it's safer to give birth than it is to put up the Christmas tree lights. I could have socked him.

I know differently, you see. I know it can happen. I know what it's like when your baby is limp; when the midwife grabs her back from you, lays her down and tries to resuscitate her. I've felt blind panic as the little body turns that horrible colour of the dying. I've gabbled out prayers, begging God for help, moaning in terror. I've felt the milk coming, ready for a child who will never drink.

So when Simon phoned me from the hospital and said that Carmela was in labour at thirty-four weeks, I didn't feel excited. I didn't feel happy. I just felt very frightened, because I knew that the lungs of babies who are born prematurely struggle to work properly. And, of course, the first thing I did was phone Luke. I didn't think twice. I wanted him to help carry the fear. He was entertaining Kate and her friends at the flat. I didn't mention the fact that I'd been to the solicitor. Too much of a coward.

'Are you all right?' he asked.

'Absolutely! It'll be fine. Lots of babies are born this early. I just thought you'd like to know.'

'Shall I come out there to be with you?'

'No need,' I said. 'I'll be turning in soon. After all, there's nothing I can do. No doubt Simon will let me know when there's any news.'

It was a charade. He knew I wouldn't sleep. I knew he wouldn't, either. We'd both keep vigil through the night.

'I don't think I'll ever forgive you,' I blurted, 'but I do miss you.'

I decided to avoid alcohol in case I needed to drive to the hospital. I drank tea, then more tea. I turned on the radio. I checked my emails. I tried to read a book. All I could think about was the new grandchild who was struggling into the world. I considered lying down, but I dreaded that empty bed.

At midnight I picked up the phone to call Luke. Then I put it down again. It was over. I was going to divorce him. I had to manage alone, and so did he.

At about three, I found myself outside. The air felt clean after the rain; the temperature had dropped at last. The world was very still and very, very dark. There were no stars. I made my way across the wet lawn and stood between Charlotte's tree and Robert's sapling. Perhaps those two dear people knew what was happening; perhaps they had some influence with the powers that be up in heaven, and would put in a good word for this newest member of the family. I felt as though the night were hiding me in its black cloak. It understood me. It let me think my thoughts.

In the end, I said a kind of prayer. There was nothing else for me to do. I begged two favours of the God I hoped existed: I asked that Carmela's baby arrive safely in this world, and breathe, and be strong; and I asked that Luke might be my Luke again, and come home to me.

Luke

Still no news. I'd rearranged all the things Kate had dropped off; I'd ironed a week's supply of work shirts and a silk blouse I'd bought online. I tried to concentrate on drafting some documents, but got nowhere. Perhaps this was a punishment. Perhaps Carmela, Simon and the baby were paying for my depravity. It wasn't a rational theory, but at three in the morning anything can make sense.

It's hard to imagine being a grandparent until you are one. Why do we care so deeply about our children's children? It used to irritate me when my father fretted about Simon and Kate—he used to say we shouldn't let them use the lathe unsupervised, and he nagged me to fence off the pond. I thought him an old fusspot.

Now I paced around the flat, worrying about a small human being who shared my genes. I imagined horrors. I'd seen horrors.

Charlotte was born at home, but I'm not convinced things would have turned out differently at the hospital. Eilish went into labour without warning, and before we'd understood what was happening, the baby was on her way. Our midwife came tearing over. 'It's all right,' she cried as she rushed up the stairs, 'the cavalry have arrived!' She thought everything looked good. It wasn't the quick births she worried about, it was the ones that were too slow. I saw Charlotte's head appear in this world and a few moments later we were welcoming our little girl with tears and laughter. Then, suddenly, something wasn't right. The midwife had taken her back from Eilish. She was trying to make her breathe, snapping at me to call an ambulance. I'll never forget how I fumbled in my panic. I'll never forget the helplessness.

And now my grandchild was arriving too early. It was all happening again. By daybreak I was climbing the walls. I called the hospital and was put through to the maternity unit. A female voice answered, sounding friendly and helpful.

'You're a relative?' she said. 'Oh yes, the grandad. Carmela Livingstone. Okay, just wait a minute.'

She was gone far longer than a minute. I waited, and I waited. Perhaps the nurse had been called away to some emergency. The sky was lightening outside.

Then she was back, but she didn't sound so chirpy. In fact, her attitude had changed completely. 'Are you still there?' she asked, with buttoned-up formality. 'Um, I'm afraid I can't give you any information.'

'But you must be able to tell me something,' I protested.

'You'll appreciate we have rules about this. Confidentiality. We can't go handing out information to everybody who calls.'

'Carmela Livingstone is with you, isn't she? She went into labour last night.'

'I can't actually confirm that we've admitted a person by that name.'

I sat down on the bed. Something was very wrong, that much was obvious.

'I'm sorry,' she said. 'You'll appreciate—'

'That you have rules. Yes. Yes, I do see that. But I'm rather anxious, you see. This baby isn't due for another six weeks. My wife and I lost a baby once, so we tend to be . . . and the fact that you won't tell me anything seems a bad sign. I'm . . . well, I'm very frightened.'

There was a pause, followed by a sigh. 'Look, all I can say is that we've had a quiet night,' she said. 'No problems we couldn't handle. The five babies born in the past twelve hours are safe and well, and so are their mothers.'

It took me a few moments to understand her meaning. When I did, I felt immense gratitude.

'Thank you,' I said. 'Thank you so much.'

•

I had a conference call booked for eight, and a partners' meeting over lunch. They couldn't be put off. I was dressed in a suit and tie, and was about to leave the flat when the phone rang. I pounced on it.

'You have a new granddaughter,' said Eilish's voice. 'Rosa Catalina. Four pounds, two ounces.'

'Thank God. All well?'

'She's in the neonatal care unit, but she's breathing by herself. Carmela's fine.'

'When are you going to see her?'

'Once everyone's had some rest and settled down.'

I walked around the table, carrying the phone. 'Rosa . . . ?'

'Rosa Catalina. It has a rather classy ring to it, don't you think?'

We talked. We were just two tired, relieved, joyous grandparents. Eilish relayed all she knew about the events of the night—Carmela's waters breaking, and Simon getting the neighbour to babysit Nico; their dash to the hospital; what time this happened, and that happened, and how long it all took.

'She was born just after five,' said Eilish.

'I called the hospital at half past! They wouldn't speak to me.'

'I know you did. I know they wouldn't.'

The penny dropped, heavily, with a hollow clunk. Simon had had me blacklisted.

'So I'm an outcast,' I said.

She sounded exasperated. 'What in heaven's name did you expect? You're never going to meet this child. You'll never have anything to do with her or Nico.'

'Surely Simon and Carmela wouldn't be so harsh.'

'No, Luke. Never. Not unless you stop what you're doing. They're adamant. They don't want Rosa and Nico to have a . . . I don't know what to call it.'

'A tranny granny.'

'Why do you joke about the destruction of our family?'

'I'm sorry,' I said. 'I don't think it's funny. Perhaps I've finally had enough of Simon's anger. Perhaps I feel a little angry myself? I'm those children's grandparent. I love them like any other grandparent, whatever gender I am or think I am. Why does it matter so much? I'm not evil and I'm not dangerous. I've been fretting all night, just the same as you. I want to play with my grandchildren. I just want . . . you know.' My voice was cracking.

'Then give up what you're doing,' she said. 'It's not too late. You can have it all, everything, just the way it was. But give it up now, or Rosa will never even hear your name.'

Twenty-seven

Luke

It was difficult to forget everything else and concentrate on the acquisition of one massive financial institution by another. An associate solicitor and a trainee were with me during the eight o'clock conference call. Afterwards I told them about Rosa, and the news soon spread. All morning, colleagues were punching me on the shoulder and congratulating me on my new granddaughter; all morning, I felt a weight in my chest. *You asked for this*, I told myself. *You chose it.*

Judi Wells, who headed our HR department, dropped by just as I was calling the florist. I wanted to send flowers to Carmela. After all, what harm could it do? In years gone by, I might have asked a secretary to organise this for me—but times have changed. Judi saw I was on the phone and hesitated, but I waved to her.

'What message would you like?' asked the woman taking my order.

'Um . . . hang on.' I hadn't thought about the message. When Nico was born, Eilish and I went together to see him. We bore gifts, like two wise men. 'Let's go for: *Congratulations on the safe arrival of Rosa. With love from Luke.*'

After I'd finished the call, I saw that Judi's eyebrows were up.

'When are you going to see this little angel?' she asked.

'Not till she's out of the neonatal unit.'

Judi had recently turned fifty—I knew that for a fact, because Eilish and I had been invited to her half-century bash. I was cheered by the sight of her spray of curls and flowing clothes. She was on the borderline between plump and very plump, but she wore her curves with panache. She could walk elegantly in high heels, something not many women can do, and that I was sure I never would. She and her long-term partner spent all their holidays going on gastronomic tours of Europe and came back with eye-popping descriptions of the menus they'd sampled. I'd never heard Judi talk about dieting, or aerobics classes, or changing herself in any way. She was completely happy with herself. I couldn't imagine such a luxury.

She stood in the doorway, eyeing me. She was wearing a chiffon kaftan today, with a dark blue necklace to match.

'So, these flowers,' she said.

'Mm?'

'They're just from you.'

'Just from me.'

'And you're living at your London pad nowadays.'

'Um, yes. At the moment.'

She slid the glass door shut behind her, and leaned her back against it. 'Have you got something to tell me?'

'No.'

'Sure about that?'

I really shouldn't share intimate secrets with Judi, or with anyone in the firm. Not yet; not until I'd told the management team. So I began to lie, as I always had. It felt awful, as though I were lifting my burden again.

I stopped in mid-sentence. I was finished with lying. I put the heavy burden down.

'Actually, yes,' I said. 'There is something I should tell you.'

•

'This may disappoint you,' said Judi, as we sat in her favourite French cafe, 'but I'm not surprised.'

'You're not?'

To my astonishment she was looking faintly smug, rather than shocked. 'Completes the jigsaw. You know how there's always one piece missing, down the back of the sofa or in the Hoover bag? Drives you nuts. Well, I've just found it. I knew you weren't gay. I knew you weren't having an affair, because I've seen that many a time and I know the signs. But I was bloody sure you were hiding something fundamental about yourself. And I was right.'

'You don't think I'm mad?'

She snorted. 'Heck, no. Why would I think it's mad to want to be a woman? It's great, being a woman. Look at me! I love it. Mad *not* to want to be a woman. The more the merrier, so far as I'm concerned. Are you taking hormones?'

'Not yet.'

'Well, I am. HRT. I can tell you all about it.' She cut her *pain au chocolat* in two, and handed me half. It was a casual gesture of friendship, or even—was I imagining this?—of sisterhood. My relationship with Judi had shifted subtly in the past half-hour. She'd relaxed some kind of guard in herself. She liked me as I was. I liked that.

She took a bite of her half, and tapped the table in front of her. 'So what's the plan, Luke?'

'I'm playing this by ear. It's new territory.'

Her eyes narrowed as she chewed. Judi's a problem solver. She weighs up possibilities and finds solutions, and that was precisely what she was doing now. 'No good,' she said briskly. 'If you're going to become a woman you must have your ducks in a row. We'll have to coordinate the rollout of the new you—and we need a time frame. How long do you need?'

'Whoa! Hang on!' I cringed at the idea of coming out to colleagues and clients. Hundreds of people would be watching me take my first tottering steps as a woman, smothering laughter, making crude jokes about my genitalia. No.

'I'll have to resign,' I said.

'Rubbish! This is nothing new. I read a piece in the paper . . . yesterday's, was it? . . . anyway, it was about this really macho guy, a US Navy SEAL from the unit that carried out the final raid on Osama bin Laden. Trained killer. Beard. Tattoos. Colossal gun. He's come out as a woman. Isn't that amazing? And remember that City trader? His bank were very understanding. And now I think about it, there's an army officer in Australia. Stunning woman.'

I knew about these people, but it wasn't helping me now. Their battles were not mine. 'It might be easier for Eilish if I quietly resign,' I said. 'She's very hurt.'

'I'm sure she is, poor lass.' The line of Judi's mouth softened, and she touched my upper arm. 'Luke, listen. Your marriage has been a success. You've amassed a million good memories; but sometimes enough is enough. For richer, for poorer; for better, for worse, blah blah blah—but not necessarily till death do us part; not if you're bloody miserable. Thousands of people reach our age and want something else out of life—though, I'll grant you, what you're after is a bit . . . um, unusual. D'you know how long the average marriage lasted in the twelfth century? I'll tell you: eleven years and six months. That's because somebody always died—normally the poor woman, in childbirth. And d'you know how long the average modern marriage lasts? Take a wild guess.'

I took a guess. 'Eleven years and six months?'

'Exactly. People don't die all the time anymore, so they have to get divorced instead. You and Eilish have been together nigh on three times the national average. You've seen your children into adulthood and beyond. That's more than can be said for most parents.'

'She still believes our marriage can be salvaged.'

Judi looked sceptical. 'Just as long as you promise to throw away your satin camiknickers? I don't see how she'd ever trust you. Can't see how she'd ever fancy you again, either. It's not exactly sexy, is it?'

'I don't own any camiknickers, satin or otherwise.'

'No? Well, now I know what to get you for your birthday.'

I didn't smile. My head was filled with Eilish, with Nico, and with Rosa, who might never hear my name. I could be father and grandfather and husband. I could pretend to be those things. I needn't end my days as a lonely joke.

'Luke.' Judi leaned closer and looked me in the eye. 'If you're going to U-turn now, you'd better be bloody sure. You seriously think this genie will fit back into the bottle?'

I imagined burying Lucia deeper than ever before; burying her alive, just as she'd begun to breathe. I could almost hear her screaming. I imagined the suffocation stretching on, and on, to the end of my days.

•

I tried to phone Simon that evening. He must have installed one of those gadgets that tell you who's calling. The handset was lifted—I heard a childish voice, but faintly, as though in the background—and then put down again.

I tried again, hoping Nico had accidentally cut me off. Same thing.

Finally I got hold of Kate. She'd been to the hospital already, and was buzzing.

'She's *unbelievably* ugly,' she said fondly. 'Like a baby-shaped walnut. She's in an incubator at the moment, but you can touch her.'

'Was Nico there?'

'Yep. Being proprietorial and talking nonstop.'

I felt an ache—really, a physical ache. Nico would have taken my hand and led me to see the new arrival. 'So he's pleased with his sister?' I asked.

'He's pleased with the pedal car she's given him.'

'Did you take any photos?'

She groaned. 'Yes, but Simon doesn't want you to . . . oh, bugger Simon. Yes, I've got some on my phone. I'll send one.'

We were about to end the call when I had a thought. 'I ordered some flowers,' I said.

'Um . . . they were delivered.'

'And?'

'Simon gave them straight back to the nurse. She said she'd find a home for them.'

I was thinking about those flowers—feeling sorry for myself—when the magical photo arrived to distract me. I sat and stared at it. I suppose, really, it was just a baby in an incubator. We've all seen pictures like that before: the babies in them look vulnerable and exposed, so small as to be barely human. This one had long black lashes and curled-up toes. She was wearing a little red hat. Behind her loomed the round face of her brother, looking in with wide-eyed wonder. His hair was tousled, his nose flattened against the perspex.

I printed out the picture of my grandchildren and leaned it on my bedside table.

That night, I dreamed of a baby in a forest. It was very dark. There were wolves.

•

It was a Saturday morning, and Rosa was ten days old. I took a cup of tea back to my bedroom, smiling at the latest photographs of her and Nico. Thanks to Kate, I was amassing quite a collection. Rosa had been allowed out of the neonatal unit, and today they were taking her home. She already had her mother's determined pout. I could see that Nico was growing up, too. He'd started at school, and had a proper boy's haircut. He'd just turned five. I'd sent him a card. I hoped it had got to him.

I took a shower with soap that smelled of roses, and dressed in a calf-length skirt and pale blue jersey. My hair was growing. If I brushed it forward around my face, it looked quite feminine. Not young—a bit granny—but feminine.

The post had arrived. Letters and leaflets lay scattered on the wet doormat, next to my umbrella. While my coffee was brewing I flicked through them. Mostly advertising. All except one: a brown envelope. It had rain spots on it, and was slightly creased. I had some vague thought that it might be about my father's will, though that had all been finalised months ago.

I slid a knife under the flap and pulled out its contents.

I should have expected it. But I didn't.

She'd walked up the aisle to Mendelssohn. The church was full to bursting, its ancient air scented by flowers. The world had come to my wedding; all except Gail. Dad had bought a new suit for the occasion; Mum had bought herself several outfits. Benjamin Rose caught my eye as he came into the church, and winked. I sat in the pew near the pulpit, straightening the collar of my morning coat and checking that Toby still had the ring. Then I heard the sudden silence, the shuffling, and I knew she'd arrived.

This was it: the first moment of my new life. I was twenty-five years old, and from now on I would be whole. I was going to be the son my father wanted; the husband Eilish deserved; the father my future children needed. I made a solemn promise both to Eilish and to myself that day.

My new mother-in-law was weeping under her designer hat. Katrina French never pretended to like me much; I think she saw through me. As the music began, and Toby and I rose to our feet, he muttered in my ear: *Last chance to make a break for it, cuz.*

I didn't want to make a break for it. I wanted to see her. Unable to resist, I turned around.

She was breathtaking. There's no other word for it. She was a beautiful woman on her wedding day. It was a dazzling October morning outside, and the light from a stained-glass window tinted the lace of her dress and the ivory flowers in her hair. She looked supremely relaxed, holding her father's arm and mouthing *hello* to people as she passed them. Tom looked far more nervous than his daughter. Good old Tom; we did love him—though how he ever came to marry her mother is a mystery to me. Then she met my eye, and we both smiled.

She walked up the aisle to Mendelssohn, to stand by my side. We stood side by side for the next thirty years. Our story began in the magical light of a stained-glass window.

And what heralded its end? A damp, slightly creased brown envelope from the county court, containing a petition for divorce.

Twenty-eight

Eilish

The weeks passed. The sky became higher, the mornings sharper. The poplars in the copse were embossed with gold. When I left for work each day, Gareth's tractor was already rumbling along the rows. I like autumn, but this time the dying of the year felt melancholy. Our wedding anniversary came and went. I wept for it alone. No party. No fireworks.

Instead, the divorce ground on. Luke behaved impeccably. He returned the acknowledgement of service to the court and agreed to everything my solicitor and I wanted. In the days and weeks that passed we talked often about the practicalities of our divorce. It was a bit like arranging a funeral: you're grieving, you're denying, but you still have to choose the readings and organise a caterer. We agreed to divvy up some of the savings now and take account of it in the final settlement. We talked reasonably and sensibly, as though we were no more than business partners. And all the time my heart was tearing right across the middle. I could actually feel it. I think his was too.

He wanted news of the children. He pressed me for every tiny detail, and chuckled adoringly when I described seeing Nico kiss Rosa one day when he thought nobody was looking.

'It was a big, smacky kiss,' I said. 'Right on her nose.'

'Little chap!' After a short pause he added, 'I wish I could see them.'

'You *could* see them.'

I was blackmailing him, as I had the day Rosa was born. I knew it, even as I said it—and why not? Surely I had a right to use every weapon in my arsenal to salvage our marriage? I'd spoiled the conversation. Soon after that, we ran out of things to say.

We're resilient, us human beings. More so than we think. I kept going; I functioned. One Sunday morning in late October, I had Neil Young on the stereo and was designing a series of lesson plans. I hadn't been to church that morning. In fact, I hadn't darkened its doors for several weeks. People were becoming more insistent when asking about Luke, and I wasn't prepared to answer their questions. I hadn't told anyone but Stella that we'd separated, because . . . actually, why hadn't I? Because they would ask *why* he'd gone.

I'd made quite a bit of headway when I spotted Jim Chadwick's green MG driving by the window with its roof down.

'Chadwick!' I cried, stepping outside to greet him. I thought fleetingly of the moment I'd last opened this door to Luke; that morning back in July, when he came in soaking wet, and our world changed forever. By contrast, Jim looked confident and uncomplicated and definitely male. That was something I used to take for granted in a man.

'Is this a bad moment?' he asked.

'On the contrary, your timing is inspired. I was about to stop for coffee.'

'Oh good. I've come to drum up your support,' he said, getting out of his car. 'We have battlements to storm.'

It was cheering to see my colleague striding towards me across the gravel. I found myself admiring the laughter lines around his blue eyes, and his sandy hair, receding a little. He brought energy and honesty at a time when I needed both. I felt my spirits lift.

'Neil Young!' he exclaimed, as he stepped inside and heard the singer's reedy voice permeating the house. 'Takes me back to my misspent yoof.'

'Luke says the man's a poet.'

I made coffee while Jim explained his mission. He was dean of year nine, and wanted my alliance in his latest skirmish with the school's management. It had been triggered by a gifted but chaotic boy who could read anything, but was unable to write legibly. Jim wanted him to be allowed to use a laptop in all his classes.

'I've hit a brick wall. Wally Wallis says it'll open the floodgates,' he complained, as I pottered around the kitchen. 'He's hell-bent on screwing up this kid's education. I'm not having it. Could you assess him, and write a report that Wally can't ignore?'

'It sounds rather like dysgraphia. If I . . .' Suddenly, I felt tears crowding into my eyes. Treacherous things. I fiddled with the coffee plunger, blinking them away. 'Luke's left,' I said. 'We're in the throes of divorce.' I pressed down on the plunger, listening to Jim's silence. 'You don't take milk, do you?'

When I turned around, he was staring at me. 'I'm so sorry, Eilish.'

'Sorry, perhaps, but I doubt you're surprised. You must have been wondering by now. Everyone must be wondering. It doesn't matter. I'm fine.' I laughed at myself even as I spoke. What foolish, empty words! Why do we deny our grief?

'It *does* matter. You and Luke are an icon of conjugal bliss!'

I turned off the music and led the way through the folding doors. It was still warm enough to sit outside. We sat looking across the garden, exactly as Luke and I used to do. Charlotte's maple tree had turned a deep red. Nearby, Robert's sapling was thriving. Luke's daughter. Luke's father. It felt odd to be there with someone else, another man, knowing that Luke was gone forever.

'What happened?' asked Jim.

I began with that July morning, and told the story as best I could. Jim's characteristic energy was now channelled into listening. He leaned forward with his elbows resting on his knees, gazing at the paving stones, nodding sharply from time to time. There wasn't the flicker of a smile. No remarks about dresses. No hint that he found Luke ridiculous.

'What's especially hurtful,' I said, 'almost inconceivable, is that he's prepared to lose contact with Nico and never meet Rosa. Luke and Nico were like *this*.' I held up two fingers twined around one another. 'They're a mutual appreciation society. I just don't understand how Luke can break that bond. It's as though he's infatuated with this idea of himself as a woman.'

'Hmm.' Jim pushed a pebble around with his foot. 'Maybe it's evidence of his desperation?'

'Or—as Simon thinks—that he's a kid in a sweetshop. He wants it all, and he wants it now, and he doesn't seem to care who gets hurt. He's going to wake up one day and realise what he's lost.'

'Maybe.'

I wasn't impressed with my friend's reaction. I was the wounded wife, after all. I was the innocent one and I expected outrage on my behalf. I told him so.

'Sorry,' he said. 'We can take it as read that you are blameless. I didn't think it needed to be said.'

'But I feel stupid.' I smiled unhappily. 'I mean, how blind and gullible can you be? I shared a bed with that man for three decades.'

'It's not your fault. You know that. I know that. The gossips in the village pub and the staffroom will certainly agree. So you can take blaming yourself off your to-do list. Have you researched this problem of Luke's?'

'Of course.'

'And?'

'I'm not alone. You spot a new story in the paper every week once you start noticing. There are lawyers and accountants and prostitutes. There are famous people: a *Vogue* model called

April Ashley. Jan Morris, the writer. She was the *Times* correspondent—male—with Hillary and Tenzing when they made it up Everest. She and her wife have stayed together. Um, who else? That American whistleblower . . . Memory like a sieve at the moment, I can't remember his name.'

'Bradley Manning.'

'That's the one. There's even a clinic in London that helps children. I covered this once in training, but I've never come across it in the classroom. Have you?'

To my surprise, he nodded. 'More than once.'

'What did you do?'

'Left it to the school counsellor.' He was tapping out a drum solo on the bench with his hands. He's a restless type, is Jim. More like rapids, where Luke is deep and still.

'Actually,' he said, 'I knew someone at university.'

'Really?'

'Mm. Francis Bates. Fran. She was flamboyant, wore miniskirts. She was taking hormones. I didn't know her well. None of us did, though she was very affable. She asked us to use the feminine pronoun, which we didn't do because we were so bloody small-minded. We used to call her Frank, just to be clever. The university put her in a male hall of residence. Nowadays there are rules about that kind of thing.' Jim stopped, rubbing his cheek. 'One night she was attacked by a gang of yobs. Young, pissed people coming out of a club—girls, too—who objected to her using the female public toilets.'

'What happened?'

'They chased her onto the roof of a multistorey. Seven floors up. Baying for blood. They got her down on the ground and they all kicked her. It came out in the papers that one of them was flashing a knife around. He said he was going to finish the job. You know. Cut off her genitals. Later, he claimed that he never really meant to mutilate anyone, just to teach "that pervert" a lesson. Anyway, we'll never know, because someone was monitoring the CCTV cameras and the police turned up.'

'That was lucky. Was Fran badly hurt?'

Jim reached down between his feet to gather a handful of pebbles. He began to throw them, steadily, one by one. He was aiming at an empty flower pot. Every time he hit the pot, his pebble bounced off with a soft *ting*.

'A black eye, and nasty bruising. A week later she climbed the stairs, the same route they'd chased her, right to the top of the same car park. She took a takeaway coffee and a Mars bar with her. She loved Mars bars. She sat down on the parapet and wrote a letter to her parents. Several people saw her writing. Nobody spoke to her. She ate her Mars, drank her coffee.' Another pebble. *Ting.* 'Then she jumped.'

I'd seen it coming, but still I gasped. 'Seven floors up!'

'Yep.' *Ting.* 'Killed instantly.' *Ting.* 'You know, Eilish, the nastiest, most depressing aspect of the whole business was that *nobody cared.* Sensation! Gossip! A weird cross-dresser got turned to pizza in a car park. Nobody shed a single tear. Nobody, including me, even asked about the funeral. Everyone seemed to think she'd brought it on herself. The jokes began on campus within two hours. *How d'you like your pizza, thin crust or tranny?*'

'You were young.'

'It wasn't because we were young. It was because we didn't see Fran as a person. She was a caricature. It was a lot easier to joke about her death than it was to question the part we'd all played in it.'

'It wasn't you who chased him with a knife.'

Jim's next pebble missed the pot. 'Why was she alone that night? I never knocked on her door and invited her along to the bar with the rest of us. I met her parents when they came to collect her things. They wanted to talk about her. I've never, before or since, seen two such shattered people. That's when it finally dawned on my stupid, ignorant twenty-year-old brain that Fran was someone's child. She was loved.'

He threw down the rest of the pebbles in a handful. They scattered across the paving stones.

'What d'you think made Fran want to be a woman?' I asked.

'I don't know, and I don't really care. There's no single blueprint for a human being. If there was, you'd be out of a job. This is what Wally can't understand.'

'Wally can't see beyond his own ego,' I said, relieved that the conversation was back on the safe ground of school politics; Fran's story had unsettled me. The shortcomings of our headmaster continued to be a shared passion, and we were soon talking shop. Jim seemed in no hurry to leave, and I was very glad of his company, so I suggested a stroll across the fields. Casino appeared from Luke's carpentry shed and fell in, trotting along beside us. He likes to go for a walk.

That walk was a tonic for me. We wandered all the way to the farmyard and back, talking about all kinds of things. I felt as though I were having a holiday from my failure as a wife. We were on our way back when Jim came out with something astonishing.

'I've been very slightly in love with you for a long time,' he said as we crossed the last stile. 'I think you know that.'

I was speechless. It's one thing to flirt with a colleague, quite another to be fighting off declarations. I'd forgotten how it felt to be desired by someone other than Luke. Then again, despite the toe-curling awkwardness, I felt a bubbling champagne rush of pleasure. There's a teenager in all of us, and mine was blushing.

'It's all right,' he said. 'You don't have to knee me in the balls. I'm going to leave now. I won't do anything embarrassing.'

'I think you just have.'

'Better get used to it. When the news comes out that you're separated, you're going to be fighting them off. Men you've known as friends and colleagues will look at you differently. Wally Wallis is going to be a royal pain in the backside.'

'Wally? He's not interested in me!'

'Ha! Believe me, I know how it works. I've been through the divorce machine myself.'

'So you're getting in before the rush?'

'Precisely.'

'I'm flattered.'

We'd arrived at his car. 'Thanks for coming around,' I said as he opened the door. 'And don't worry about your student. We'll have him using a laptop in no time.'

Autumn sunlight has a special brilliance. It lit up Jim's eyes, with their fan of smile lines. I felt the old spark, the fizz of possibilities.

'I just wanted you to know,' he said.

Casino and I watched him drive away. I'll admit it: I was smiling. After all, I'm only human.

•

Later that week—thirty years and seventeen days after we married—a judge in Oxford pronounced decree nisi. We were halfway to divorce. Neither Luke nor I was there to hear it. Our case was read out as one of a long list of failed unions. Production-line divorce. My marriage was in its last gasps.

Twenty-nine

Luke

It was like landing in the middle of a sitcom. The coffee was dreadful, but the armchairs were comfortable. I'd never been to a support group before; I didn't think of myself as that kind of person. I was in danger of giggling, out of sheer nerves.

It was Usha Sharma's idea. If she and I had been stuck on a desert island together, one of us would have built a raft very quickly; but as a counsellor she did me good. I'd arrived in her room all wound up, and spent our session talking about the decree nisi. She asked me about what she called my 'transsexual community' and 'support networks', as though my life were a social whirl.

'What community? I don't know anyone like me,' I protested. 'Only online. Wish I did. D'you want me to be visiting clubs in Soho or somewhere?'

'Hmm. Perhaps not. They can be quite, um, well . . . let's just say I don't think you are their target customer. But there are some groups. Hang on.' She swung around to her computer, printed out three addresses and gave them to me. The most convenient was the parish lounge of a church in Barking, once a week. The Jenny Marsden Trust.

'It's a peer support group,' Usha said. 'People at every stage of transition. Why not give it a try?'

'What do I wear? Will they throw me out if I don't turn up cross-dressed?'

'There are no dress codes.'

'As a male I feel like a fraud. As a woman on the tube, I'll probably get beaten up.'

'Well. What are your options?' Usha sat with one raised eyebrow, waiting for me to answer my own question. She had this obsession with me finding my own solutions. It was irritating, because sometimes I just wanted information. I daydreamed occasionally about getting revenge: she'd come into Bannermans and ask me for urgent legal advice on some corporate matter—not likely, I know—and I'd sit back and smile enigmatically, like the Sphinx, and say, 'Well now, Usha. Let's unpack that, shall we? What are your options?'

'All right,' I conceded huffily. 'Perhaps there's a middle course.'

At four o'clock the following Wednesday, I was on my way to Barking. In the end I'd settled on black trousers, a silk blouse and my mulberry jacket. I kept my head down on the tube and didn't notice anyone staring at me. Another milestone.

According to the map, the place wasn't far from the station. Yes, there it was—a brick-built church squashed in among jumbled housing and an Italian restaurant. A door at one end stood open. I read a board propped up against the wall: *Jenny Marsden group*. My steps faltered; then I scurried right past. I couldn't do it. I couldn't walk into that place, and meet a bunch of strangers, and try to be one of them. My limbs felt shaky, so I sat down on a low wall.

It was one of those times when I felt too tired to go on. I missed Eilish. I missed being able to walk down the street or travel on the tube without fear. I felt panic, deep in my chest, and had to shut my eyes and mouth to stop it from breaking out in a great yell.

I didn't hear the footsteps.

'Hi,' said a voice.

I looked up quickly, brushing my eyes on my sleeve. Jesus was standing there. Well, he looked like the Jesus you see in children's picture books. He was a young man, thin as a breadstick, with a wispy beard and soulful eyes. He was smiling gently at me. I half expected him to hold out his hands and show me the wounds. Perhaps that meant I was Doubting Thomas.

'I'm Neil,' he said. His accent was East London, rather than first-century Palestine. 'Were you looking for the Jenny Marsden group?'

'I was, but I've just remembered . . .' I began to stutter, racking my brains for some excuse to run away. 'I've just remembered this appointment . . . Okay. Yes, I was.'

'You've found us. Come on in.'

It was impossible to refuse. He led me back along the street, chatting all the way. He wondered whether I might be Lucia. He'd read my email. People often missed the place. They needed a bigger sign.

The parish lounge had been partitioned off from the body of the church, carpeted and given a false ceiling. I gathered, from all the crayoned pictures on the walls, that a Sunday school met there. People stood around in small groups, and I heard a murmur of conversation.

'What's your poison?' asked Neil, stopping by a hatch into a kitchen. 'Coffee? Right.'

'Who was Jenny Marsden?' I asked.

He pointed to a glossy photograph on one of the noticeboards: a smiling girl wearing a mortar board and academic gown. It was the sort of graduation photo that people display proudly on their mantelpieces and Facebook profiles. 'Jenny was a research scientist,' he said, handing me a mug. 'She was also a trans woman. She took her own life.'

'When?'

'Back in the nineties. Her family didn't want anyone else to feel as isolated as she did, so they set up the trust in her memory.'

I looked again at the picture. Jenny had curly hair and apple cheeks. She didn't look despairing.

'It's easy to smile, isn't it?' said Neil. 'When people are watching you.'

'True.'

'You're welcome to come along on the twentieth of November. That's the Transgender Day of Remembrance. We light a candle for Jenny as well as the others.'

I'd had no idea such a day existed, and made a mental note to look it up; but I didn't have time to ask more because Neil was steering me across the room. 'I'd like you to meet Chloe,' he was saying. 'She's here today for the first time, like you, and she's a bit nervous. In fact, she accidentally walked straight past, too.'

Seconds later, I found myself face to face with a young warrior princess, albeit one sporting a leather miniskirt and cut-off top. She was standing awkwardly holding a glass mug, though she should have been driving a chariot.

'Chloe,' said Neil. 'Meet Lucia. This is her first visit as well.'

Chloe's features melted into a wide and artless smile. She was a beautiful girl; tall—strikingly tall—with dramatic features, a bronze complexion and long, braided hair.

'Hi,' she said. 'So you're another new kid on the block.' It was a deep voice, unmistakably male. For a moment I was tongue-tied. I'd lived with gender dysphoria all my life but never knowingly spoken to a real-life trans woman before, let alone one in a miniskirt. I wanted to scuttle outside, leap into a taxi and hightail it back to the flat. This was a world outside of my experience.

Hypocrite! I scolded myself. *Snob!*

I wasn't sure of the etiquette. Should I shake Chloe's hand, or would that give me away as a stuffy old trout: white, middle-aged and middle-class? She was wearing perspex platform shoes. Dear God, I thought, why does someone with legs like that need platforms? There was a generation gap even with us outcasts.

Chloe didn't seem to notice my confusion. She was happy

to talk; all I had to do was listen, and that suited me. Within a couple of minutes Neil had moved on, leaving us deep in conversation. Chloe had a habit of laughing uproariously when she got to the most painful parts of her story. It was unsettling. She told me that she was twenty-two, and from a town near Manchester. She'd started taking hormones when she was fourteen, in an attempt to stop her adolescence in its tracks.

'Fourteen?' I was surprised. 'So . . . were you at the children's clinic?'

'The where? Oh, the kids' place! D'you think my mum would let them anywhere near me? No!' Laughter. 'I bought the stuff myself. Internet.'

I was shocked at the idea of a fourteen-year-old ordering hormones on the black market and experimenting alone. I was so rattled that I didn't think before I asked my next question; it was a stupid mistake. I asked her what she did for a living.

'I'm a working girl.' She said it carelessly, assuming I'd understand. When I didn't, she dissolved into more laughter. 'There are guys out there who'll pay a premium for what I've got. I'm a bit of a niche market.'

'Oh!' I was desperately trying not to look scandalised. 'I see. At least, I think I see. That must be . . . um, actually, I've no idea what that must be like.'

For once she didn't laugh. She shrugged, and her eyes were blank. 'Pays the bills,' she said. 'I've got qualifications, just can't get a better job.'

'What's your training?'

'Computing, catering . . . I used to be duty manager in a restaurant. Anyway, that's enough about my boring life! How about you? How do you pay your bills?'

This vibrant young woman had just revealed that she was a prostitute. As life stories go, it was a hard act to follow. I had to confess that I was a city solicitor and spent most of my days helping multinationals to push vast sums of money around. I've never felt so square. Chloe lit up, however, because her cousin was a legal executive. She and I were getting on like a house on fire when Neil called the group together. My new friend stuck to me like glue, folding her long legs into the chair next to mine and whispering that she didn't know anyone. I felt protective.

We were a mixed assortment of human beings: men, women, people whose place on the gender continuum was impossible to categorise. To my astonishment, it turned out that Neil had begun life as a girl. There were twelve of us in all, sitting in a circle. That's when I felt the bubbles of nervous laughter inside me. I wished Eilish were there. Perhaps I could phone afterwards and tell her about it? No, perhaps not.

They didn't make me say anything, so I said very little beyond introducing myself. Other people talked about their week; about their challenges and triumphs. One person was upset about a speeding ticket, another was worried about her father's dementia. A girl called Joanne had at last received her new birth certificate, and brought along birthday cake to celebrate.

When the meeting broke up, Chloe left with me and we walked together to the tube station. I noticed some sidelong glances. I suppose we were a bizarre duo: a glamorous young Amazon in perspex heels, striding beside a middle-aged androgynous creature wearing a blue silk blouse. Chloe was Kate's age, and yet she'd already faced down the world. I wished I'd had her mettle when I was young. We chatted as we walked. She said she was almost two years into her RLE. Ah yes, the Real Life Experience.

'How's it going?' I asked.

'Oh. My. God.' Chloe made an anguished face. 'You know.'

'I don't, actually. I haven't done it.'

'It got a lot easier once I had help with my hormones. But will my body behave? No, it won't! Those ole levels are still up and down like a kangaroo. I've had my moments.' She held up crossed fingers. 'But I'm getting there.'

'What brought you to London?'

'Um, well, to be honest, my home town got a bit small. I lost my job. They said it was a redundancy but . . . you know.

And my family aren't talking to me. My mum reckons I'm dead to her.' She chuckled fondly, as though her mother was terribly witty. 'My brother said he'd make sure I was *really* dead if he saw me again.'

She told me she'd been for an interview the day before. It was at a cafe that was looking for a manager. Right up her alley; she could have done it standing on her head. I asked how it had gone, and she shrugged. 'As soon as they saw me they said they had somebody else in mind. That's okay. No problem. Something will come up.'

We walked on. I imagined the cafe owner hearing Chloe's deep voice and thinking, *No way.* I felt angry for my new young friend. My mind was skimming across the employment laws, wondering if she should take a stand.

'It's okay. If they don't want me, I don't want to be there,' she said, as though she'd read my thoughts. 'I can almost pass, most of the time. I just need to work on my voice.'

'You certainly can pass. I don't know if I'll ever be able to.'

She looked me up and down with a critical eye. ''Course you will! You've got the face for it. You're not too tall. Just wait till you've been on hormones for a while, and get boobs.'

'I can't even walk right.'

She took my arm and danced me down the street. She seemed hopeful and vital and oddly naive. I hated to think of her plying her trade.

'Watch and learn,' she said, laughing. 'Watch and learn.'

Thirty

Eilish

November the tenth was my birthday. Jim Chadwick buttonholed me at school, and asked if he could take me out for dinner. I was able to say no without having to search my conscience, because Carmela—such a thoughtful daughter-in-law—had invited me to London to spend the night with them.

Jim was undeterred. 'How about some other time? Absolutely no strings attached. I promise.'

'Not for a couple of weeks, anyway. I've got parent meetings and reports and the school play.' I was making excuses; putting off the decision.

He grinned. 'Good enough for me,' he said, before pelting away to stop a violent brawl in the quad. I could hear him yelling, 'Break it up! C'mon, break it up! Haven't you lads heard of the Queensberry Rules?'

A parcel from Luke arrived on my birthday. I opened it to find emerald earrings glowing on a velvet cushion. They matched my engagement ring. What was the proper response to such a gift from the man I was divorcing? Should I mark the parcel *return to sender* and shove it in the nearest post box? Should I give it to charity?

I did neither. Instead, I stood in front of the bedroom mirror and slid them into my ears. They were single stones set in gold, and truly beautiful. Luke had chosen well. He always did have good taste. I closed my eyes and allowed myself to imagine that he was standing very close behind me. We were still happy, still together, still off to Tuscany next year.

I was deep in this daydream when the phone rang. Talk of the devil.

'Sorry to bother you,' said Luke. 'Happy birthday.'

I never admitted it to him, I barely admitted it even to myself, but I felt warmer when I heard his voice. You can't just drop a friendship like ours into the recycling bin.

I thanked him for the earrings. 'They're perfect,' I said. 'Though I've a feeling my solicitor would disapprove. We're supposed to be dividing our assets, not giving more of them to each other.'

He asked about work, and I fumed about the size of Walter's ego, which was in inverse proportion to his competence. Luke was worried about the Rayburn—did it need servicing? Was the house warm enough? And how were the grandchildren?

Once we'd covered all these topics, there was a long pause. Neither of us wanted the conversation to end. This can't go on, I thought. I have to understand his new world. If I don't do that, I can't even be his friend. I took a breath.

'So,' I said. 'What's happening about your . . . gender problems?'

He sounded pleased, but wary. 'You don't really want to know.'

'I think I'd better. It's probably time my head came out of the sand.'

He talked; slowly at first, hesitantly, as though afraid I'd slam down the phone. He'd been to a gender clinic but had taken no hormones yet. He was also seeing a counsellor, though he wasn't sure why.

'That's good,' I said. 'You've got professional help.'

'The further down this road I go, the more I feel as though I'm coming home. Do you know what I did last week? Well, of course you don't know.' He gave a small, nervous laugh. 'I'm going gaga.'

I sighed. 'All right. What did you do last week?'

'I went to a group. A peer support group. I met people I never knew existed.'

He was obviously bursting to tell me about it. As he talked, I was struck by the animation in his voice. The old Luke never used to bubble over with news; he was reticent and careful. The new Luke was forging a new life. He'd taken the tube to Barking and gone into the community room of a church, a room filled with strangers. He'd befriended a transsexual prostitute from Manchester. He used other words for it (*trans woman*, *escort*) but we both knew what he meant.

'What's, um, he or she like?' I asked, genuinely curious.

'Her name is Chloe. She's brave. Bright, I think. She's also vulnerable, despite towering over me at six foot two. She's almost exactly Kate's age.'

'How sad. She's got no future, has she?'

'I hope you're wrong about that. Here's something that surprised me . . . On the twentieth of November, they're all meeting up for a candlelight vigil to mark—this is extraordinary, Eilish, I didn't even know this existed—to mark the annual Transgender Day of Remembrance. It's held all over the world, to remember everyone who's been murdered because they're trans.'

'Actually murdered?' This was a new worry; it hadn't occurred to me. 'Are you safe?'

'Oh, I think so. I'm too old and ugly to attract any attention.'

I was talking to Luke; and yet it wasn't quite Luke. This person was . . . not exactly happy, he was too anxious for that, but . . . *hopeful.* Yes, that was it. There was a light at the end of his tunnel. It was heartbreaking, and yet intriguing.

I heard a knock on the kitchen doors downstairs, and Stella's voice, calling, 'Yoo-hoo, where's the birthday girl?'

Luke laughed. 'I heard that all the way from London! You'd better go. Give Stella my love.'

'Thanks for these lovely earrings,' I said.

'Happy birthday, my darling.'

•

That afternoon, I babysat Nico. We got out his Lego. He built a spaceship, flew it around—*whoosh!*—and carefully landed. Then he stopped playing. He just sat and looked at the ship. He was mouthing words silently to himself.

'What are you thinking about, monkey?' I asked.

'Thinking about a wooden plane. Is Grandpa home again?'

I didn't expect it. Not coming out, just like that.

'He isn't,' I said.

'Is he in the little house? The one with a door under the ground?'

'Yes.' I swallowed, making a supreme effort to keep my voice light. 'Yes. He's been busy at work, and the door-under-ground house is handy for his work.'

'He should be at *your* house.' His brow was furrowed. I stood up, brushing down my trousers as I wondered how best to distract him.

'Daddy shouted at Grandpa,' he said.

'Shall we go out into the garden?'

He picked up the spaceship and flew it through the air in front of him, whispering *Whoosh*. 'Is Grandpa dead?'

'No, darling, he's not dead. He's—he's—' My throat closed up. Yes, I thought, Grandpa is dead, in a way. Or at least dying. He's never going to come back to us.

'Whoosh. Whoooosh. We were going to make a plane out of wood. In his shed. He promised.'

'I'll tell him.'

'You'll tell him we have to make a plane?'

I nodded and smiled. I was thinking that perhaps Luke could come back to Smith's Barn for a day, and Nico could come too. Why not? Surely Simon would agree, if I offered to be present at all times. I imagined Luke back at home, making a plane with

Nico. It was such a happy idea. They could potter about in the shed. I could bring them cups of tea and juice. It would be just pretending, but it would be like old times.

Nico was energised; he jumped up and ran across to the telephone. 'Shall we phone and tell him? You dial the number, please, Granny, and I will talk.'

'He'll be . . .' I shook my head. 'We have to ask your dad and mum.'

His face crumpled. I ran over to him, picked him up and squeezed him tight. 'Don't cry! Grandpa will make your plane with you,' I said. 'I promise.'

•

'Absolutely not,' said Simon.

'But if—'

'Not happening. Please drop the subject.'

We were sitting at the breakfast bar in their kitchen, eating paella Carmela had rustled up. Simon had arrived home later than expected, via the pub ('just a couple of drinks'), and was now knocking back prosecco at a rate of knots. Carmela looked dog-tired but refused any help. Nico was in bed, Rosa asleep in her carrycot in a corner of the kitchen. She was a stunner, my little granddaughter; still the size of a newborn baby, with olive skin and cherry-red lips. Kate had joined us too. She seemed rather smitten with her new niece, which amused me because she'd never before—at any age, or any stage—shown the slightest interest in babies, or kittens, or ponies. She kept taking photographs of Rosa.

'Simon,' I said sternly—he might be almost thirty, but he was my son and I wasn't going to be bullied. 'Let me finish my sentence. I just thought Luke could come to my place for the day. Obviously he'd have to promise to . . . you know. Be male. Nico can stay over with me.'

'Nico asks about Luke all the time,' said Carmela. 'But I'm afraid it's not going to happen.'

Kate scowled. 'Why not? Because Simon can't behave like an adult?'

Simon wasn't sober, and he was struggling to stay calm under fire. I knew the signs; his jaw was tight. 'What d'you suggest, Miss Cleverclogs? D'you want Nico and Rosa to grow up with a drag queen for a role model? What are they supposed to tell their schoolmates?'

'God, you're a pompous douchebag,' retorted Kate. 'Is this about what's best for your kids, or is it really about punishing poor Dad?'

Simon looked as though he could cheerfully strangle his sister, which was nothing new. They'd begun arguing when Kate was two, and there haven't been many ceasefires since then. Still, I think they love one another. I hope they do.

'It'll be very hard on Nico if Luke simply disappears from his life,' I ventured.

'Mum, think about the practicalities,' Simon said, refilling our glasses. 'Let's assume Dad goes ahead as planned: takes hormones, grows breasts, has his bits cut off, goes the whole way. People do. I know they do. Nico and Rosa are not—repeat *not*—going to have to deal with that kind of . . . weirdness. How do you propose to explain to Nico that Grandpa is a lady boy?'

'Well,' said Kate, 'you could just tell him the truth. He'll take it in his stride.'

'Shut up.'

She didn't shut up. 'So you'd rather cut Dad out altogether? Seriously—you're going to be that bigoted?'

I saw Carmela touch her husband's shoulder, flashing Kate a warning glance. 'We have to decide whether we're happy about our children having a transsexual person in their lives. There is a stigma, Kate. And Simon feels that the answer is no.'

Transsexual. I didn't like the word. It conjured images of *The Rocky Horror Picture Show*. Fishnet tights. Transylvania.

'If Luke has a lovely day with Nico,' I suggested, 'he might change his mind.'

'You can't use Nico as bait,' said Simon, who'd begun slamming plates into the dishwasher.

'No! Not bait. Just a reminder of what family life is all about; what he's missing.'

'You'd trust him again? I wouldn't. Come on, Mum. He's history. Find yourself somebody else.'

I was shocked into silence. Simon's words sounded too final. Mercifully, Rosa was woken by the crashing plates and began to wail, providing a distraction. I slipped away to the bathroom and stood with my hands on the basin, facing my imperfections in the mirror. My eyes weren't as clear as they used to be, and when did those bitter-old-bag lines appear beside my mouth? I wasn't young anymore, but Luke didn't mind. I'd always relied on that. He and I were supposed to grow old together.

Come home, Luke, I whispered. *Just come home.*

My handbag was on the chest in the hall. I took out my phone as I passed, and saw that I'd missed two calls. One was from Luke. The other was from Jim. I didn't call either of them back.

Thirty-one

Luke

London is at its glittering, magical best in the run-up to Christmas, with late-night shopping under cascades of lights, and trees glimpsed through open curtains.

But, by golly, it can be lonely. The only events on my social calendar were Wednesday afternoons with the Jenny Marsden group—and I rarely had time to get to that—and the entertaining of Bannermans clients. Eilish and I had plenty of friends in London but I wasn't ready to face their questions, so I avoided them all. Sometimes as I set off for work in the freezing pre-dawn, I fantasised about taking a train home and walking into the house as though nothing had happened. I imagined the pond lying very still under a mist. I imagined Eilish alone in our bedroom, waking up and beginning a new day. Perhaps she wouldn't be happy to see me.

There were other moments, though, times when I felt a tremendous sense of hope. Week by week, shyly, Lucia was taking over and becoming me—or perhaps I was becoming her. I'd begun seeing a speech therapist, who thought we could do a lot towards feminising my voice. He gave me exercises to practise, using a dictaphone so that I could hear myself.

'Listen carefully when you're out and about,' he said. 'There's a pitch overlap between the sexes. Find that, and you've found the key.' We had a long discussion about the melody of different voices. I found it truly fascinating, but I smiled to myself as I imagined what Kate's reaction would be (*Men and women use different language? Women's voices are more sing-song? Oh, for frig's sake! What utter patriarchal patronising bollocks*).

Far more frightening was the issue of my beard. I don't enjoy pain; who does? But I took my courage into my hands and booked myself into a clinic for laser treatment. The grim-faced woman who wielded the laser said it would take about a year to get rid of my facial hair: at least eight sessions, six or more weeks apart, and maybe electrolysis after that, and she couldn't guarantee that that would be the end of it. Laser treatment is meant to be quicker and less painful than electrolysis, but—believe me—it's screaming torture. The first session had me gritting my teeth and breathing through the pain. I had to go home and have a stiff drink afterwards, and I felt pretty traumatised. Had I really lifted my chin and let that psychopath of a woman inflict this upon me? I was halfway through a glass of whisky before I felt steady enough to phone Chloe. She'd understand what I'd just gone through.

'Hi there, Lucia!' she cried when she heard my voice. 'What's happening?'

I told her about the torture, and she laughed merrily. 'It's okay, it gets better. Third or fourth time you'll have less to take off, and then you'll look in the mirror, and *then* you'll feel good.'

'Third or fourth? I don't know if I can go back and do it again, even once.'

'Oh yes, you can! No pain, no gain. Take a couple of ibuprofen half an hour before, and a good old swallow of Jim Beam.'

She told me she'd had a phone call from her mother—a short one, just to ask for a cousin's address—but still, a call. She seemed very buoyed by this.

'Hey,' she added, 'you're doing well with the voice.'

I knew she couldn't possibly afford a speech therapist—she

sometimes struggled even to pay her rent—so I passed on everything I'd learned. She wanted to know if I'd come out at work yet, and thought it hilarious when I groaned and said I certainly had not and that I thought I'd rather retire.

'All those posh lawyers,' she said. 'You'll make their day!'

'Five hundred people work in our firm. How can I face five hundred people?'

She was chuckling away. 'And every one of them wondering if you're going to have your nuts cut off! Oh my Lord, Lucia, they'll cross their legs when you walk by.'

By the time the call ended, I was smiling.

Eilish

I was crammed into my room in the prefabricated block with two malodorous year tens. They were clearly counting down the seconds until the final bell of the week. So was I.

One of them was texting under the table while I turned a blind eye. The Christmas term was coming to an end, after all, and concentration levels were dropping all round. The other was choosing, from the box I'd given him, a book to take home. I noticed a face at the window, and waved. Jim Chadwick. He saw I was busy and moved away, but I was pretty sure he'd wait until the end of the lesson.

'Got one, miss,' said the boy with the books. He was holding out a paperback with a picture of a soldier on the front, bristling with bandoliers and murderous weapons. He often picked that one. He loved a bit of gore.

'You've read that already, Zane. About five times. But that's okay, you can borrow it again. You've done really good work today. Jamie, who are you texting?'

'Santa,' Jamie replied promptly. 'He says he's got his sleigh parked outside.'

The bell rang while I was deciding whether to laugh or hand out a detention.

'Go on,' I said. 'Have a good weekend. Say hi to Santa from me.'

As they opened the door they almost ran into Jim.

'What're you reading, Zane?' he asked, holding out his hand for the book. 'Ah. *Crack Shot*. Nice one.'

The two boys set off for freedom, joining a great throng that milled across the quad. Jim stepped into my room and closed the door behind him.

'It's Friday,' he said, folding his arms.

'Yes. I know that, Jim.'

'Dinner at The Lock, tonight?'

'Tonight? Um . . .'

He sat down in the chair Zane had just vacated. 'Yes, you can. I know for a fact that you were meant to be helping with a rehearsal for the school play this evening. I know for a fact that the rehearsal has just been cancelled. So, unless you've got yourself another date in the past hour, you're unexpectedly free.'

I could get all dressed up, and go to a gorgeous restaurant by the river. I could spend the evening laughing with Jim, sharing a bottle of wine, enjoying adult conversation of a kind I craved, especially since Kate had left. *And let's face it*, said the wicked floozy inside me, *he's easy on the eye.*

But Luke.

He walked away. You owe him nothing.

That's true.

Don't risk it, counselled the prude in me. *Dinner doesn't come for free. You go to The Lock, the next minute he's pouncing on you in some taxi, and then you're back at his place, taking off your clothes. Nobody but Luke's seen you naked in thirty years! Do you really want to show those stretch marks?*

'I promise you,' said Jim, who seemed to be a mind-reader. 'Not a single string. I'll behave impeccably. Unless you don't.'

I was teetering at the top of a fairground ride, fearing to launch myself onto the crazy loops and whoops of the roller-coaster.

I was being asked on a date. An actual date, with a man I liked very much.

Luke's gone. He didn't love you enough.

'All right,' I said.

•

Was the blue and white top a mistake? *Avoid horizontal stripes at all costs*, my mother used to say. *They'll make you look big, Eilish; and when I say big, I mean fat.* On this occasion she was wrong, because I seemed to have the opposite problem. I'd lost weight since Luke left. The figure in the mirror looked like a bustless bag lady in those unforgiving stripes.

I hadn't got dolled up in months; I was out of practice, couldn't even find a pair of tights without a hole in them. It was daunting but—I had to admit—fun.

Discarding the stripes, I tried on my little black dress. *You can't go wrong with a little black dress*; that's my mother's wisdom again. It looked good, but . . . no. Luke loved that dress. He helped me choose it. I couldn't date another man in a dress Luke chose. I took it off.

Trousers? No, too dowdy. This little skirt? No! Much too short.

What does a fifty-something almost-divorcee wear on a date?

'This is ridiculous,' I said out loud. 'Stop pratting about, Eilish Livingstone! It's just Jim. It's not a visit to Buckingham Palace.'

In the end, I plumped for the black dress because nothing else worked so well. Then I caught myself searching through my drawers for a matching lace bra and knickers. The prude in my head was scandalised. *What d'you think you're up to? Who's going to see them?* Nobody was going to see them. All the same, best to be colour-coordinated. Ah, here they were. They still fitted perfectly.

Kate phoned as I was blow-drying my hair. She wondered if she'd left a particular book in her room; her tutor wanted it back. I looked and found it, and promised to post it.

'Owen asked to come round,' she said gloomily. 'Says he wants to talk.'

I was pleased she was confiding in me. Kate and I had broken through some barriers in those weeks when she lived back at home, just after our world had imploded. There was more honesty between us now than I could ever remember. Perhaps she saw me as more human and fallible; for my part, I'd learned that she was an adult.

'Did you say yes?' I asked now.

'Mm. I'm meeting him at eight, in the local. Can't bring him back here—Mathis and John would have a fit. The thing is, Mum . . . I've still got a soft spot for the guy. But if we get back together, I know where we'll end up.'

'Do you want my advice? Feel free to ignore it.'

'All advice gratefully received.'

'Okay.' I was struggling to put in earrings with one hand, but gave up and sat down on the bed. 'I don't think Owen's the man for you.'

'Really? I thought you approved of him.'

'I was being polite. Let's face it, Kate: he's a wimp and you're not. If I've learned one thing from this disaster with Dad, it's that it's best to be honest right from the start. Otherwise there's just a whole lot of misery in store.'

There was a brief silence. I was afraid I'd annoyed her.

'Okay,' she said. 'You're bang on. There's no future in it, and I'll have to tell him so. He can be very persuasive, though. If he turns on his lost-boy routine . . .'

'I think you'd better stay sober, and in a public place. And if I were you, I wouldn't invite him in for coffee—especially if Mathis and John aren't in. No coffee, no matter what.'

'Good plan.'

I asked about an essay she was writing—it sounded fascinating, actually, made me wish I'd been an archaeologist—and we talked for a time, but I had one eye on the clock. At seven-thirty I said I had to go. She was instantly curious.

'Go?' she echoed. 'Go where?'

I had no choice. I had to tell her. As I'd expected, the news had quite an effect. I could almost hear her falling off her chair.

'*Mr Chadders*?' She gasped, caught somewhere between hysterical mirth and revulsion. 'Sorry . . . sorry . . . let's just get this straight. My old science teacher and my mother are going out on a . . . on a . . . Oh, Lordy Lordy!'

'It's not a date,' I declared tartly. 'It's just two colleagues meeting up out of the work environment. We'll probably talk about education all evening.'

'Yeah, and work colleagues never hook up. What are you wearing?'

'Just a, um, a dress.'

'You're wearing that black lacy thing, aren't you, Mum?'

How the hell does she know that?

'The Lock is only a tarted-up pub,' I said. 'I'm meeting an old friend in a pub. Just as you are, in fact. That's all. I've insisted on driving myself, so I won't be drinking.'

'It's a date, Mum. Face facts. The Lock's a very romantic spot, especially at night.'

I felt anxious. Perhaps I was making a mistake. 'Do you think I shouldn't go?'

She'd stopped laughing. 'No, no. I'm sorry. Of course you should go. I've got a lot of time for old Chadders, one of the best teachers I ever had. Quite hot too, in a lab coat and Bunsen burner sort of way. And now it's my turn to hand out advice. Feel free to ignore it.'

'Let's hear it.' I was looking under the dressing table for my handbag. I'd be late if I didn't get a move on.

'Stay sober,' she said. 'And in a public place. And don't invite him in for coffee—'

We finished the sentence in chorus.

'No matter what.'

Luke

I locked the front door of the flat with the Yale, and then with the deadlock, and then I bolted it. Simon's visit had made me wary.

Out on the streets, the weekend had begun. I heard the footsteps of children on their way home from school, galloping along the pavement, whooping at one another. I heard the tapping of a stick and knew it was the old man who lived on the top floor. A little later I heard female voices, and caught a glimpse of court shoes.

But I was in my own world. I was about to do something terrifying and wonderful.

In my bedroom, I pressed the first dose out of their packets and laid them in a careful row on top of the chest of drawers. I'd finally been given the green light to begin hormone therapy. The endocrinologist had calculated my dose of female hormones, which would send the signal to my body that I was indeed a woman; then there were antiandrogens to suppress the testosterone and turn off the male tap. A double whammy. Don't expect miracles, they'd all warned me; it's hard to get this right. There will be a lot of finetuning.

I viewed the pills with fearful reverence. I wouldn't turn into a page three girl overnight; at first the war would be fought at a cellular level. Yet this was the first real physical step. Over weeks and months my body really would change: I'd become more and more of a woman; less and less of a man. Imagine that.

This was it. I was about to cross the Rubicon.

Or was I?

I took off Luke's suit and shirt and tie, and became Lucia. That made me feel stronger. For a long time I stood absolutely still, looking at those pills. I picked up the glass of water, and raised my eyebrows at the person in the mirror.

'Sure, now?' I said aloud. 'Is this really what you want?'

The last time I'd tried to change myself physically, I was three years old. My mother and Janey's mother put us in the bath together. I remember we had a new kitten, a soft tortoiseshell who regarded the entire world as a toy. I looked at Janey as we blew soap bubbles, and spotted something I'd never noticed before.

'Janey's hurt herself,' I said to Mum. 'She's got no willy. Where's she put it?'

The two mothers fell about laughing. They kept trying to control themselves, then catching each other's eye and bursting out again. Janey's mum was actually crying with the hilarity of it all.

'She's not hurt!' she gasped, wiping her eyes. 'She's a girl, you silly peanut. Girls don't have willies. They have tuppences.'

I had no idea what this meant, but I didn't want them to laugh at me anymore. We got out of the bath and into our nightclothes. I was truly amazed by the news. So it wasn't Janey who was faulty, it was me. I envied her. I wanted to have a tuppence. Then I had a good idea.

A few minutes later, when everyone else was playing with the kitten in the sitting room, I trotted away and into the kitchen. I had to climb on a chair to get to the knife block. I chose the biggest one, slid it out of the block and carefully lowered myself from the chair. Then I took off my pyjama bottoms and sat cross-legged on the floor. I was frightened that this was going to hurt but I was very, very determined. I was going to be the same as Janey.

I don't know what would have happened if my mother hadn't walked in. Fortunately I was ineffectual with a knife, and I wasn't nearly as brave as I thought I was; but Mum kept it razor sharp and I'd managed to break the skin. It hurt far more than I'd expected, and I was howling with the pain and the terror of seeing so much blood. Poor Mum. I still remember her horrified shrieks, and Janey's mother running in. I remember bawling my eyes out, and Mum yelling, *Don't ever, ever do that again!* Later, when we were sitting by the fire, she gave me a piece of chocolate cake, pressing me against her chest and whispering in my ear, *We won't tell Daddy about this, eh?* And we never did, because one thing my mother and I both knew—but never said—was that Daddy must be looked after and shielded from the nastier things in life. I did that, right up until the day he died. But now he was gone, too far gone even to be spinning in his grave.

These hormones looked a lot less savage than my mother's carving knife. I was doing this for that small child, sitting on the kitchen floor. I was doing this for the misshapen woman who watched me from the mirror. She was so hopeful. She was willing me to go on.

I threw the pills into my mouth, swallowed, and chased them down with water. The Task Force was on its way.

'Feeling any different yet?' I asked.

Lucia smiled.

•

That night, I dreamed of a baby in a forest. I felt the milk coming and knew it was for her. As I fed her, she gazed up at me as though I were a goddess. I had never known such love; I'd never felt such happiness and peace. Everything in the world was hushed.

The forest was a cathedral with green glass windows. Shafts of silver poured through the canopy, glowing in droplets on the leaf litter all around me. It was morning. We were safe. And no wolves came.

Eilish

It was long, long after midnight. I lay in a Lukeless bed, gazing up through the skylight. A brilliant moon shone full onto my face. I'd been close to happy this evening, and yet I was crying. Is this how it feels, I wondered, when a marriage finally slides out of your hands?

Oh, Jim. He'd given me such a gift. I hadn't been on a date with anyone but Luke since I was twenty-four years old; yet there we were, off school turf and in our glad rags. Kate was right about one thing: The Lock's a romantic place for dinner. Our table was nestled up to a window, right above the water. There were candles, and the reflections of coloured lanterns gleamed and rippled out in the darkness. I took that first sip of wine, savouring the rich depth of it. It seemed a crime to be here and not in love.

I wasn't going to talk about Luke. I wasn't going to act the jilted wife. I asked Jim about his sons, Bill and Matthew, who were roughly Simon's age. Jim was very amusing on the subject of Bill's latest girlfriend, who sounded completely off her head. By the time the venison arrived, we'd moved on to Kate's dig in Israel. Jim was on his best behaviour until I noticed that he was gazing at me much too intently.

'Lipstick on my teeth?' I asked.

'You're beautiful,' he said.

'Flatterer!'

He shook his head. 'No, I don't just mean you've got a frock on and you scrub up well. I mean really beautiful, in every way.'

I thanked him. It was wonderful to hear someone say that, because I harboured this nagging fear that I must be frumpy, or boring.

My phone beeped from the depths of my bag.

'Sorry,' I said, reaching for it. 'Infuriating when people text over dinner. I'd better turn it off, before you confiscate it.'

I glanced at the message, saw it was from Kate, and laughed out loud.

SOBER?????

I typed quickly. *As a judge. How is Owen?*

OMG he stood me up. Hello to Chadders. Remember no going home 4 coffee.

'Kate,' I said, as I turned off my phone. 'Keeping an eye on me. She says hello.'

'And hello to Kate from me. I bet she said some other things as well.'

'Well, yes. She does have views about her mother and her physics teacher cavorting around the countryside. But she's level-headed. She's coped with Luke's coming-out far better than Simon has.'

I saw Jim's eyes flicker, and wondered what he was thinking. He was holding the bottle of pinot over my nearly empty glass. I half-heartedly protested; said I had to pace myself, muttered something about having to drive. He mentioned a taxi.

'Simon's struggling?' he asked, as he poured.

'That's putting it mildly.'

'Is he all right?'

'I don't know, Jim. I'm not sure he is all right. His dad was his hero. If Luke was in the carpentry shed, Simon was too. If Luke was in his study, Simon took his homework in there. Luke's a keen cricketer and—whaddaya know?—so is Simon. Career decisions, business problems, worries about Nico, Simon ran them all by Luke. And then one day, out of a clear blue sky . . . well.'

Bugger. I'd been determined not to talk about Luke, but here I was, burbling on. I described Simon's anger, his drinking, his adamant refusal to let poor Nico see Luke. 'He's a bit of a mess,' I concluded.

'Sounds like it.' Jim looked thoughtful. 'He was doing so well, wasn't he? Career, lovely wife. On an even keel. It was good to see.'

Odd choice of words. *Even keel.* I wasn't aware that Simon had ever been rudderless.

'He wasn't unhappy, was he?' I asked. 'When you taught him?'

Jim shrugged. 'Well, you know. He had his moments.'

'I'm not sure I do know.'

'He hasn't always found life easy, has he? Bit of a loner. He had people he knocked about with. Not sure he liked them much.'

And that's probably true, I thought as I tried to remember Simon's teenage years. To my shame, it was all a bit hazy. I was working full-time; Kate was young and turbulent; Simon seemed focused on his A-levels, and, anyway, he tended to talk to Luke more than to me. He didn't seem to be a squeaky wheel, so he got no oil.

Dessert arrived then, and the conversation moved on. The rest of the evening passed in laughter and warmth. Jim and I always had plenty to talk about, but tonight there was an extra energy. Even without Luke, I thought in surprise, there can be good moments.

'New Year's Eve,' Jim said, as he was helping me into my coat. 'My place. I'm having a party. Be there, or be square.'

'I can't have an affair with you, Jim.'

He feigned indignation. 'The invitation was to a New Year's Eve shindig, not my bedroom! But, purely out of interest . . . why can't you?'

'I'm not quite divorced,' I said. 'It would be adultery.'

'Semantics.'

'And you're a colleague.'

'That's never stopped anyone before.'

He was right. Sometimes you could cut the atmosphere in our staffroom with a butter knife.

'Okay,' I said, as I pulled on my gloves. 'I'll rephrase. I can't have an affair with you *yet*, Jim. Luke's only been gone five months.'

'And I've waited fourteen years for you.'

'I hope you're getting a taxi home,' I said severely.

He opened his arms. 'This isn't the wine talking! I'm shtone-cold shober.'

I grinned, and deflected him, and soon we were laughing again. Jim was so buoyant compared with Luke; he was lighter in his being. We were among the last to leave, stepping out of the warm restaurant into a frosty night. The moon had risen. We chatted for a while, loitering between our two parked cars.

Finally I looked at my watch, saw that it was after midnight, and said I'd better go.

'I've had a wonderful evening,' I said. 'Thank you.'

'Another time?' he asked, holding my door as I got in.

'New Year's Eve,' I said. 'Thank you. I'd love to come.'

Thirty-two

Kate

Frigging Owen. Half an hour late. She sat in a corner of the George and Dragon, reading *Private Eye* and trying not to look as though she'd been stood up. There was a band on that night, but the place wasn't hopping because their music was truly awful. It was a middle-aged man and woman, each with a guitar, playing what sounded like seventies folk and singing in really annoying nasal voices. At the end of every song they'd stop and drone on about what the next song was trying to say—as though anyone cared.

'This one's really important to me,' the man was saying. He dipped his head down to the microphone like a rock star. 'You know, it's about my journey, really, because I just realised I wasn't fulfilled, and now I'm just in a really good place, so, yeah, this is sort of my story.'

And they were off again, warbling away. The song sounded exactly the same as the last one, and the one before that. Kate looked at her watch and cursed. Owen was now thirty-seven minutes late. Another ten, and she'd leave. She was meeting her dissertation supervisor at nine tomorrow, and there was some work she needed to do before then.

Mum would be at The Lock right now, with Mr Chadwick. Bloody hell. Those two teachers were bound to get tipsy and giggly. It didn't bear thinking about! To pass the time, Kate sent Eilish a text; then she grinned at the reply. This thing with Mum and Mr Chadders was funny . . . except that it wasn't. What about poor Dad?

There was a guy across the room, sitting with some other people. She'd spotted him when she first came in. Quite hot. Open-necked shirt, jacket, jeans. Might be thirty, might be younger. She could see him looking her way. When she caught him out, he smiled at her. Kate went back to *Private Eye*. She wasn't here to pick up men. She was here to meet Owen and listen to whatever it was he had to say.

Then again, he ticked all the boxes, that guy. She found herself speculating about him as he stood up and headed for the bar. He had friends, and he was buying a round. Not a loner, then. Or a loser.

He'd just passed Kate's corner when he hesitated, laughed to himself, and swung back to speak to her. He looked her in the eye but seemed slightly diffident, slightly wary of being told to piss off. Just wary enough. Any more would make him awkward; any less would make him an arrogant twerp.

'Um, can I get you a drink?' he asked her.

Oh, she did like his voice. Low, but not a growl. Just enough of a northern accent to be sexy.

Play it cool. She raised her eyebrows. 'A drink?'

'Yep, that's all. I'm not suggesting anything else. This is a genuine offer. You don't have to join us if you don't feel like it. You might have sneaked out to the pub for a bit of me time.' He gestured at his friends—two women and a man—who were playing some sort of game with the beer mats. 'Though you're welcome.'

She glanced again at her watch. Owen was now fifty minutes late; he obviously wasn't coming. The singers were taking a break, which was a mercy.

'Why not?' she said. 'Thanks very much. A half of Guinness, please.'

He nodded and made for the bar. She kept him under surveillance. Dark-blond hair and a bit of stubble. Heavy eyebrows. Long legs. That nose was probably too big, if he was wanting to be a model, but the effect was rugged. This washout of an evening was looking up.

After a decent interval she joined him at the bar, and he held out his hand to shake hers.

'Peter,' he said.

'Kate.'

Ouch. Bit of a firm handshake.

They talked as they waited to be served. Kate said she'd been stood up by a complete idiot. Peter told her he wasn't a local. He was visiting his sister, who'd just got engaged. When their order was ready he picked up four glasses, and Kate took hers.

'Join us?' he said. 'Don't expect intellectual conversation from this rabble. We're building a house of beer mats.'

She accepted the offer and nipped back to the corner for her magazine. That was when she felt fingers gripping her arm, and heard an all too familiar voice.

'Kate. Thank God you're still here.'

Frig's sake, Owen! She could have clouted him. He stood there looking tousled and wide-eyed. Little boy lost, wearing an awful anorak.

'*Now* you show up,' she hissed. 'What time d'you call this?'

'Baffy ran away. He's nuts, that dog. Took me ages to find him.'

'Yeah, well, you're too late. I'm busy now.'

He thrust his hands into his pockets. 'But I have to talk to you. I've come all the way across London.'

'You could have sent me a text, at least. I've been sitting here like a lemon.'

'My phone's flat.'

She ground her teeth. 'Oh, for God's . . . okay. Grab yourself a drink.'

Peter was standing at his table, waiting for her. She mouthed the word *sorry*, and pointed at Owen with both hands before miming the act of throttling him. Peter obviously got the message; he smiled and shrugged before turning away. To make matters worse, the singers had started up again. They were murdering other artists' songs now, starting with 'Scarborough Fair'.

'Right,' she began, when Owen returned with a glass. 'Shoot. But I'd better say right now, Owen: we're not getting back together. Just putting it out there.'

He gaped at her. 'You and me?'

'Not going to happen.'

'Um, Kate . . . this is really embarrassing. I thought you might've heard.'

'No,' she said. 'No, I haven't heard anything. D'you think you could possibly get on with it, before I tip this drink over your head?'

'Okay. I'm with someone. We're very serious, actually.'

This was an intriguing development. 'Really? Who?'

'She works with me. Eva Jones. I'm moving into her place tomorrow.'

'Great news! Woo-hoo! So what's she like?'

'What's she like?' Owen looked shifty. 'She's, um, a lot more mature than you. Don't take that the wrong way . . . I mean, she's had life experience. She's got two boys, and they're . . . um, the older one's eighteen.'

It was Kate's turn to gape. 'How old is this woman?'

'Why does her age matter?'

'Hang on, I'm doing the maths. You're twenty-three. She's got a son aged—'

'Forty,' snapped Owen. 'She's forty, okay? And we're great together.'

Kate leaned back in her seat, smirking. So Owen had found a surrogate mother at last, and Eva now had three kids instead of two. Perhaps they *were* perfect together.

'Well,' she said, holding up her glass. 'Here's to you and Eva Jones. What I don't get is why you couldn't just tell me on the phone? Why trail all the way across town?'

'Yeah, that's a bit more difficult to . . . You might not . . .' Owen started nibbling at his cuticles. 'Look, come outside and you'll see.'

'See what?'

He tipped back his drink and stood up, not quite meeting Kate's eye. She knew that look. He was trying to find the balls to ask a favour.

Eilish

'So I went outside the George and Dragon with him,' said Kate. 'And what d'you think I saw? You'll never guess.'

It was Saturday morning. Stella had already dropped by for coffee, and was all agog when Jim phoned to say how much he'd enjoyed their evening at The Lock. Once Stella had gone, Luke phoned to say he'd signed some transfer documents, as requested by my solicitor. And then—lovely surprise—Kate's face appeared around the door from the lobby.

'You alone, Mum?' she yelled, her eyes screwed shut. 'I hope I'm not going to be traumatised by the sight of Mr Chadders in a bathrobe?'

'Kate!' I ran to kiss her. 'No naked physics teachers, you're quite safe. You've just missed Stella. How did you get here?'

'Borrowed Mathis and John's car. I brought lunch—unless you're going out? I've got to tell you about Owen, and . . . well, I'll explain.'

'I thought he stood you up.'

'He did—then he didn't. It's a bit of a long story. I'll get the kettle on.'

She was bearing flowers as well as goodies from a delicatessen, and I had a nasty feeling these offerings were designed to soften some blow. I laid the table for lunch while she told her story. It seemed Owen was in deep disgrace: partly because he'd been so late to arrive at the pub, and partly because he'd arrived at all.

'Sounds as though he saved you from being abducted,' I said when she described the man who'd tried to pick her up. 'Probably a serial killer, preying on single women in pubs.'

'Peter was out for a drink with his sister and her fiancé. I don't think he fits the profile of a predatory killer, Mum. It wasn't even a pick-up, really.'

'Hmm . . . you never know. Anyway, Owen's happy with this woman, Eva?'

'Seems to be. But don't you think it's all a bit kinky? He's not much older than her sons.'

'I don't think our family is in a position to judge the kinkiness of others,' I said. 'What I can't quite follow is why he had to make such a meal of telling you. Was he afraid you'd be upset?'

'Ah.' She looked at me with a half-smile, and I knew that this was what she'd really come for. 'Good question. At that point, I discovered what a total wanker Owen really is. He said he wanted me to come outside. So I went into the street with him, and who d'you think I saw?'

'Was it Mrs Jones and her teenagers?'

'Thankfully not.'

'Um . . . Owen's parents?'

'Nope.'

'I give up.'

'Wait here. Brace yourself.' Kate hurried out of the front door and over to her borrowed car. Curious now, I stood watching. Suddenly the quiet was shattered by a wild bark, and something came hurtling across the gravel: something white, fluffy, and far too energetic to be cooped up in a car. He ran right around the house before galloping up to me.

'Baffy!' I bent down to pat the dog. 'I thought we were rid of you.'

'He was tied up outside the pub, freezing cold,' said Kate. 'Wearing a stupid tartan coat, but still shivering. I had to rush him straight home to get him warm. I nipped back to the pub later, but the serial killer had left.'

'So Owen's going on holiday, and wants a dog-sitter?'

Kate watched as Baffy charged off again, barking at some birds. 'Mum, here's the thing. Eva and her sons are allergic to dogs. Well, so she says, sounds like bollocks to me. She's probably just a control freak. Poor old Baffy is now surplus to requirements in Owen's life. So he brought him over and dumped him on me.'

'He can't do that! Baffy's no angel, and Mathis and John have just redecorated that place. It's their pride and joy.'

'That's right.'

'You're on the first floor. No garden.'

'No garden, not so much as a balcony. And he goes insane if he can't get outside.'

The awful truth was dawning on me. Lose a husband, gain a dog.

'Um,' said Kate. 'I have a favour to ask.'

Thirty-three

Simon

An enormous Christmas tree was not designed to be carried in a small car.

He and Nico had chosen an extravagant one from a stall outside the tube station, but getting it home proved a challenge. In the end he managed to cram it into the car by moving Nico's seat to the front. The top of the tree poked between them and covered up the gearstick. By the time he'd parked outside their house, Simon had a faceful of pine needles.

'Magnificent!' cried Carmela, as her menfolk carried it through the front door—Nico holding only the very tip, and making this-is-heavy groaning noises. 'Birnam Wood is come to Dunsinane! Coffee's ready, Simon, just the way you like it, and then would you go into the cellar and find the decorations? I tried to do it but the light has blown and I tripped over something. It's chaos down there. I would have changed the bulb, but I don't think it's such a good idea with this passenger I'm carrying.'

She smiled over her shoulder. Rosa was fast asleep, tightly strapped to her mother's back in a bright red cloth. Only the upper part of the baby's face was showing. She seemed soothed by the warmth and movement. Simon could see her dark lashes fluttering, as he stooped to nuzzle one softly curled ear. She smelled of milk, and he felt his heart swell. It was one of those good moments. This—now—was all he wanted. Nico wandered off to play with his Lego.

'I've been thinking,' said Carmela.

'That's a worrying opener.' Simon made a mock-frightened face. 'You're planning on real reindeer this year? Think of the mess.'

She walked away, into the kitchen, and he followed.

'Christmas can't be a family gathering at your mother's house,' she said. 'Not this year.'

'No.' Simon felt his shoulders sag. No more happy family events.

'So I think we should invite your mother to come here.'

'Great idea! But she'll bring that maniac of a dog. I can't believe Kate dumped him on her.'

'We can cope with Baffy,' said Carmela, smiling as she handed him a cup of coffee. 'So shall we also ask Kate, and Meg, and even Wendy? Let's gather them all here, around our tree. The children will keep things happy.'

Simon drew her closer to him. She was so thoughtful; so good at caring for his family. He knew how much she missed her own.

'You are a wonderful, wonderful girl,' he said fervently, kissing her. 'I'll phone Mum.'

'And what about your father?'

The perfection of the moment died. Simon dropped his arms. 'He's out of the picture,' he said flatly. 'We agreed.'

'It's Christmas, Simon, and he's alone.'

'For Christ's sake! Do we have to have this conversation? He's made his bed.'

'It is still Christmas, and he is still alone. He has not even seen his granddaughter.' Carmela reached back, touching the fluff of Rosa's hair. 'She is the most precious treasure, and he's excluded. He sent presents today, they came in the post. And . . . you know what? I think you miss him.'

Simon drained his coffee. 'I'll change that light bulb,' he said, and stomped out of the room.

Carmela was tenacious. She followed him to the top of the cellar steps, her shape outlined in the light from the hallway behind her. Simon was up a ladder by then, changing the bulb.

'Why won't you admit that you miss him?' she asked.

He ignored her. This wasn't fair. Nobody should have to argue with a stubborn woman when they were risking their neck in a pitch-black cellar.

'Why, Simon? Nico asks all the time, "Where is Grandpa, where is Grandpa?" What shall we tell him?'

Sometimes, if he was dogged enough in his silence, she'd give up. But not this time.

'This is your problem too,' she persisted. 'What do we tell Nico?'

'Fucking bulb, it's broken off in the fitting. Hang on . . . bloody hell, now I've cut myself, I'm bleeding all over the place . . . Look, do we really have to discuss this now?'

'I think we do.'

'Ouch, that's sharp. Okay. How about we tell him Grandpa's ill?'

'And have him develop some morbid fear that Luke is about to die? No.'

'All right. We'll say he's been really, really naughty and we don't want to see him anymore. That's the truth.'

She sounded doubtful. 'Naughty?'

'Do you have a better idea?'

'I know what will come next. He'll ask if Luke's sitting on the bottom stair. That's where naughty people go, in Nico's world. The bottom stair.'

'Try the switch now.' Simon felt a dull satisfaction as the light went on. 'Bingo! And then there was light. Right, where are these decorations?'

'In the plastic box. No, not that one. There, behind those rolls of wallpaper.'

Simon carried the box upstairs, licking his forefinger as Carmela bolted the cellar door behind them.

'You tell him, then,' she said. 'You tell him his grandpa can't be his friend anymore.'

'Okay, I will.'

'Now?'

'Next time he asks.' Simon dumped the box next to the Christmas tree. 'He might never ask again. It's been months since he saw Dad. He'll soon forget.'

Rosa stirred in her papoose and opened her eyes. She was a sleepy little clam peering out of its safe place. Simon stroked her head. He had to protect her, and Nico too. He hated to think of the sniggers and teasing, if other children knew they had a freakish grandparent. He'd heard that kind of laughter before.

•

Even in broad daylight, the girl from the club was a work of art. Jessica Stent was her name: a real live person, not a lager-induced mirage. He kept his hands to himself now that they were both sober. They sat by the river, talking all afternoon, sometimes kissing. They cared about the same things. Jessica was one of two siblings, like him, and she also had a father who was a lawyer. She liked Simon. She really liked him. Someone as wonderful as her liked geeky, awkward Simon Livingstone.

He didn't tell his friends; he knew how they talked about women. At night he imagined tearing her clothes off; but by day, when she firmly removed his hands from her bottom, he respected her for it. This wasn't just about sex. She was special. He caught himself daydreaming about her all the time. He thought he was falling in love with her.

They were walking through the botanical gardens when he told her so. It was raining, and he'd lent her his jacket. She stopped in her tracks, grasping his hands.

'You mean it?' she whispered.

'Of course.'

'Yes, but you really mean it?'

Simon sank down onto one knee. 'Allow me to express my undying adoration.'

'Thank you! Oh my God, I never thought this would happen to me. But you'll change your mind when you know me better.'

'Of course I won't.'

She laughed, shook her head, laughed again—and promptly burst into tears. He put his arms around her, feeling baffled. Weren't girls meant to be pleased when you said you loved them?

'You'll hate me,' she sobbed. 'You will.'

When he got home, Quinn—one of his housemates—was eating noodles out of a bowl. The two students punched their knuckles together in greeting.

'Been in the library, Livingstone?' asked Quinn.

'Nope.'

'Why are you grinning like a blithering idiot?'

'I'm not.'

'You are!' Quinn paused with the fork halfway to his mouth. 'Did you just get laid?'

'Is that all you think about?' Simon was opening a tin of baked beans. Nobody in the house ever did any washing up. Plates and other crockery lay in piles over every surface. New life forms had grown in the fridge, and the pantry was home to the fattest, sleekest colony of mice in the world.

Quinn finished his noodles and dumped his bowl in the overflowing sink. 'Who is it?' he asked, wiping his mouth. 'You can tell Uncle Quinn.'

'Okay. It's the girl from Moroney's.'

Quinn stared. Then he chuckled uncertainly, as though hoping Simon had just made a joke.

'You're kidding, right?'

'Why would I be kidding?'

'Seriously, Livingstone. You're banging that blonde we saw you hooking up with in Moroney's?'

'I'm not banging her. I'm just . . . seeing her.'

'Whew.' Quinn wiped his brow. 'Lucky.'

Simon was annoyed. 'What the hell are you on about? She's a stunner.'

'The chambermaid from the White Hart? Legs up to her armpits? Mate . . .' Quinn had begun to smirk. He seemed embarrassed, but at the same time he was obviously enjoying himself. 'Look, you've got to know. Um, how do I put this? She's not a *she*. She's a *he*.'

'You've got the wrong girl.'

Quinn was trying to hold in the laughter, but it escaped in a great gush of sound. 'He's a tranny!' he gasped, as he sobbed with mirth. 'He's packing all the tackle you've got, and more. Fergus was chasing him a while back. The DJ warned him off. Sorry, mate, we should have told you. We thought you'd grope him and get the fright of your life . . . but you came home and never said anything, and I haven't seen you since.'

Simon remembered Jessica gripping his hands, tears on her cheeks. 'You're having me on.'

'Mate, that's a tranny. Ask the DJ at Moroney's, his sister works at the White Hart. That leggy blonde was seen taking a shower. He's got tits! He's saving up for the op, going to have it in Thailand.'

Without another word, Simon retreated to his bedroom. He sat on the floor, feeling sick. Soon he heard his other housemates coming home. At first there was suppressed laughter, and then gales of it. They weren't good at keeping their voices down, and what he heard made him hate them all. *Snogged a lady boy! . . . Is he a shirt lifter? . . . Poor old Livingstone, didn't know he was that desperate!*

He wanted to kill somebody. When he opened his bedroom door, someone said, 'Hi, Simon,' as though nothing had happened. Then they all exploded. They slapped him on the back—in a friendly, patronising way—and asked him how it was, and were her tits real, or silicone?

He smiled weakly and accepted the cans of warm lager they offered him. He drank quite a few of them. Later, when the others were watching *Doctor Who*, he quietly left the flat. His blood was racing by the time he got to the White Hart. His mind was on fire. He'd got down on one knee . . . he'd said the word *love*! Hell, he–she would be laughing at him now. Simon would make him–her stop laughing.

It was dark behind the hotel. Very dark. Not quiet, though, because people were coming home from the pubs. Beer bottles lay discarded beside the recycling bin. He picked one up by the neck, and smashed its base against a wall. Then he sent a text.

Come out. I'm round the back, by the bins. I've got something for you.

•

They decorated the tree together, singing along to Christmas carols on the stereo. The fairy lights didn't work, and Simon had to nip out and buy some more, but that was all part of Christmas. Even Rosa seemed interested, until she began to whimper, and then wail.

Nico gently touched her face. 'She's hungry,' he said. 'You'd better stick her up your jumper, Mummy.'

'There are already some presents to go under the tree,' Carmela told Simon as she swung the baby off her back. 'In the cupboard where I keep my shoes. Could you get them?'

Simon looked through the pile of presents, leaving aside the four with his father's handwriting on them. He'd give those ones away. He put the rest into a pillow case, slung it over one shoulder and carried it downstairs, making Father Christmas ho-ho-ho noises.

'You're not fat or jolly enough to be Santa,' said Carmela. 'And if you ever grow a white bushy beard, or prance about with a pack of elves, I shall divorce you.'

Nico had parked himself on a stool, watching his mother feed the baby. He'd got used to the sight and didn't seem at all jealous.

Later that evening, Rosa would be grumpy, and her parents would carry her up and down, up and down; but right now she was tucking in with happy murmurs.

When Simon emptied his sack under the tree, Nico scrambled off the stool. 'Will the proper Santa be coming?' he asked, looking at the treasure.

'Mm. Down the chimney.' Simon felt guilty about lying to his son. He considered himself an honest man, and yet here he was, spinning a right old whopper. Next year, he thought, I'll tell him the truth. Or maybe the year after that.

'Does the sleigh come down the chimney, too?'

'The sleigh . . .' God, what lie was he supposed to tell now? 'Um, I think it stays on the roof. But, hey, we're going to ask Granny and Kate to come on Christmas Day, and see our tree.'

'Will Grandpa be coming?'

Simon's smile froze.

'Well?' asked Carmela, her eyebrows raised in sarcastic inquiry. 'I think you'd better answer the question. Will Grandpa be coming?'

Nico was standing beside the Christmas tree, fiddling with the front of his T-shirt. His excitement had been popped, like a pin in a balloon. Simon remembered how it felt to be small and anxious. He sat down and drew Nico close.

'Shush,' he said. 'Let's not worry about that now.'

'He will be coming, won't he?' Nico's voice was high, and he twisted the front of his T-shirt in both hands.

How could Dad do this to us? How could he be so selfish?

'No,' said Simon. 'Grandpa can't come anymore.'

Thirty-four

Lucia

I got dressed, looked in the mirror, and knew I had to do better. I had higher standards now. Genetic women have had all their lives to learn how to be women; even the ones who wear jeans and trainers. They're socialised as women. They *are* women. When Kate was younger she had a stack of teen magazines, full of make-up and fashion and hair. She pretended to despise them, but she still bought them. She can do femininity when she wants to.

I'd tried to give myself a crash course, but the internet was no longer enough. The wig was too young for my face—I saw that now. My make-up was clumsy, my clothes were dated, my posture wasn't quite right. I gave myself away with a thousand tiny signals.

I needed help.

When I phoned her at home, Judi sounded as though Christmas had come early.

'You want me to do a Trinny and Susannah on your wardrobe?' I could imagine her rubbing her hands. 'How about tomorrow morning? I'll come around to your place.'

When Judi says she's going to do something, she delivers. She arrived bang on time, clutching two suitcases full of her cast-offs, which, she said, dated from skinnier days. Some of the clothes looked brand new.

'Off you go,' she said briskly, holding out a swirling skirt and a blouse. 'Let's see these on you. I bought them in a sale and it was a big mistake, but I think they'll suit your colouring.'

'You want me to try these on? *Now?*'

'I'll wait here while you change in your room. Don't forget your shoes and falsies, will you? Never try on clothes with the wrong shoes or underwear. That's the first rule of shopping.'

'How d'you know I even own falsies?' I asked, feeling myself blush.

'Lucky guess. It's nothing new. Flat-chested women have been wearing padded bras forever, and I know more than one who owns a pair of bottom-enhancing knickers. Why not? Been going on ever since Henry VIII padded out his codpiece.'

I changed slowly, mortified at the idea of parading around cross-dressed in front of a colleague. I had to steel myself to walk back into the kitchen, but Judi was supremely relaxed. 'Give us a twirl,' she said, and I did. By the time we'd got to the third outfit, I was having fun. There were dresses, skirts, smocks and voluminous blouses; a sumptuous, impossibly soft pashmina and a floaty cardigan. Of course they didn't fit perfectly. Many were too roomy, especially across the bust; some were too tight in the shoulders or the waist. Judi made them work—a belt here, or a scarf, or a button moved across; she'd brought a needle and thread for the purpose.

Leggings were a revelation to me. 'They're marvellous,' I said, as Judi showed me how to layer them with dresses or smocks. 'Neither Eilish nor Kate owns a pair, I'm pretty sure.'

'Eilish is too classy. Kate would probably rather be seen dead. I love 'em, though. They're forgiving to those of us whose waists aren't exactly hourglass.'

We took a break for coffee while she looked through my existing wardrobe with a critical eye. I felt intensely self-conscious, as though she were reading my diary. I'd begun hiding clothes the day I locked a stolen petticoat into my tuckbox in the attic. I had never shown anybody before.

'Hmm, quite old-fashioned,' said Judi, holding up a blue dress. 'The colour's not right for your skin, it'll be ageing. I think the whole effect is a bit . . . granny. You're not old, Livingstone, you're in your prime! Rock it! And what's this? Oh my God, no . . . Where in the name of Hades did you get this monstrosity?' She was staring in horror, as though it might bite her, at a frilly pink blouse.

'That? Oxfam.'

'What were you *thinking* of?'

'I liked the colour,' I admitted sheepishly. 'What's wrong with it? A bit too lurid?'

'Nothing's wrong with it—except the cut, the colour and the fabric. It has to go, unless you plan on standing on street corners?'

Next, she pulled a chair in front of the mirror and suggested a make-up lesson. Eilish wore very little; she had a natural kind of beauty. Kate neither needed nor wanted warpaint. Judi, on the other hand, was the sort of woman who never left the house without lipstick. The golden rules, she said, were subtlety and contouring. She showed me how to apply foundation while avoiding the mud-pie effect, and blusher without it making me look like a Russian doll. She warned me off red lipstick. 'You need less flashy colours,' she said, producing one from her handbag.

As she messed about, we discussed the 'rollout of Lucia Livingstone', which was what Judi called my transition at work. She treated it like any other office project, including the major software overhaul we'd endured the previous year.

'You'll have to let the management team know well in advance,' she said. 'Give them a date when you're going to be fetching up as a babe.'

'I don't want to do it.'

'They can't kick you out. Look down . . . look up . . . See how I'm just brushing that onto your upper lashes? Keep still, if you don't want to be a panda.'

'Come on, Judi. There are ways and means of levering me out. We both know that.'

'What date do you have in mind? How about January? New year, new woman.'

'Far, far too soon.' I couldn't move, because she was still wielding a mascara wand millimetres from my eyes. 'Maybe the following year.'

'Your hair's getting quite long,' she said, spraying it with water. 'I think we can do something with it. I had a talk to my stylist last night, and he gave me some tips on—I'd stress that these are his words, not mine—on making guys look like gals. Ultimately, he says, you need a fringe, just to soften your forehead. That'll make a huge difference.'

I'd never had mousse in my hair before. Actually, I didn't know such stuff existed. I was fascinated by the way it expanded with a quiet fizz when Judi sprayed it into the palm of her hand. She made me tip my head upside down and blasted it with a hairdryer ('to give it bounce,' she explained, as I spluttered), and then dried my hair in layers so it framed my forehead and jaw. I watched the transformation in the mirror, and I wanted to dance.

'You're a genius!' I cried. 'An artist!'

She put down her hairdryer and regarded my reflection with a half-smile. 'D'you know what, Lucia? You scrub up pretty well. I think those hormones are having an effect already. It's hard to put my finger on it . . . D'you think your skin's softer?'

'Impossible,' I scoffed. Secretly, though, I agreed with her. Perhaps it was my imagination, but I did feel different: more serene, somehow. My sex drive was definitely less—I wasn't sure if that was a good thing or not, but it was a fact. And that morning, for the first time, I'd noticed a soreness and sensitivity across my chest.

'Let's go out for lunch,' she said.

My euphoria slid away. 'I can't. I've never eaten in public. People will read me.'

'*Read* you? What does that mean?'

'It means that they'll see me for what I am.'

'Well, that's all right then, because what you are is a friend of mine.' She picked up a pair of earrings and handed them to me to clip on. '*Your* first visit to a cafe as a woman. *My* first visit to a cafe with a transsexual woman. Sounds like fun! Let's go.'

•

I lay in bed that night with a cup of tea by my side, wishing Eilish were there to share my triumph. Things were happening! I'd filled my wardrobe with new clothes; I'd been made up, my hair blow-dried. I'd wandered through Spitalfields market dressed in a long, full skirt, and browsed the jewellery stalls, before eating tagliatelle and sharing an excellent bottle of chablis with a girlfriend.

I never thought I'd see the day.

Thirty-five

Kate

This was her first Christmas as the child of a broken home. She had friends who'd been through it when they were small; they talked about shuttling from Mum to Dad and back again, eating two Christmas dinners, opening two lots of presents and generally being carved up like little Christmas turkeys. They always ended up blubbing by the end of the day. Christmas was a nightmare for them.

Kate's memories couldn't have been more different. The routine had been the same, year after year. She and Simon got up early and sat on each other's beds to open their stockings. At ten, the family walked along the lane to church. Afterwards, Kate, Simon and the other village children would play kick the can in the graveyard while their parents were queueing up to shake hands with the vicar.

There was always a crowd at lunch: lots of family, and whichever cat they had at the time scoffing turkey giblets from a bowl on the floor. Normally there'd be a distant cousin or aunt, or some waif or stray with nowhere else to go—like Stella, when she was between husbands. To Kate, as a child, it was all perfect.

So she had no right to grumble about the fact that at the age of twenty-three she finally had a broken-home Christmas. Simon and Carmela had issued a general invitation; general to everyone, that was, except her dad. Kate was wondering what to do about this when she had a call from her grandmother.

'Carmela's so kind to ask me,' said Meg. 'I think I should meet this new baby. But what about poor Luke? I hate to think of him alone on Christmas Day.'

That was when Kate made her decision. 'Granny, don't worry. Go and be gobbed on by Rosa, who, I must admit, is quite cute. I'll have lunch with Dad. We'll sit around and pull sad and lonely crackers, and get quietly stonkered together.'

Meg sounded heartened. 'Would you do that, dear?'

'You think I'd rather spend the day with Simon and Wendy, wearing a stupid paper hat?'

Kate was glad she'd made that decision, because her dad perked up when she told him. How the mighty were fallen! A year ago he was Mr Popular and Respectable, hosting a houseful of guests; now he was grateful for one visitor to his bare little basement flat.

'Don't you ever look up your London friends?' she asked him.

'Well, no. Not often. They tend to ask questions about why I'm living here.'

'But you'll have to come out sometime,' she argued. 'Won't you? If you're really going to . . . what's the word?'

'Transition.'

'Why haven't you told anyone? Are you having second thoughts?'

There was a pause, and Kate held her breath. Maybe she'd hit the nail on the head. Maybe it hadn't worked out for him. If he was going to turn back, he'd better get a move on. Mum wouldn't wait forever.

'Our human resources manager wants it to happen tomorrow,' he said. 'Judi. You might have met her.'

Kate was surprised. 'You told her?'

'She got it out of me. She can't understand why anyone would hesitate to become a woman. We went on a shopping expedition. It was fun.'

Kate snorted, muttering about women who shopped as a pastime.

'Judi celebrates being female, Kate. It isn't a crime.'

'Actually it is a crime, if what she's celebrating is being vacuous. Women are still not respected, Dad, and why? Because they've bought into this giggly fun shopping crap.'

She heard him laughing. Nice sound. 'Don't be such a killjoy.'

'Not all women think shopping is fun. Don't expect me to go into ecstasies over totes and bright yellow Italian shoes.'

'Yellow shoes?' He sounded intrigued. 'I must hear more! The Italians make bright yellow shoes?'

Kate sighed, and said she'd see him for lunch on Christmas Day.

She'd been feeling sorry for her father, thinking of him as a Nora No-Mates, but when she fronted up on Christmas morning he wasn't alone after all. She could see two figures in the kitchen as she passed the window. One was her dad; the other was a young woman, sitting at the table. Her head was thrown back and Kate could hear laughter. She also caught a waft of roast chicken, and a blast of Neil Young from the stereo.

The basement door was locked—unusually—but Luke came trotting over to open it, beaming out through the glass. He was in his shirtsleeves, wearing a plastic apron Kate had given him after a trip to Florence. It had a picture of Michelangelo's David on the front, arranged artfully (or possibly tastelessly) to make the wearer look improbably well hung.

Luke's eyes were bright as he held out his arms. 'Happy Christmas, darling girl!' he cried. 'Now, come and meet someone.'

As Kate followed him into the kitchen, his visitor unfolded herself from the chair. Beautiful, thought Kate, but not pretty. She wore thigh-length boots, like Puss in Boots, and a red silk scarf around her neck; braided hair cascaded from a high ponytail. Above all, she had terrific posture. Kate had seen women with her kind of looks on the cover of *Vogue*—all cheekbones and legs—though she suspected that their clothes cost a thousand times more than this woman's outfit.

'This is Chloe,' said Luke. 'My daughter, Kate.'

Chloe's reaction was wildly enthusiastic. She held out her hand, then seemed to change her mind, laughed, and grabbed Kate in a bear hug.

'This is great!' she cried. 'You're the archaeologist, right? You dig stuff up? Lucia's told me all about you.'

Gender, eh? It was funny; when you were with people like her dad and Chloe, you stopped thinking of it as a binary thing. It confirmed what Kate had long believed: that the world isn't yin and yang, it isn't black and white, and it certainly isn't bloody Venus and Mars; it's so much more fun than that. Chloe couldn't hide her male voice, and the silk scarf covered an Adam's apple, but she *was* female. There was no hint of a chip on her shoulder when it came to education or money or race or gender. They'd broken the conversational ice before Luke had got around to pouring Kate a glass of bubbly. Chloe already had her own, and clinked it against Kate's, saying, 'Cheers, m'dear.'

Luke had cooked a chicken (a turkey wouldn't fit in that silly little oven) and Kate contributed a Tesco's Christmas pudding. To her immense relief, nobody was wearing a paper hat. It was a blue-sky day outside. As the sun sank lower, they were dazzled by a little square of brightness, shining right on their faces.

'Do you want me to pull down the blind?' asked Luke, seeing that Chloe was squinting.

'No!' She waved him back into his seat. 'It feels like a blessing.'

Two glasses down, and they were well away. Kate told the story of Owen, and Baffy, and the stranger in the pub. Chloe sympathised completely.

'That guy sounds *gorgeous*,' she cried. 'You didn't get a phone number? Oh, that's tragic. And the poor dog—your ex needs a kick up the backside.'

'What about you, Chloe?' Kate leaned her arms on the table. 'What's happening in your life?'

Chloe was disarmingly open about herself; said that she was on the waiting list for surgery but God knew when that would happen. She'd be applying for her certificate just as soon as she'd saved enough for the fee. When Kate asked, she explained that this would mean she was legally a woman. Then she mentioned, casually, that she'd been in a car accident the day before.

Luke was fussing about with the oven, a tea towel over one shoulder, but now he whirled around. 'Chloe! Are you all right? I didn't even know you had a car.'

'I don't! It was a client's car. One of my regulars. We were on our way to a hotel.'

'What happened?' asked Kate.

'This bicycle courier rode straight across the road, and—oh my God—next moment we'd hit him.'

'Was he okay?'

'I thought he was dead. My client was bricking it, you can imagine—I mean, he's married for one thing, and guess what he does for a job?'

Luke and Kate shook their heads. Chloe paused for effect, looking from one to the other.

'A bishop?' suggested Kate. 'A judge?'

'Politician?' added Luke.

Chloe leaned forward, whispering. 'He's a policeman. High up. That's all I can say.'

Her audience made fascinated, scandalised noises.

'Not another word.' Chloe zipped up her lips. 'Take it from me: he's very senior.'

'And this man is married?' asked Luke, who was shaking his head.

'Hey, Lucia, don't be too quick to write him off. He's all right. Anyway, the bloke on the bike had a heck of a wallop and it took a while for him to get up. He just lay there looking like he was dead. People were running up. My client was trying to get his seatbelt off but he was in a state, he was freaking out—"Oh my

God, oh my God, I've got to call an ambulance, I'll be caught with you in my car, this is the end of my career, end of my marriage, end of everything, panic panic panic"—and I pressed the button to release his seatbelt, and said, "Just go and help that poor sod lying in the road, and don't worry."'

Kate was hanging on Chloe's every word. She could see it all: the senior policeman with a transsexual prostitute in his passenger seat, and the lifeless cyclist, and onlookers beginning to gather. Mobile phones, with cameras, would be coming out. Someone would be calling 999. Imagine the headlines! The clock was ticking on that guy's career.

'What happened?' she asked.

'I got down low in my seat, oh my God, I was practically sitting on the floor. While everyone was standing around the bloke in the road, I managed to get my door open and crawl away. It wasn't too easy, but he'd fallen on the driver's side, so I was hidden by the car. I got around a corner. Then I started running.'

Kate laughed at the idea of Chloe, all six-foot-something of her, crouching behind a car. 'Anyone see you?'

'Nope. Got away with it. The cyclist turned out to be okay, just cuts and bruises and hurt pride. My copper's car had a dent but he just wanted to get away, so they agreed to call it quits. He texted me to say thanks.'

'He was lucky,' said Luke. 'Your policeman. You covered for him. He's also lucky that you aren't the type to blackmail.'

Chloe drew her head back, a little offended. 'You have rules in your job, right? Rules about keeping things under your hat and not talking about your client's business? Well, so do I. I'm not there to ruin a man's life.'

'It's a dangerous job, though, isn't it?' said Kate.

Chloe shrugged. She looked bleak suddenly. Kate cursed her own tactlessness and changed the subject. 'Christmas pudding,' she said. 'Tesco's own. I shoved a pound coin in, so watch your teeth, Chloe. Dad, got any brandy? Let's do the flame thing.'

After lunch, Luke suggested a walk. This was a family tradition. Every year, just as Kate and her grandmother were settling down to the BBC's annual showing of *The Sound of Music* (Granny's crush on Christopher Plummer was no secret), her dad would suggest a bloody walk. 'Come on,' he'd say, rubbing his hands and throwing wellies around, 'let's make the most of the daylight! Chop-chop, and we'll be back in time for the Queen's Christmas Message.' Simon and Kate complained like buggery, but they always gave in. They'd slide out across the icy terrace, crunch their way through hoarfrost or drizzle or gale-force winds, and come back feeling as though they'd earned the right to scoff half a Christmas cake.

So when Luke tabled the idea of a stroll, Kate wasn't surprised. But Chloe was.

'Walk?' she squeaked, shivering as though Luke had suggested they all go for a bracing dip in the North Sea. 'Why would we want to do that? It's brass monkeys out there, and we could be opening another bottle and sitting in this nice warm flat. Have you lost your tiny mind, Lucia?'

Luke laughed and said yes, he certainly *had* lost his mind. Then he went off to the bathroom.

'I guess I could manage a quick dash up and down the street,' said Chloe, once he'd gone.

'It's a tradition,' said Kate, sighing, and explained about *The Sound of Music* and the Queen's Christmas Message. 'Think yourself lucky it's a sunny afternoon, no hurricanes or blizzards.'

'Erm . . .' Chloe looked thoughtfully at Kate, and a smile spread across her face. 'Can I negotiate? Don't jump down my throat, but . . . okay, here's the deal. I'll go for your Christmas walk, if Lucia comes too. As Lucia.'

Kate knew exactly what she was driving at, and was appalled. It was like being asked to meet the monster under your bed. She was still haunted by Simon's description of the clown in tights and lipstick and a wig. She knew her lovely father did this stuff, but she didn't want to see it.

'He's my dad,' she protested.

'Are you scared?'

'Yes, I am.' Kate was drumming her fingernails on the table. 'I'm very, very scared.'

'Guess what?' said Chloe. 'Lucia's scared too. It's okay, Kate. She looks great. She doesn't look like a freak. She needs you to accept her.'

'I don't know if I can.'

'Yes, you can.' Chloe wagged her forefinger. 'Transition is the hardest . . . fucking . . . thing e-*ver*. I should know. If people, people she cares about, don't help Lucia, she might not get through all this. And from where I'm sitting, people she cares about is . . . you.'

The patch of sunshine had moved on. It was gloomy now in the kitchen. Kate got up to switch on the fan heater and stood warming her calves. Her dad had showered her with pure, unquestioning love since the day she was born. He'd loved her through two-year-old tantrums and ten-year-old ones and teenage ones. He'd taught her to drive—ye gods, that must have taken nerves of steel. He'd cleaned up after her twenty-first party, when she tangoed with Owen up and down the kitchen table before vomiting. He'd let her pierce her tongue (closed up now, thank God) and dye her hair, without saying anything judgemental. Despite all her cock-ups, all the times she'd behaved like a total bitch, he'd never stopped being proud of her.

'There's nobody else,' said Chloe. 'You're the only one who's got enough love to stand beside her.'

The bathroom door was being unbolted; she could hear her dad's measured footsteps, walking into his room and out again. She was running out of time. The next moment he'd reappeared in the kitchen, wearing a waxed jacket and a paisley scarf.

'Ready to go?' he asked, with his quiet smile. 'Anyone need to borrow sensible shoes?'

Kate made her decision.

'Dad,' she said. 'Um, I don't know how to put this, but . . . do you think this Christmas walk could include Lucia?'

•

Well. As bizarre, screwed-up and yet oddly lovely experiences go, this won the rosette. Kate had never thought of herself as a conventional person: she'd snogged a girl when she was in year ten, in a determined but doomed attempt to be gay; she owned three pairs of Doc Martens and not a single pair of kitten heels; she'd done things with a carrot that she seriously wouldn't want posted on Facebook; but this was one Christmas Day walk she would never forget. She took it in the company of two women, one of whom was her father.

He—no, sorry, *she*—took ten minutes to change. Kate stood in the kitchen, drinking coffee and wanting to run away.

'It'll be okay,' Chloe kept saying.

'I hope so.'

'Keep calm, young Kate!' said Chloe, imitating a royal voice. 'Keep calm, and keep smiling.'

Suddenly the kitchen door opened, and there she was: the woman who was Kate's father. She'd transformed herself. She was wearing a simple dark blue dress and a grey pashmina, pearls around her neck and in her ears, and low court shoes. Kate could tell there was make-up, but it was subtle, and it made her face look feminine. It was rather a professional job, actually. She wasn't wearing a wig—Kate was relieved about that—but she'd done her hair differently, across her forehead and around her jawline and somehow fluffed up, and it worked. She didn't look like a pantomime dame. She looked like someone you might see in church, arranging the flowers.

Chloe wolf-whistled. Kate was too stunned to speak.

The new woman stood like a coiled spring, shifting her weight from one leg to the other and trying to smile. She seemed ready to bolt back into her bedroom. Kate needed to pull herself together, and fast. She put down her coffee, hurried across to Lucia and took both her hands.

'Dad,' she said. 'You look really . . . nice.'

And Chloe was right. It was okay.

Thirty-six

Lucia

New Year's Eve was almost upon us. Kate said she'd be helping out behind the bar at the Bracton Arms. My mother was off to a bash at her golf club. Chloe was working (I tried not to imagine what this meant). Maybe Eilish was going to be alone? I thought perhaps she and I could spend the evening together, as old friends. Last year we'd celebrated on top of East Yalton hill. It would be nice to do that again.

I was in my office when I summoned the courage to ask her. Most partners spent this holiday week with their families, but I'd been going stir crazy in the flat. No time like the present, I thought, lifting the phone.

Stupid of me. Presumptuous. Did I really think a woman like Eilish would be sitting around, waiting for her ex to call? No, she was going to a party at Jim Chadwick's place. She mentioned it casually, trying to make it sound like a bore ('All that booze and bonhomie and "Auld Lang Syne"! I'd rather be in bed with a good book') but I knew Eilish very, very well. I could tell Jim was becoming more than a colleague and friend. There was a tinge of embarrassment, even excitement, in her tone.

I told her I had to end the call because my desk phone was ringing. It wasn't. Then I grabbed my coat and got out of the building as fast as I could. Benjamin, who was semi-retired now, tried to stop me in the corridor—*Ah, Luke, can we talk about this seminar we're hosting?*—but he must have read the anguish in my body because he let me go without another word. Winter hit me as I stepped outside. The streets were grey, the sky was grey; there was ice in the air. I walked faster and faster, across the river and back, trying to escape the pain of it. The dreaded, inevitable thing was happening. I was losing her.

Jealousy is a torment. It eats you from the inside. My sexual desires had diminished since I began hormone therapy, but my emotions were as strong as ever. I had no right to question Eilish's private life; I had no right to anything, but I felt violent bitterness towards Jim Chadwick. I knew the man and had always liked him. Why was he taking Eilish from me?

It wasn't until that evening, back at the flat, that I took control. I gave myself a mental slap across the face and told myself not to be so bloody selfish. I loved Eilish, didn't I? Felt guilty for ruining her life? Right. So I had to let her go. I had to be pleased for her, and for Lucky Jim.

When New Year's Eve arrived, I resolved not to think about what she was doing. I treated myself to my favourite Thai takeaway. Then I put on a comfortable skirt and jersey, and spent the evening in an armchair in the company of Virginia Woolf and a bottle of whisky. They were good companions. I kept one eye on the clock. The birth of a year is still an occasion, even if you're alone.

Just before midnight, I wrapped Judi's pashmina around my shoulders and stepped out into the garden. It was a crisp night. Very still. After a few minutes, I heard the countdown from the television in an upstairs flat, and joined in: *Three! Two! One* . . . and then the world went crazy. It was like being in a celebratory war zone. I was too far away to see the public display; these fireworks were being lit by ordinary families, huddled in tiny back gardens. I imagined a city full of human beings, all hoping and praying and believing that this year would be a good one. We were in the middle of a global recession; there was unrest and brinkmanship and civil war all over the world, and the ice caps were melting. And yet as midnight struck, thousands of fireworks blazed above the rooftops of London. Sometimes you have to love the human race for its sheer bloody optimism.

I stood in the darkness, my head tilted towards the iridescent, gunshot exploding sky, and found myself quietly weeping. I couldn't tell you whether they were tears of love or euphoria or loneliness. All three, I think. Perhaps the hormones were heightening my emotions, or perhaps it was the whisky. Whatever their cause, the tears felt right and good, and there was nobody there to see them. I cried for Eilish; I cried for Nico, and for Rosa, and wished them a happy New Year. I promised Lucia that I would not abandon her. This year, I would become the person I was always meant to be.

Eilish

The last seconds of the dying year. Such precious seconds! Big Ben. Party poppers, streamers, everybody kissing everybody. I was counting down and party popping with the best of them. Jim's friends were many and varied, his energy infectious, and his mulled wine not for the faint-hearted. My feet ached from dancing; my high-heeled shoes had long since been kicked into a corner. Jim threw one hell of a party.

As the final bell tolled, I stood still. The world around me seemed to move in slow motion, as though I were watching a film. This couldn't be real. This was the last second of the year in which I lost Luke.

Then Jim was beside me: his arms around my shoulders, his eyes smiling into mine. I'd been expecting him; the spark between us was as highly charged as ever. He bent his head to speak into my ear, because the celebrations were deafening.

'I've a feeling it's going to be a wonderful year,' he said. I felt the warmth of his mouth on my ear, my hair, the nape of my neck, and on my mouth. I felt my stomach twist with longing.

I kissed him. I did. I kissed Jim Chadwick as the streamers floated around us. I felt his hands pressing on my back and I swayed against him. After all, I thought, why not? There is life after divorce. Jim's intelligent and attractive and fun. He doesn't suffer from black moods. He doesn't try on my clothes when I'm not around. Why not?

The thing is, though, that Jim wasn't Luke. He didn't kiss like Luke. He didn't feel like Luke in my arms. He didn't say the things Luke would say.

Another guest grabbed him—a perky divorcee who'd been pursuing him all evening—and, after her, another. Meanwhile, the friendly couple I'd met during dinner came rushing up, enveloping me in hearty New Year hugs.

The moment had passed.

Under cover of all the revelry I found my shoes and jacket and slipped out, through the kitchen and into the back garden. It was another world out there. The sky was cloudless, the stars brilliant, the air bitter. No moon. Jim's cottage was deep in the fields, but I could see fireworks going off over Cottingwith.

This time last year, Luke and I had climbed East Yalton hill with champagne and plastic glasses. This time last year, Luke was on the verge of depression again. I knew it, but I ignored it. I hoped the problem would soon go away. It didn't fit with my plans. Which of us was the selfish one?

Luke's alone tonight. He might be alone forever.

Sounds of celebration rose and fell behind me, muffled by the weathered walls of the cottage. I remembered that there were some garden chairs on the lawn and made my way across to them. They were wooden, and very solid. For a long time, I sat silently beneath the dazzling chaos of the universe. Alone out here, I knew myself better. In the darkness, I saw things clearly.

I heard the back door open and shut, footsteps on the grass, and there was a touch on my shoulder.

'Hello,' said Jim. 'I lost you.'

'I'm sorry.'

He sat in one of the other chairs. I could make out the pale shape of his face. 'You're sorry? I don't like the sound of that.'

'Half the women in that house are after you, Jim. You've made me feel a whole lot better about myself. I'm so grateful.'

'God. Please don't be grateful! Anything but gratitude. It implies . . . what does it imply? . . . polite obligation. I was hoping for something quite a lot more passionate.'

'All right. I'll try to be ungrateful.'

'Better.'

I collected my thoughts. There were things I had to say, and I wanted to get it right.

'You and I go way back,' I said. 'You know how much I value that. You're top of the list of men I'm tempted to sleep with. In fact, you *are* the list.'

'But?'

'But . . . Luke.'

'Eilish, Luke's been gone for months.' He sounded exasperated, and I didn't blame him.

'Nearly six,' I agreed. 'And I'm about to apply for decree absolute.'

'And he's about to become a woman. I like him, I admire what he's doing, and I really do hope he'll be happy . . . but you've got the rest of your life ahead of you, and you deserve to be happy too.'

One last firework shot up. A rocket; brightly coloured. It hung high above the horizon before bursting apart with a distant crackle.

I sighed. 'You're right. That's why I thought perhaps I could let go now, tonight, and start a new life; but it doesn't work like that. I can't just forget the last thirty years and fall joyously into bed with you. Not yet, anyway. I'm very, very sorry, because it would have been a lot of fun.'

'It would.'

He was silent for a time. I heard him shift in his chair.

'Don't worry,' he said. 'I can take rejection on the chin. What I want to hear from you is a promise that this won't change things. We were bloody good friends before—and we still are. Right?'

'Right.'

'And you promise to call on me if you need anything?'

'I promise.'

'And you'll come inside now, and help me hand out cups of coffee to fifty drunk people?'

'I'd be honoured,' I said.

He stood up, and reached for my hand.

Thirty-seven

Luke

On New Year's Day, I woke to a hangover and low spirits. The emotion of the night before had worn off and left me flat. For a time, I found I couldn't even get out of bed. It would take too much effort to get dressed or make coffee or eat. I'd felt like this before, and I feared it. 'Watch out for depression,' Usha had said. 'Be alert to it.'

I wondered whether it might help to go to a local cafe, just for some human company; but I pictured myself sitting alone at a table, surrounded by couples and families all in holiday mode. I picked up the phone to call Eilish, then remembered she'd been to a party and might not appreciate her no-good cross-dressing husband waking her. Anyway, what if she wasn't alone? What if she and Jim . . . ? Appalling possibility. It made me feel far, far worse.

I had to fight this descent. I had to get up and get going, to behave like a useful human being with a role in life. I decided to go into Bannermans, where I had plenty to be getting on with. At that thought I took a shower and dressed in Luke's going-into-work-on-a-public-holiday clothes: corduroy trousers, a collared shirt and a jersey. It was a costume that felt more and more alien. My hair was becoming too long for conventionality now, curling down the back of my neck. On a whim I pulled a ribbon out of the drawer and tied my greying locks into a ponytail. It was a very small ponytail, like a paintbrush, and it looked silly—ageing rocker meets square solicitor—but it felt rebellious and made me smile, so I left it there.

Our divorce was well underway. Papers lay beside the toaster where I'd thrown them in disgust, but I couldn't ignore them forever. I leafed through the pile, wondering whether today was the day to tackle them once and for all. I had already offered far more than half of our joint assets to Eilish, including Smith's Barn, but it seemed that her solicitor was not a trusting person. She wanted bank statements; she wanted valuations; she wanted details about the pension; she wanted sworn affidavits; she wanted exhaustive lists. All of this was leading inexorably towards decree absolute, the death knell of our marriage.

I was shovelling the papers into my briefcase when I heard the sound of shoes on the area steps, and a female voice. Tearing the ribbon out of my hair, I swung around to peer through the window. The door was locked and bolted; there was no need for me to behave like a scared rabbit. The next moment I saw who it was and my heart leaped—I mean really, it leaped with joy. I rushed to the door, fumbled with the locks and threw it open.

And there they were. Carmela stood in jeans and boots and padded jacket, looking nervous. A bright-eyed baby gazed at me over her shoulder, strapped to her back by a band of cloth. Holding his mother's hand, hopping from foot to foot and yelling, *Grandpa!* at the top of his lungs, was a small boy whom I loved.

'Happy New Year,' said Carmela.

•

Five minutes later, Nico was drinking hot milk and looking at me over his mug, talking and talking because he had a million things to say. I was sitting with one arm around his shoulder, ruffling his hair. Carmela had taken Rosa from her back and was feeding her (*She gets milk from there*, Nico whispered knowledgeably. *It doesn't hurt Mummy because Rosa hasn't got any teeth yet*).

'Carmela, does . . .' I stopped, and reframed the question. Nico had big ears. 'Have you notified all parties of this official visit?'

She raised one eyebrow. 'Not yet. All parties have been called out to an emergency involving a canine and a large red passenger service vehicle.' I think she saw my concern, because she smiled. 'Don't worry about the reaction of all parties. It's my problem.'

Distracted by our talking, Rosa stopped sucking and tried to pull herself upright. She was a curious little thing, interested in all the goings-on in her world. I couldn't take my eyes off her.

'Would you like to hold her?' Carmela asked me.

'Could I?'

By way of a reply, she lowered my granddaughter into my arms.

She had tiny curling feet, and round cheeks. I held her carefully, mesmerised by such miniature perfection. At first she whimpered and looked back at Carmela, but when I said her name she turned her head to see who I was. Her fingers closed around my shirt front. Nico tickled her toes while I burbled nonsense and made idiotic grinning faces, tucking her closer into my arms so that she felt secure. Suddenly, she seemed to get the joke. Her mouth opened and her face split into a toothless smile.

'She likes you, Grandpa,' said Nico.

I tried to speak, but I couldn't. For the second time in twelve hours, I was in tears.

Simon

He was on duty over New Year, so he had to keep off the booze. Probably a good thing. There were two calls in the night but neither concerned anything life-threatening. The first real emergency came at seven, just as he was stepping out of the shower.

'Fred Bibby here,' said a quiet voice. 'My dog's Floss. Wire-haired terrier.'

After a moment's thought, Simon remembered. Fred Bibby was an ex-serviceman in his eighties, and Floss was a complete airhead.

He reached for his clothes, dressing as he talked. 'Go ahead, Mr Bibby. What's up?'

The old man sounded asthmatic, wheezing with each breath. 'She took off after a bloody cat. Wouldn't come back no matter how much I called, got across the road, and I thought she'd be all right, but then she turned around, tried to get back to me and jumped out right in front of the bus. Wasn't the driver's fault. He was white as a sheet, white as a sheet, you never saw a man so upset. She can't get up. Can I bring her in?'

Simon was dressed and grabbing his car keys in three minutes flat. His family were eating breakfast in their nightclothes.

'You have to go?' asked Carmela.

''Fraid so.'

'How long will you be?'

'Hard to say. Maybe not long. Not many dogs get hit by buses and live to tell the tale.' He kissed each of them. Rosa waved her arms and beamed at him. She was four months old now, and undeniably a person in her own right.

As it turned out, Floss had been lucky. Her pelvis was fractured but the prognosis was good. Simon stayed at the surgery for the rest of the morning, doing the rounds in the clinic and phoning owners. He arrived home at two o'clock, with the beginnings of a headache, to find his family pretty much where he'd left them. Rosa was lying under her baby gym, kicking the toys.

'Jeepers!' cried Simon. 'Haven't you lot left the room since I've been gone?'

'Have some lunch,' said Carmela. 'We treated ourselves to quiche from the delicatessen. I've kept it warm for you.' She crossed to the oven and took out a plate.

Simon picked Rosa up and sat with her on a stool. '"This is the way the ladies ride,"' he sang, bouncing her gently. '"Trit-trot, trit-trot. This is the way the gentlemen ride. Gall-op! Gall-op! Gall-op!"'

The baby screeched with delight. Nico joined in, shouting the words—not an elegant sight, as his mouth was full of quiche. Father and son yelled the last lines together: '"This is the way the drunkard rides! Slip . . . slide . . . And DOWN we go!"'

'She likes that bit,' said Nico. 'Daddy, guess where we've been? We've been somewhere a *loooong* way!'

'Shh, Nico. Not now,' said Carmela, quite sharply.

'A dastardly secret!' cried Simon, thinking this was all a game. 'Where have you been? Let me think . . . To the North Pole, to try and persuade Father Christmas you've been good?'

'No!'

'No? Um, to the moon?'

Nico laughed raucously. 'No, silly! We saw someone. Guess who we saw?'

'The Queen?'

'We saw Grandpa!' Nico was prancing around in a circle. 'We went to his house under the ground.'

'Nico,' snapped Carmela. There were crimson spots on her cheeks. 'I think Rosa has a dirty nappy. Could you be a very grown-up boy and fetch the changing bag? And if you choose a story from your bookcase, I will read it to you. Off you go, please.'

Nico stopped prancing. 'I'll get "The Magic Crayon",' he said happily. The next moment, his footsteps were clattering up the stairs.

There was a very nasty silence in the kitchen.

'I looked at Rosa,' Carmela said. 'And I looked at Nico. I saw the joy they bring. I knew it was wrong to shut him out.'

'Jesus Christ!'

'Shush,' warned Carmela, but it was too late. Rosa was startled by the shout, so close to her ear. She wailed tragically, holding out her arms to her mother.

'I don't believe this,' snapped Simon, handing the baby over. 'Go on, then. Go back to Mummy.'

'Don't be such a child. It isn't her fault.'

'No. It's yours.' Simon stood up, reaching for his jacket. 'The one thing you knew I didn't want to happen, and you waited until my back was turned and did it anyway. It was a bloody deceitful, downright shitty thing to do.'

'He is the grandfather of my children! And you know what? I'm not sorry. If you'd seen the look on his face when he spotted us at the door! He held Rosa. He wept. If you had seen Nico's happiness, I don't think you would be so angry, Simon. I really don't.'

Simon imagined his dad holding Rosa. His father, and his baby—it should have been such a precious moment. He was afraid he might be going to cry. He needed a drink.

'I'm going back to work,' he muttered.

'You can't keep running away, Simon.'

'If I stay here any longer there's going to be an almighty row. D'you want that?'

Her eyes shone with fury. 'Maybe there are things that need to be said. I want an adult husband, not a little spoiled brat who thinks only of himself.'

Simon strode out, letting the door slam behind him.

He found a thousand things to do in the surgery, then went to the pub and sank several pints. He sat hunched over, hands hanging between his knees. His head was pounding. He didn't trust many people in this world. For much of his life he'd felt alien, as though he were gatecrashing a party to which everybody else was invited; but he'd trusted his dad, and he'd trusted Carmela. Those two people had conspired against him today, and he felt as though he'd been run over by a steamroller. He'd never asked for this. He'd never asked for any of this.

•

The White Hart looked solid and respectable. A light rain was starting to fall, tiny drops forming an aura around the streetlights. He waited in darkness. The shards of his bottle were jagged. They could do horrific damage to a human being. The back door of the pub opened and shut, followed by quick footsteps.

His fist tightened on the neck of the bottle. He'd smack it into his–her face. This was one lady boy who would never again lure an innocent man into its web.

'Simon?' she said softly.

Yes, he could hear it now: it wasn't an ordinary woman's voice. It was husky and low. He shivered in disgust, because he'd thought it sexy.

'Here,' he said.

'Why are you skulking back there?'

The footsteps came closer until the slim figure appeared, just visible in the light from the hotel's windows. He felt a tug of affection. There was a halo of mist around her hair, and her smile was as sweet as ever.

No, he corrected himself, not *her* smile. *His* smile. And it wasn't sweet, it was false. This was a cunning trickster.

'Simon? What's up?' Jessica seemed puzzled by his silence. She came closer. Then she saw what he was holding.

'No,' she said. 'No, Simon. Oh my God.'

'What's your name?'

'Jessica.'

He stepped right up to her, and put a hand on her throat. 'Don't fucking give me that. I want your real name.'

She was shaking. She looked down at the splintered glass in his hand.

'Joshua,' she whispered.

Simon swung the bottle. 'You should have been drowned at birth,' he said.

Light flashed on dagger shards. The he–she person didn't try to run away, or even to defend herself. She simply stood with rain and tears on her cheeks, waiting for her boyfriend to maim her. Five hours and twenty minutes ago, he'd said he loved her.

Thirty-eight

Eilish

New Year's Day. Kate was nursing a hangover and—to my shame—so was I. The pair of us drooped around the house, knocking back the Alka-Seltzer and tripping over Baffy, who seemed anxious that he might be abandoned again.

'So,' Kate said. 'Did you play tonsil hockey with my old science teacher?'

I felt myself blush. 'What a very unattractive expression that is.'

She nodded calmly. 'I'll take that as a yes. Eew. How come you're home, then? How come you didn't stay for a night of passion—or whatever passes for passion when you're talking about two teachers in the sack?'

'Because, when it came to it, he wasn't your dad. Would you have minded?'

'I probably would, but it's none of my business who you shack up with. It's only a matter of time, anyway. The sharks are circling. Mr Chadders will get you in the end—or if he doesn't, somebody else will.'

In the afternoon we summoned enough energy to walk with Baffy across the fields. He seemed to think this was a trip to heaven, full of rabbits and streams and dead things to roll in. The little dog was growing on me; there was something appealing about his zealous stupidity. Casino didn't find him appealing at all, but the two animals had come to an understanding. It was pretty simple: the cat was boss. Poor Baffy had the scars to prove it.

I'd invited Meg for dinner, and then to stay the night. I thought she'd like to see Kate. At five o'clock the hybrid ladybird puttered up to the house. Neither Kate nor I was up to cooking, so the three of us went out to the Bracton Arms. It's a marvellous pub in winter: open fires, stone flags, and oak beams around the bar. As a bonus, Ingrid and Harry had gone on a cruise, so we were able to order meals without being cross-examined.

'Bloody lucky,' whispered Kate as we settled ourselves into an alcove. 'Ingrid's getting harder to fob off, bless her mule slippers. When I said Dad's working on some bloody enormous deal and the commute's just too much for him, she actually stuck her tongue into her cheek.'

'It's her job to know about everyone,' said Meg. 'It's better than living in a big city where nobody knows or cares.'

My mother-in-law was her usual dapper self—in appearance, at least. I wasn't sure what was going on underneath. She raised her glass to us in salute . 'Here's cheers. Let's hope this year turns out better than the one that's just gone.'

'Cheers,' chimed in Kate. 'Right. Now you're both here: hit me with it, oh ancient ancestors! How was Christmas Day at Simon and Carmela's?'

I looked at Meg, and she looked back at me.

'Mmwell . . . it was a beautiful meal,' she began, twisting her mouth. 'Carmela did a special pudding that she said was a Spanish delicacy. She's a clever girl.'

Kate giggled. 'When people start yakking about how terrific the food was, I know the whole event was fucking dire. Come on, Granny.' She rapped her knuckles on the table. 'On a scale of one to ten, just how bad was it?'

'Ten,' said Meg promptly. 'No, nine and a half, because I have to admit those children are a delight. But the elephant took up so much space, there wasn't room for anything else. I mean, how do you celebrate peace in the world when there's a son not speaking to his father? Or even *about* his father? And Eilish, I have to say this . . . he's drinking too much. He was slurring his words by the time I left. Carmela looked so upset. It wasn't good, was it?'

I agreed with her. Carmela had done her best, but the day was a disaster.

'And then there was Wendy,' I said.

Meg covered her eyes with a hand. 'I sometimes wonder whether she's really mine. She got all tearful, Kate. Said she's lost her only brother. Which I suppose she has, in a way.'

I was sticking to sparkling water that evening; I just don't have the stamina anymore. Kate was nursing a half of Guinness. She claimed to like it, though I wondered whether it was an image thing. 'And what about you, Granny?' she asked. 'Have you lost a son?'

Meg thought about this question for quite some time. I waited, intrigued. Finally she put down her glass. 'Fifty-five—nearly fifty-six years ago, I gave birth to a child. He was gorgeous from the first day. I don't have favourites, but if I did—' a guilty little grin '—well, no prizes for guessing which it would be. Now that child has grown up into an adult and had children of his own. Turns out there were things about him I didn't understand, but the fact remains that he's the one I gave birth to. He was always kind and thoughtful, and he's still kind and thoughtful. He was always clever; he's still clever. I always loved him, and I can't see that changing now.'

'You're a saint,' I said.

'No, no. I wish I was.' Meg shook her head. 'He was suffering. That's what I can't get over, that's what keeps me awake at night. I keep thinking back and remembering how that boy of mine never smiled. I *knew* something was up but I didn't ask. I was too scared. I let myself get caught up in the farm and the girls and Robert, and things I wouldn't give a bar of soap for now.' Her hand was trembling as she took a sip of her wine. I reached out and touched it, and she murmured, 'It's all right, dear.'

'Mothers aren't mind-readers,' said Kate. 'They can't know everything their children are thinking. You mustn't blame yourself.'

A waitress—Sophie—turned up with cutlery and serviettes. She was a friend of Kate's who'd built many a hut by our pond, and she stopped to chat. I listened vaguely to the small talk, smiling in the right places, but I was fretting about what Kate had just said.

She's wrong. Isn't she wrong? Mothers can almost be mind-readers. I remembered the jolt I'd felt when two-year-old Simon touched an electric fence—as though the shock had bolted through my own body; and what about those sleepless, tearful nights when Kate was being bullied? Luke and I felt what our children felt, feared what they feared. I'd be horrified if I learned that Simon had been depressed as a youngster and I hadn't even known.

Then I remembered the hints Jim had dropped, over dinner at The Lock. *He hasn't always found life easy, has he? Bit of a loner.* I hadn't known my husband, after all; perhaps I hadn't known my son either. Perhaps we never really understand our families at all, any of us. Perhaps those we love the most are really a bunch of strangers, with secret thoughts and inner lives. I didn't like the idea.

After Sophie left, Kate rolled up her sleeves.

'Now,' she said. 'There's something I have to say. I want to talk to both of you about Christmas Day with Dad. I'm not sure either of you is going to like this, but I think you have to know.'

Meg and I listened with increasing astonishment—and, in my case, indignation—as she described her day. By the time she came to the end of the story, I imagine our jaws were touching the table.

'Sorry,' I said, blinking in bafflement. '*Sorry?* You're telling me you went for a sedate little promenade around East London with two . . . with two . . .'

'Two women.'

'Both of whom had . . . ?'

'Wedding tackle,' suggested Meg helpfully.

Kate nodded. 'Wedding tackle. But two women, all the same.'

'One of whom was *my* husband and *your* father,' I said.

Kate opened her hands. 'I can't describe it in any other way, Mum. I'm telling you, I felt as though I was out and about with two women. I was *not* in the company of men. Their . . . I don't know, their life force was female.'

I don't do New Age, and I wasn't going to start talking about life forces now. 'You never met Chloe when she was Carl or Geoffrey or whatever she was,' I said. 'Fair enough, I can see how you might suspend your disbelief about her. But surely you can't do that when it comes to your own father?'

'Yes. No.' Kate pressed her fingers to her temples. 'Aargh, how do I explain this? Yes *and* no. I don't think gender's about wedding tackle, or the lack of it. The problem is this obsession we've got with categorising people into discrete little boxes.'

I sat back in my seat. 'Kate, I'm appalled! How could he ask this of you? He never used to be a selfish man—never, ever. Maybe Simon's right, he's gone completely mad.'

'I asked him to do it.'

Meg was swirling her wine around in the glass. It caught the light from the fire.

'Seeing him,' she said. 'That's going to be a real test. I don't know how I'll cope with that.'

Kate was positively evangelical, as though the sight of her father cross-dressed had been a road to Emmaus experience. 'Granny, I was dreading it too, but, believe me, it was okay. I think I understand now. When I picture Dad as I grew up, he was gorgeous, but somehow . . . there was something dark. It's hard to put your finger on it.'

I knew exactly what she meant.

'A shadow,' said Meg. 'That's how I see it.'

'Bang on!' Kate clapped her hands. 'Well, I think Dad's shadow is finally lifting. And I'll tell you what, he's bloody convincing as a woman. He's been practising. *She's* been practising. That doesn't mean it's easy. It's not. He's lonely and he's scared. Chloe seems quite worried. She reckons transition is a dangerous time . . . actually, she said it's the hardest fucking thing ever and if we don't front up, Dad might not get through it. I think she means suicide.'

The word winded us all. Our meals arrived; we made appreciative noises and said no thanks, we don't need ketchup. Then we let our food go cold. We were a silent trio of women, all of us thinking about the same man.

Meg recovered first. 'Right,' she said, pulling her knife and fork from a serviette. 'I'm not having that. I failed him when he was a kid and I'm not going to make the same mistake now. If you can face seeing him like that, Kate, then so can I. It's lucky Robert's gone. This would definitely kill him.'

'Have you heard from Gail?' I asked. I barely knew Luke's eldest sister.

'Oh, Gail.' Meg rolled her eyes. 'Yes, I've heard from her. She phoned the day she got his letter. She said she always knew he was a freak. She said she never wants to hear his name again. I told her that was her business.'

'She's a piece of work, isn't she?' said Kate.

She and Meg talked for a while about Gail, but soon their conversation began to range through quite a sweep of topics: Owen's new girlfriend (Meg disapproved—old enough to be his mother), Meg's appointment at the audiology clinic (Meg disapproved—there was nothing wrong with her hearing), and a pop star who'd frolicked about completely naked for her latest music video (thereby objectifying all women, according to Kate; Meg just thought the poor lass looked cold).

I half listened, even chipped in from time to time, but my mind was on Luke. I wondered what he was doing right now, tonight, and whether he was safe from himself. For the first time, I began to imagine what kind of a woman he would be.

Kate thought his shadow was lifting. If that were true, then all this might be worth it.

•

The new term began. Every day, somebody in the staffroom would complain about the fact that it was January. I was tempted to have badges printed for them to wear, save them the trouble of moaning out loud.

'Nothing left of Christmas but the overdraft,' someone would drone gloomily, opening their packed lunch. 'Hate it. Don't you hate it? Forecast says more rain for the weekend. Been raining for weeks. Thank God we're going to Tenerife for half-term.' There would be general nodding and tooth sucking from the chorus. Then someone would look out of the window and mutter, 'It's so . . . bloody . . . *dark*.'

I hate to sound like Pollyanna, but I've always rather liked January. There's something clean about it. I like the skeletons of bare trees against the sky; I like the frosty mornings when the pond has a thin rime of ice, and leaves crackle under your feet. Luke was gone, but that wasn't the fault of the season. I'd been dreading that first Christmas apart from him, and was relieved to have got through it. The immediate agony had dulled to a constant throbbing. In the evenings I'd close my curtains and tell myself to be grateful for the warmth of the Rayburn. There were refugees who'd lost everything, who didn't even have a blanket or food for their children, and all I'd lost was my husband. Sometimes I managed not to think about him for . . . ooh, minutes at a time.

'For goodness' sake,' I protested, when I'd heard the January lament once too often. 'We don't live in the Arctic Circle. The sun does actually rise, you know.'

'Not for long,' mumbled one of the Eeyores. 'Dark by four, never see my house in daylight; so depressing.'

I was on my way out. During Friday lunchtimes I ran a Brain Gym club. The most restless and uncoordinated teenagers in the school would already be waiting for me in the drama room, so I was in a hurry to get there before anarchy broke out.

Mick Glover looked up from his tablet. He spent his life gazing at its screen; I was sure he watched porn on there. 'You and Luke going away at half-term?' he asked.

'Probably not.'

Out of the corner of my eye, I saw heads swivel my way. They were all wondering.

Mick raised one eyebrow. 'Still working on the Big Project?'

The cynicism in his tone set my teeth on edge. *What do you know about love, or loyalty?* I thought furiously.

'Actually,' I said loudly, 'Luke and I have separated. Permanently. We're getting divorced.'

The effect was rather satisfying. The staffroom fell silent, coffee mugs halfway to open mouths. It was a bit like being in one of those westerns when Clint Eastwood walks into a saloon and asks for a whisky, and the pianist stops playing, and everyone ducks except the barman.

Mick had the grace to look embarrassed. I heard a general murmur: *I'm sorry*, and *I don't believe it*, and *Eilish, I had no idea*.

'It's perfectly amicable,' I told them. 'No fault attached, neither of us has anybody else. I am fine, absolutely fine.'

With those words, I barged out through the saloon doors.

School staffrooms are the most gossipy places in the world—and it's mostly the men who do the gossiping, in my experience. By the time I left the building at five o'clock, every adult in the school knew that my marriage was over. People were kind. They touched my upper arm, adopting the sad eyes and sober smiles reserved for funerals. Even the lab technician—who lives in her storeroom and never speaks to anyone if she can help it—said she'd heard things weren't going well for me, and she'd been through it too.

Not one of them could hide their curiosity, though they tried to do so, with varying degrees of tact. Of course they were curious; I would have been, too. When a plane crashes, they look for the black box because they want to understand what happened and avoid it happening again. It was the same with Luke and me. They wanted to understand why, after thirty years, the most stable marriage in the world had suddenly foundered. Someone had to be at fault. Someone *must* have had an affair. I later heard that the staff were divided roughly fifty-fifty on which of us had been playing the away game. A small but vocal majority thought it was me, with Jim Chadwick. The rest thought it was Luke, perhaps with Penny O'Neil, headmistress of St Matthew's Primary. Apparently he'd been seen in her office a lot—which was hardly surprising, since he was chair of her board of governors.

I wondered how they'd react if they knew that Luke's days as a man were numbered. When that news breaks, I thought grimly, the old saloon piano really will stop playing.

Thirty-nine

Lucia

My bedroom curtains were glowing in the light of a February sunrise. Everything was exactly the same as it had been the day before, and yet something was different. It was me. I felt . . . happy. I lay still, revelling in this unfamiliar serenity, prodding it to see if it was real. Something had left me; some deep ache of unhappiness. It was like waking up after having an infected tooth extracted, to find the pain is gone. Call it what you like: the placebo effect, hysteria, pure madness—but, for the first time in my life, I felt right. I fitted.

A new year, a new woman. Kate had seen and accepted me at Christmas; and in January my mother had rung to ask what I was doing for my birthday on the fourteenth. When I confessed to having no plans, she suggested we go to a P.G. Wodehouse adaptation that was on in the West End. We arranged to meet in Trafalgar Square.

'And, Luke.' She had a determined edge to her voice; I knew it well. 'You can be a girl. It's time I met this daughter of mine. I won't swoon.'

I'd tried on three different outfits that day, looking for one that wouldn't shock her too much. Chloe had given me a string of green glass beads for my birthday. I was very touched, because I knew she was often short of money. I put them on, wanting a little of my friend's panache. It was a drizzling afternoon. I felt cripplingly self-conscious as I walked up to my mother, who was waiting by one of the lions. I watched her eyes come out on stalks when the smiling woman in a dove-grey pashmina and pearl earrings turned out to be her son.

'It's all right, dear,' she said stoically, though for several seconds she'd been doing a fair imitation of a goldfish. 'I'm not going to have a heart attack.'

'Please don't,' I begged her. 'Not right under Nelson's Column, which Kate tells me is really a giant phallus and symbol of the filthy patriarchy.' My voice sounded quite feminine now; I'd found that pitch overlap after hours of practice, and the new inflections and intonations were coming more easily. It made all the difference to people's reactions.

Mum stepped back to look at me. 'I'm not going to pretend this isn't a strange moment. But I will say this—I'm impressed.' There was incredulity in her voice. 'Classy, not brassy.'

We went to the play, which was hilarious; and then out to dinner in a nearby restaurant.

'People stare,' whispered Mum, her eyes flicking around at the other diners.

I shrugged. 'Some do. Not all. Most don't even notice nowadays.'

'You're amazing,' she said, shaking her head. 'Just amazing.'

I didn't ask her what she meant. She tucked into her steak, and we talked about golf for the rest of the evening.

That had been a turning point. I now had my mother's approval, as well as my daughter's, and Lucia blossomed. Each evening, a conventional man in a suit carried his briefcase into the flat in Thurso Lane. An hour later a woman emerged, holding her head high. I rarely saw my neighbours—mostly Somali refugees, with problems of their own—and I honestly don't think they noticed anything unusual. I travelled on buses, went ice-skating with Kate and Chloe (they skated, I was the admiring audience), and had lunch in a bistro with some of the Jenny Marsden group. My friend the Che Guevara man would always remember if Luke had bought *The Big Issue*, and not ask Lucia.

People who become fluent in a second language tell me they actually think in that language; they aren't translating. It was like that with me. I began to think in Lucia's voice, with her words. She was the reality now. Luke was a fancy-dress costume I donned for work. It was a strange double life; it took me an hour or so to change from one person to the other—not physically, but mentally. Sometimes I accidentally used the wrong voice or body language. It was a strain, but I wasn't sinking.

As I took a shower on that glorious February morning, wincing at the increasing soreness across my chest, I noticed something new. It was very slight indeed, but nevertheless it was there. My body had begun to change. Fat and muscle were redistributing themselves. Even my face seemed different, when I looked in the shaving mirror.

I dressed in a white blouse, cardigan and flowing skirt and did several hours' work. At about ten I made a sortie to the newsagent's for more milk. On my way back, I picked up a magazine from Che Guevara man. He too was feeling chirpy, he said, because spring was on its way and soon it wouldn't be so effing cold. I stopped to chat for a while. He told me he used to sell sound systems and had a home and family. Then he'd fallen into gambling, become a total arsehole (his words) and lost everything.

I had appointments in the office that afternoon, and was reluctantly changing into a suit and tie when Chloe phoned. I told her about my euphoria.

'I feel so calm,' I said. 'Everything's lovely today.'

I could hear the smile in her voice. 'You know what that is? The hormones. For the first time in your life, your body isn't fighting your mind.'

'You could be right.'

'I *am* right! That's how cis people feel all the time.'

She meant cisgender people—those whose bodies matched their identities. I was pretty sure Mr Che Guevara didn't feel calm and happy all the time; quite often he felt cold and lonely. Still, I didn't argue.

'Will it last?' I asked.

'No.' She laughed. She was always laughing; I knew it was to cover up the pain. 'Hang on tight, Luce, you've boarded a roller-coaster—up, down, up. But when things get tough, remember how you're feeling today. Hold on to that and don't let go.'

'And where are you?' I asked her. 'Where on the roller-coaster?'

The laughter carried a flutter of panic. 'Not so good today.'

Poor Chloe. She'd tried to phone her mother the previous evening, and it hadn't gone well. Her mother insisted on calling her Callum ('Why does she do that? I haven't been Callum since I was fourteen years old!') and gleefully announced that her grandparents had changed their will to cut Chloe out. *They don't even want to hear your name, Callum.* Chloe had hung up on her. I suspected she'd then spent the night in tears and this was the real reason she'd phoned me.

'I wish there was a pill,' she said, in one of those rare, bleak, not-laughing moments, 'to make them feel what we feel. Just for a day. Just for an hour. Then they'd stop hating us.'

I told her I'd a good mind to take the first train up to Manchester and have words with the old bat. Chloe said her mum wasn't old, she was forty-six, but she was a bat.

'Thanks,' I said, as we ended the call.

'What for?'

'Well, you know . . . putting up with a fuddy-duddy like me.'

I could hear her laughter as I hung up.

I was still floating several feet above the ground when Judi turned up in my office. She was wearing some kind of trouser suit in dark crimson. Apparently, she'd had it made while on holiday in India.

'That's enough about my outfit,' she said. 'You've been on the hormones for a while now. You should come out before questions are asked.'

'They can't have had any noticeable effect,' I protested. 'It's like adolescence. It takes months. Years.'

She looked me up and down with a sceptical half-smile. 'You're changing fast, Luke,' she said. 'And you know it. It's not just a visual thing. Maybe it's some kind of sixth sense, I don't know, but my radar tells me you're changing. I don't even think of you as male anymore, to be honest. Not sure I ever did, but I certainly don't now. I see you as kind of . . . hinterland. You just don't . . . I don't know . . . you don't *smell* male. You don't talk male, or walk male. Your skin's not male. Lucia is taking over. People will notice. Then they'll talk.'

I knew she was right. It terrified me. It delighted me.

'Let's have a timetable for this rollout. May I?' she said, opening my desk diary with her manicured fingers. 'You must be the last person in this firm to use a real diary as well as a virtual one. Christmas present, was it?'

'Good guess. From my mother.'

'What else do you need to do?'

I scribbled a list on a memo pad. More voice training, deportment coaching, finish the electrolysis, allow time for the hormones to take effect; time for our divorce to be finalised, which I hoped would make things easier for Eilish, give her time to distance herself from me.

Judi was leafing through my diary. 'Weren't you meant to be taking a three-month sabbatical this year?'

'We were going to Italy. We cancelled it.'

'Okay. Well, let's aim for July. You'll have been separated from Eilish a year by then. In mid June, we brief the management committee and give them time for feedback. On July eleventh, you disappear for two weeks. While you're gone we send out a memo to everyone, and change your name on the website and stationery. You get a working woman's wardrobe together—I'll help with that. Have your hair done, get another laser zap on your face. What else? Leg wax, eyelash tint. Ear piercing.'

'Ouch.'

'Man up! And, for God's sake, have those eyebrows sorted out by someone who knows what they're doing.'

'Femininity is so complicated and painful.'

She sighed. 'Darling, try being in labour for thirty hours with an eleven-pounder. After that, everything's a cinch. Anyway, you return to work on the twenty-eighth of July as . . . drum roll, please . . . Ms Lucia Livingstone.'

I glanced anxiously at the diary. 'That's only five months away.'

'Probably too long. If you leave it any later than that, you're going to be outed before you're ready. Disastrous.'

'True.'

'Shall we make it a fixture?' Her pen was poised.

'Wait . . . wait.' I was spluttering. 'Think about it, Judi! This is it. This is no going back; goodbye, Luke.'

'I thought you'd already made that decision.'

'Yes, but . . . I'll have to walk in here with a new name, new clothes, a new gender. You won't be able to move for people laughing. Clients will take their work elsewhere. I'll bring Bannermans into disrepute.'

Judi had rested her chin on the back of her hand, and was nodding as though I were giving her a shopping list. 'Yep . . . yep . . . yep. All of that.'

'I'm seriously thinking about early retirement. I could move away, somewhere nobody knows me, then quietly transition. That'd be easier for Eilish. Much less public.'

Judi let me finish, and then she tapped the desk. 'Listen. Are you listening? This is a really, really big thing for you. I know that. But it isn't a really big thing for this firm. There are over five hundred people in our London office alone, and every one of them has their hang-ups. Over the past ten years I've seen 'em come and I've seen 'em go. We've had partners caught having sex in the lift. We've had someone become a reality TV star. We've had someone arrested for shoplifting. We've had three people die, in various ways. Those are just the things I can remember off the top of my head. The thing is, Livingstone—and I mean this nicely—you aren't such a big deal. There will be tranny jokes for a few weeks, but after that you'll be old news. You'll just be Lucia, who's as competent and decent as Luke ever was. Only better dressed.'

'I think you underestimate how disturbing this is for people.'

'I think you underestimate their tolerance.'

I still got a kick out of my job; at the moment, it was all I had. I needed the income, too. Divorce is very expensive and I hadn't planned for it. I couldn't afford to retire.

'You win,' I said. 'July it is.'

Judi couldn't suppress a victorious chuckle. I watched the words appear, flowing from her pen and onto the page of my diary. Magical, dangerous, exhilarating words. I had dreamed of them. I never thought to see them.

Lucia's birthday.

•

I began to have doubts as soon as Judi left my office. They started as a niggle, but by the end of the afternoon I was in a cold sweat. It was almost March now . . . how could I be ready by July? I was staring at the words she'd written in my diary when my desk phone rang. It was Izzy, at reception.

'I've got Penelope O'Neil on the line for you,' she said.

I was pleased, if a little surprised. Penny O'Neil, headmistress of St Matthew's school. We got on well. I liked her earthy sense of humour and straight talking.

'Penny!' I cried expansively, when she'd been put through. 'What a pleasure.'

There was no warmth in her voice. 'I think it won't be a pleasure,' she said. 'Luke, we've got a problem.'

Forty

Eilish

'You need to get rid of all this,' said Stella, emerging from the downstairs cloakroom with an armful of Luke's jackets and coats.

'I will,' I promised, taking them from her. 'I'll send them on to him. I just haven't got around to it yet.'

'Darling, it doesn't get easier! I should know. Why don't you let me sort everything out? He's not going to come home and wear them.'

She was helping me with the spring issue of the parish newsletter. I'd first offered to edit the publication a decade ago, and still hadn't found another mug to take it on. Luke thought this hilarious; he reckoned I did it in a desperate attempt to put credit in the heavenly account. The newsletter came out once a month, but in early March we pushed our bumper issue through every letterbox in the parish.

It had been a heart-lifting day, tinged with the first softness of spring. I'd picked a bunch of daffodils and they were in a vase on the kitchen table. I was writing the editor's letter while Stella organised the layout—she's a whizz at that kind of thing. The sun went down as we worked, Turkish-delight colours flaming through the copse.

'You should announce it in here,' Stella said, as she typed and clicked.

'What?'

'Luke. In your editor's letter. *It's been a busy and exciting year for East Yalton and Cottingwith parish. We have a dishy new vicar, the Reverend . . .*' Stella's brow furrowed. 'Damn. Can't remember the Rev's name.'

'Somebody Vallance.'

'That's it. *Somebody Vallance, who looks about eighteen and is adored by all the flower-pot hats. St Matthew's Church of England Primary School is proud to announce that they have a new IT suite, at vast expense, and also that its chair of governors is to be known henceforward as Miss Lucia Livingstone.*'

'There'd be fireworks,' I said. 'Luke's been such a pillar of the community, and for so long.'

'Mm. And the higher your pedestal, the more satisfying a crash you make when you fall. I discovered that after Steve got arrested.'

Once we were on the home straight, we opened the bottle of wine Stella had brought with her. I was just beginning to think about supper—I had a stew in the crockpot—when I noticed her peering out of the window.

'Little green sports car. Shall I nip out and see who it is?'

'I know who it is,' I said. 'I'll go.'

I wasn't surprised. Jim was still a frequent visitor, utterly unabashed by what had happened—or rather hadn't happened—on New Year's Eve. Today, though, he looked harassed.

'Sorry not to phone first,' he called out, hurrying across from his car. 'Just on my way home. I need to talk to you. Urgently. You've got somebody here?'

I stood back to let him in. 'Stella, this is Jim Chadwick. Jim, Stella Marriot . . . It's all right. Neither of you has to be discreet. You both know about Luke.'

Stella was charm itself, but as soon as Jim's back was turned she made meaningful faces at me. When he realised he'd left his lights on and ran back out to his car, she clutched my arm.

'Is this the one who was chasing you? Phwoar!'

I chuckled. 'Stel-*la*! We aren't teenagers, and this isn't the youth club. We don't snog behind the bike sheds.'

'So? Whoever said teenagers get a monopoly on romance? I'd be inviting him in for more than a glass of plonk, if I was in your shoes.'

Before she could warm to her theme, Jim strode back inside and took a glass out of my hand. Stella and I settled on the ragged sofa beneath the gallery, leaving an armchair free for him, but he didn't take it. He paced around—across to the big windows, then back again.

'You had something to talk about?' I asked.

'I did.' He scratched his head. 'I hate to be the bringer of bad tidings, but . . . well, really, I think I have to.'

'Get on with it then. And for heaven's sake, take a seat. We're getting sore necks just watching you.'

'Okay.' He threw himself into the armchair. 'It's out.'

'What's out?'

'Luke's out.'

I heard an intake of breath from Stella.

'He's been seen in London,' said Jim. 'Wearing a skirt and carrying a handbag.'

'Who saw him?' I asked.

'I've traced it to a lad who left school last year. Went to be a chef in one of the hotels. Ricky Tait? He had a job in the Bracton Arms for a while.'

I knew Ricky. I'd taught him. A good-looking lad; quite a charmer.

'Is he sure it was Luke?' I asked, clutching at a very small straw. 'I mean, wouldn't he look very different in those clothes? And it was probably just a glimpse. Ricky can't actually *prove* it was Luke. Nobody's going to believe him.'

'Eilish.' Jim leaned forward in his chair, demanding my attention. 'Luke stopped to talk to a *Big Issue* seller. Ricky had time to take photographs on his phone.'

A photograph on a teenager's phone. It took a moment for the significance to sink in. When it did, I stopped breathing. I put my hands to my face.

'He shared them?'

'They were all over the internet within ten minutes,' said Jim. 'They've been shared on Facebook and Twitter and Instagram and WhatsApp and Snapchat, and other media I don't even know about. They're still being shared, right now. Those pictures are everywhere.'

'WhatsApp?'

'Smartphones. They were causing a sensation in the staffroom just as I was leaving. Mick Glover, Graeme Nelson . . . everyone knew. By tomorrow morning there won't be a soul at Cottingwith High who hasn't seen those photos.'

I felt faint. 'Oh my God.'

'Look, I think you should take a few days off work. It's far too late to get them off the internet. It was too late the moment Ricky shared them, and that was ten seconds after he took them.'

'Stable doors,' said Stella.

'And bolting horses,' agreed Jim. 'I'll go and see Wally tomorrow morning, make him think about a damage limitation exercise.'

'Have they looked at them?' I asked. 'Mick and Graeme, and the others?'

Jim looked sickened. ''Fraid so. Mick had them on his tablet. He was flashing them around. I threatened to ram the bloody thing down his throat.'

'Quite right,' muttered Stella. 'This Mick's an idiot, whoever he is.'

'Have *you* seen them?' I asked Jim.

'No. But those who have assure me that it is unmistakably Luke.'

My private grief had become public gossip. It was breaking news, all over the district, right now. *Guess what? Guess what? Have a look at these . . . Oh my God, that is a crack-up!*

'Couldn't we pretend he was on his way to a fancy-dress party?' suggested Stella.

'The pictures were taken this morning, in broad daylight. Apparently they don't have a . . . fancy-dress look about them.'

'Poor Luke,' I said.

Jim smacked his hands on his knees. 'Eilish! For God's sake, never mind poor Luke. You must understand—you must be ready. This is going to make your professional life bloody difficult. And your personal life.'

'I'd better warn him straight away, before those photos get to Bannermans.'

'Darling,' said Stella, reaching for my hands. 'Luke isn't your problem.'

The phone rang. I stood up to answer it, but my mind was elsewhere. I was trying to take in what this meant; trying to focus on what I must do. There was absolutely no chance of hushing the whole thing up. I'd never been a great fan of social media—I'd only ever been on Facebook so I could see Kate and Carmela's photos—but I knew that once an image has been released into the wild, it can never be recovered.

'Eilish. It's me.' Luke's voice.

'If you're phoning to tell me that you're a celebrity, don't bother. I already know.'

'Oh, my love.' He sounded shaken. 'I'm sorry. I am so sorry. I didn't think it would come out like this . . . I thought we'd have time, it could all be kept under control, you could distance yourself from me in advance. This is a nightmare. I don't know how it's happened.'

'I do.' I told him about Ricky Tait. 'The kid should go into journalism,' I said bitterly. 'He has the killer instinct.'

'I don't blame him. Mrs Livingstone's husband in drag! Quite a scoop.'

My mobile rang—stopped—then rang again. I didn't look at it. Luke and I talked around and around the situation, both of us trying to understand the implications of what had happened.

The news hadn't reached Bannermans yet, but the clock was ticking because several of Luke's colleagues lived in our area. He'd arranged to meet the management committee that same evening.

We were in for a hell of a storm. A part of me thought—as Kate would say—*Bring it on! Screw the bastards.* So Luke was cross-dressed. So he and I were a spicy scandal. So what? Real friends would stick by us; fair-weather ones would head for dry land.

'I've a feeling we're about to find out who our friends are,' I said, watching as Stella put the kettle on, mouthing *Tea?* at me. In the background, Jim was quietly answering a call on his mobile phone. From his closed expression and hushed voice, I gathered it was about Luke.

My own mobile beeped. I had two missed calls and a text, all from Simon.

Call me. It's about Dad.

'It looks as though Simon's heard the news,' I said. 'His hair will be standing on end.'

'Oh dear—already? It's like the Big Bang: from nothing to everything in a nanosecond. And it's still expanding exponentially. People will be sharing it and sharing it, on and on.'

'How did you find out?'

'Penny O'Neil phoned. She laid it on the line, because she's been getting calls from parents who want me to resign. The logic seems to be that I cross-dress so I must be sleazy. Well, that's fine. I've given her my resignation. I was struggling to do the job properly anyway, living in London.'

Oddly, this news made my blood boil. St Matthew's owed a lot to Luke. He'd helped to turn the place around after they'd had an incompetent head, and they'd gone from strength to strength ever since. It was all voluntary, though clients of Bannermans would have paid a zillion pounds for that much of his time. How dare they condemn a man who'd been their friend for so many years? Which of them could cast the first stone?

'It's *not* fine!' I said indignantly. 'It's shoddy and it's bigoted and it's a bloody disgrace. After all you've done for them! Did Penny want your resignation?'

'She didn't see any alternative.'

'Spineless.'

'Darling, truly, this doesn't matter. All that matters now is you. I've brought shame on you.'

Jim had answered his mobile yet again. He'd turned away from me, but he was clearly agitated and I overheard a snatch of his conversation. *Why the hell should she bow out?* He got to his feet suddenly, and marched to the window and back. *You're out of your mind! You think we have SEN teachers of her calibre coming out of our ears?*

We're in trouble, I thought, Luke and I. Both of us. For better, for worse . . . and this is worse. Our world has changed again. It's no longer safe.

I said the next words before I'd thought them through. They came out instinctively, but I knew they were right.

'Will you come home?'

He didn't answer me.

'I want you to come home,' I said clearly. 'Just until this storm's blown over. You can wear any damned clothes you want. You can call yourself whatever you want. We have to face this together.'

Forty-one

Simon

He couldn't stop looking at them. Every time he looked, he wished he hadn't.

They'd arrived by email, from an ex-schoolmate who said Simon might like to know what was doing the social media rounds; and was he aware that his father was a transvestite? It couldn't have been much worse. Simon instantly recognised Luke, and yet it was a woman—wearing a skirt, a white blouse and a cardigan. She was nose to nose with a *Big Issue* seller. They seemed to be great mates.

Simon's life was falling apart. Carmela had moved into the spare bedroom after their row on New Year's Day. She said he snored when he'd been drinking. He hadn't forgiven her for taking the children to Thurso Lane; she hadn't forgiven him for reacting as he had. Stalemate.

'Are you trying to blackmail me?' he'd demanded one morning when he couldn't take any more of her cold politeness. 'Is this all about Dad?'

'No. This is all about you.'

So he went to work without saying goodbye, and in the evening he lingered at the pub. This soon became a routine. It seemed easier than going home and trying to put things right.

The girl in the club was haunting him again, as she had years ago. Sometimes he dreamed about her—graphic, erotic dreams—and woke up to find himself aroused. On those mornings he couldn't look anyone in the eye. He couldn't even look himself in the eye.

And now this. His father, the drag queen, plastered across the internet.

Nico was looking for him, running around the house. 'Daddy! Where are you? We have to go to swimming now.'

'In a minute,' Simon yelled back. 'You get ready.'

'I've got my things. I don't wanna be late. The teacher tells us off if we're late.'

The woman in the photos had changed since Simon saw her in the kitchen of Thurso Lane. She was much more convincing in her disguise. She had a different stance: one hand on the strap of her bag, the other delicately touching her own cheek as she listened intently to whatever the *Big Issue* seller was saying. There was no wig now. She wore her own dark hair like a woman's. Her eyes seemed wider, her mouth fuller. She looked disturbingly feminine.

Jessica was convincing, too. Even after she admitted what she was, and lay sobbing in the rain, she seemed like a real girl. That was what was so creepy about these people.

'Daddy, come on!' Nico charged into the room, and Simon quickly closed the page. The first thing to do was to look after Mum. This was going to blow her apart. He must warn her before she heard it from someone else.

'Shush a minute, I'm busy.'

'I'll be late,' whined Nico. 'I don't wanna be late. I'll be late, I don't wanna . . .'

Jesus, I can't hear myself think. The phone at Smith's Barn was engaged. No luck with Mum's mobile, either. He began to write a text.

Nico tugged on his arm. 'Pleeease! I don't wanna be late . . .'

'For Christ's sake, shut up!' snapped Simon. 'Selfish little brat.'

Nico burst into noisy tears. Carmela must have heard the commotion, because she appeared in the doorway, holding Rosa on her hip.

'What's going on?' she demanded. Nico ran to her, still wailing, and she bent to comfort him.

Simon looked up from his phone. 'What's going on is that someone's managed to take photos of my father in drag, and the pictures have gone viral.'

'No!' Carmela blinked several times, processing the information. 'So the secret's out? Poor Eilish.'

'Yep. The world is laughing at the Livingstone family right now, as we speak. I told Dad! I warned him—and now he's done this to us.'

'I'm sorry, Simon. We'll talk about it later.' Carmela looked at her watch. 'But Nico's going to be late for swimming if you don't set out right now. It's a good ten minutes' walk.'

'Does it matter?'

'It does,' she said firmly. 'Especially with all this stress. He needs normality.'

'Fine.' Simon stood up. 'I'll take him to his sodding swimming.'

Weird places, public swimming pools. There was something hellish about the smell of chlorine and the echoing water. Parents sat along the spectator benches, pretending to watch their children but actually gossiping and messing about with their phones. Perhaps they all knew. Perhaps they were looking at the pictures—yes, there were two fathers laughing at something on a screen. He couldn't face them. He helped Nico to change and then quickly left, searching for a refuge.

There was a licensed cafe across the road; its lights beckoned through the gloom. He hid in a warm corner with a bottle of Heineken. And then another. And one more. From time to time he stole a horrified, fascinated glance at the pictures on his phone.

He was heading for the toilets when Carmela rang.

'Where are you?' she asked.

'Nowhere.'

'I've just had a call from the receptionist at the pool. I think you forgot our son.'

There can be no sight more forlorn than that of a five-year-old boy clutching his swimming bag and waiting all alone. Nico was wearing only one sock, his jeans were wet and his sweatshirt was on inside out.

'Buddy,' cried Simon, rushing into the pool's foyer with outstretched arms. 'I'm so sorry!'

Nico must have been putting on a brave face for the receptionist; but when he saw his father, the facade crumpled.

'You left me,' he whimpered, and burst into tears.

'He thought you weren't coming.' The woman wasn't amused. 'The other children have been gone half an hour. He thought you didn't want him anymore.'

Simon dropped to his knees and hugged the little boy.

'Heartbroken,' added the woman, whose job description seemed to include making parents feel as guilty and inadequate as possible.

'D'you want some crisps, Nico?' asked Simon. 'Or chocolate?'

Even bribery didn't work. Simon gathered the wailing child into his arms, thanked the receptionist—who managed a frosty smile—and carried him outside.

'You left me,' said Nico, between sobs. 'You left me, Daddy.'

'Shush, buddy. I'm sorry. I got held up.'

'Held up where?'

'Shush.'

'You left me.'

Simon carried his son all the way home, which was no mean feat. 'You're getting heavy,' he puffed, but Nico just pressed his face closer and held on tighter.

As they turned into their street, Nico seemed to cheer up a bit. 'Nearly home. Mummy's going to be cross with you.'

'Yep. I'd say that's a fair assumption.'

'The swimming pool lady was *very* cross with you. She said she was sick of people using her as a babysitter.'

Carmela was waiting at the front door. Nico scrambled down from Simon's arms and ran to her. She took one look at her husband, guessed exactly where he'd been all evening, and was furious. He knew the telltale spots of crimson on her cheeks.

'You were drinking,' she said.

'Just a swift half.'

'Or two.'

'He's fine,' protested Simon. 'He's just been chatting.'

'He's not fine. He was really distressed. They told me when they rang.'

Simon looked at Nico, who had his face buried in Carmela's jersey. 'What's up with him nowadays? He never used to cry all the time.'

'He senses things, Simon. He feels the atmosphere. He's not stupid.'

She swept the child away, hissing insults at Simon in Spanish. For the next hour, she was completely focused on the children. She gave Nico supper and a bath, and tucked both him and Rosa up in bed. Meanwhile, Simon sat in the kitchen, feeling truculent and demolishing a bottle of wine. He was distinctly the worse for wear by the time Carmela reappeared.

'I don't believe it!' she cried, glaring at the bottle. '*More* alcohol? After you forgot our son?'

'In for a penny, in for a pound. Grab yourself a glass.'

She turned around and walked out of the room.

'Might as well be hung for a sheep as a lamb,' he yelled after her. He knew he was drunk; he was too drunk to care. 'And other clichés.'

He desperately wanted her to storm back into the kitchen and yell at him. She didn't. After half an hour he began to feel uneasy. He walked around the house looking for her. In the end he found her sitting at the writing desk with her face in her hands. He made his way to an armchair—stumbling once or twice—and sank into it. God, what a bloody awful day this had turned out to be. He didn't know what to say; he couldn't think how to put all this right.

'What're you doing?' he asked.

She shrugged.

'Look, I'm sorry. I was thinking about those photos. I lost track of time.'

'We can't go on like this, Simon.'

This sounded ominous. 'What d'you mean?'

'You are drinking too much. You are angry too often. You are not a good father anymore. The children will suffer if this continues, and I have to protect them.'

He stared at her, processing what she'd said. *Not a good father?* Christ almighty, that wasn't fair.

'Are you serious? I was late collecting Nico—okay, I put my hands up for that heinous crime; fair cop, probably a capital offence—but the world didn't end.' When she didn't respond, he punched the arm of his chair. 'Fuck's sake! Why does every little mistake I make have to be a massive drama?'

'There you go again. Shouting and swearing. Angry straight away. Why so angry?'

'Too bloody right, I'm angry! Today was the day my father's perversion got splashed across the internet. Everyone will know by now. And you took my children to see him. I can't get over that.'

She was shaking her head sadly, as though he were a hopeless case. 'You know what? I think you are grieving for your father. I think you feel as Nico did this evening. Abandoned. Bewildered.'

'Oh, God. Now we're an amateur psychologist, are we? I'm not five years old.'

'No, Simon, you are not. So get over it, and forgive, and move on.'

He wasn't up to this. He felt very drunk now, and unpleasantly close to tears. He stood, swayed, and grabbed the back of a chair. 'I can't handle a fucking stupid conversation. I'm going to bed.'

'No. Don't run away again.'

He wanted to be somewhere else, away from her. 'I've had enough of you telling me how to think, Carmela. I've had enough of the whole lot of you. I've had enough, okay?'

'Go then!' shouted Carmela, as he hauled himself up the stairs. 'Run away, you coward. You will lose more than your father.'

He managed to get into the bathroom, where he took a pee. The walls seemed to be whirling slowly, as though he'd just stepped off the roundabout in the playpark. As he lurched across the landing he heard Rosa begin to cry. His baby girl would be pleased to see him, even if nobody else was.

She was sitting up in her cot, wearing her red all-in-one suit and gripping the bars like a miniature prisoner. When she saw him, she held out her hands and cried extra loud. Even in his addled state, he knew that he loved her.

'C'mon moppet,' he said, lifting her out and sitting down in the one small armchair that would fit in the room. There was a child's cup of water standing on the table. She reached for it as he handed it to her, and held it to her own mouth. Clever girl. He heard the slurping sound she made, and held her closer still.

The room was in darkness except for a nightlight in one corner. Rosa's little body relaxed, and he felt her head lolling against his chest. His own head felt heavy. He closed his eyes.

•

At the age of nineteen, Simon Livingstone learned something about himself. He learned that he wasn't capable of pushing broken glass into the face of another human being. He hurled the bottle against the wall.

'I should kill you,' he said. 'Someday, someone *will* kill you.'

She reached to touch his face, and he felt her fingertips. He took hold of her shoulders and pushed with all the strength of his fury. It was like knocking over a rag doll. She hit the ground hard, and lay in a puddle.

'I am Jessica,' she sobbed, again and again. 'I am Jessica.'

For a moment he felt sorry for her. Then he remembered the sniggers of his flatmates. This freak had made a fool of him, and he–she was still manipulating; still trying to get sympathy. Well, the games were over. He strode out of the car park and away through the centre of town. He'd fallen for a guy. He had touched and kissed and lusted after a guy. What did that make him—gay? Perhaps he was. After all, he'd been attracted to another man. He felt filthy. He felt betrayed. He couldn't imagine ever feeling happy or normal again.

The next day, Quinn reported that the lady boy had left his job at the hotel in the middle of the night, without stopping to collect his wages. At around the same time, a text arrived on Simon's phone. He read it, deleted it, and blocked the number. But he couldn't erase the girl in the club from his memory.

So so sorry I didn't tell you before. Thanks for the happiness. I am Jessica.

Forty-two

Luke

Judi had gathered nine members of the management committee in a conference room, and made sure there was coffee. I was pleased to see both Benjamin Rose and the senior partner, Sarah Arkwright. The managing partner, a bean counter called Giles Lea, and some of the practice heads I knew very well; others less so. They were politely baffled to be collared in this way, looking at their watches.

'I need to be away by eight,' warned Sarah. 'I've got another meeting elsewhere.' She was an indomitable warhorse who struck terror into the hearts of trainees.

'You will be, Sarah,' I said. 'I'll talk fast.'

I was getting much, much better at this. I had my spiel ready, and it took exactly three minutes. When I'd finished, there was a lot of leg shuffling, and throat clearing, and Benjamin asking unhurriedly, *Let me just understand this, Luke. You're telling us that you are transsexual?* One of the litigation partners—Hugh Tolly—fired up his iPad and began reading emails. Others looked stunned, or intrigued, or amused.

'What are the implications?' asked Sarah. Her voice was crisp. She wanted to cut to the chase so that she could get away.

I began to answer, but was interrupted by Hugh Tolly. 'Are you going to have a sex change?'

'I've already told you that I'll be presenting as female. So yes, that will be a change of gender.'

'Oh, come on.' There was a taunting, school-bully ring to his voice. 'You know exactly what I'm talking about. Are you going to have The Operation?'

I smiled at him. 'If you mean will I be having gender reassignment surgery at some point in the future, the answer is that I haven't yet made that decision. Also that it's none of your business. It isn't generally regarded as polite to ask intimate medical questions.'

'Why haven't you resigned?'

'I'm not sure it's called for.'

'Of course it's bloody called for. I'm calling for it. From what you've told us, there are compromising photos of you all over the internet.'

Judi leaned towards him across the conference table. 'You'll be aware of the discrimination laws,' she said pleasantly. 'If you look at our website, we do rather brag about our equal opportunities record. Look on the bright side! This will be a feather in our diversity cap.'

'This isn't about discrimination,' said Hugh. 'It's about loyalty to this firm. We rely on professional relationships. We're going to lose half our clients if they have to take advice from a wolf in Granny's nightie. He needs to clear his desk.'

Sarah had clearly heard enough. 'Shut up, Hugh, before you get us all into expensive trouble.' She had a very penetrating voice. Hugh shut up.

To my own surprise, I found I was thoroughly enjoying this meeting. I was running on adrenaline and it felt terrific, like flying. After years of hiding, years of fear and shame, I had finally broken cover and was standing in the open. I was who I was. My mind was clear and focused.

'I would like to transition at Bannermans,' I said. 'That means present myself full-time as female. Judi and I *had* planned to roll it out in an organised way: give out plenty of information, allow the whole thing time to normalise. It's been done before, as you know. There are transgender people in the legal profession—well, in every walk of life. We had a detailed timetable, working towards July.'

'But you've been outed,' said Benjamin, without rancour.

'I have, Benjamin. And I'm sorry.'

He brushed away the apology. 'Which changes everything. So your new plan is . . . ?'

'We have hours, days at the most, before these photographs arrive on the first screen here. Once that happens they'll be on *every* screen. It's no good hoping people will refuse to look or share them—of course they will. Heck, I would, if Hugh was wearing his Spider-Man costume.'

There was some laughter. Hugh scowled at me.

'We'll have to pre-empt the arrival of those photographs,' said Giles Lea. 'Damage limitation.'

Judi took a stack of paper from a file, and slid copies of a document across the polished surface of the table. Like me, she was in her element. 'I've already prepared a memo. Here it is. My suggestion is that I send it out at eight o'clock on Monday morning, by email, to absolutely everybody, including support staff and caterers. You can see I've included links to a website—it's excellent, very informative about gender identity. I've also sourced an organisation who can come in and run training workshops, if you think that's necessary.'

Hugh snorted and asked how many man hours did we intend to squander? Political correctness gone mad, he said.

'I hate to agree with Hugh, but I can't see why training would be necessary,' remarked Sarah, who'd scanned the letter within five seconds. 'Surely we can educate ourselves. Have we taken advice on how to handle the situation?'

Judi nodded. 'I've just come off the phone from an ex-colleague of mine who's experienced something very similar. The advice is that Luke should stay at his desk for the next week. It won't be much fun for him, with these images floating around, but if he simply disappears it'll fuel more speculation—quite apart from the practical difficulties of rescheduling his diary. From next Friday, he'll take some leave. While he's gone, we change the website details and letterheads and do other admin. He'll return to Bannermans in the new gender role on March the ninth. We'll send out another memo closer to the time, about feminine pronouns and other landmines to avoid.'

'By "new gender role",' said Hugh, 'I take it you mean as a transvestite.'

'No,' I said. 'That's something different.'

'Christ, I loathe doublespeak! Don't we have a dress code for partners? Are fishnet stockings on the list?'

'Nothing wrong with fishnets. I look smashing in them myself,' said Sarah. There was another ripple of laughter, and I was grateful to her.

'Right.' She stood up. 'Sorry to break up the party, but I have to leave now. This is all perfectly simple. There's no point in chucking your toys around the cot, Hugh. We can't by law discriminate against . . .' she glanced down at the letter '. . . against Lucia, even if we wanted to. It's a pity we've been bounced by these wretched photographs, but there it is. Let's get on with the job. Good work, Judi. Best of British to you, Luke.' She was getting ready to leave as she talked, throwing a black velvet cloak around her shoulders.

The meeting broke up. Judi said she'd speak to me over the weekend and hurried out. Hugh stomped away, but most of the others managed to meet my eye. One said I knew where she was if I wanted to talk, and asked how Eilish was coping. Another muttered, 'You're a bloody dark horse,' but he looked more stunned than revolted.

Benjamin and I were the last to leave.

'I've caused a scandal,' I said, with a grimace of apology.

'Makes a refreshing change from adultery.'

I thanked him for staying late, and he said it was no trouble because he'd planned to visit his mother in her nursing home and she preferred him to arrive after her favourite television program. He and I took the lift together, watching the numbers counting down.

As we reached the ground floor, he spoke again. 'Nature or nurture, do you think?'

'Not nurture. I'm pretty sure I was born with this conflict.' The lift doors opened, and we stepped out into the lobby. 'I don't know, Benjamin. The fact is that nobody knows why I am as I am. Psychiatrists and geneticists and endocrinologists, and theologians from every religion, and . . . nobody has a bloody clue. My sister says I'm a sinful but curable soul.'

'Do you agree with her?'

'I know I'm not curable. Perhaps I'm a sort of divine conversation piece, like a Rubik's cube.'

We parted company outside the revolving doors. Benjamin flagged down a taxi for himself.

'What about you?' he asked, as a driver pulled in. 'Where are you headed now?'

I smiled. 'I'm going home.'

Eilish

He was a figure in an overcoat, walking up the dark platform.

It was after eleven when I collected him from the station. I'd hit a traffic diversion on the way into town, and was almost late. I hurried across the bridge and down the steps just as the train was pulling away. There he was: my husband still, though I'd applied for decree absolute. He halted when he saw me. I stopped too, with my hand on the staircase rail and my foot on the bottom step. It was Luke; Luke with his dark eyes, and the reticent smile I knew so well, and the way he always held his head—upright and steady, like a gentle soldier. The other passengers passed us by. We were alone.

I spoke first. 'Dr Livingstone, I presume?'

'The very same.'

I stepped forward, barging into him, and we clung to one another. I kissed him for the first time in all those months—it was the only right, natural thing to do. I tasted the salt of my own tears, and perhaps of his too. We walked to the car with our arms around one another and talked all the way home. It was difficult to know where to start, because there was so much ground to cover. I wanted to know how Bannermans had taken his news; I pressed for every detail of his conversation with Penny O'Neil. We talked about my job, about my world; about what was to come.

'Kate's coming on Sunday,' I said, as I parked outside Smith's Barn. 'She thinks this world is too big and bad for us to manage it without her. And here we are. Welcome home.'

He reached out to my hand on the steering wheel. 'I've missed you,' he said. 'So much.'

I leaned across and kissed him again. He seemed to hesitate for a moment, but then his arms were around me. I wanted to arouse him, to persuade him to come back into my bed. I wanted my husband back again—not Jim, not anyone else; I wanted Luke. I slid a hand under his shirt, feeling the warmth of his body as I ran my fingers across his ribs and up towards his chest.

'I'm not the same.' His voice was sharp with warning. 'The hormones.'

I froze, terrified of what I might have been about to touch. Then I fell out of the car and rushed into the house. I heard him follow me into the kitchen. My hands were shaking. I didn't know what to think, or what to say.

You idiot, I told myself. *You knew he was taking oestrogen. We all know what happens when a man does that.*

It was no good. I couldn't skirt around this subject. I had to ask. 'Are you growing breasts? And what else . . . ? Oh my God.'

'The hormones are ending the war inside me. They're bringing peace. They're also changing me—very, very gradually.'

I watched as he took off his coat and cradled a fanatically purring Casino in his arms. He was Luke. He was still Luke. I'd known him in a thousand roles and moods: as an embarrassed young man at the ballet, and a confident professional; as a father, a lover, a son. I'd seen him shattered as he held Charlotte's lifeless body; joyous at Simon and Kate's achievements; I'd seen him making sandwiches for Robert on their last outing together, gently helping the old man into his car. I'd seen him overcome by lust, and pain, and love, and rage, and helpless laughter. I'd seen him drunk. I'd seen him depressed. I'd seen him singing and dancing on a table in a skirt. I had walked with him through thirty years of light and shade and changing seasons.

And now here he was in my kitchen, and he was different again; but he was still the same person. There were physical things: his hair was much longer now, curling around the nape of his neck. It looked rather stylish and piratical. He'd never been plump, but in the last seven months he'd lost a lot of weight. His shoulders were not quite so broad as I remembered, his jaw not quite so strong nor so stubbled; in fact, his complexion seemed almost boyish. There was a new quality about him, something translucent and light and comfortable. He was beautiful in a strange, gypsyish way; but . . . well. Younger. Not quite male; more androgynous.

'You look good,' I said. 'Whoever you are.'

He smiled at me. 'So do you.'

'You're really going to go on with this?'

There was no evasion, no embarrassment, no uncertainty. 'I'm really going to go on with this.'

Everything had changed since that awful day, back in July, when he'd walked all night in the storm before coming home to confess. That day he was broken. Now—perhaps for the first time since I'd known him—he was whole.

I knew now. I knew what I wanted to do.

'Then be her,' I said. 'If I can't have Luke back, I want to get to know Lucia. Tomorrow we'll go out together and face the gossips. They'll all have seen your picture by then, so let's give them the real thing. The pub, the shop, everywhere.'

'You want me to walk into the Bracton Arms?' he asked, looking apprehensive.

'Oh yes. I've a good mind to take a picture of Ingrid's face when she sees you, and share it on Facebook.'

We sat side by side on the sofa, in the warmest spot in the kitchen. From time to time we held one another's hands. We're awfully fond of one another's company, I thought sadly, for an almost-divorced couple. Casino draped himself over Luke, his purrs dwindling to happy sighs. Baffy snoozed on the cushion I'd bought him.

Luke had seen Ricky Tait's photographs. Apparently they weren't hard to find.

'How bad?' I asked.

'I look like Beethoven on a bad hair day.'

'That's the paparazzi for you.'

It was almost two when I looked at my watch and said I'd better turn in. Luke's bed was made up in the study, but at least he was in the house. I slept well that night; better than I had for a long, long time. I heard him going to and from the bathroom, and tried not to imagine what he was wearing. But it was all right. I was all right. The world was turning, and I was not going to be flung off.

Forty-three

Kate

They were definitely off their heads.

She'd been dropped at home by a friend half an hour ago, to find her parents just setting out for church. That wouldn't have been unusual, except for the fact that her father was presenting himself to the good folk of East Yalton as a woman. The pair of them seemed hell-bent on public humiliation.

'The new vicar invited us,' insisted Eilish. 'He collared us in the Bracton Arms yesterday, said he was expecting us in church this morning.'

'Yeah, well,' scoffed Kate. 'Everyone knows the C of E is super-trendy nowadays. The Reverend Niceguy probably thinks the whole resurrection thing is just a metaphor. This is all very modern and inclusive, but it won't stop Colonel Smyth from turning purple and threatening to horsewhip you. It won't stop Hattie the ancient verger fainting. What if the servers point-blank refuse to hand over the bread and wine, Dad?'

Luke looked anxious. 'I'm sure the vicar wouldn't allow that. But you don't have to come with us, Kate.'

Of course she had to go. Someone had to shield her parents from the viciousness of the human race.

'We stopped for a drink in the pub yesterday,' reasoned Eilish as the three of them were walking along the track towards the village. 'Nobody fainted, and nobody horsewhipped anybody. Mind you—gosh, folk can be rude. A couple of people actually got up and walked out.'

'Bloody rednecks! Who were they? I'll pay 'em a visit.'

'Never mind. Ingrid and Harry were very welcoming.'

'Yeah.' Kate rolled her eyes. 'I know. I heard all about it from Sophie. By the way, Dad, you've got a new fan. Sophie thinks you make a very impressive woman. She waxed lyrical about your eyes, and how you're so tall and slim.'

'Really? Well, that's kind.' Her dad was almost blushing. He was—

Kate stopped her own train of thought in its tracks. She was going to try to use the right pronouns from now on, even when she was only using them in her head.

She was immaculately made up, wearing a midnight-blue dress with her pashmina. Leather boots, which Kate rather envied. Gold earrings, and a beret. Kate had always thought a beret would suit Luke, and she'd been proved right. The new woman looked a bit too chic for a country church, but that had to be a fault on the right side.

'Ingrid and Harry came bustling over the second we arrived,' said Eilish. 'Leaned on the bar and asked intrusive questions. Such personal things! Suddenly, Luke's genitalia becomes fair game as a subject for discussion. Everyone wants to know whether he's having surgery. People are obsessed with the surgery! Why is that? It's ghoulish. I was so relieved when the vicar came over and interrupted them.'

'The clergy are getting younger and younger,' sighed Luke. 'Or am I getting older and older?'

Kate wondered whether this interfering do-gooder had any idea how much courage it was taking for her parents to front up in church. Well, she'd give him a piece of her mind. She flexed her fingers. If she saw a single sneer this morning, or heard a snide remark, she was going to let fly. She felt very protective of her mum and dad. They'd been through enough.

There were three bells in the old tower, of three pitches, and whoever was ringing seemed to be tolling them entirely at random. The sound was comforting. This church had stood right here, in these fields, for hundreds of years. It had witnessed the Great Plague, the Industrial Revolution and two world wars. It didn't give a damn what her father was wearing. She opened the back gate and followed her parents down the path, their footsteps crunching. Kate knew every corner of the graveyard from playing all those games of kick the can. She could recite the family names on the stones: Samuels, Smyth, Donaghue, Bell, Roach. She'd hidden behind the tiny, tragic graves of infants, and the massive family mausoleums. Hundreds of real people over the centuries, each *Beloved* or *At peace* or *Taken from us too soon*. Every one of them has a story, she thought. They've had their tragedies and love affairs. Perhaps some of them were like Dad. If so, they took their secret to the grave. She was glad her father wasn't going to do that.

Near the church, their winding path drew close to the main one. They'd been spotted, and it was clear that the news was out. People glanced sideways at them. One or two waved but hurried on, as though they didn't quite know what to do or say. Finally, an elderly couple approached. Kate knew them from her days in Sunday school, where they'd been teachers. Mr and Mrs White, she used to call them then. Olly and . . . oh bugger. What was Mrs White's name?

Eilish laid a hand on Luke's arm as the Whites came up to them. 'Hello there, Yvonne and Olly,' she said breezily. 'Lovely morning.'

'Eilish!' bellowed the man. His voice was a little too jolly to be natural. 'Am I in time to get a notice into the parish newsletter?'

'Oh dear—too late, I'm afraid. I emailed it to the printer yesterday afternoon.'

He saluted her, for reasons best known to himself. 'Never mind, ma'am, my fault. Next month will do.'

There was an awkward pause, before Yvonne cleared her throat.

'Um . . . It's lovely to see you, Luke,' she said.

It was all too much for Kate, who had the nervous giggles. 'It's okay, Mrs White! You don't have to pretend everything's tickety-boo. Dad's wearing a dress, for Pete's sake. She's got earrings and heels and bouffy hair. You're allowed to be a bit gobsmacked.'

Mrs White laughed too, slightly hysterically. 'I wasn't sure of the etiquette,' she said. 'To be perfectly honest, I've never met a . . . a . . .' She looked wildly to her husband for inspiration. 'Oh dear, I don't even know the right vocabulary . . . I'm totally at sea. What do I call you? I've never been in this situation in my life before. Neither has Olly, have you, darling?'

Luke smiled. 'Look, Yvonne. Olly. It's very simple. We've known one another for years. I hope we can still be friends now that I'm Lucia. Don't worry about the vocabulary—I won't take offence as long as you don't call me a freak.'

Yvonne began to shake Lucia's hand, then changed her mind and air-kissed her instead—but carefully, as though she were afraid of creasing Lucia's clothes. 'You do look . . . well, marvellous, actually. Come and share a pew with us,' she said. 'We'll be your bodyguards.'

When they reached the porch, Kate lingered a little behind the others. The organ was wheezing away gently; she could already smell dust, damp and furniture polish. She smiled at the sight of Hattie the ancient verger, with her hymnbooks, peering myopically out at them. Some things never changed. Hattie spoke to someone over her shoulder, and Kate glimpsed a figure in a surplice. The new vicar, presumably.

She watched as her parents paused, side by side, on the threshold. Their hands touched, then briefly entwined. She was proud of them. They were about to be divorced, but when the chips were down, they were a team.

'Right,' said Lucia, taking her wife's arm. 'Let's face the music.'

As they stepped inside, Kate could just make out the vicar shaking their hands. Full marks, she thought grudgingly. He'd made sure he was there to meet them. He was waiting to greet Kate, too. It was gloomy in the old building, after the brightness of the day. Her eyes took time to adjust, and for several seconds he was a silhouette against the east window. When he came into focus, she saw that he was staring at her incredulously.

'Kate,' he said, and she felt a grip on her hand.

She began to laugh.

Forty-four

Simon

It had been another long day. He didn't finish writing up his notes until after seven.

His dad had moved home now, and was living as a woman; called himself Lucia, apparently. So he was the village joke, like something off *Little Britain*. Simon was baffled. Mum, Kate, Granny, even Carmela, seemed able to perform some kind of mental gymnastics that he couldn't understand. They were lucky, because they hadn't lost the person they'd loved.

He found his colleague Sven in the clinic, injecting a diabetic cat with insulin.

'Coming for a drink?' Simon asked.

Sven was in his forties, and had teenage children. All the clients, both animal and human, loved him; his bedside manner was irresistible. Simon wished it were contagious.

Sven looked at his watch. 'It's a bit late.'

'Never too late.'

'Why don't you go home, Simon?' Sven lifted the cat back into its cage and stroked its head for a moment. 'You have a family. What's the point in all this hard work if you don't go home to them?'

'You think I'm drinking too much.'

'I think you should go home. Straight home.'

To his own surprise, Simon took Sven's advice. He'd try to make it right with Carmela. The troubles had gone on too long; he missed the old days, when they were happy. He was home by seven-thirty, dropping his keys on the table the hall. Carmela wasn't around, and there were no sounds from upstairs. Nico was probably asleep. He got so tired now that he was a schoolboy.

Shrugging out of his jacket, Simon wandered into the kitchen. Carmela must have been having a spring clean, because the place looked pristine. He took a bottle of wine out of the fridge. Something steamed in the slow cooker, but he wasn't hungry.

He walked back to the kitchen door, looking towards the stairs. He stood in his shirtsleeves, a glass in one hand and the bottle in the other.

And he listened.

The house was quiet. Very quiet. No footsteps, no murmur of the radio. No yells from Rosa, who loved to party at this time of the evening.

'Carmela?' he called.

To him his voice sounded uncouth, as though he'd shouted during a funeral. He hoped she would appear at the top of the stairs, with a finger to her lips and a sleeping baby in her arms. She didn't.

Suddenly frightened, he shouted again before sprinting up the stairs to look in every room. It was like a horrible detective game. Their toothbrushes were gone from the bathroom. Nico's duvet had been taken from his bed. The baby's travel cot was no longer on top of the cupboard on the landing, and neither was Carmela's big suitcase.

There was no text on his phone, no missed call. It took him a long time to find the note, though she'd left it where he should have seen it straight away. It lay on the table in the hall, right next to the keys he'd dropped so casually.

Dear Simon,

I feel that I have no other choices. I have taken the children away from what is happening to us. We'll be staying in Suffolk, by the sea. You'll be angry, you'll probably think that I'm being manipulative, but I am not. Nico needs a holiday from the tension, and so do I. I have informed his school. As for the future, I don't know.

I think it would be kind if you don't tell your parents yet. They're going through this terrible time, and they would only blame themselves. It's not their fault. It is our fault.

I will turn my phone on from time to time, in case there are messages. I think this is a good thing for you as well as for me. You and I both need time to think, and time to decide what is best.

My love, take care of yourself.

Carmela

P.S. Soup in the slow cooker. Your dry-cleaning ticket is pinned to the noticeboard.

All the wine in the house couldn't dull the pain.

He imagined them in a holiday cottage by the sea, happy and excited. He imagined Nico playing on a beach, running and shouting; he imagined Carmela with Rosa on her back, and saw her hair lifting in a breeze. He wished—fiercely, desperately—that he were with them.

It took him most of the night to write a simple text. He composed it first on the back of an envelope, since it was probably the most important message he'd ever send. The envelope was soon covered in his handwriting. The problem was that he wasn't sure what he wanted to say. He drafted long and convoluted messages; he drafted bitter messages, pleading messages, irrational messages. He paced around the garden in the dark, trying to get it right. What did he want to say?

He tried to be angry with her. That would be so much easier than being angry with himself. He tried to think her faithless, selfish, a total bitch; but the truth was that even as he'd feverishly searched the house for his family, he'd known they were gone, and he'd known why.

I drove them away, he thought, staring at his scribbles on the envelope. Why was I so destructive? Perhaps it was a form of self-harm, like cutting myself. I thought I'd grown out of that; haven't done it since I left school.

By the time he lay down on his bed, he still hadn't sent any message. According to the bedside clock it was three-eighteen. He felt light-headed with exhaustion, but he wasn't at all sure he'd sleep. He'd been going to bed alone since New Year's Day, and hated it. This was far worse. He slid under the covers and lay very still, listening to the emptiness. There was no life in the house. No Carmela, no Nico, no smiling Rosa; no hope that tomorrow would be different.

Finally, he knew what he wanted to say.

Five words.

Terrified. Please come home soon.

Forty-five

Luke

I was grateful to Ricky Tait, who'd invaded my privacy and shared my secret with the world. He was the super-cool teenager who'd pushed me off the edge of the cantilevered platform. I'd been hesitating, looking down into the abyss, until he gave me that final nudge. I dived into thin air, and so far I had survived. So had Eilish.

Of course the world gossiped about me. I'd have done the same, in the world's shoes. I was too alien for some: those parents who called Penny O'Neil and demanded my resignation; Hugh Tolly, who never did quite meet my eye; the couple who walked out of the Bracton Arms that first day; the woman beside me at the altar rail who turned the chalice around as though afraid she might catch transgender-person germs. My sisters. My son.

Ah, but then there were the others—so many others, who looked beyond their fear and revulsion and accepted me. It came from the most unexpected quarters, and it carried both Eilish and me through those first days.

Two weeks after Ricky took his photographs, a tall fifty-something woman walked up to the main doors of Bannermans. It was eight o'clock in the morning. An expert had done her hair; it was very dark, but with streaks of silver, and it bounced around her face in waves, softening the lines of her jaw and forehead. Another expert had chosen her understated clothes: a cream blouse and charcoal skirt suit, beautifully cut; she had pearls around her neck and in her ears. Her make-up was subtle, her shoes elegant. Her nails were polished and carefully shaped. She drew few second glances from passers-by. One or two stared just a little too long, as though puzzled, but she kept smiling. She felt intensely feminine, determined and nervous in equal measure.

She didn't allow herself to hesitate. Up the steps. In through the revolving doors.

The two women at reception had been well primed.

'Morning, Ms Livingstone,' said Izzy, with a bright smile.

Ms Livingstone returned the greeting warmly, crossed the lobby—her heels tapping on the marble floor, feeling eyes on her back—and swiped her security card before calling the lift.

Behind her, she heard Izzy pick up a phone and whisper to someone: *He's here. No, sorry; shit, I've done it already . . . God, this is going to be impossible . . . I mean,* she's *here.*

The lift doors opened. Empty, thank heavens. She stepped in. What a relief: for about half a minute she was alone, and could lower her guard.

She had a busy day ahead of her.

'I'm afraid you're straight in at the deep end,' Judi had warned her. 'Your secretary tells me they've had to schedule two client meetings for your first day back.'

'Clients still want me to act for them?'

'Livingstone, you're more in demand than ever. Apparently they've been fighting 'em off. Don't kid yourself, though—this popularity isn't because of your incisive legal brain. They couldn't give a toss about that. They just want to see how you've done your hair. Welcome to womanhood.'

I wish I were, thought Lucia now. *I wish I were welcome to womanhood.*

The lift reached her floor. There were—as always—several people around. She was back on display, and she had to walk down the corridor. She thought of a small child in green shorts, sobbing on her first day at school. One or two colleagues said hello, how nice to have you back, and she smiled brilliantly at them. She guessed they'd all had the fear of God put into them: no staring, no smirks, no careless remarks that might be taken to an employment tribunal.

At last she reached her own office. The sliding door was open. Judi was waiting by the desk, holding an immense bunch of flowers.

'You made it, then,' she said.

'I made it.'

For a moment they smiled at one another, taking pleasure in a hard-fought victory. Then Judi nodded towards the open door. 'Did you notice something?'

Lucia stepped back outside to look. When she saw the new nameplate, her heart almost burst.

•

'*Flowers?*' echoed Kate. She sounded incredulous. 'They gave you bloody flowers? Have they ever given you flowers before, in the decades you've worked there?'

'Well, no.'

'So what kind of naked stereotyping is that?'

I laughed. I could see where this was going. 'The good kind.'

'You know what the implications are, don't you, Dad? Female equals soft and sweet-smelling and non-threatening. We'll never smash through the glass ceiling with flowers in our hands.'

'Never mind the flowers—what about my new nameplate? *Lucia Livingstone.*'

'Yeah,' conceded Kate. 'That was cool.'

'I had two meetings today, both with large teams of people, during which my advice was listened to, flowers or no flowers—though I did notice quite a few people staring at my boobs, obviously trying to work out if they're real or not.'

'*Are* they real?'

'Not very. Not yet.'

'Men look at women's chests,' said Kate. 'It's what they do. They can't help themselves. They don't even know they're doing it.'

'Not all men,' I said mildly.

'No. Well, I'm sure you never did. You weren't that sort of man.'

We'd met for a drink at the station to celebrate my first day as a full-time woman. Kate had Guinness. I asked for a white wine spritzer and remembered to sit in the way I'd learned: knees together, ankles tucked to the side. The satin lining of my skirt felt luxurious. Still, I couldn't relax in case I made a mistake; I hadn't been able to relax all day. I was triumphant but dog-tired, and longing to get back to Smith's Barn. I knew I'd have to learn to do without Eilish, but for now she was my refuge.

'You know, Kate, I'm fighting a pretty big battle here. I think I can safely say that as a transgender woman—technically, a lesbian transgender woman—I'm a bit of a pariah. It seems to bring out a primal fear in some people. Like a snake does.'

'Can't deny that. A lawyer, too! Ouch. Triple whammy.'

'I can't fight on two fronts,' I said. 'I applaud your ideals. I do. I think you're right, there is a glass ceiling, and having heard the way many men talk at the urinals, I know we've a long way to go before it's shattered. But I can't—and I won't—feel angry when someone gives me flowers or holds open a door. I'll just be grateful. If there's a glass ceiling for me, it isn't because I'm a woman. It's because I was once a man. You do realise you've got foam on your nose?'

Kate had the grace to grin as she wiped her face. 'Sorry,' she said. 'Just me banging my drum again. The flowers were a lovely touch. Judi's a star.'

It had been an odd time for me; a revelation. Broadly speaking, people were divided into four camps: the openly hostile; the slyly hostile; the genuinely relaxed; and the oh-my-God-I'd-better-be-cool-about-this brigade, whose eyes were rigidly fixed on my face but occasionally strayed to my chest.

Kate held up her glass. 'Here's to you! I'm so proud of you. You are the bravest, cleverest, most beautiful father in the world!'

With that she leaned across the table—knocking menus to the floor—grabbed my face in her hands and kissed me on the cheek, three times. *Mwah! Mwah! Mwah!* People glanced around at us. A middle-aged woman met my gaze and muttered something to her companion, who promptly turned to stare.

Kate had spotted her. 'Excuse me,' she said loudly. 'You—yes, you, madam, in the grubby anorak. Do you have a problem with my father?'

The woman pretended she hadn't noticed. I heard laughter from other tables. 'Shush, Kate,' I whispered. 'No. Don't do it.'

'Let me tell you something about my father.' Kate's voice carried across the hushed room. 'She's a bloody good woman. She's a hell of a lot better-looking than you. She's a very successful lawyer but she's got time for everybody. And she doesn't judge other human beings after one glance.'

'Kate!' I hissed. 'Stop right now, or I will leave.'

The two women gathered their shopping bags and hurried out. I felt mortified, but to my surprise there was a flutter of amusement and even appreciation in that crowded bar. I think it was Kate's charisma that did it, rather than any sympathy for me.

I shook my head at her. 'You can't square up to every single person who gives me a sour look,' I told her. 'Thanks . . . but please don't do that again.'

'She was a cow.' Kate downed the rest of her drink. 'I'll be home at the weekend.'

I was surprised. 'Again?'

She looked evasive, flicking non-existent crumbs from the table. 'Yeah, well. I'm having dinner with someone. Anyway, I think we should celebrate your coming out. Why don't we get a few people round and open some bottles of bubbly?'

'People won't come.'

'They will if you ask the right ones. Granny, for one. Stella. Mr Chadders—he's got the hots for Mum, but he won't hear a word against you. People like Mr and Mrs White—they were fantastic, weren't they? Sophie, Ingrid and Harry from the pub, Bryan the postie . . . and, um, Peter will definitely come.'

'Peter?'

'Peter Vallance. The vicar.'

There was something in her tone; the penny dropped. 'You aren't . . . it's not him you're meeting for dinner?'

'And why wouldn't I be?'

'Well, because he's a . . . clergyman.'

'Is he? I hadn't noticed. He looks a bit like Sean Bean, don't you think? I met him in a pub in Swiss Cottage, believe it or not, while I was waiting for Owen. Anyway, relax, Dad. It's not sex. It's just dinner.'

I was still reeling from this piece of gossip when Kate nipped along to the bathroom. I wanted to go too but didn't dare. I wasn't yet confident enough to use the ladies' room, and the men's was out of the question. I'd just have to tie a knot in it, and wait for the unisex one on the train. When my phone rang, it took me several stressful seconds to locate it. I felt in my breast pocket, where it normally lived . . . damn, I didn't have a breast pocket anymore . . . so where was the bloody thing? Ah—my handbag! I scrabbled to pull it out, saw who was calling, and grinned.

'Chloe!'

'So how did it go?' asked my friend, without bothering to say hello. I felt safer for hearing her voice. She was so young, but she cared so much.

'I did it!' I gasped.

'And you're still alive?'

'I'm still alive.'

'Woo-hoo! Go, Luce! Did the guys all wince and cross their legs when you walked by?'

'Oh yes,' I said. 'You never saw such leg-crossing and wincing.'

Laughter. 'So . . . how d'you feel?'

I ruffled my hair, then realised I'd be messing up the blow-dried waves. 'Oh gosh, Chloe, how do I feel? I'm sitting in a bar at the station, wearing a skirt suit, and nobody's thrown me out. The name Lucia Livingstone is on my door at work. I can't take it in. I can't believe it's real.'

'It's real, all right.'

'I feel wonderful. I also feel . . . knackered. And tomorrow I'll get up and dressed and do it all again.'

'And the day after that, and the day after that. It gets easier. Soon you won't have to think about every move you make.'

Kate was coming back, threading her way between the tables. She was wearing her usual drab clothes but moved with artless grace. I saw people glance admiringly at my daughter as she passed, and felt proud.

'What about you?' I asked Chloe. 'What's happening in your world?'

There was a slight pause, then a rush of words. 'I've got a date, actually. I'm going to the cinema with a real-life, very lovely guy who isn't a client.'

'That's great! Who is it?'

Chloe was wildly excited. I could hear it in her voice. 'I met him in the supermarket. We got chatting in the queue, then we carried on chatting after we'd gone through, then we went to Starbucks and he asked if he could see me again. His name is Adam, he's taller than me and he isn't a weirdo.'

'Does he know . . . ?'

'Come on, Lucia. Everyone knows as soon as I open my mouth. How long did it take for you to clock me? We'll work that side of things out.'

I felt joy for her. Chloe deserved to be loved. Kate was gesturing to ask if I'd like another drink. I looked at my watch, saw that my train left in a few minutes and shook my head.

'I think that's wonderful news,' I told Chloe. 'But if he isn't a gentleman, you let me know and I'll handbag him.'

She said she'd take a selfie of the two of them for me, and that we needed to catch up. How about grabbing a bite to eat one evening? Thursday? And could Kate come too?

'You're on. I'll ask her.' I stood up, thinking about the train. 'In the meantime, you take care, you hear me?'

She sighed, imitating a grumpy teenager. 'Yes, Mum.'

Kate came as far as the barrier with me. I relayed Chloe's news as we ran.

'You're not the only one with a date,' I said. 'Though I bet her fella isn't wearing a dog collar.'

'Nobody uses the word fella anymore, Dad. Not even incredibly old, decrepit people like you.'

We arrived, panting, on the station concourse. They'd just opened the barriers, and the crowd was moving very slowly through the bottleneck. I joined the back of the queue and Kate kept me company.

'There was one other thing I wanted to run by you,' she said.

'Go ahead.'

'I'm trying very hard to get my head around this thing you're doing.'

'I know you are.'

'Mm.' We were inching forward, packed like sardines in a can. 'But every time I call you "Dad", it trips me up. For me the word "Dad" conjures up male things. It's you . . . but it isn't you. And you sure as hell aren't Mum. I've got a mum already, and one is enough. So I thought, if you didn't mind, I'd try calling you Lucia.'

We'd got to the barrier. I turned back to give her a grateful hug. 'Please do,' I said. 'That would be perfect.'

The train was full, and I didn't get a seat until three stations before my own. I didn't mind. It was as I stood in the aisle, letting my body move and sway with the train's rhythms, that I finally grasped what I had achieved that day. The nameplate on my door wasn't a dream, it was real. The woman looking back at me from the dark windows of the train wasn't a dream; she was real. *You are me*, I thought. *I am Lucia Livingstone.*

A young man was sitting at a table, watching a film on his iPad. I don't think he cast more than a glance in my direction, but perhaps he registered the grey in my hair, because he stood up and offered me his seat. I declined it with a smile, but my soul was singing.

Woo-hoo, I thought. *Go, Luce.*

Forty-six

Eilish

What makes us who we are? Countless things; more than humanity is ever likely to understand. All I know is that by becoming a woman, Luke didn't lose himself. She found herself. For seven months I'd raged and grieved for what I'd lost. I still grieved, but now I also celebrated her new-found peace. I'd loved him enough to love her, too.

She made mistakes, of course. In her first week at work I twice had to stop her from heading off to work looking like a Christmas tree.

'So many pitfalls,' she complained on Thursday morning, as I made her remove a silk scarf that clashed with the rest of her outfit. 'I used to open the wardrobe and grab the first clean shirt. Now it's just a constant stream of decisions.'

'Um, I'm afraid that necklace doesn't show above your collar,' I said. 'Here—d'you want to borrow mine?'

She looked into the mirror, touching the string of green glass beads. 'This was a birthday present from Chloe. I thought she'd be pleased if I was wearing it this evening.'

'And it's lovely, but it's the wrong length. Hang on, I think I can adjust it.' I managed to clip the necklace several links further down, so that it was short enough to show. 'How's that?'

I wanted to protect her fragile happiness. I wanted people not to sneer. Her hairstyle softened the outlines of her face, and she was humming under her breath. Sometimes it was difficult to remember that she was once Luke. She turned around with a smile. 'Perfect! Thank you,' she said, and kissed me on the cheek.

She was drinking coffee while I pottered about. I'd made it for her in our one remaining red and yellow cup. Bryan turned up with the post as well as the newspaper, and I looked through the mail. Two bills, a bank statement, an invitation to somebody's silver wedding anniversary.

And one other.

I tasted bitterness in my mouth when I saw that last one. I'd been expecting it. I didn't want to open it.

Lucia looked up from her newspaper.

'From the court?' she asked. 'Go on. It might just be a speeding ticket or something.'

With a heavy heart I slid my hand under the flap, took out the paper and scanned its contents. 'Decree absolute,' I said. 'We're divorced.'

That bitter taste grew stronger. For a time, we were both silent. There were no words for this. I couldn't look at her.

'We knew it was coming,' said Lucia. 'I can't expect to stay here with you forever.'

I put the letter to one side, and took her hand. 'But we're still family, aren't we?' she added, with a desperate smile.

I agreed that we were. Then I rushed off, saying I must get ready for school. Those wretched tears arrived as soon as I reached my bedroom. I had to hide for a while; in fact, it was a good half-hour before I felt composed enough to come out.

'We're both running late. I'll give you a lift to the station, if you like,' I called, as I hurried along to the bathroom to brush my teeth. When Lucia didn't reply, I came out of the bathroom onto the gallery, holding my toothbrush. She was standing by the kitchen table.

'Luke? Oops, sorry, Lucia? Did you want a lift?'

She looked blankly up at me, rocking slightly on her heels, backwards and forwards.

'What's happened?' I asked.

'He's . . .' She walked right around the table, hitting herself on the upper arms. It was a primeval gesture, as though she were a creature in pain. I dropped the toothbrush and ran down the stairs. As I reached her I saw that she was horrified. Her eyes were wide.

'You have to tell me,' I said, frightened now. 'Is it Kate?'

When she finally managed to get the words out, they seemed to choke her.

'He killed her,' she said.

•

Police have released the identity of a transsexual sex worker found dead in a South London bedsit on Monday evening. The mutilated body of Callum Robertson, 22, who also used the name Chloe, was discovered by police after a neighbour reported hearing screams. Adam Stuart Walsh, aged 35, was arrested near the scene. Police are not seeking anyone else in connection with the incident.

An autopsy has yet to be carried out. Police sources indicate that the attack involved a sharp object or objects, and described it as savage and sustained.

The neighbour, who asked not to be named, told reporters that she looked out into her hallway after hearing sounds of a struggle in the bedsit next door. 'I saw a man walking towards the stairs, covered in blood,' she said. 'He told me, "I think I've killed something." So I locked myself in my room and called the police.'

Callum's mother, Kirsty Robertson, has made a plea for the family's privacy to be respected. 'We are broken-hearted. Callum was a good lad who made some wrong choices. We just want to get him home. He needs to be among his family again.'

Lucia

'I was going to see her,' I kept saying. 'I was going to see her. D'you think, if I just give her a call, it might turn out she's fine?'

'No,' said Eilish, who'd rung Bannermans and asked them to cancel my appointments. 'I'm so sorry, but I don't.'

I felt sickened by the gleeful prurience of the newspaper, with its mention of blood and mutilation and the transsexual sex worker called Callum Robertson. All I could think of was Chloe lying with her throat cut and God knows what other cruelties inflicted upon her. *Mutilated*, the paper said. And I was wearing her green glass beads.

The wolves had dragged Chloe out from her hiding place in a hollow tree, and they'd torn her apart. I couldn't save her.

'I should have warned her to be careful,' I said.

'Darling.' Eilish touched my hand. 'From what you've told me, she was far more street-wise than you will ever be. I know she was young, but if anyone seemed able to take care of herself it was Chloe.'

Which was true. In fact, it was Chloe who had done the caring. Chloe, with her nervous laugh and her perspex heels. She cared for me.

When I couldn't stand inactivity a moment longer, I rang her local police station. After a lot of explaining I was put through to Detective Inspector Dave someone-or-other. I told him what I knew about the man Chloe had planned to meet. He took my details. Although they'd already made an arrest, they wanted to piece together the last hours of Chloe's life.

'Look, there's a mistake in the paper. She wasn't Callum Robertson,' I said. 'That wasn't the name she used. She was a woman called Chloe.'

Yes, he said. They were aware that the deceased had an AKA. They'd looked into the appropriate response. She had made no application for a gender recognition certificate, and the next of kin wished her to be referred to by her male name.

I felt impotent rage. '"Chloe" wasn't an AKA. It was *her* name. Look at her—she was obviously trying to be a woman! She didn't have the money to apply for the certificate yet, but she was a woman.'

'Your view is noted,' he said tersely. 'Thank you.'

I asked him for the family's contact details. No, he said, he couldn't help me there. There were issues of privacy. If I wanted to give them a message he would pass it on.

'Please ask them to phone me,' I begged him. 'Tell them I was a friend of hers.'

He sounded doubtful.

'I'm a solicitor,' I added, as though my profession made any difference.

He'd had enough of me, and ended the call. I stood helplessly in my warm kitchen in my trendy converted barn. I felt disgustingly privileged. Chloe was lying in a cold morgue, to be dissected by someone who would find her body a fascinating example of the preoperative transsexual. To the press she was a lurid weirdo, a creature who lived underneath a stone. Her family would take her back to Manchester. They'd talk about their son and brother who'd gone wrong, and who had paid for it with his life. They'd cut her hair. They'd force her to be Callum forever.

'I wish I could stop them,' I said to Eilish. 'I can hear her now, laughing and saying, "Bloody hell, no, don't let that mob get me."'

'You've got no say in it, surely? They're her family.'

I had to try. I phoned the newspaper, and quoted the Gender Recognition Act at them. It's meant to protect the privacy of trans people. They didn't care. 'Sex-swap' stories sell papers, so Chloe's murder boosted their sales. Privacy wasn't too high on the priority list.

Then I called Neil, of the Jenny Marsden group. He too had only just heard, and was horrified. We talked for a time, and he said he'd let everyone else know.

I'd run out of practical things to do, but I just couldn't keep still. That's the thing about grief: it hurts, and it can't be escaped. I paced around and around the kitchen until Eilish suggested a walk in the garden. She took my arm, and we stepped out through the folding doors into a morning that felt alive and mellow. A gauzy haze hung across the lawn, but the sun was breaking through. There were leaf buds on the trees and even the first bursting of blossom. Chloe couldn't smell the spring. She was twenty-two, and she'd never laugh again.

'I can't believe she's dead,' I said. 'I can't believe it. So much hope, so much vivacity.'

I hadn't even realised I was crying until Eilish handed me a tissue.

'Thanks,' I said, as I took it. 'Sorry.'

'Luke would have had a large white hankie in his pocket, ready to whip out if his nose was running.'

'Lucia is hopelessly disorganised. I find the lack of pockets confusing.'

My father's tree was coming into leaf. Nature goes on, even when life ends. The sun still rises; the world is still beautiful. As we neared the pond, a pair of ducks glided away, leaving a wake on the glassy surface. Their serenity clashed with the images of violence and hatred in my mind. I imagined Chloe happy and excited, getting ready for her date; I imagined the terrible moment when she realised he was going to kill her.

Eilish and I stood quietly, our two figures reflected in the water.

Forty-seven

Kate

If Adam Stuart Walsh, thirty-five, were sitting in an electric chair right now, she'd cheerfully throw the lever.

'But *why*?' she asked Eilish, who'd met her at the station. 'What kind of moron murders a lovely person like Chloe?'

'He panicked. That's what he's telling the police, according to the latest reports. They've charged him with murder.'

'Panicked!' Kate kicked the car, before getting into it. 'What, because she laughed too much?'

'He didn't know she was transgender. He says they'd had a good night out, gone back to the bedsit for . . . well, coffee. He assumed that meant sex. Then she mentioned it in passing, as though he already knew. He lost his head.'

'Oh well, that explains everything,' said Kate, as she slammed the door. 'I mean, if someone doesn't walk around with a big placard saying "trans woman", obviously they deserve to be hacked to death.'

'He did think that. Exactly that. He said he thinks they're vermin. He says Chloe brought it all on herself. He thought she'd tricked him.'

Kate kept her eyes fixed on the familiar road unfolding ahead, battling an urge to burst into tears. She'd only heard the news last night, when Lucia phoned. It had been the worst phone call of her life; she'd felt sick ever since. She couldn't get Chloe out of her head. They'd had Christmas lunch together, gone for a walk, joked about *The Sound of Music*. They'd been ice-skating. Now Chloe was dead, and all because some lowlife had a hang-up.

'She was a great person,' she said. 'Honestly, Mum, I wish you'd met her.'

'I wish I had, too.'

'She loved Dad—Lucia.'

'I make that mistake all the time.' Eilish waggled her head. 'Dad, Luke, Lucia. I'm getting better at it. I thought it would be impossible and stupid to think of Luke as a *she* . . . after thirty years of *he*. But it's not impossible, is it? You get used to it. I think it just takes time.'

Kate could almost hear Chloe's laughter. 'How's Lucia doing?' she asked.

'Sad,' said Eilish. 'Just very, very sad. He—no, get this right—*she's* been researching the law, but she can't see any practical way to make the family respect Chloe's wishes. Her only victory was forcing the paper to print a tiny addition, saying that Chloe was living as a woman and wanted to be known as Chloe.'

'Are you worried about her?'

'About Lucia? You mean do I think she might have some kind of breakdown?' Eilish narrowed her eyes, thinking. 'No, I think she'll come through this. There's a whole group of them, all supporting one another. They're going to hold a memorial vigil soon. I thought I'd go along.'

'I'll come too.'

They'd reached East Yalton; past the church, up the lane. Kate knew every pothole. It all seemed so peaceful and ordered, and a million miles from Chloe's world.

'Mum,' she said. 'Now Dad's home . . . Lucia's home . . . how long is she going to stay? What's the plan?'

Eilish glanced quickly at her, then looked back at the road. 'Decree absolute came through yesterday. We're divorced.'

'I don't think that answers my question.'

'No.' They were turning into the driveway of Smith's Barn. 'No. I don't think it answers any of my questions either. Love's a complicated thing, isn't it, Kate?'

Kate wasn't sure how to phrase her next question. They'd passed the copse and parked at the front door before she came out with it.

'You can't stay together, can you? I know some wives do stick it out, but I really can't imagine it working unless you're a little bit bi. Are you a little bi, Mum? I mean, it's a continuum, isn't it?'

'*A little bit bi*?' There was embarrassment in Eilish's smile. 'This is not a conversation I ever expected to be having with my daughter.'

'It's not a conversation I expected to be having with my mother, either. But then, quite a few things aren't what we expected.'

Eilish turned off the engine, and rested both her hands on the steering wheel. 'No, Kate, I really don't think I am. Not even a little bit. I had a crush on the head girl when I was at school. I was eleven, so I don't think it counts. But . . . *but* . . . I think I really do love your father. I mean, what is love? I've no idea, I only know how it feels. When I married him I was infatuated, couldn't keep my hands off him. I don't imagine you want to hear about that.'

'Certainly not.'

'After ten years I appreciated him more than ever . . . his empathy, his wisdom, his friendship. We'd lost Charlotte, we had you and Simon. I knew he wasn't perfect and he knew I wasn't, but we rubbed along. By the time we got to *thirty* years he was simply part of my landscape. There's a depth of understanding after all that time. Our marriage didn't rely on sex, certainly not by then.'

'Hell, no!' exclaimed Kate. 'I bet it didn't—not after thirty years with just the one guy. Doesn't bear thinking about.'

'I didn't mind.' Eilish sighed. 'And then my man became a woman. So now I'm having to rethink it all. One of the things

I'm thinking is that this is still the same person. I loved him. I love her.'

'But without sex?'

'Well . . . yes, I think so.'

'You can't be celibate forever!' Kate was appalled. 'No, no, no. That's just awful, even if you are fifty-six . . . I mean, sorry. I'm not saying fifty-six is old. It isn't very old, nowadays. Anyway, you don't look it.'

Eilish was smiling. 'If you're in a hole, stop digging.'

'Dad wouldn't ask you to give up your sex life forever. You didn't sign up for that.'

'Nuns do it. They're celibate all their lives. They do it out of love. What's the difference?'

Kate had a brief, surreal image of her mother in a wimple. 'You're not a nun, Mum,' she protested, chuckling. 'You snogged Mr Chadwick on New Year's Eve.'

'What if my husband had been in a car accident, had a spinal injury and was wheelchair-bound and impotent forever? Or what if he'd got cancer, and the radiotherapy meant . . .'

'Meant he couldn't get it up anymore? That's different.'

'Why? Why is it different? If he were impotent as the result of an accident, would you want me to leave him? Would *I* want to leave him?'

'Well, no. Obviously not.'

'What's the difference?'

'The difference is . . .' Kate thought for a moment, and then gave up. *Love*, she thought. *Love. I never really believed in it until now.*

'I'm getting used to it already,' said Eilish. 'To her. You told me, that night in the Bracton Arms, and you were right. At first I was upset by the effect of the hormones, but now it just seems a good thing, because it's making her whole. I can hug her, kiss her on the cheek at least. I'm having to think again about what intimacy means. After all, it's just what we make it.'

Neither of them made any move to get out of the car. It was an oasis of quiet; time to think and talk. Kate watched a pair of blackbirds flying in and out of the copse. They might have been the descendants of birds she'd watched when she was ten years old. Some things didn't change.

'In an odd way,' said Eilish, 'I feel as though my love for Luke had been dozing for years. Lazily and complacently dozing. All of this has reawakened it—reawakened me. I've had to question everything I thought I knew.'

'You and me both, Mum. So . . . you two might stay together?'

The front door opened, and Lucia appeared on the step. Eilish immediately unclipped her seatbelt.

'We've tried living apart,' she said, 'and we didn't like it. If giving up our sex lives is the price we have to pay for being together—well. I think we might decide to pay it.'

Kate's mind was reeling from this conversation, but it was time to think of other things. Lucia was already hurrying across to the car, and Kate leaped out to throw her arms around her.

'I'm so sorry!' she cried. 'So sorry. Poor Chloe, oh my God. Twenty-two years old. I can't believe it. The frigging bastard.'

Lucia looked as though she'd thrown her clothes on. Her face was deathly pale, her eyes red-rimmed. A string of bottle-green beads had somehow become caught up in her hair, but she seemed too distressed to notice.

'The coroner's released the body,' she said.

'So there'll be a funeral?'

'Yes, but—Kate, it's so awful. They're going to make her be Callum. They'll dress her in a suit, they'll cut her hair. A private cremation in her home town. Family flowers only; I can't even send her flowers. I can't say goodbye. I can't do anything for her. I'm letting her down!'

'How do you know all this?'

'I looked online. There was a notice in the family's local paper. In the death column. *Callum Robertson, beloved son and brother.*'

A cold breeze had sprung up, and Eilish shepherded them indoors.

'Why would her family do this?' asked Kate, as she stamped her feet on the mat. 'After all she's been through, why deny her now? I just don't get it. Is it to punish her?'

'I think it is,' said Lucia. 'And to control her.'

'Do you think so?' asked Eilish. 'Maybe they just want their son back? They lost him once, probably never understood what it was all about, and now they can have him back in some way.'

It was warm in the kitchen, and there was a lovely smell from something in the oven. It felt like home again. Her mum was looking after Lucia. She made suggestions and cups of tea, and constantly touched her arm or her back. They were physically close—like sisters, perhaps? No, that wasn't quite right. In the end, Kate gave up on trying to understand. Other people's relationships often seemed baffling.

Later, when Eilish was drawing the curtains, she paused to peer out into the darkening garden. 'We should plant a tree for Chloe.'

Lucia came to join her. 'We're going to end up with a vast rainforest out there, at this rate.'

'I think there's room for Chloe in our forest,' said Eilish.

Forty-eight

Simon

Their things were all around: Nico's favourite cereal, Rosa's baby gym, books Carmela had been reading; even her scent followed him everywhere. That was why he spent more time at the surgery than at home. He didn't stop by the pub anymore. It didn't bring any comfort. Carmela had sent short texts each day, and twice he'd spoken to Nico on the phone. They were having a lovely time, apparently, and from the Visa bills it looked as though they'd been eating in a lot of cafes.

'Carmela's in Suffolk,' he told Eilish when she phoned for advice about Baffy's diet. 'Bit of a holiday with the children. I'll join them if I get the time.'

She didn't notice he was lying. The only person who seemed to have rumbled him was Sven.

'Simon,' he said one lunchtime, after Carmela and the kids had been gone about ten days. 'This holiday in Suffolk. How long's it meant to be?'

'Couple of weeks.'

'Then they're back?'

'Absolutely.' Simon picked up the phone. He had a list of owners to call with progress reports on their animals. 'Absolutely.'

Sven's expression was cynical. 'Okay. And where are they, exactly?'

'On the coast . . . Hello, Catherine? Simon Livingstone here; yes, the vet. I've got good news about Gandalf's results.'

Fortunately, Sven had been called away to an emergency appointment before he could ask more questions. Simon made several home calls, which took up the rest of the afternoon. The last one was to euthanise a labrador with heart failure. She was a beautiful creature and had grown up with the family's children, two of whom had come home to say goodbye. The whole family was in tears. Simon wasn't confident in the pastoral side of his job, but he did his best to say the Right Thing.

The mother saw him to his car. She was clutching a tissue. 'Sorry we got so emotional. It's the end of an era, you see. She arrived as a puppy when George was four, and she's been such a friend ever . . . oh dear. Sorry.'

'Don't apologise,' said Simon. 'She was part of the family.'

'That's so true. She was. It won't feel like home anymore.'

He remembered her words later, as he walked along his own street. He longed for his empty house to be full again—of noise, of chaos, of getting ready for swimming lessons and cheering when Rosa managed to sit up by herself. He even longed for a good old tantrum from Nico.

He was almost at his front door when he noticed a familiar car jammed into a very small space on the street outside. It looked like Carmela's. He shouldn't get his hopes up; lots of people owned dark blue Passats. He walked closer, not taking his eyes off it. Yes—surely that was Nico's car seat? And there was Rosa's mobile!

He broke into a run, wrestled with the key in the lock and burst through the front door. He heard childish shouts, and the next moment Nico had galloped out of the sitting room and been swung into his father's arms.

'Hi there, big fella!' cried Simon. 'You've grown!'

Carmela appeared at the kitchen door. She'd lost weight—surely she couldn't have lost so much in ten days? She was wearing her pre-baby jeans, he noticed, and her hair was clipped up in a messy bun. She seemed wary of him.

'Hello,' she said.

Relief made Simon euphoric. Still carrying Nico, he strode across the hall, threw his free arm around her, and kissed her.

'You're home,' he said. 'Thank you for coming home.'

Meanwhile, Nico hadn't stopped talking. He wanted Simon to know about the little house they'd had, and the beach, and the noisy seagulls, and how he slept in a top bunk but sometimes he went and found Mummy in the night, in case she was scared of the dark. Then he remembered he was starting a museum, and had collected a whole box of sea glass.

After climbing down, he trotted off to fetch this treasure. Simon left his arm around Carmela's shoulder as they walked into the kitchen. To his shame he hadn't been looking after the place, and she'd obviously decided to air it. All the windows were open. Simon looked into the garden and noticed that the sun was shining, despite a fresh wind. The neighbour's apple trees were all decked out in pink blossom. When did that happen? Winter was over, and he hadn't even noticed.

'I'd have tidied up, if I'd known you were coming,' he said.

'I didn't know we were. We made the decision this morning. Just like that. Nico said it's been a very nice holiday, but is it nearly time to go home and see Daddy? And I agreed with him.' She put one of Rosa's bottles into the microwave and pressed the buttons. *Beep . . . beep.*

'Where's Rosa?'

'Asleep. She was tired and grumpy. But she should wake up now, or there will be hell to pay tonight.'

'I'll get her,' said Simon eagerly. He set off with the bottle in his hand, but turned back at the door.

'Please don't go away again,' he said.

She didn't answer him.

•

It was a happy evening, despite the anxiety of it all. Simon and Nico went to collect a takeaway pizza, and the family ate together around the breakfast bar. Rosa seemed delighted to be home, banging her cup and crowing with laughter when her dad—who was folding the washing—put a sock on top of his head. At bedtime, Simon read to Nico while Carmela pottered about downstairs. The house phone rang while he was reading, and he heard Carmela's voice. She was having a very long conversation with someone.

He found her in the kitchen, checking her emails.

'Tea,' she said, pushing a mug in his direction.

'Did I hear the phone earlier?'

'You did. It was Eilish.'

He leaned over her with his arms linked around her neck. Mum was probably still worrying about that silly little dog of Kate's. No need to call her back tonight. He didn't want to think about his parents. He wanted to forget them, just for a while.

'Your father's had a terrible thing happen,' said Carmela. 'Terrible.'

He felt a lurch of fear. 'He's been attacked? Shit, I've been expecting this. How bad?'

'No, no. He's not hurt. This thing happened to a good friend of his. D'you want to know about it?'

Simon straightened up. He really didn't want to know.

'Suit yourself,' said Carmela.

He really *did* want to know. 'Tell me. What's happened?'

'You promise not to interrupt?'

'Okay.'

'Right. Sit down.' She patted the stool next to her. 'It's a horrible story. Your father had a friend called Chloe. A good friend. She was a great support to him.'

'A friend? Was she a—'

'Yes, she was also a transgender woman. Now, shush!' Carmela pouted, touching her finger to his lips. 'You promised not to interrupt.'

She seemed to know all sorts of details about this Chloe, who—Simon had to admit—sounded like a nice person. He kept his promise and listened to the story without a word, until she came to the ghastly part at the end.

'Stabbed to death?' he repeated incredulously. '*Stabbed*? In her own bedsit?'

'It was even worse! He continued after she was gone. He cut her private parts. He mutilated her.'

Simon remembered the smashing of a bottle, in the car park of the White Hart.

'Christ,' he said. 'That's . . . What a screwball.'

'Yes, a screwball. Apparently, Chloe was so happy about her date. She thought somebody valued her for herself, at last. Isn't it sad?'

Jessica was standing in the botanical gardens, clutching his hands, smiling and crying. *You mean it? You really mean it?*

I surrender, thought Simon. He felt the relief, the freedom of it. *I'm coming out. My hands are up.*

'Poor Dad,' he said. 'Must be gutted. Is he all right?'

The words were a white flag, and they both knew it. For a moment—just a moment—he saw a smile of triumph on Carmela's lips. She got to her feet.

'Shall we have another cup of tea in the sitting room? I've put the heater on in there. I have to name all Nico's school clothes. Can you believe it? We had a bossy email from the school while I was away. Rules, rules, rules. All so that they can turn him into a totally up-himself middle-class Englishman. Over-privileged and smug. A yawn a minute.'

'Like his father,' said Simon. He heard her laughing as she walked away.

He made more tea, and found some chocolate in a drawer. When he joined Carmela, she had Elgar playing on the stereo. The Enigma Variations. She'd arranged herself gracefully, cross-legged on the floor. Nico's school uniform lay folded in a pile beside her, and she was wielding a marker pen.

'We must label our son,' she said, shaking her head in disgust. 'He must know who he is!'

'Can I help?'

'With *your* handwriting? When Nico loses his gym shorts they will be given to somebody called Joe Bloggs. But you could just rub my shoulder, here. Can you feel it? I've strained something. Nico kept climbing into my bed in the night, and jamming me into one tiny corner. Every day I woke up with a crick in my neck.'

She began to label one garment after another: *Nico Livingstone. Nico Livingstone.* Simon sat behind her, on the edge of the armchair, digging his thumbs into the muscles of her upper back. She wriggled and said, 'Down a bit . . . left a bit . . . there; ooh, that's lovely.' Neither of them mentioned the fact that she'd almost left him.

Elgar's melody was immaculate. For some reason, it was bringing tears to Simon's eyes.

'Why *Enigma*?' he whispered. 'Puzzle, paradox . . . What did Elgar have in mind?'

Carmela chuckled. 'I don't know.' She picked up a grey school jersey, looking for somewhere to write Nico's name. 'Some puzzles aren't meant to be solved,' she said. 'They are a work of art in themselves.'

A work of art.

'I knew a transsexual once,' he said. 'When I was nineteen. She was . . . a work of art. I fell in love with her.'

He saw the marker pen stop moving, halfway through the word *Livingstone*. Carmela swivelled around to stare at him in astonishment. 'I have known you more than six years, and you've never mentioned this before.'

'Even up-themselves, over-privileged, smug English males have skeletons in their closets.'

'Tell me.'

He told her. He talked about the nightclub, and the river, and the botanical gardens. He only faltered when it came to describing what happened outside the White Hart, in the darkness and rain. That part sounded barbaric, especially after the news of Chloe's murder.

'I don't feel good about it,' he said. 'I discovered a vicious side to myself. I didn't even know it was in me.'

Carmela had put aside Nico's clothes as he spoke, and was resting her elbow on Simon's thigh. 'You were touchy about your sexuality. I've got four brothers, remember? I know how they think. You were afraid of the feelings you had for her. Did you wonder if it meant you were gay?'

Simon nodded.

'And, after all,' reasoned Carmela, 'you didn't actually hurt this Jessica.'

'Not physically.'

'Have you ever seen her again?'

'Nope. Never again. After that one text, I blocked her number. A couple of years later I heard a rumour that she'd gone for surgery. Might be true, might not. You never know with student gossip.'

'You must have wondered.'

He shrugged.

'Simon!' she said, slapping his knee. 'Of course you wondered.'

'I just wanted to forget it. I wanted to forget that I was the one who fell for a lady boy. That whole event buggered up university life for me. I've never made friends easily, Carmela. I'm not like you. I didn't trust anyone after that, didn't even trust myself. I didn't really like myself again until . . . well, until I met you.'

She was resting her chin on his knee, smiling at him. Her hair had come loose from its clip, and her eyes seemed very dark.

'You didn't like yourself?'

He felt her fingers untying the laces of his shoes and pulling them off, one by one. It was just a light touch, but it was glorious. The next moment she'd kneeled up in front of him and was deftly unbuttoning his shirt.

'I like you,' she said. 'Shall I prove it to you?'

Forty-nine

Lucia

I'd done all I could for Chloe. Her mother never got in touch. I called the police again, and this time was put through to the family liaison officer assigned to the case. I asked for the family's permission for myself and some of Chloe's other friends to attend her funeral. The liaison chap was more helpful than D.I. Dave, and agreed to ask them.

My hopes weren't high. He came back to me with a curt message, which he'd written down and read out verbatim:

> *Please respect our grief. We have no wish to know about Callum's other life. Leave us in peace with memories of our son and brother.*

They were cremating her on Wednesday. The service began at twelve.

It was one of those calm, almost-sunny March days. Sparrows and swallows were nesting under the eaves of the house, flitting in and out, diving across the lawn with straw in their beaks. Eilish had a full day at the school; I had a vast backlog of work, so I got up at six, tackled the most urgent tasks and made several phone calls.

Just before midday, I pulled on my gumboots (Eilish had fetched them from the loft, where she'd thrown them) and took Baffy for a walk across Gareth's fields. At the footbridge I stopped and played solitary Pooh sticks for a while. There wasn't a breath of wind. The sticks floated sedately beneath the bridge before bobbing out the other side, around the corner and away on their journeys. Chloe, too, was going on a journey. *Safe travels*, I murmured as I watched the sticks disappear. *There will be a place for you, on the other side.*

At twelve-thirty, I said goodbye and thank you.

By one o'clock I knew it would all be over.

I dropped Baffy back at the house but I didn't want to go in. Instead, I crossed the lawn and let myself into the shed. As soon as I stepped through the door, I was overpowered by the scent of wood shavings. Eilish kept her gardening equipment in here, but my things were all exactly as I'd left them: the power tools, the circular saw, the router and an old lathe. They were my heritage.

My father's woodworking shed was legendary. As soon as I was tall enough to reach the bench, he showed me how to use all his tools—even the circular saw, which looked so fearsome. I grew up with the resinous scents of wood and linseed oil in my nostrils. By the time I was ten, I could identify a timber by its smell, which came into the house on Dad's clothes. His socks reeked of resin as they dried on the Aga; when he shook out his jerseys, sawdust rose in a cloud. Dad and wood resin went together. He made me my first ever blocks, and my first ride-on truck. One wonderful day, he and I worked together and a little biplane emerged from the timber. That was why I'd made one with Simon, years later. I'd promised to do the same for Nico.

When Dad died, they made his coffin out of timber from his farm. It was newly milled. I breathed in the living scent of pine as I carried him out of the church.

Now I stood in the shed, inhaling that familiar smell and thinking about my father. He gave me most of his tools. Even when he knew he was dying, he and I would come in here and make things. It used to calm him, and me too.

I pictured him climbing a ladder to rescue me from a tree. I heard him calling to me from his tractor, inviting me to ride beside him in the cab. I sat under the table while he played poker with his friends, and felt his calloused hand ruffling my hair. I saw him sitting beside me in the car park at East Yalton hill, a blanket over his knees, shrunken and ready to meet death. Then I looked down at myself. I was wearing a pleated skirt and a mauve cowl-necked sweater. My hair grew in heavy waves. I had a definite bust now, even if it was only a size AA. My pierced earlobes ached slightly under their gold studs.

'Hello, Dad,' I said. 'Are you here? This is who I am nowadays. I hope you don't mind.'

He didn't speak, but I thought perhaps the scent of resin had grown a little stronger.

My last project was lying on the workbench. It had been there since last July: a wooden shower mat, designed out of crisscrossed pieces of elm. The fun part was that it involved so many joints. There were the next pieces, waiting to be attached. I turned on the compressor and blew away eight months worth of cobwebs.

Several hours later, Eilish came home to find me working away. She brought me coffee and cake, kissed my cheek and left again. Later still, I heard a car in the drive. I thought it might be Stella.

I'd finished the coffee and was gluing an especially tricky joint—very tricky indeed—when the door opened again.

'Just a minute, darling,' I called. 'I can't move. Bit of a critical moment.'

When she didn't reply, I looked around. It wasn't Eilish; it was Simon. He was half in, half out of the doorway, as though not sure of his welcome. I turned back to my handiwork.

'I've got glue on here,' I said. 'I can't clamp it, the angle's impossible.'

He took a quick look, and immediately saw the problem. I'd taught him well.

'Is this the next bit?' he asked, holding up a piece of timber. 'Okay. I'll sand it.'

Have you ever watched two small boys playing Lego? They talk nonsense, especially if they're good friends who know one another well. They're concentrating on the job at hand, and words just bubble out of them. Eilish calls it 'Lego talk'. Simon and I were like that. We worked side by side, and we talked nonsense. It saved us from having to talk sense, which was far more risky. There was a moment when he began to apologise for what happened in the flat that day, but I stopped him in mid-sentence.

'How about a clean slate?' I suggested. 'On both sides.'

He didn't look up from his sanding, but I saw him nod. 'I can live with that.'

We were gluing the final piece when he said, 'I heard about your friend. Sorry.'

'Her funeral was today. They wouldn't let me go.'

'Well, she was . . .' Simon hesitated. I steeled myself, expecting him to say something insulting about Chloe. 'She was their child. They've lost their child.'

We laid our wooden creation flat on the bench. I was wondering how to make sure it stayed flat while the glue finished drying. Simon suggested we cover it with a board and then put weights on it; so we did that. It worked very well.

'Must be supper time,' I said.

As we were leaving, he stopped and looked around the shed. 'We've spent a few hours in here, over the years.'

'We certainly have.'

'Nico was hoping you'd make one of those little biplanes with him. You know, like mine. Would you do that next weekend, Dad?'

'I'd be honoured. And when Rosa is older, she must come in here and make one too. I won't have Kate accusing me of gender stereotyping.'

Simon smiled, and turned out the light.

Fifty

Lucia

The first thing I saw was a vase of flowers: long stems, and bright yellow petals. I was sure they hadn't been there earlier.

There was a clock on the wall. The hands stood at ten past seven, but I had no idea whether it was morning or evening. It seemed just a few moments ago that I was lying in an ice-cold operating theatre, with music playing, sweating with terror as I talked to the anaesthetist. I had the vaguest memories of the journey back to my room, lying on a gurney. I remembered a voice saying that all had gone well. I remembered a familiar hand holding mine, as I drifted away.

When they took me to theatre I was wearing a loose set of hospital pyjamas. Now, somebody had replaced the trousers with a pink sarong. The air was very warm, and it smelled of flowers and antiseptic. Sounds began to trickle into my consciousness: the drone of traffic, car horns and the sudden whine of a motorised rickshaw. White curtains covered one wall, filtering the light. It was a pleasant little room, more like a sparsely furnished hotel than a hospital. I saw a drip in my arm, and to my right stood banks of equipment.

I'd done my homework, and talked to other women who'd been through this surgery. I knew there was morphine pumping into me. I knew that I had a catheter. I knew that the next days and weeks would be shot through with agony and indignities; but right now I felt very little pain. I felt light, as free and light as thistledown, as though all the worries and anxieties of my life had been lifted away. I'd never felt so right. I didn't even know it was possible to feel like that.

I had a picture in my mind: my own legs and hands when I was a small boy, sitting on the kitchen floor. I felt the heaviness of the carving knife, and heard my own fast breathing. I remembered the fear and the pain, and the sheer desperation to get rid of these things that stopped me from being like the other girls.

I smiled in victory. *You did it*, I told myself. *At last, you did it.*

The white curtains fluttered. I heard a gentle cough before her slender figure stepped inside, pulling the door shut behind her. She was wearing a linen shirt and shorts, and fanning herself with her book. Two years had passed since that stranger on a train had persuaded me to carry on living, but Eilish seemed as young and vigorous as ever. Her hair was pulled back into a ponytail, and auburn wisps stroked her neck. My beautiful ex-wife. She tiptoed closer, peering to see if I was awake.

'Hello,' I said. My voice sounded slurred. I had a sore throat—from the intubation, I supposed. I didn't care. Who cared about a sore throat? Why would I ever care about anything, ever again?

She sat on a chair next to the bed, resting her fingers on my arm. 'Eight hours,' she said, smiling at me. 'Long time to be under. The doctor's very pleased with the way it all went. Apparently he'll be coming in to see you soon.'

My voice was a croak. 'Thank you for being here.'

She fetched a brush from my sponge bag, saying she'd tidy up my hair before the doctor arrived. It was a soothing sensation. I tilted my head, revelling in a fizz of pleasure and calm. My hair hung over my shoulders now, and I had a wispy fringe.

'How do you feel?' she asked. 'Apart from the screaming agony, of course.'

'Lucky,' I said. 'So lucky. And no screaming agony yet.'

The Thai surgeon who ran that clinic was an artist. I'd seen photos of his work before I chose him. He gave trans women the only gift they'd ever really wanted. He gave it to me. I wished Chloe could have had this gift. She was the one who really deserved it; she was honest about who she was from the very first. She had courage. I was a coward who'd blundered around the china shop for five decades, breaking precious things with my denial.

'The flowers?' I whispered.

'Ah. They're from Kate and Peter. They came with a cryptic message. Hang on.' Eilish picked up the card and read it out. '*Congratulations on smashing through your glass ceiling.*'

I remembered our conversation in the bar at Paddington, and smiled. 'She's going to make a terrible vicar's wife,' I said.

There were footsteps in the corridor before my door opened. It was an orderly, carrying a tray. She grinned widely at both of us, dipped her head and cried, 'Breakfast!' We did our best to thank her in Thai. I'd met this same woman when I first came in, and knew she didn't speak much English. I didn't want to eat. I didn't want to sleep, either; I felt no need to do anything except savour these wonderful moments. Soon the pain relief would wear off, and my joy would be tempered by the grisly realities of such major surgery.

The orderly left the tray on a side table as she walked across to the curtains and pulled them wide open. It was mid-morning when I'd been wheeled into the operating theatre, and night when they brought me back. Now a new day had dawned, and its glory blazed into the room. The sun lit up Eilish's face, deepening the creases of laughter and life around her eyes. It shone on the sheet that covered me. The new me.

The woman approached my bed, still smiling. She looked excited, as though she had a present for me hidden behind her back. I have never forgotten her next three words.

'Good morning, madam,' she said.

Fifty-one

About thirty miles from the city of Florence, nestling among vineyards, there is an old stone villa. It has wooden shutters, a loggia covered in vines—perfect for lazy lunches, with peaches and red wine—and a swimming pool painted a hot cerulean blue, like the sky. On a burning August day, this is as close to paradise as most of us are ever likely to come.

Two small children played in the villa's garden. One, a boy of six, ran around it—round and round and round. He held a toy plane high above his head, and was making it fly. As he ran he grinned, and as he grinned he shouted to the world. He used no words; it was a long, joyous yodel. His sister bobbed in the pool, held up by a pair of bright red water wings. She was a toddler and very merry, with rosebud lips and dark curls—a smaller version of her mother, who swam close by. The little one kept splashing her hand in the water, making it sparkle in the dazzling light. From time to time she spurted some out of her mouth and then roared with laughter. Her mother tweaked her nose and said she was a monkey.

Two older women—not old, just older—reclined in deckchairs in the deep shade of a covered terrace. They wore large, floppy sunhats and colourful summer dresses. Both were holding books, but instead of reading they were watching their grandchildren. From time to time they called out, joining in the laughter.

The small boy ran up to the taller of the two and grabbed her hand. She was a striking woman, with dark eyes and strong features. Her hair was caught up with a mother-of-pearl clasp. Green glass beads glittered around her neck.

'Watch me dive in, *Abuelita*?' he asked.

'Like a hawk,' she said. 'I'm not going to take my eyes off you.'

'Hold my plane, then.'

He rushed to the side of the pool—he did nothing slowly—and belly-flopped into the water with a loud splash. He came to the surface a second later, dog paddling furiously. His two spectators clapped and called for an encore, so he got out, ran around the pool and went through the whole performance again. And again. Their hands were beginning to smart when they were distracted by a man stepping out through the door of the house, carrying a jug and some glasses. A towel was slung around his neck, and he wore board shorts.

'Here we are,' he announced, laying his wares on the table, next to the wooden plane. 'My special recipe.'

'You're a marvel, Simon,' said the dark-haired woman as he handed her a glass. 'Have you seen Nico diving? I think he's going to end up with a sore tummy.'

'He's better at diving than at cricket,' replied Simon. 'But, frankly, that's not saying much. He learned from an expert, though I do say so myself. Watch this!'

He dumped the towel on a chair, took a run-up to the pool and hurled himself in, curling up into a ball so as to create a small tsunami. His wife and children cheered, but the women on the terrace shrieked as water cascaded over them. One of them—freckled, and with auburn hair—flapped her novel to dry the pages.

'Vandal!' she cried. 'You're just a big kid!'

Simon laughed at them, then grabbed a floating ball and began to play pig-in-the-middle with his family. The two grandmothers tried to go back to their books, but after a few minutes they laid them down on their chests. It was too perfect a day to be buried in a thriller.

I reached for my glass. It was ice cold. Beside me, I heard Lucia drop her book onto the ground, sighing contentedly.

'Well,' I said. 'We made it.'

She knew what I meant. Of course she did. After all, we were as close as it's possible for two human beings to be.

'We made it,' she said.

That sunlit garden rang with splashes, shouts and the gentle slapping of water against the tiled edge of the pool. Lucia and I sipped our drinks and chatted quietly about this and that. I was beginning to feel a little sleepy when the vineyard's owner walked by. He glanced over the garden wall, nodding affably at us two grandmothers.

'*Ciao, signore*,' he called.

•

Perhaps this is the end of the story, but I doubt it. We have adventures to come, Lucia and I. Maybe our tale will end when death parts us. I doubt that too.

Girl meets boy. They fall in love. They marry. For thirty years, they share one another's lives. Thirty years.

And then a new journey begins.

About the author

Charity Norman was born in Uganda and brought up in successive draughty vicarages in Yorkshire and Birmingham. After several years' travel she became a barrister, specialising in crime and family law in the northeast of England. Also a mediator, she is passionate about the power of communication to slice through the knots. In 2002, realising that her three children had barely met her, she took a break from the law and moved with her family to New Zealand. Her first novel, *Freeing Grace*, was published in 2010 and her second, *Second Chances*, in 2012 (published in the UK as *After the Fall*), was a Richard and Judy pick. *The Son-in-Law*, her third novel, was published in 2013.